The Form
and The Shatter

Being the Second Movement of the
Song of the Crickets

Emmett Burgess

Copyright © 2024 by Emmett Burgess

All rights reserved.

No part of this publication may be reproduced, distributed, or transmitted in any form or by any means, including photocopying, recording, or other electronic or mechanical methods, without the prior written permission of the publisher, except as permitted by U.S. copyright law. For permission requests, contact Windmill Publishing, LLC at the website below.

The story, all names, characters, and incidents portrayed in this production are fictitious. No identification with actual persons (living or deceased), places, buildings, and products is intended or should be inferred.

Any references to historical events, real people, or real places are used fictitiously. Names, characters, and places are the products of the author's imagination.

ISBN: 979-8-218-50981-1 (Paperback)

Cover art and design by Ethan Coates

Published by Windmill Publishing, LLC

First print edition 2024.

www.windmill.ink

Table of Contents

Foreword..............................13
Prelude...............................19
Canto 1...............................22
Canto 2...............................73
Canto 3..............................171
Canto 4..............................214
Canto 5..............................244
Canto 6..............................287
Canto 7..............................374
Coda.................................473

Appendices
A: Keuleno Calendar..........480
B: Glossary........................483

About the author....................486

Other works in the Continuum:

The Lone and Level Sands
Emmett Burgess

Outcast
Giancarlo Vanzzini

For Mrs Deboodt.
—EB

For Grandpa Robert.
—EG

For the crunch of leaves beneath your feet
on a crisp autumn day.
—JT

Is he not sacred, even to the gods, the wandering man who comes in weariness?

—Homer, *The Odyssey*

The Form
and The Shatter:

Being the **Second Movement**
of the
Song of the Crickets

taken from the epic poem
Sos Mao Brikhweg by Kanwas

adapted and translated by
Emerson Grey

—here transcribed by
Emmett Burgess

Foreword

A note on the original epic

The Form and The Shatter is an epic poem by the same name, attributed by tradition to a bard named Kanwas. Whereas *The Lone and Level Sands* was recounted to me by the mouth of John Talbot himself, this installment within the *Song of the Crickets* is translated from its original.

The original epic poem is titled in the Late Keuleno language *Sos Mao Brikhweg* and consists of several small stories that weave together tales of the characters you will read about here. Of Kanwas herself, little is known for certain.

Kanwas probably lived ca. 3E 1500 (about 3500 CE, or 1500 AA according to Berenstain-reckoning). A native-born Keuleno, she was educated from a young age in Mitho Gorikhwa where she developed a talent for poetry and prose. We know of hner only through third-parties, as none of her works have survived save for *Sos Mao Brikhweg*.

Kanwas married a woman named either Hessa or Lyn (sources differ), and together they lived out their lives on a small island south of Saulen. Kanwas died at the age of 73 of unknown causes. Her grave is a site of pilgrimmage for writers from all over the world.

A note on translation

I am not a poet; I am an historian and a writer of (by my own standards) passable prose. Therefore, I have elected not to attempt to recreate the intricate meter and rhyme-schemes employed in the original epic. As an example of the Old Keuleno text, here are the first few lines of Canto I:

> *Kleumo iwe mei*
> *A baithaisin mewaisin tefwaisin e gleumaisin*
> *Segai gweryge ensero ys*
> *Derais tenai ubyenn derais aum ir e ngwenai*
> *Greyenn i dherevain idan niyud gorgaith*
> *Megwenai gellun brikhwo*

Of all the languages I have studied, I have found Keuleno one of the most intricate—both in grammar and semantics. Entire meanings of phrases can be changed simply by affecting word order or adding a small affix to a single word out of a dozen. As I am not a poet, I hope the reader will excuse me for giving a straightforward translation. After all, my translation of the epic would be in my own native language, which is unknown to Emmett Burgess's audience. Emmett himself is tasked with translating my work into his own form of early twenty-first-century Berenstain American English. If he and I worked together to accurately capture the meter and rhyme of *Sos Mao Brikhweg*, it would pass through three different languages before appearing as this book you are now reading, and all characteristics of the original would be lost.

—Emerson Grey
Jemston, New Amrika
9348 AA

Pronunciation of Keuleno words

Those who spoke Keuleno, as well as Kanwas herself, did not use the Latin alphabet—neither does Emerson. But I do. So, whenever a Keuleno word must be spelled, I've chosen to keep the spelling as uniform as possible (a trait I wish my twenty-first-century Berenstain American English shared). For the most part, just read the words how they're spelled.

I find Spanish to be a good example for Keuleno vowels:

a = f*a*ther
e = b*e*d
i = mach*i*ne
o = b*o*at
u = l*u*te
ai = *ai*sle (never as in *ai*m)
ei = w*ei*ght (never as in w*ei*rd or st*ei*n)

y = This sound doesn't exist in English, though you may pronounce it as *u*. Using the International Phonetic Alphabet, it is pronounced /j/ when between or before vowels, and /y/ when between or before consonants.

I took a note from Tolkien and decided to always write a final "-ë" with an umlaut (as well as in a few diphthongs, like in Tobëa) so you remember that it's never silent.

Consonants are pronounced the same as in English and most other languages that use the Latin alphabet. Here are some odd ones to remember:

dh = *th*at
th = too*th*
kh = lo*ch*
j = *j*ump

I hope this isn't too complicated. Try reading Emerson's Gaian handwriting.

—Emmett Burgess
Illinois, North America
2024 CE

Prelude

On the coast near the taiga lives a song. No one knows how it came to be there, or how long ago it was written. No one has heard it in its entirety. It is difficult to find, and if you find it you would be lucky to hear even a single verse.

Those who have heard it say it is elegant and sad, layered and haunting. It is chasmic, complex as a concerto, familiar as a fairy tale. Some hear deep tones from a duduk while others are convinced the chief instrument is the sorathryu. Most agree that several instruments play the song, and some even hear lyrics.

As with any mystery, those who know of the song cannot make any sense of it. Those who hear only music cannot agree on which instruments it is played, and those who hear lyrics cannot understand them. No one knows why the song is there, what purpose it serves, or even whether one should hear the song at all.

But the song is there. You can find it if you listen for it.

Often you can find it at night when the moon is full and the aurora dances across the sky. Look out over the water and listen to the surf wash against the shore while the owls hoot and foxes yip in the dark woods behind you. All of these are part of the song, so listen.

Then, *žužžánije*. This is what the locals call the chirring of insects. If the night is warm, which is rare on the taiga coast, žužžánije will be steady.

When you have listened to žužžánije for enough time that your mind places it in the backdrop of sensation and you lose your focus on all that is around you, the song will begin. Or rather, you will hear it then—the song has no beginning.

The melody will rise and circle around you. Perhaps you will hear the thump-thump-thump of the drums, and the bass will hit you in the heart like a steel-tipped spear. You may hear a lute played with light notes that border on the sound of tiny silver bells. And you may hear the lyrics. Don't worry if you don't. Those who do are often disappointed when they find they cannot understand them.

But you will feel these things:

Harsh sunlight against hot sand, and winds that bite in the snow.

Excited for young love, saddened by loss, the joy of fast friends, and the dreadful crawl of slow death.

The curiosity of holding a new instrument. The betrayal of dying before playing anything worth hearing.

The sting of tears that slide down your cheeks as

you struggle to choose between duty and love.

The taste of salt spray from that ocean that has no end, and the pride of discovering what lies beyond.

An uneasiness in the belly that comes with the sound of a sour-milk voice.

Razor claws that rake and tear flesh from bone.

The color orange.

The smell of burnt almonds.

You will forget what brought you there, the choices that shaped and formed your sorrows and joys, that determine where you will journey next. And later you will forget the music. You will forget the lyrics, if they came to you. The experience will leave your memories like snow melting in sunlight. You will remember only that the song exists, and that you were lucky to have heard a single measure.

I am not lucky.

I have heard the entire song.

This is a small piece.

Canto 1

Kleumo iwë mei!

Listen to me, all of you!

Of Baithais, Mewais, Kleumais, and Tefwais, tales have reached our ears: Derais—those chosen Holders, men and women both, anointed by the Derevai to shepherd humankind with the Shatter's mighty Powers.

There was Kes-Solodath, Mewas, king of Sakhdo Mor, who for his people forsook his faith, and whose progeny, Kes-Eroth, last bore the title King o'er that domain. His crown to the Kelai he did relinquish, and with it died their ancient gods.

There was Angai, holy to her kin and loyal to her land. 'Twas she who held the Sun aloft when Akho's raiders said, "With dusk's arrival our fires your houses will burn"—thus Angai endured, and with her the Tefwais.

Of the Kleumais, scarce a whisper, less a tale is known. They lived ere the time of Ice and Giants, ere the First Folk ventured from the northern waste. Should they persist this day, they dwell beyond the Aikhwë.

Also was Panaikh Polekheft, who led his kin's array, a multitude of souls, from lands where their forebears in Dol-Nopthelen fell; eastward he guided them to peace; he, taught by wolves and crows, his wisdom to his descendants imparted, and in Keulen's vast and snowy plains he settled. There his fame as king did flourish, til all who in that realm resided, and those across the emnet folds where nomads ply their wheeled and skiffed ships, gave ear to him and tribute rendered—of his afterbear I shall sing.

Brenn Ragnir he was called—harried and beleaguered, thrust into unbidden quests manifold, pursued by Easterlings for the Power he bore, a witness to many a city, a traveler amongst diverse tribes, he imbibed the customs of sundry civilizations and their speech, traversing the world, his friends scarce, his secrets held close within.

His adventure was vast—by foot, by steed, by ship—he sought the solace of seclusion. In time he chanced upon it in Koraithlen's rugged and cloistered land, at the very cusp of the world, where none but the Erkhesgur, the Bear-folk, allies of Brenn, would dare to tread.

But hold, O listener, and lend thy patience; I travel through the streams of yesteryears, to times when Brenn Ragnir's name was but a murmur in his soul's recess. Cast thine eyes instead upon young Gwennotir Ker, in the Spring of his years, amidst the mournful chill of his brother's funeral rite.

Behold, there was a Baithas, Deugwer Ker by name, born a full six millennia after Panaikh gave up his heavy crown. (No longer did kings and queens from Baithais' lineage reign, though the affection of the Derevai endured for them, as did the love of their folk.) Unto Deugwer was given an heir, a babe whom the Derevai sent to help guide the folk of Edorath.

Kolewa's fame did spread both near and far—the first-born son of Deugwer, lord of Albogorwë, and Holder of the Power of Speech. In the days of Kolewa, knights and nobles alike did ally with him, and he found no lack of companions when the drums of war did sound; for nobility is not a birthright but a stature earned through valiant deeds.

Across the breadth of Keulen, ten thousand leagues, did Deugwer and Kolewa ride with the legions of King Gwalo, unto the river Gwelulo where Khesi Addeu, the malevolent Mewas and Prophet to his folk, had cast his eye of conquest upon Edorath. At Gwelulo's shore, Deugwer and Kolewa did confront Addeu's forces, engaging them in a battle fierce and unyielding, spanning four days and nights.

But come the fifth morn, the evil Addeu did pierce Kolewa's gut with his blade, and thus the gallant young Baithas was ushered into the Shatter. Along the lengthy Gwelulo did his father Deugwer carry him, then across the icy plains of Keulen did the warriors bear him homeward to the Valk, to Albogorwë. Thereupon the noble King Gwalo did proclaim: "Of princely virtue was Kolewa Ker; not a prince of Keulen, but a prince unto all Edorath's children. Dear was he to his liege, and his absence shall be deeply felt."

Upon the shore did the people erect a pyre; they placed the deceased Baithas, beloved by all who had known him, in majestic repose atop. Riches and relics were gathered from verdant Mitho Gorikhwa, from the level lands of Markhlen and the sea-locked isles of Saulen, from the humid realm of Maikhethlen and the scattered islands of Pellen, yea, even from the arid reaches of Deulen and the expansive kingdoms of Mithoër. Never was there a pyre of greater splendor recounted. About him they arrayed treasures; upon his breast they rested his sword—Pukhso was its name, a blade that felled many a foe ere it found rest in the fire.

Tiny snowflakes danced in the breeze, mingling with the smoke from Kolewa's great pyre. The essence of the Baithas now was but vapor, and Gwennotir, his younger brother, was loath to accept that Kolewa had forever left this mortal Form.

The day was gripped by frost, yet the grand blaze that ushered Kolewa to the Shatter offered no solace of warmth. A great assembly had come, from Keulen's heart and lands afar, even the distant corners of Edorath, to honor the Speaker's fall—for the death of a Holder was a sorrow universal. Those nurtured in the Valk, of eastern blood, were untroubled by the chill as strangers stood by, swaddled in their furs like infants in their cradles. Yet Gwennotir felt a deeper cold that day, not born of snow nor the gloom of the heavens, but from a solitude profound, a feeling unknown since the departure of his father and brother to war, leaving him with his mother and loyal wolf.

Song of the Crickets

The multitude cried out, "Hail, Baithas!" and "Eternal be the spirit of Kolewa," whilst warriors brandished their steel in homage to the fiery bier.

Lord Deugwer drew nigh to the blaze, his eyes closed in solemnity, his hands, smeared with ash, raised for all to witness. His loyal wolf, Wind, kept vigil, lamenting the loss of his friend. Segwi Ker's gaze was lost in the flickering flames, searching in vain for quickness in her eldest son's form. Deugwer's eyes then met his younger son, fixing upon Gwennotir until the youth writhed, uncertain of his bearing. The lord then spoke, reciting from the Dwal-Fontho, their hallowed scripture:

"But when mine heart did yield to wisdom's call and I did ponder o'er my toils beneath the Sun, lo!—all was naught but vanity and chasing after the wind. For no man can grasp the wind, nor can he lay hold upon shadow, nor can he capture smoke, for it is fleeting as life itself."

Further words were uttered—by the dorovayan as he conducted Kolewa's final sacraments, by many of Kolewa's brothers-in-arms, and by King Gwalo. But Gwennotir heeded not the speeches, for his heart had been deaf to all since his father had returned from the fray with his brother's lifeless form. All was but a phantasm to Gwennotir, and he yearned for the morrow when he might awaken, and Kolewa would beckon him to ride through the Polgwelë woods.

Yet the ghastly vision persisted, and the flames did roar. Within the span of an hour, the crowd dispersed, each soul in search of hearth and food, with ale to chase the inner chill. Gwennotir tarried beyond all others, outlasting even his mother Segwi. But Wind, the devoted wolf, approached and tenderly nudged the boy's hand, prompting Gwennotir to caress him behind the ears. The wolf urged the lad away from the dwindling mound of ashes carried off by the sea's breath, and Gwennotir yielded. The Moon reigned supreme, and the Sun would not greet them til Spring's return, and the cold gnawed at the boy despite his eastern blood.

From the shadowed Polgwelë, a fox emerged, its approach graceful. With a tail that danced, it raised its snout to the heavens and howled. Its lamentation ceased, the creature locked eyes with Gwennotir, its gaze profound, before vanishing into the forest's embrace. Silence there was once more.

The pyre crumbled, and a frigid gust swept the land, chilling Kolewa's living brother. It was the chill of mortality, the inexorable cold of the Shatter. Gwennotir trembled; this desolation would haunt him ever more.

In the grand Ker estate, Deugwer held a feast to honor his departed son. The hall was aglow with warmth and food. As Gwennotir entered, many a gaze turned, eyes filled with compassion. Yet the merriment persisted.

Navigating the revelry, Gwennotir sought his place by his mother's side. Yet before he could settle, Lord Deugwer beckoned: "Nay, my son. Tonight thou shalt sit at my right." The hall fell silent as all understood the gesture. Reluctantly, Gwennotir took the honored seat, meeting only his mother's eyes, which bore sorrow's great weight.

As the feast continued, Deugwer rose. "Hear me, for I would speak of Kolewa's valor." But Gwennotir's heart was elsewhere, and he heard not his father's words.

Soon the conversation and movement and music began once more, and Gwennotir turned his attention to the roast pork and onions on his plate, though he could do little more than poke at them with absent fingers. To his right, a man cleared his throat, and Gwennotir looked to see the king himself smiling at him.

"Forgive me, King," said the boy with a low nod. "I did not realize thou wast here; else I would have greeted thee properly."

"Banish the thought," said Gwalo, placing a hand upon the boy's shoulder. Drawing his chair closer, Gwalo met Gwennotir's gaze, not as sovereign to his subject, but as one heartbroken to another. "My brother, Melis, was a beacon of valor. He was both my confidante and my shield. How I yearned instead to shield him from the world's cruelties! Yet, fate deemed otherwise, and he was taken from me." A heavy sigh escaped Gwalo's lips. "Much like thee, I too grappled with false hope surrounding my brother's demise. But know this, young Gwennotir, Kolewa would not wish that thou wast ensnared by guilt or regret. He would desire that thou shouldst embrace life with fervor, cherishing each day as a gift. What is it that thine heart truly seeketh, Gwennotir?"

With trembling voice, the young boy answered, "I would that my brother yet lived."

Gwalo then said, "Thy brother was a paragon of

courage. He met his end with honor."

But Gwennotir's anguish was unshakable. "I care not for tales of courage and valor. It matters not how he met his end, but why."

Deugwer, sensing the rising tide of emotion, gently placed a hand on his son's arm, a silent warning of restraint. Gwennotir, in his grief, was heedless of his father.

Gwalo, with a firm voice, declared, "Kolewa laid down his life for Keulen, for his king, and for his folk. Such a sacrifice is worthy of the loftiest hymns. I pray that thou wouldst find the courage to give all for thy kingdom when the time comes."

Defiant, Gwennotir rose, his eyes locked hotly on the king's. With a gesture, the king signaled Deugwer to allow the young lord his moment of expression. Gwennotir spoke thus: "There is no honor in death. I would not die for any." He then fled into the night.

Beneath the starry vault, in frigid waste, did Gwennotir flee, his heart a leaden weight.

Exhaustion claimed him, tears gave way to sleep, and in a dream he wandered shadowed woods. His soul yearned for the forest's fond embrace, to speak with the ethereal fox, yet the path eluded him. A distant glade beckoned, but as he neared, the trees like sentinels grew dense, their limbs entwined to bar the way. Though he endeavored to break through, the thorns and branches tore at his flesh, drawing forth his blood. In desperation he retraced his steps, but Polgwelë in cryptic will denied him. His cries rang out in vain; he found himself forever trapped in nature's labyrinth.

Dawn's light then broke the spell; he woke to find the faithful Wind atop him. Tender care from the wolf brought fleeting solace, yet a part of Gwennotir wished night's cold embrace had claimed him to the Shatter's realm with Kolewa. In silence save for crunching snow, they journeyed homeward. Arriving, Segwi rushed to him, a mother's love unmeasured in her arms. Relief and unease mingled in her words: "Warm by the hearth, my son; thy meal awaits."

Yet Gwennotir spied a strange horse without and queried of its presence. Segwi's face darkened as she replied, "Thy brother's death is fresh, yet for the ritual they press."

Inside the hall, in sacred garb adorned, the dorovayan Rirth with Deugwer spoke. His visage painted in the earth's own hues, the shaman turned to Gwennotir, urgent, stern. "Young lord, dost thou not grasp thine absence's weight?" His tone, ill-suited to address nobility, rankled the boy, who quickly retorted thus:

"Rirth, my brother's passing rawly scars mine heart."

Steeped in tradition, duty-bound, Rirth said, "To Shatter's realm a Speaker has now gone. The line of Power teeters on the brink. Well knowest thou the purpose for which I am here."

Within, the boy's anguish fiercely burned. "Before I bear this burden, may I not be granted time to mourn and find my peace?"

Lord Deugwer's patience visibly grew thin, but Rirth reacted with astonishment, as if the boy had

The Form and The Shatter

uttered blasphemy. "Burden!" his voice like thunder echoed round, divine fury resounding. Wind's ears perked; Segwi recoiled, surprised. "By Odol's gaze, I marvel that his wrath in lightning form doth not strike where thou standest. Hast thou yet eaten?"

The boy replied, "Nay, but I was nigh to doing so."

The priest then said, "Refrain. The ritual awaits; its timely execution is for all our interest."

Gwennotir looked to Segwi, seeking solace, who, with a helpless shrug, conveyed the rite's imminence. Deugwer, though Albogorwë's lord, was not exempt from Derevais' decrees. The dorovayan's word could not be breached. With a stern nod, Deugwer signaled to the boy to heed the shaman's call. A sigh bespoke his apprehension as he trailed behind Rirth to the bathing chamber, his parents noticeably absent—small mercy—for Rirth, divinely urgent, bade him strip. The chamber, warmed by the stove, held a frothing tub, its surface stirred by hidden heat below. As Rirth intoned his cryptic invocations—invoking Derevai and arcane powers—he cast grey powder in; the water foamed.

"Enter," Rirth commanded.

Gwennotir stepped in, exclaiming, "The heat is unbearable!"

"Endure," said Rirth, "let Odol's flames purify thee."

Despite discomfort, he submerged himself, the scalding water threatening his skin. A final act: he plunged his head beneath, engulfed by searing liquid. Rising, gasping, "Rise," Rirth ordered. Swiftly, the boy emerged, skin flushed, and wrapped in woolen blanket's folds.

Within the main hall, parents waiting anxiously, their son, still drenched, in naught but a blanket draped, sat at the table. Rirth then brought a vial of viscous yellow elixir. Anointing the boy's brow with the sap-redolent substance, he bade him taste—spiced honey on the tongue.

Upon the table lay a cloak and relics of ancient rites. Arms wide, Rirth then unfurled the cloak, cascading it on youthful shoulders. Coarse, fish-odored, it scratched against his skin. Atop his head, Rirth placed a headdress grand, mirroring his own, with antlers and ringing bells.

In hand, a willow wand etched with the runes that whispered the sacred names of Derevai. From it hung shells and tokens—red, yellow, white, and black—hues matching the face-painted priest. With a resonant voice, the dorovayan spoke:

"In the time before time, when naught but the vast sea reigned, two logs, one of ash and one of willow, were set adrift. Upon the ash alighted a pigeon and an owl; upon the willow, an eagle and a hawk. 'Let us forge the world,' they declared, 'lest we be consumed by the abyss.' From the ash, they sculpted the tangible realm; from the willow, the ethereal. The ash they named Form; the willow, Shatter. These architects then transcended their bodies, becoming the unknowable Derevai.

"From the Form sprang forth the first of people and beasts, the living tapestry of the world. The Derevai, in their wisdom, chose four among the humans, bestowing upon each a divine Power: Space, Time, Mind, and Speech. Gib, the recipient of Speech, became the forebear of the Baithais.

"The sacred Power, a birthright, shall pass to the eldest offspring. In the absence of an heir, the next in line shall bear this mantle. By the decree of Odol, Nao, Eno, and Parthu—Kolewa Ker, a Speaker, has journeyed to the Shatter. Gwennotir Ker, his younger brother, shall now bear the mantle of Baithas."

With swift motion, Rirth cast earthen powder upon the boy—ancient forests in its scent. As Gwennotir recoiled, Rirth carried on, chanting in tongues long lost to mortal ears, known only to those steeped in eldritch lore. The boy's mind swam betwixt waking and the dream.

The sacred powder lingered on his tongue—a symphony of life's antinomies: triumph, defeat; passion and raging conflict. A transformation stirred inside his being. No more just Gwennotir Ker—son, brother—but a vessel of a power greater still: the ancient trees; antlers and shadow-fur. Embodiment of Odol and the First Folk.

Perception stretching far beyond the mundane, he saw Polgwelë sprawled before him now—a testament to nature's timeless cycle. The towering trees, lush underbrush, and wonders that words could neither encompass nor convey. Time's march played out in cryptic visions then: green meadows turned to barren waste, where grass once swayed, steel fortresses and banners rose. Jub Khewi glimpsed—seat of an ancient empire—foretelling of a cataclysmic war where gods would clash with mortal kind, and one—a Holder—would the fatal blow deliver. A lineage emerged of Power and Blood, culminating in one beyond all reckoning.

From shadows came a figure, robed in leaves, wielding a yew bow, one with the woodland realm. Then shifting: man and woman, hand in hand, one and the same, cradling a bundled babe that wept, the couple weeping with the child.

The visions fading, Gwennotir returned to mundane time and place, the ritual's taste still on his tongue. He sought the answers then from the enigmatic Rirth: "What sorcery is this that thou hast wrought?"

With reverence, Rirth replied: "I merely called; the Derevai gave answer." A final flourish of his wand, declaring, "The rite is done. May he sire heirs before his own journey to the Shatter's distant shores."

With clarity restored, the father neared, offering his son both pride and consolation: "How dost thou feel now, my son?"

The boy replied, simple yet profound. "Hungry," Gwennotir said.

In darkness deep, while all in slumber lay, Gwennotir, his senses dulled and slow from verdant broth and drowsiness's soft sway, did mumble low, "Methinks I shall go to bed." Segwi, gentle, helped his faltering steps to the chamber where, ere reaching bed, he slept.

Awakening to silence profound, the house enwrapped in night's bewitching spell, bereft of the Sun's fair light to guide around, he pondered whether to rise and break his fast ere heart-fire warmed the dwelling's quiet halls.

"...alone..." a whisper echoed, source unknown. His eyes, alarmed, sought ember's faintest glow beyond the door, yet none could be seen. "...dead..." the voice returned, a chilling sound.

"Whence cometh yon voice?" he asked, perturbed.

Roused by his master's call, Wind stretched and rose, the noble wolf, to offer comfort's nuzzle. "Didst thou perceive another's voice?" Gwennotir posed, as one might query a companion, puzzled.

"Nay," Wind replied, his voice in a mental stream. "All are ensconced in slumber's restful dream."

A cry of terror broke from Gwennotir's throat, causing the wolf to cower, tail between his legs. Swift Deugwer came, with servants in his coat, demanding, "What tumult disturbs the peace? Gwennotir, whence comes this distress so raw?" The boy, overwhelmed, could not speak for tears.

As he composed himself, Wind then addressed Lord Deugwer with profound eloquence: "He heareth my voice within." Realization dawned on the father, who, with tender patience, approached his frightened son.

"Fear not, my child," he soothed, extending a hand in comfort mild. "Such revelations, though they startle thee, are a legacy of blood, our family tree. I too was once taken aback by this, as was Kolewa. 'Tis a rite, not amiss."

Gwennotir, tear-streaked, gazed upon the wolf and said, "His voice resonates in my very soul!"

Deugwer drew him close, whispered words to quell: "My sire died ere I came into my role. Alone I navigated these strange waters, yet I am here for thee, my son." Wind then declared his true wolf-name with gravity, a name of meaning, history, and levity, speaking of nature's dance, the seasons' cycle.

Recovered some, the boy asked, hesitant, "Hast thou always comprehended my words?"

Wind, with a sagely tilted head, replied, "The question's slant applies to thee as well."

Deugwer interred with gentle mirth, "Thou shalt discern in time, Wind's wit surpasses that of many beasts."

"Tell me, Father," Gwennotir asked, "do all creatures converse thus?"

"The more enlightened ones," Deugwer replied, "speak more clearly, predators and birds astute prove most lucid. The wolf in wisdom's guide exceeds the common hound."

Wind, resolute, fixed gaze upon Gwennotir, eyes piercing deep. "Thou art wary of me," he intoned.

The boy replied, "Nay, 'tis just too much to fathom."

"Seek not full understanding," said Wind. "Rejoice instead in our new communion."

Gwennotir smiled, inhaling deeply to send away his tears, and with perspective true, beheld the wolf, so human-like in gaze, as friend and guide in this newfound life.

In that moment of profound astonishment, fear's grip on Gwennotir began to ease, as wonder filled his heart and mind alike. The scope of his new Power now laid bare, a turning point had come within his troubled soul.

Deugwer, who saw this transformation swift,

spoke words of love and wisdom to his son: "Gwennotir, thou, now Baithas called, must serve and wield this gift for the greater good. No small or trivial task, but one replete with joy and purpose true. Embrace thy role, for thou art not alone, but part of something grander than thyself."

As father and son shared this precious time of deep, unbounded love and unity, King Gwalo, drawn by the commotion's sound, arrived, his presence filling the room. His eyes alight with pride and grave respect, he spoke, his voice gentle, rumbling, low. "My boy, I heard thy cries and came to thee to offer heartfelt praise. Thy new Power is cause for celebration and for joy—a sign of thy great destiny unfurled. I know the path ahead may seem dim, the weight of duty pressing on thy soul, but I am here, thy liege and faithful friend, to guide thee as thou growest in thy role."

And thus Gwennotir, a Baithas born anew, with Wind beside, and family, king, and country at his back, faced the uncertain future—though he would not admit that within him grew a great unease, hesitance at this new mantle.

In Kers' grand hall, where morning moonlight streamed through windows, casting a soft and gentle glow, stood King Gwalo, his presence commanding all to heed his words. Anticipation thick in the air, tinged with a sense of dread.

"My loyal subjects," Gwalo's voice rang clear, "the time has come for us to take a stand against the threats that gather at our borders. The Methyo Genlas front demands our strength, while Len

Khalayu's shadow looms over us. Deugwer, my trusted friend, to thee I charge with the task of leading our brave knights to face the foes that would assail our southern bounds. And Gwennotir, our newly risen Baithas, shall journey with me to Len Khalayu, to lend his Power to our righteous cause."

Startled by this sudden call, Gwennotir spoke, his voice a mix of fear and doubt, "My liege, I beg thee, reconsider this. I am but newly come into my role, ill-prepared to face the trials of war. My place is here, with family and kin, to learn and grow, not on the battlefield."

Gwalo, brow pulled low, replied with force, "Young Baithas, thou dost forget thy sacred duty. Thy Power is not thine to hoard and keep, but rather to be used in service of thy people and thy king. Thou shalt obey my command and join me in this fight. Dost thou not desire vengeance for thy brother's death? For it was at the hand of Khesi Addeu, Mad Prophet of Len Khalayu, that valiant Kolewa fell."

Deugwer, sensing tension in the air, stepped forth, his voice a mix of love and steel: "Gwennotir, my son, heed well the king's words. Thy reluctance, though born of honest fear, is misplaced in this time of grave import. We owe our lives, our service to the crown, and to the people to whom we are sworn to protect. Thou must embrace thy role, thy fate, and stand beside our king in this dark hour."

Chastened by his father's words, Gwennotir bows, his voice a whisper tinged with pain: "Forgive me, Father, and my lord the king. I spoke in haste, mine heart overwhelmed by doubt. I shall obey and journey to Len Khalayu, to lend my Power to our noble cause, though heavy lies the weight upon my soul."

Deugwer, his eyes a mix of pride and grief, embraced his son, the moment bittersweet. "Be strong, my boy, and trust in thy new strength. Thou art a Baithas, born to lead and serve, and though the path ahead be fraught with peril, know that mine and thy mother's love and faith go with thee always."

Gwennotir, fighting back the tears that threatened, returned his father's embrace, then turned to face the king, his voice now steady with resolve. "My liege, I am thy servant, now and always. Lead on, and I shall follow, to Len Khalayu, to face our foes and safeguard our fair land."

And so, with heavy hearts, yet wills steadfast, father and son prepared to part, one to the south to guard the border's keep, the other west to stand beside his king and face the gathering storm ahead. Though fear and doubt still lingered in their hearts, they knew their duty and would not be swayed—for they were Baithais, father, son, and in their veins ran courage, strong and true.

In Ker Manor's courtyard, beneath the shine of the Moon and stars, soldiers and the household gathered round, their faces etched with tension and unease. The king's knights, resplendent in their armor, marched forth, a prisoner bound and dragged between them, his fate sealed.

Before them, the man of foreign visage, bound and kneeling, looked upon Gwennotir with eyes pleading for mercy. The boy, unfamiliar with this captive, surmised from his complexion that he hailed from Len Khalayu, as tales of their darker hue had reached his ears through Deugwer. Yet, the vast expanse of Edorath held many realms unknown to Gwennotir, and the captive's origins remained a mystery.

From the king's hand extended a sword of renown: Pukhso, once wielded by Kolewa.

"Thou hast taken this from my brother's pyre?" Gwennotir asked. "In the ethereal Shatter, how shall he defend himself, partake in celestial battles, bereft of his trusted blade?"

King Gwalo, with regal air, responded, "In life, the blade was Kolewa's, but in death, all that was his became mine. For Kolewa, though noble, was my subject. This blade, exquisite in craftsmanship, reminiscent of the famed Sauleno forge, is befitting of a king. Yet, I bestow it upon thee, for as this sword is not thine instrument, yet art thou mine."

With reverence, Gwennotir grasped the hilt, feeling its history and weight. Memories of Kolewa surged within him, and the blade seemed to resonate with his emotions, reflecting the pale moon's glow. "What task, O King, dost thou set before me?"

With a commanding gesture, Gwalo indicated the captive. "End his mortal time; execute with precision and might—for though thy frame is imposing, I deem thy spirit is yet untested. It shall demand all thy vigor, both of body and soul, to sever this man from life."

Gwennotir, aghast, implored, "Wherefore this grievous task? Is it not sufficient that I bear the mantle of Baithas, especially in my fledgling state?

Must I also be an instrument of death, mine hands stained so early in my years?"

"In my court," declared Gwalo with authority, "no soul, be it man or woman, shall remain unblooded, not least one bearing the mantle of Baithas. The divine decree of the Derevai doth not absolve thee; rather, it requires the act all the more. As thy king, I command: end this man's life."

Young Gwennotir, a mere fifteen summers old and yet unblooded, stood in contemplation. Many, including Deugwer and Kolewa, had tasted blood at a younger age. Kolewa, at the tender age of twelve, had vanquished his first foe, a rite of passage marking the awakening of his Power. Deugwer had beamed with pride, though Kolewa, overwhelmed, had retched in the aftermath.

The king's edict was absolute; defiance would mean Gwennotir's doom, and the onlookers might be compelled to enact the sentence. Yet, the sacrilege of slaying a Holder was universally abhorred. The tragic demise of Kolewa, heirless, had nearly plunged the world into chaos. The audacity of Addeu, a Holder himself, to strike down a Baithas was unfathomable. Rumors painted Addeu as a fiend deserving of the direst fate. But the sin of his execution seemed large.

Such profound reflections eluded Gwennotir in that fraught moment. Youthful and impressionable, he grappled with the weight of obedience and the dread of the act. His voice quavered. "I pray thee, let not this burden be mine." Tears glistened in his eyes and rolled down his cheeks.

The captive, bound and desperate, uttered words

in the foreign tongue Kalayo. Yet, Gwennotir, with his newly realized Power, comprehended him as if he spoke the familiar Keuleno: "Mercy, I implore! I have family, a wife, and children. I am no disciple of the proclaimed Prophet, Khesi Addeu. He laid waste to mine homeland, slaughtering the innocent before advancing to thy realm."

King Gwalo, intrigued, asked, "What words spill from his lips? Heed them not, Gwennotir. Act swiftly, lest his serpentine speech, in service of the Mad Prophet, ensnare thee."

Torn between duty and compassion, Gwennotir, with a heavy heart, did the unthinkable: he struck the man down. The blade Pukhso, wielded by trembling hands, did not achieve clean severance, but bit deep, causing the man to convulse before succumbing.

In the aftermath, what little composure was left to him then departed, and Gwennotir was overcome with shame. As the king's attendants pulled away the fallen, the prince, with cruel jest, mocked Gwennotir's distress.

"Behold, Father!" jeered the prince. "In this trepidation, he has soiled himself!"

The king's response remained unknown, for Gwennotir, consumed by fury, lunged at the prince, landing a blow that drew blood and shattered a tooth. The prince's outcry, a blend of pain and wrath, echoed, but Gwennotir, aflame with righteous anger, readied himself for the next blow.

The prince, with swift reflex, parried Gwennotir's impending strike, his arm rising in defense, and retaliated with a fierce punch to the Speaker's face. Though no bone broke, a dark contusion, the color of a ripened plum, would spread from chin to neck, marking the aftermath of the assault.

Kregeth Gollapo, with virtuous intent, intervened, pulling the fervent Baithas from the prince's reach. As Gwennotir writhed and Gwalo the Younger, in his wounded pride, spat bloody disdain, Kregeth sought to restrain the Speaker. A sharp reprimand from the king halted his actions.

"He bears the mantle of Baithas, Kregeth," the king proclaimed for all to hear, "and unto him is due a reverence which I expect thee to bestow. Dost thou comprehend my decree?"

Kregeth Gollapo, with a deferential nod, released Gwennotir, who, in his youthful indignation, recoiled with vehemence, casting daggers with his gaze upon Kregeth and the prince, yet shunning the king's piercing eyes. Kregeth, undeterred, challenged, "Shouldst thou not address thy king and prince?" Gwennotir looked upon Kregeth, noting his long white scar that stretched from cheek to neck.

With cheeks aflame, tears coursing, and pain evident, Gwennotir, eyes cast downward, humbly intoned, "To thee, my liege, and to Prince Gwalo, I convey my profound contrition." He bowed, a gesture of respect and submission. The prince's face darkened, but the king, with a hearty laugh, clapped Gwennotir's shoulder.

"Banish the memory, young one," said the king. "Many a soul, upon their blooding, fancied themselves as paragons of valor. Yet, in truth, none emerge unscathed in spirit. Thy brother, Kolewa, was overtaken by nausea; thy father, by tears. Thou standest neither above nor below them in this rite."

Gwennotir, sensing the weight of many an eye upon him, yearned to ask of the king's own blooding, yet propriety forbade such a query. His gaze found the prince, pondering the nature of the Younger's initiation. The thought of the prince, in a moment of vulnerability, would have been a balm to Gwennotir's wounded pride. But such a vision was not his to witness.

"Thy grace is boundless," Gwennotir said, bowing once more. But the king, with a paternal gesture, raised the boy to face him.

"Commit this day to memory," the king said with a solemn voice. "Recall the weight of life taken, the resistance of steel meeting flesh, the pleas of the fallen, and the tumult within thy soul. Remember the aftermath, the lifeless form dragged away, the warmth of thy shame, the sting of thy wounds. Recall the fire of thine anger, the bitterness of thy tears, and the loathing thou harborest for me. But above all, etch upon thine heart the profound aversion ever to wield death again."

On the bustling camp on the road to Jub Khewi, two months since Gwennotir's fateful deed, the morning routine did unfold, a hive of ceaseless activity, as soldiers and retainers went about their sundry tasks. Amidst the clamor of the waking camp, a messenger arrived, breathless and stained with the dust of travel, bearing urgent news for King Gwalo himself.

The king, surrounded by trusted council, grave of mien, received the messenger, his brow knit as he broke the seal and read the tidings that did chill him to the very core. Gwennotir, drawn by the commotion's sound, approached in time to hear the words that shattered his already fragile soul.

The king, his voice a knell of somber import, read: "I bring thee a grim report from the pursuit of Khesi Addeu at sea. Thy loyal servant, Deugwer Ker, and all his crew have been forever lost, their lives claimed by the deep, in service to thy cause and to the realm."

Gwennotir, stricken by this most cruel blow, cried out in anguish: "Father! O cruel fate! Is this to be my lot, to lose all those I hold most dear to violence and death? Is this the price of being Baithas-born, to watch as all I love is rent asunder?"

The king, his heart heavy with the weight of this most grievous loss, turned to Gwennotir, his voice a mix of sorrow and resolve: "My boy, I know the pain that thou dost feel, for Deugwer was a friend and loyal knight, but we must not let grief overcome our duty to press on, to see our mission through."

Gwennotir, eyes wild with dark despair, rounded upon the king, his voice a bitter cry: "What mission, what duty can justify such senseless waste of life? All that awaits us on this path is death, a yawning void that swallows all we are and all we love. I cannot bear this burden, cannot face the inevitable end that looms before us."

With these words, he fell upon his knees, his body wracked with sobs, his spirit broken by the weight of sorrow and fear. The camp fell silent, all eyes fixed upon the young and shattered Baithas, his anguish a stark reminder of the toll that war exacts on even the most high and favored souls.

The king, moved by the raw despair of

Gwennotir, knelt down beside him, placing a hand upon the trembling shoulder of the youth, his voice a gentle murmur meant to soothe: "Gwennotir, I know the path ahead seems dark, fraught with perils no man should face, but thou art not alone in this grim hour. We stand beside thee, and together we shall face what trials may come our way. Thy father's sacrifice, though bitter, shall not be in vain, for we shall see this through and bring an end to this most bloody strife."

Gwennotir, his tears still flowing, looked into the king's compassionate eyes and saw there a flicker of the strength he must find within himself to carry on. With shuddering breath, he rose to his feet, his voice a whisper, trembling: "My liege, I shall endeavor to be strong, to honor my father's memory with deeds that would make him proud, though mine heart quails at the dark road that lies ahead. Lead on, and I shall follow, though my steps be heavy, and my soul burdened with this weight of grief."

The king, his hand still resting on Gwennotir's shoulder, nodded his approval, a small, sad smile upon his lips. "Together, then, we shall press on, my boy, and face the gathering storm with heads held high, in memory of those who gave their lives for king and country, and for the greater good. Though the path be dark, we shall not falter, for in our unity we find the strength to bear the burdens this war demands."

With these words, the king turned to face the camp, his voice ringing out: "My loyal subjects, soldiers, knights, lords and ladies, hear me now, and know that we have suffered a most grievous loss, but we shall not let sorrow stay our hand, nor turn us from the righteous path we tread. In Deugwer's name, and in the name of all who have laid down their lives for this great cause, we shall press on until our foes lie vanquished, and peace once more reigns over this troubled land."

A cheer went up from the assembled throng, a defiant roar in the face of grief and pain, as the king's words ignited a flame of hope within their hearts, a flicker of resolve that would not be extinguished by the dark and gathering clouds of war and loss. Gwennotir, his heart still heavy, stood tall amongst the clamor, eyes fixed upon the distant horizon where the road to Jub Khewi and destiny awaited.

In the still of night, when slumber's gentle hand lay heavy on the camp, Gwennotir stirred, his heart a tempest of conflicting tides. Despair and fear, twin specters of the mind, urged him to flee, to seek solace in flight from the grim path that fate had laid before him. With furtive steps, he made his cautious way toward the king's pavilion, where Pukhso lay, a symbol of the duty he now spurned.

Beneath the cloak of shadows, Gwennotir crept, his breath a shallow whisper in the gloom as he sought out the blade that marked his station, and gathered what meager supplies he could to aid him in his desperate bid for freedom. His task complete, he slipped into the night, a wraith amid the slumbering host, his goal the tethered steeds that might bear him away from war's embrace.

Among the horses, Gwennotir paused, his gaze alighting on a sturdy beast, its coat a midnight hue, its eyes agleam with what he fancied was a kindred spirit, a longing for the open road and skies. With gentle words, he coaxed the steed to calm, his voice soothing in the still air: "Come, my friend, for I have need of thee to bear me far from this accursed place, where death and duty circle like fell beasts, waiting to claim my soul for their dark ends. Together we shall break these bonds of fate and seek a path that leads to life and hope."

The horse, hearing Gwennotir's plea, nuzzled his hand and said, "To bear my rider is my duty, but I would welcome flight from certain death. Therefore, mount and take my reins, and lead me as any other would."

In that moment, a bond was forged between the troubled youth and his new steed, whom he now christened Boriwar, a name that spoke of a wellspring in barren wastes.

With practiced ease, Gwennotir mounted up, his heart a thunder in his aching chest, as he urged Boriwar to a gentle trot, seeking to put the sleeping camp to rest. But as they neared the perimeter, a sound of footsteps sent a chill through Gwennotir's veins, and hastily he reined Boriwar in, seeking shelter in a nearby copse, where shadows draped their forms in obscurity.

Scarcely daring to draw breath, Gwennotir watched as a lone sentry passed, his eyes roaming, seeking signs of trouble in the night, but blind to the boy and horse lying in wait, their hearts a-hammer with the fear of capture. Long moments stretched, an eternity of held breath and fervent, silent prayers—until at last the guard moved on, his steps receding into the distant dark.

With a shuddering sigh, Gwennotir urged Boriwar forth, his voice a whispered plea: "Swift now, my friend—for we must put this place far from our sight before the morning birds reveal our absence to the waking host. The road ahead is long and dangerous, but we shall face it side by side, as one, united in our quest for freedom's light."

Beneath the velvet cloak of night, Gwennotir and Boriwar made their escape, two figures fleeing from the specter of a fate decreed by powers beyond their ken, seeking solace on the unknown road ahead, where hope, however faint, yet flickered.

On Southern road, as morning's light pierced through the canopy's dense embrace, Gwennotir stirred, his heart a restless beat, as he prepared to quit the woodland camp. The sounds of nature, a symphony divine, filled the air with life's sweet melody, a stark contrast to the turmoil that raged within the young Baithas's troubled mind.

Suddenly, the tranquil scene was rent by the appearance of an armored knight. Astride a mighty steed, his presence grim and purposeful, a herald of the king's uncompromising will. With a voice that rang with stern authority, the knight declared: "Gwennotir Ker, by order of his majesty, King Gwalo the Elder, thou art commanded to return forthwith to the camp, to take thy rightful place beside thy liege and face thy destiny."

Gwennotir, his heart a tempest of defiance, stood his ground, his voice a steel-edged blade: "I shall not return, nor bend my knee to the fate decreed by others. My path is mine to choose, and I have chosen freedom's uncertain road over the grim certainty of war and death."

The knight, unmoved by the bold words of Gwennotir, urged his steed forward, his hand upon his hilt. "Thou hast no choice, young Baithas. The king's word is law, and thou art bound by oath and duty to obey. Come now, and let us end this folly, ere it brings thee to a doom most dire."

Gwennotir, his eyes alight with desperate fire, drew Pukhso from its sheath, the blade a gleam of deadly purpose in the dappled light. "I will not go, not now, not ever more. And if thou wouldst compel me, then thou must first best me in the dance of blades and blood."

The knight, dismounting, drew his own sword, edge a whisper of impending doom. "So be it, then. Though it grieves me sore to raise mine hand against a Baithas, I shall not shirk my duty to the crown."

With the clash of steel on steel they met, two figures locked in mortal combat's throes, the forest ringing with the savage song of blade on blade, as each sought to overcome the other's skill and strength. Gwennotir, driven by the fury of desperation, pressed the knight hard, his every blow a plea for freedom, for the right to choose his fate.

The knight, a seasoned warrior, met each strike with a riposte, his movements sure and graceful. But Gwennotir, fueled by the fire within, would not relent, his onslaught fierce and wild, until at last, with a cry of savage triumph, he found an opening, his blade a blur of motion, as he sent the knight's sword flying, leaving him defenseless, at his mercy.

The Form and The Shatter

In that moment, charged with tension's crackle, Gwennotir stood, his sword at the knight's throat, the power of life and death within his grasp. The knight, his eyes wide with sudden fear, spoke in a voice that trembled with his dread: "Thou hast bested me, young Baithas. My life is thine to take or spare, as thou dost choose. But know that if thou strikest me down, there is no turning back, no hope of reconciling with thy king, thy country, or thy fate."

Gwennotir, his heart a maelstrom of conflicting tides, hesitated, the weight of choice a crushing burden on his weary soul. To strike, to kill, to sever the last ties that bound him to his past, his duty, his destiny—it was a choice that would forever change the course of his life, his very being.

With shuddering breath, Gwennotir spoke, his voice a whisper, heavy with the weight of his decision: "I cannot turn back now, not after all that I have lost, all that I have risked for this chance at freedom. Forgive me, knight, for what I must now do, but I will not be shackled to a fate not of mine own choosing."

And with these words, Gwennotir brought his blade down in a swift and deadly arc, its edge biting deep into the knight's unguarded flesh, a spray of crimson staining the forest floor, as the warrior crumpled, his life's blood ebbing into the thirsty earth. Gwennotir stood, his sword dripping with the knight's blood, his eyes wide with the horror of his deed, as the realization of what he had done crashed over him like a tidal wave, sweeping away the last vestiges of his former self, leaving him forever changed, a man baptized in blood and death on this lonely road to destiny unknown.

In the depths of ancient Hloëd Wood, where towering trees and tangled undergrowth create a world apart, a sanctuary from the cares and conflicts of the realm, Gwennotir wandered, his heart heavy with his recent deeds and future fears. The path he chose, less trodden and obscure, wound through the forest's heart, a ribbon of uncertainty, leading he knew not whither.

Suddenly, the dense canopy above parted, revealing a small clearing bathed in shafts of golden light, a respite from the gloom that pressed in from all sides. And there, to Gwennotir's surprise, he saw a figure seated by a crackling fire, a man he knew yet had never thought to meet in such a place, at such a time as this.

Rirth, the dorovayan, who had bestowed upon Gwennotir the Power of Speech, looked up, his eyes alight with recognition, and spoke, his voice calm: "Gwennotir, well met in this secluded glade. Come, share my fire, and rest thy weary limbs. For fate, it seems, has brought us here to meet."

Gwennotir, his mind a whirl of doubt and fear, approached with caution, his hand upon his hilt, his voice a wary whisper in the stillness. "Rirth, what brings thee to this lonely place? What purpose hast thou in seeking me out, here in the depths of Hloëd's ancient boughs?"

Rirth, his gaze unflinching, met Gwennotir's stare and spoke, his words a riddle and a plea: "I am here, young Baithas, for the same reason that thou art—a quarrel with the king, a price upon mine head, a need to flee the consequences of my choices past. Like thee, I seek a path apart from that which fate and duty would impose upon me."

Gwennotir, eyes narrowed in suspicion, replied with a tone a mix of doubt and hope. "Thou speakest of choices and of fleeing fate, yet thou art here as if in wait for me. What game dost thou play, what web dost thou weave, that thou shouldst find me in this lonely wood?"

Rirth, his smile enigmatic, shook his head. "No game, no web, young Baithas. Merely a sense that our paths, though separate, are entwined by forces greater than our mortal ken. I am here to offer thee my aid, my counsel, in navigating the twists and turns of life that lie ahead, if thou wilt have me."

Gwennotir, his heart a battleground of trust and apprehension, paused, his mind awhirl with memories of betrayal and deceit, of powers granted and of burdens borne. Yet in Rirth's eyes, he saw a glimmer of understanding, of shared experience, that called to him despite his every fear.

With a sigh, Gwennotir lowered his guard and spoke, his voice a mix of resignation and tentative hope: "Very well, Rirth. I will hear what thou hast to say and judge the merit of thy words and thine intent. But know that I am wary and will not be easily swayed by promises or platitudes."

Rirth, his nod a gesture of acceptance, replied with a tone of gravity and aught akin to admiration: "I would expect no less from thee, Gwennotir. Thou art a Baithas, after all, and one who has seen the darker side of Power's coin. But trust me when I say that I am here as a friend, not a foe, to help thee find thy way through the labyrinth of destiny's design."

And with those words, Rirth gestured to the fire, inviting Gwennotir to sit and share the warmth and light amidst the forest's gloom. Gwennotir, his heart still heavy with the weight of doubt and apprehension, accepted the offer and settled by the flickering flames, ready to hear what Rirth had to impart and to confront the mysteries that lay ahead.

In the tranquil depths of Hloëd Wood, beneath the canopy of ancient trees, where Rirth had made his solitary camp, a small fire crackled, casting dancing shadows across the faces of the two who sat in contemplation as the night drew near.

Rirth, his countenance a mask of solemn introspection, broke the silence first, his voice a low and earnest whisper in the stillness of the forest's listening heart: "Gwennotir, I would share with thee a tale of disillusionment and shattered faith that brought me to this lonely place in search of truth beyond the reach of Derevai."

Gwennotir, with skepticism, replied, his tone bespeaking doubt and interest: "Speak on, Rirth, and I shall listen, though I make no promises to trust or follow whither thy words may lead. Mine own path is already fraught with perils and uncertainties."

Rirth, his gaze distant, seeing far beyond the flickering circle of the fire, continued, his voice a steady stream of pain and revelation: "I once believed, as thou dost now, in the power and wisdom of the Derevai, the guiding hands that shape our lives and destinies. But as I delved deeper into the mysteries of the world, I found a truth that shook my faith to its very foundations and left me adrift in a sea of doubt."

Gwennotir, his interest piqued, leaned forward with eyes intent upon Rirth's face: "What truth was this that could so shake the faith of one who served the Derevai with such devotion and conviction? What could drive thee to abandon all thou once held dear?"

Rirth, his smile a bitter twist of irony, replied, his words a hammer blow: "The truth, young Baithas, is that the Derevai are not the benevolent guardians we have been taught to revere and obey. They are capricious, cruel, and indifferent to the suffering of those who bear their mark. The Powers they bestow are not a gift, but a burden, a yoke of servitude that binds us to their will and robs us of our own agency and freedom."

Gwennotir, his mind a whirl of conflicting thoughts, struggled to reconcile Rirth's words with his own experiences and beliefs, his voice a strained and hesitant whisper: "But what of the good that Holders do, the lives they save, the peace they bring to troubled lands? Are these not proof of the Derevais' grace and wisdom?"

Rirth replied with sympathy and conviction: "The good that Holders do is not the work of Derevai, but of the human heart and will. It is the choice to use the Power for the sake of others, not the Power itself, that makes a Holder true and worthy. But this choice is one that each must make alone, without the weight of divine expectation or command."

Gwennotir, full of doubt and longing, fell silent,

his gaze turned inward as he grappled with the implications of Rirth's words and his own growing sense of unease with the path that fate had laid before him.

Rirth, sensing Gwennotir's inner turmoil, leaned forward and with a gentle voice offered thus: "I see the struggle in thine eyes, Gwennotir, the same struggle that I once faced myself. But know that thou art not alone in this, that there are others who have walked this path and found a way to wield the Powers free of the Derevais' influence and control. If thou wilt trust me, I can guide thee to a place beyond their reach, where thou canst learn the truth of thine own Power, and the Powers of Space, Time, and Thought, unfettered by the chains of divine obligation."

Gwennotir, with a sudden leap of hope and trepidation, met Rirth's steady gaze: "I will hear what thou hast to say, Rirth, and learn what thou canst teach me of the Powers and the path to freedom from the Derevai. But I make no promises to follow whither this knowledge leads, only to listen and to weigh the merits of thy words against the weight of mine own heart and conscience."

Rirth, smiling, nodded, his hand outstretched in silent pact, as the fire's glow illuminated the darkness of the forest's heart; and the path ahead, uncertain still, was now filled with promise of revelation and discovery for one Baithas seeking truth and freedom in a world of shadows and false divinity.

Across the landscape of the south, through forests dense and meadows sprawling wide, o'er rocky outcrops and through winding vales, Gwennotir and Rirth journeyed side by side, their path a winding ribbon through the wild, marked by the passage of the turning days.

As they walked, Rirth shared the ancient lore of Powers and the teachings of the Keulenu, his voice a steady stream of wisdom flowing, revealing truths long hidden from the world. He spoke of origins and roles ordained, of those who wielded might beyond the ken of mortal men, and how their fates were bound to a greater purpose than they could know.

Yet even as he spoke, Rirth's voice was tinged with fading faith, his own life once entwined with the Shatter's mysteries, now unraveled by the doubts that grew within his heart, like cracks in a foundation once thought unshakable and true.

In a moment of reflection, as the Sun hung low upon the horizon's distant edge, Rirth turned to Gwennotir, his voice a gentle invitation to a path less trodden on: "Gwennotir, let me share with thee a practice that has brought me solace in these times of doubt. It is the art of meditation, of turning inward to find the strength and wisdom that reside within oneself, rather than seeking validation from deities or others who would claim to hold the keys to truth and destiny."

Gwennotir replied with hesitation and curiosity: "Rirth, I hear thy words, but struggle to embrace them fully. All my life I have been taught to seek approval from those above me, to doubt mine own worth and abilities, to rely on the guidance of the Derevai and the Powers they bestow. How can I trust myself to be the source of mine own strength and purpose?"

Rirth, with an understanding smile, said with empathy and encouragement: "It is a difficult path to unlearn the lessons of a lifetime and to trust one's inner voice. But know that this is a path worth taking, for it leads to a deeper understanding of oneself and the power that resides within. Let me guide thee in this practice, and together we shall explore the depths of being and find the truth that lies beyond the veil of expectations and external validation."

And so, beneath the colors of the setting Sun, upon a hill that overlooked the world in all its wild and untamed beauty, Gwennotir and Rirth sat, cross-legged and still, their eyes closed and their breath a steady rhythm, as Rirth led Gwennotir through the winding paths of meditation, teaching him to sit within the stillness of his own soul's depths.

Gwennotir struggled, his mind a tempest of doubts and fears, of memories and regrets, a whirlwind of distractions that threatened to pull him from the present moment's grasp. But slowly, with each passing day and night, with Rirth's guidance and his own determination, he learned to let the thoughts drift by like clouds caught in a pool's reflection, to anchor himself within the steady beat of his own heart, the whisper of his breath.

And then, one evening, as the world was bathed in hues of gold and crimson, as the breeze whispered its secrets through the rustling leaves, Gwennotir felt a sudden shift within, a moment of pure clarity and peace; a veil had lifted from his eyes, and he saw himself, perhaps for the first time, not as a pawn of fate or destiny, but as a being of inherent worth and power, connected to a source beyond the reach of Derevai or mortal expectation.

In that moment, brief but profound, Gwennotir felt a sense of liberation, a lightness in his heart and in his step, as a weight left his shoulders, and he breathed more deeply than before. He turned to Rirth, his eyes alight with wonder, and spoke, his voice a whisper of revelation: "Rirth, I think I understand now what thou didst mean about finding strength and purpose from within. It is a feeling unlike any I have known, a sense of connection to something greater than myself, yet also deeply rooted in the core of who I am, beyond the label of Baithas."

Rirth, with a smile bespeaking pride and understanding, replied with a warm and supporting voice: "Yes, Gwennotir, that is the essence of the path we walk, the truth that lies beyond the stories and the legends we were taught. It is a truth that cannot be bestowed by any external force or power, but must be discovered and embraced within oneself, through the quiet practice of turning inward and listening to the wisdom of the heart."

And so, beneath the painted sky of sunset, two figures sat in silent contemplation, their journey far from over, but their path now illuminated by a new and brighter light, of power understood and purpose found, not in the dictates of divinity, but in the depths of their own being's truth, a truth that would guide them through the trials and triumphs yet to come, these seekers on the winding road of fate.

Song of the Crickets

Beneath the vast expanse of the starlit sky, in the depths of Hloëd Wood, where ancient trees stood sentinel and wise, Gwennotir and Rirth made their humble camp, their horses and a flickering fire their sole companions in the night's encroaching darkness.

As crickets sang their timeless lullaby and gentle breezes stirred the leaves above, Gwennotir sat apart, his form composed in meditation's still and silent pose, seeking the inner peace that Rirth had shown him how to find, beyond the world's turmoil.

Deep in the reaches of the mind's expanse, where thoughts and feelings swirled like eddies in a vast and uncharted sea, Gwennotir suddenly perceived a presence, a being of immense and ancient power that spoke directly to his startled soul.

"I am Yog," the voice intoned, its timbre rich with wisdom's weight and knowledge's vast domain, "and I have come to guide thee on thy path, to show thee truths beyond the mortal realm."

Gwennotir, awed and shaken by this strange intrusion on his meditation's peace, replied with hesitation: "Yog, thou sayest, but how can I be sure that thou art not just a figment of my mind's imagining, a trick of stress or fevered fantasy?"

Yog, knowing Gwennotir's doubt and fear, responded with a demonstration clear, a gentle breeze that swirled a single leaf in patterns intricate and mesmerizing, an unmistakable sign of presence beyond the bounds of mortal conjuring.

"Dost thou believe me now, young Baithas?" Yog

asked, its voice a mix of mirth and power. "For I have much to share with thee, if thou wilt follow where I lead, along a path marked by a tree of shape and form unique, that lies in wait upon the southward road."

Gwennotir, grappling with the weight of this encounter strange and wondrous, agreed to follow Yog's instruction, though his heart was filled with trepidation, uncertain of the meaning and the scope of this new manifestation.

As he emerged from meditation's calm and shared his tale with Rirth beside the fire, he found his mentor's reaction less than kind, a skeptic's dismissal of his claims as nothing more than stress-induced delusion or wishful thinking born of faith's excess.

"Gwennotir," Rirth said, concern and condescension biting through his words, "thou must be wary of such visions grand, for oft the mind, when strained by circumstance, can conjure phantoms that seem real enough, but are mere shadows of our own desires."

Gwennotir, stung by Rirth's dismissive tone, retorted with a passion born of truth: "I know that what I experienced was real, a presence vast and ancient, wise and kind, that spoke to me in ways I cannot doubt and showed me signs of power manifest!"

The tension between mentor and student grew thick and palpable beneath the stars, as each defended his own certainty, one born of skepticism's cynical edge, the other of conviction's fervent fire, both grappling with the dire implications of powers beyond their understanding and control.

"Enough," said Rirth, his patience wearing thin. "I shall not debate the truth of thy delusions but caution thee against the dangerous road of blind belief in voices from within, that may lead thee astray from reason's path and into madness's dark and tangled depths."

Gwennotir, isolated and misunderstood, withdrew into a silence cold and deep, his heart a storm of doubt and longing fierce for validation of his strange encounter and guidance in the face of destiny's inscrutable and ever-shifting tides.

As the night wore on, and embers dimmed, two figures sat in silent contemplation, one lost in thoughts of visions grand and strange, the other in the certainty of doubt, both unaware of how this debate would shape the path of fate's unfolding dance, and lead them to a future yet unknown, where gods and mortals intertwine and clash in the eternal struggle for the soul's dominion over destiny and will.

In the rugged, Sun-drenched wildlands of the southern road, where lesser-trodden paths converge and split like veins in living stone, Gwennotir and Rirth came upon a fork, a crossroads marked by a strange and twisted tree, its branches bent in patterns most bizarre, shaped by unseen hands or forces.

Gwennotir, his eyes alight with recognition, exclaimed with joy and vindication's fire: "Rirth, behold! This tree, so strange and gnarled, is the very one Yog described to me, a sign that we should take the southern path and follow where divine direction leads!"

Rirth surveyed the tree and paths with a critical eye and spoke with firm conviction in his voice: "Nay, Gwennotir, I see no reason here to trust in signs from beings we know not; the western road is safer, swifter too, and will lead us far from Gwalo's reach."

Gwennotir, with suspicion, doubt, and newfound faith colliding, replied with heat, his voice a challenge bold: "Rirth, why dost thou suddenly insist upon a path that seems to draw us closer to the very king we both have cause to fear? Could it be that thou hast hidden motives, or knowledge that thou hast not shared with me?"

Rirth, with narrowed eyes and defensive ire, retorted sharply: "Thou art a foolish boy, naïve and stubborn, to trust in visions and ignore the wisdom of one who knows these lands and dangers well. I only seek to protect and guide thee truly, not lead thee into peril's waiting jaws."

The tension thick between them as the strange tree stood witness to their strife, its twisted branches a silent jury, judging the merits of their arguments, Gwennotir with resolve a fire burning bright, made his decision, a declaration firm: "Rirth, I cannot ignore the signs that Yog has given me, nor the instinct in mine heart that tells me I must follow this southern path, even if it means parting ways with thee, for I must trust in mine own destiny and the guidance of powers that be."

Rirth, his face a mask of disappointment and something akin to pity or disdain, shook his head, his voice a bitter sigh: "So be it then, thou stubborn, stupid child. Go then, and chase thy visions and thy dreams, but come not crying when they lead thee to ruin and regret most deep, for I have tried to save thee from thyself, but thou art deaf to reason's urgent plea."

As the argument reached its peak, with tempers flaring and accusations hurled, Gwennotir and Rirth stood at an impasse, their wills and visions locked in bitter strife. But as the Sun began to dip below the western hills, and shadows lengthened deep, a moment of clarity, a pause in passion's headlong rush, descended upon them both, as if the very land itself had breathed a sigh of patience and perspective's balm.

Gwennotir, his voice a mix of firm resolve and newfound understanding, spoke once more: "Rirth, I hear thy words, and though I still believe the southern road to be the way that Yog has shown me, I would not let our disagreement drive a wedge between us, for we have come too far and faced too much to let this choice divide us in the end."

Rirth, his anger cooling in the face of Gwennotir's unexpected wisdom, replied with a measured tone, his eyes reflecting a glimmer of respect and gratitude: "Perhaps thou art right, Gwennotir, in this at least, that we should not let passion's heat obscure the bond we share, the trials we've overcome; and though I still have doubts about thy vision, I'll not let them destroy our partnership."

A silence fell between them, comfortable, as the last rays of sunlight painted the sky in hues of gold and red, a reminder of the world's continuance despite the struggles of mortal hearts and minds in conflict caught.

Gwennotir spoke once more, his gaze upon the darkening sky: "Let us then make camp here for the night, beneath this strange and fateful tree's embrace, and in the morning's light, with clearer heads and hearts, we'll choose which path to take together, as companions and as friends. For in the end, 'tis not the road we walk, but the company we keep that matters most."

Rirth nodded his assent: "Aye, let us rest then, and let the night's cool breath soothe the fires of our debate, and in the dawn's new light, we will face the choice that destiny has laid before our feet."

In the dimly lit campsite, just off the road where the fork's strange tree loomed overhead, Gwennotir sat, his mind a torrent tossed with doubts and indecision's heavy weight, as shadows danced and flickered in the light of the crackling fire, a feeble defense against the encroaching night's embrace.

With hands made busy by the evening's chores, Gwennotir stirred the pot, his thoughts a whirl of arguments, the day's debate with Rirth still fresh and raw in his mind, a wound that would not heal.

As if on cue, Rirth ventured forth into the treeline's shadowed depths, his purpose vague, returning later with a bundle of unnecessary kindling for the fire, a gesture that did little to dispel the lingering tension in the air between them.

The meal consumed in silence, heavy with unspoken thoughts and questions left unasked, Rirth soon retired to his bedroll, his breathing soft and even in the night, leaving Gwennotir alone with his suspicions, a gnawing ache that would not let him rest.

At last, unable to endure the weight of curiosity and mistrust combined, Gwennotir rose, his steps a furtive whisper as he crept towards the spot whither Rirth had gone, his heart a pounding drum within his chest, half-dreading what he might discover there.

And just past the tree-line's shadowed edge, a stack of stones stood there, deliberately placed, with Rirth's initial drawn upon the top, a mark of secret communication made, a sign that all was not as it appeared between the mentor and young Baithas.

Gwennotir stood, transfixed by what he saw, his mind a whirl of dire implications, as realization crashed upon him like a wave of icy water, shocking him out of the fragile trust he had begun to build with Rirth, despite their differences.

"What is the meaning of this?" he asked himself aloud, his voice a strangled whisper in the night, as he stormed back into the campfire's glow, the stone clutched tightly in his trembling hand, a talisman of betrayal and deceit.

As dawn's first light began to paint the sky, Gwennotir sat beside the ashes of the dying fire, his heart heavy in his chest, his resolve shaken, and unready to fight the challenge this day would bring.

Then Rirth awoke, and seeing the stone that Gwennotir held, averted his eyes, shoulders hunched, as if beneath the burden of his guilt, a posture that did little to allay the growing tension in the air between them.

At last Gwennotir spoke, his voice a mix of steady calm and barely contained rage: "Rirth, I demand the truth, and nothing less. What is the meaning of this stone, this mark of secret communication? What hast thou hidden from me all this time?"

Rirth, caught off guard by Gwennotir's words, hesitated, his face a mask of conflict as the weight of long-held secrets fought against the urge finally to confess, to lay bare the tangled web of lies and plots that had ensnared them both, unwitting pawns in a game of power, politics, and death.

With a heavy sigh, Rirth met Gwennotir's eyes, his voice laden with regret: "Gwennotir, there is much I have not told thee, much I have kept hidden, out of fear and a misguided sense of loyalty to those who do not deserve it, least of all the king, whose machinations led to the deaths of thy beloved brother and thy father."

Gwennotir, his eyes wide with shock and pain, felt the air rush from his lungs as if a blow had struck him, deep within his chest: "What meanest thou, Rirth? What role didst thou play in this vile plot, this betrayal of the ones I loved, the ones who trusted thee?"

With head bowed low in shame, Rirth said: "I was part of it, Gwennotir, a tool used by the king to shape events, to clear a path for his ambitions, his desire to have a Baithas under his control, a weapon to be wielded, not a friend or ally in the cause of peace and justice.

"Leubkherth Morhwa, thy father's second, was the one who caused Kolewa's death, a pawn in

Gwalo's game, a sacrifice to set the stage for thy ascension, thine unwitting role as Baithas, bound to serve the king's dark purposes, his lust for power."

Gwennotir then felt the tears begin to fall, hot and fast, as the depth of Rirth's betrayal sank in, a knife twisted in the wound of his own trust, his naïve belief in the goodness of the one he thought a mentor and a friend.

He asked with a ragged whisper: "And what of Leubkherth, what fate befell the one who betrayed Kolewa to his death, on the orders of the king thou claimest to have betrayed?"

With his face a mask of grim resolve, Rirth replied: "He too has paid the price, Gwennotir, killed by the very master he once served, a loose end to be tied, a threat removed, as Gwalo seeks to cover up his tracks and eliminate all those who know the truth of his foul deeds and vile machinations."

Gwennotir, with trembling hand, drew forth Pukhso, the symbol of his Power and his pain, and leveled it at Rirth, his eyes alight with fury and despair, a shattered soul laid bare before the one who had betrayed him.

"And what of thee, Rirth? What fate deservest thou for thy part in this wretched plot, this web of lies and death that hath ensnared my family, my destiny, my very life?"

Rirth, his grey eyes filled with weary sadness, spoke softly, his voice a plea for mercy: "I cannot undo what has been done, nor can I bring back those whose lives are lost to Gwalo's cruel ambitions and mine own misguided loyalty and fear. But I can offer thee the truth, at last, and the chance to chart thine own path forward, free from the lies and manipulations of those who would use thee.

"If thou wishest to kill me, I will not resist. For I have earned thy wrath, thy righteous anger; but know that my death will not bring back thy loved ones, nor will it heal the wounds that have been inflicted on thine heart and soul, though death would bring me peace."

Gwennotir, his sword hand shaking with the weight of his decision, the choice that lay before him, felt the tears stream down his face, a flood of grief and rage and bitter disappointment, as he struggled with the urge to strike, to end the life of one who had betrayed him so.

But in that moment, as the Sun rose higher above the trees, casting its light upon the scene of confrontation and despair, Gwennotir lowered his blade, his voice a whisper, saying: "Go, Rirth, leave this place, and never seek me again, for I cannot bear to look upon thy face, nor hear thy voice, without feeling the pain of all that thou hast done, the trust that thou hast broken. But know that if our paths should cross again, if thou shouldst ever seek to harm or use me, as thou and Gwalo have done before, I will not hesitate to strike thee down and send thee to the fate that thou dost deserve."

Rirth, his head bowed low in silent assent, gathered up his meager possessions, his heart heavy with the weight of his own guilt, and, mounting his horse, he turned to leave, the hoofbeats soft upon the forest floor, a figure consumed by the shadows of the trees, a memory of betrayal and trust forever lost.

Then sheathing his blade and wiping the tears

from his eyes, Gwennotir looked to Boriwar and said: "Forgive me, friend, for I have neglected thy friendship these long days past, in favor of a man whom I now despise. Wilt thou speak with me and be a warmth against loneliness's chill?"

The steed replied: "I am thy beast, and thou art my master, and there is nothing to forgive. Mount up, and we shall continue on the path that leads from pain and death."

Then Gwennotir broke down the camp, and mounting his horse, he turned his face toward the south, toward the road that Yog had shown, the path that he must follow if he hoped to find his own destiny, the role that he must play in this unfolding story.

In the depths of Hloëd Wood, where ancient trees cast dappled shadows on the forest floor, Gwennotir wandered. Amidst the quiet of untouched nature's realm, he found a place, secluded and serene, where he might seek the counsel of the divine and find the path that he was meant to tread.

With a deep breath, Gwennotir settled down, his eyes closed, his mind a calm, clear pool, as he reached out with all his heart and soul to Yog, the wisdom that had come before.

"Yog, I am lost, adrift in a sea of doubt, betrayed by one I trusted, one I thought to be a friend and ally in this twisted game of power, politics, and fate. I need thy guidance, now more than ever, to light the way, to show me whither to go, and who to be, in this uncertain world."

But silence was his only answer, a void that

echoed with the absence of the voice he so desperately yearned to hear again. The weight of isolation pressed upon him, a burden he could not bear alone.

With a sigh of frustration and resolve, Gwennotir rose, his eyes now open wide, determined to cut his own path, to be the master of his fate, no matter what the cost may be.

"If Yog will not answer, if Rirth has betrayed me, then I must trust mine own strength, mine own instincts and desires, to guide me through the wilderness of life, the tangled web of choices and consequences that await."

And so, with Boriwar, he set his course to the south, cutting through the undergrowth, the untamed wilds that lay between him and the future he would make.

As he walked, his mind a whirl of thoughts, of memories and hopes, of fears and dreams, he came upon a fallen tree, its bark etched with the words "Brenn loves Ragnir," a sign that seemed to speak directly to his heart.

"Brenn loves Ragnir," he whispered to himself, two names that felt both strange and somehow right, names that spoke of new beginnings, of a chance to leave behind the burdens of his past, the expectations, and the lies that had defined him for so long—too long.

"I am not Gwennotir Ker," he said aloud, his voice a declaration to Boriwar and the trees, the sky, the world that stretched out far and wide. "I am Brenn Ragnir, born anew this day, a man who will not be defined by others, but by his own choices, his own will to be!"

And with that revelation, that moment of self-recognition and acceptance pure, he felt a weight lift from his shoulders, a sense of freedom and purpose he had not known before, a joy that filled his heart.

No longer bound by name or destiny, by duty or by fate's capricious hand, he rode forth, ready to face whatever lay ahead, with courage and hope, with strength and will.

Brenn Ragnir now walked a path of his own making, a journey that would test him, shape him, lead him to the truth of who he was, and who he was meant to be in this wide world of wonder and strife.

And though the road ahead was long and hard, though dangers and temptations lurked unseen, he knew that he would face them unafraid, for he was the master of his own soul now, a seeker of his own truth, his own way, in the great tapestry of life's design.

So on he went, through Sun and shadow, through the winding paths of Hloëd's ancient wood, a figure small against the vast expanse of nature's timeless beauty and its might, but a figure strong, determined, and alive with the fire of self-discovery and growth, a flame that would not be extinguished by the winds of fate, the storms of circumstance, but would burn bright, a beacon in the night, a light to guide him on his chosen way, towards a future that was his to claim, and a destiny that he would make his own.

Canto 2

In a wide-open valley, vast and still, where snow-capped peaks stood sentinel in the distance, Brenn and Boriwar, two figures small and lone, pressed onward through the bitter cold, their breath a fog of crystalline despair, their steps a weary march against the howling wind.

The blizzard, fierce and sudden, had descended upon them like a vengeful god, its wrath a blinding veil of white, a frozen hell that threatened to consume them, body and soul.

Brenn, his voice a ragged whisper, spoke to Boriwar, his faithful steed and friend: "I fear this may be the end, my loyal one, for even my resolve, my newfound strength, cannot withstand the fury of this storm. We may well perish here, in this vast waste, two more lost souls claimed by Winter's rage."

But even as despair began to take its icy grip upon his heart, a sound broke through the wind's relentless roar, a cry of voices, strong and clear, a sign of life amidst the desolation of the vale.

And through the swirling snow, a group appeared, hunters on horseback, their fur-clad forms a welcome sight to Brenn's half-frozen eyes. At their head, a man of noble bearing rode, his face a mask of stern concern, his voice a command that cut through the storm's din.

"Ho there, traveler! What brings thee to this place, in such a time of peril and of strife? Thou seemest ill-prepared for this harsh clime, and ill-equipped to face its deadly chill."

Brenn, his voice a grateful croak, replied: "I am Brenn Ragnir, a wanderer in these parts, seeking my own path, but caught unawares by this fierce blizzard's rage. I fear my journey may well end here, sir, unless some aid or shelter can be found."

The nobleman, his eyes a glint of steel softened by compassion's gentle light, spoke then, his words a balm to Brenn's despair: "I am Lord Aebakhmë, master of these lands, and I will not see a traveler perish thus, not while my castle stands, a haven warm against the cold embrace of winter's wrath. Come, Brenn Ragnir, thou and thy steed alike, and find respite within mine halls until this storm has passed, and thou mayest journey on."

With gratitude and wonder in his heart, Brenn followed Aebakhmë and his crew, their horses plowing through the drifts with ease, until at last, the castle came in sight, a bastion of grey stone and flickering light, a promise of warmth, of food and rest and cheer.

Inside the keep, the fires roared in hearths of

massive size, their glow a welcome kiss upon the frozen skin of Brenn. Servants brought him blankets, mulled wine, and bread, and as Boriwar was led to safety in the stables, Aebakhmë with grace and charm bade Brenn to sit and share his table's bounty.

"Tell me, Brenn Ragnir," the lord inquired, his eyes alight with curiosity, "what quest or purpose drives thee through these lands, to brave the wilds alone, without a guide?"

Brenn, warmed by wine and gratitude alike, spoke then, his tale a winding path of woe and wonder, of betrayal and rebirth, of gods and men, of power and of fate—though he gave not the true names of those who played their parts, for he wished not that his identity should be known.

Aebakhmë listened, rapt, his questions keen, his interest genuine and deep, a welcoming balm to Brenn's long-lonely heart, a connection forged in the midst of Winter's isolation.

And as the night wore on, and the storm raged still beyond the keep's thick walls and shuttered windows, Brenn felt a sense of peace, of respite brief but precious, in the company of one who seemed to understand, to empathize with his strange tale, his journey's twisting path.

"Thou art welcome here," Lord Aebakhmë said, his hand a firm clasp on Brenn's shoulder laid, "for as long as thou needest to rest, to heal, to gather strength for the road that lies ahead. Mine home is thine, mine hearth, my meat and mead, for in thee, Brenn Ragnir, I sense a kindred soul, a seeker of truth, a wanderer in this world of shadows and of light, of joy and pain. Stay, then, and be at ease, until the dawn breaks clear and bright upon the snow-swept plain, and thou mayest set forth once more, renewed, reborn, to face the challenges that lie in wait beyond the valley's vast and silent gate."

And so, in the warmth of Aebakhmë's hall, Brenn found a moment's peace, a chance to rest and to reflect upon the winding road that had brought him to this place, this time, this strange and unexpected interlude in the grand saga of his life.

Within the grand dining hall of Aebakhmë's keep, where warmth and revelry held sway supreme, a stark contrast to the blizzard's rage outside, Brenn found himself amidst a sea of faces, attendants, guests, all gathered to partake of the lord's hospitality and cheer.

The air was thick with laughter, conversation, the clink of goblets and the savory scent of roasted meats and rich, exotic spices, a feast fit for a king, or so it seemed to Brenn, the wanderer, the grateful guest.

And yet, amidst the merriment and mirth, he felt a twinge of obligation, deep within his heart, a need to reciprocate the kindness shown to him by Aebakhmë, the lord who'd saved him from the storm's cruel grip.

With purposeful strides, he made his way through the throng of revelers, his eyes fixed upon the high table, where Aebakhmë sat, presiding over the feast with regal grace.

"My lord," Brenn spoke, his voice a humble note amidst the din of conversation's flow, "I come to offer thee my services, in gratitude for thy most generous aid, thy shelter and thine hospitality, which saved my life and that of my faithful steed."

Aebakhmë, his eyebrows raised in surprise, regarded Brenn with a curious gaze, a hint of amusement playing at the corners of his lips, as he replied in measured tones: "Thine offer is most kind, Brenn Ragnir, and yet I wonder at its nature, its intent. What services couldst thou, a wanderer, provide to me, a lord of these vast lands?"

Brenn, beneath the weight of Aebakhmë's stare, the unspoken challenge in his words, pressed on, determined to prove his worth, his gratitude: "My lord, I am a man of many talents, a warrior and a hunter, and a speaker of many tongues. Whatever task thou wilt set before me, I will strive to see it done, with all my might."

Aebakhmë, his lips now curving in a smile that danced between the lines of mirth and mischief, leaned forward, his voice a conspiratorial whisper: "Is that so, Brenn Ragnir? Well then, let us see the measure of thy resolve, thy willingness to serve my every whim, no matter how absurd or dangerous the task may be."

With a gesture grand, he pointed to the hearth, where flames leapt high, a roaring inferno: "Wouldst thou walk barefoot across these glowing coals, to prove thy loyalty, thy fearless heart?"

Brenn, taken aback by the odd request, hesitated for a moment, doubt and fear warring with his desire to prove himself. But then, with a deep breath, he nodded once, his voice a steadfast declaration bold: "If that is thy command, my lord, then I shall walk the coals, and trust in mine own strength to see me through the trial, unscathed, unbowed."

Aebakhmë, his laughter ringing through the hall, clapped his hands in delight, his voice a boom of jovial amusement, tinged with pride: "Well spoken, Brenn Ragnir! But fear not, I would not ask such a feat of thee, not yet, for I can see the sincerity that shines within thine eyes, the depth of thy commitment to honor and repay the debt you feel."

With a more serious tone, he then continued: "Thine offer is accepted, Brenn Ragnir, but know that I shall call upon thy skills as I see fit, in matters great and small, for in thee I sense a spirit true and strong, a man who keeps his word, no matter what the cost may be, to body or to soul."

Brenn, relief and gratitude mingling in his heart, bowed low before the lord, his words a solemn vow: "I am at thy service, Lord Aebakhmë, from this day forth, until the debt is paid, or until thou dost release me from my pledge, I shall be thy man, thine instrument of will, in all things, save those that would compromise mine honor or mine own sense of what is right."

Aebakhmë, pleased by Brenn's words, his loyalty, nodded in approval, then gestured to a seat at the high table, near his own, a place of honor: "Then sit, Brenn Ragnir, and share in this feast, as a member of mine household, a trusted friend, for I have a feeling that thy presence here will bring great things, both for thyself and for the realm that I hold dear."

And so, with a heart both light and heavy, Brenn took his place at Aebakhmë's side, a part of something larger than himself, a cog in the grand machinations of a lord whose motives and whose plans were yet unknown, but whose generosity and grace had saved him from the icy jaws of death, had given him purpose and a chance to prove his worth.

In the aftermath of the feast, as the last morsels were consumed and the final drops of wine were drained, Lord Aebakhmë rose from his seat, his countenance aglow with the warmth of good cheer and hospitality. "Well, that is all for me tonight. Goodnight to you all!" he declared, his voice a jovial boom that echoed through the hall.

With a swish of his robes, he turned to leave, his companions following in his wake, a procession of sated guests and loyal retainers. As he reached the threshold, he glanced back at Brenn, a smile playing upon his lips, a silent acknowledgment of the bond they had begun to forge.

Brenn, alone now amidst the remnants of the feast, turned to his right, where a servant stood against the wall, her posture one of quiet deference. "The meal was delicious," he said, his voice warm with gratitude. "I thank thee and the others for it."

The young woman, her eyes downcast, replied softly, "Thou art kind, but instead thank my master. I am his servant." Her garb was simple and unadorned, a mirror of the other servants' attire, yet there was something about her that caught Brenn's eye. She seemed to be of an age with him, her raven hair a hallmark of Mitho Gorikhwa, her voice a gentle lilt that spoke of lands beyond.

Through a high window, the moonlight streamed in, bathing her in a silvery glow, her gown seemingly woven from starlight itself. It was then that Brenn realized what had struck him as odd about her appearance.

"Thine eyes are green," he mused, "and thou art taller than Aebakhmë, who is already large for someone of his race; nor is thy skin olive, but ivory. Thou art not of this land unless I am mistaken."

The servant, her gaze still fixed upon the floor, confirmed his suspicions. "Nay, thou hast the right of it."

Intrigued, Brenn pressed further. "Wilt thou tell me whence you come?"

"I was born in Dol-Nopthelen," she revealed, "but my father took me to Mitho Gorikhwa when I was very young."

A smile spread across Brenn's face, a flicker of recognition. "The land of my forebears. No doubt we share a lineage, though it may be a connection from four thousand years ago." He paused, a sudden realization staying his tongue. He knew he should not share details of his homeland with anyone, lest word of his whereabouts reach the ears of Gwalo.

The young woman, perhaps sensing his hesitation, spoke once more. "I know little history of the land of my father. The hour is late. If thou hast no need of me, I will attend my duties."

"Before thou goest," Brenn said, "wilt thou tell me thy name?"

She bowed, a gesture of respect. "I am Baiwieth." With that, she turned and left the dining hall through the kitchen door, leaving Brenn alone with his thoughts.

As he turned back to the table, he was surprised to find Lady Luwa, Aebakhmë's mother, still seated in her chair, a knowing smile upon her face. "That was strange," she remarked, her tone laced with amusement.

"What meanest thou, my lady?" Brenn asked, puzzled by her words.

Lady Luwa's smile widened, a glint of mischief in her eyes. "Thou art a handsome young man, Brenn. Baiwieth is a beautiful young woman."

Brenn shook his head, a flush creeping up his neck. "I cannot stay long in the house of Aebakhmë. I should retire as well. Goodnight, Lady Luwa." With a bow, he took his leave, making his way to the chambers that had been prepared for him.

Once in the privacy of his room, Brenn changed into his night clothes, the soft fabric a welcome respite from the day's trials. As he settled into the bed, the mattress yielding beneath his weary form, he marveled at the comfort that surrounded him. The sheets, warm and inviting, seemed to embrace him, and it was only then that he realized the depths of his exhaustion.

Sleep, a gentle mistress, claimed him swiftly, drawing him into her sweet embrace, a temporary reprieve from the challenges that lay ahead. For now, in the sanctuary of Aebakhmë's keep, Brenn could rest, his dreams a tapestry of the day's events, woven with threads of hope and the promise of a new beginning.

A few hours thence, Brenn woke, his slumber broken by the wind's mournful howl outside his window. Like a mother hound crying for her pups, lost to winter's icy grasp, the wind rose and fell in plaintive waves, a lament that echoed through the night. Brenn listened, his mind adrift, until at last, in the early hours of morn, a light sleep claimed him once again.

Near noon, as judged by the light that streamed through his window's pane, Brenn arose, his body refreshed, his mind still heavy with the weight of dreams. He dressed, his movements slow and deliberate, before making his way to the main hall, where he hoped to find Lord Aebakhmë.

The lordling sat at the long table, his mother Luwa by his side, a spread of meat and bread laid out before them. Aebakhmë's hunting companions, Husin and Suthai among them, had joined their lord for this midday repast.

"Good morrow to thee," Aebakhmë said, his nod a greeting warm and sincere. "I trust thou didst sleep well."

Brenn, his smile a mask for the restless night he'd spent, replied, "Very well. I apologize for sleeping as late as I did. I hope I have not caused thee any inconvenience."

Aebakhmë waved his hand, a gesture of dismissal. "Nay, not at all. I have eaten and completed my morning duties, so I am free. Please eat, Brenn."

Though not as grand as the feast of the previous night, the meal was generous, the flavors rich and satisfying. Brenn ate his fill of soft bread and thick-cut ham, the hearth's crackling fire a comforting presence. The meat, sweeter than the fare of the Valk, and the bread, glazed with a thin layer of sugar, left Brenn's mouth smacking with each bite.

As his meal drew to a close, Brenn turned to Aebakhmë, his voice a mix of gratitude and obligation. "My lord, thou didst save my life yesterday, and I am in thy debt. If there is aught I can do for thee, I shall."

"That pleases me to hear," the lordling said, "but I know not what I would have of thee."

Brenn, his resolve unwavering, pressed on. "Anything within my power, I will give."

Aebakhmë laughed, a sound of mirth and possibility. "I see. Then, I suppose there is something thou couldst do. I have business matters to which I must attend in Jub Khewi. Perhaps thou wilt accompany me there."

A smile spread across Brenn's face. "'Twould be my pleasure, Lord."

"Then I will send a messenger ahead to inform my steward of our arrival. We shall leave tomorrow at dawn."

With the meal concluded, all in attendance rose, making their way to the yard, save for Luwa, who remained behind. Aebakhmë paused at the door, as Suthai and Husin went ahead.

"Come with me, Brenn," he said. "There is something I would show thee."

Brenn followed the lordling through the door and into the yard, then up two flights of stairs on the castle's side, to the roof above. From this vantage point, the woods to the east stretched out before them, while to the south, the valley lay blanketed in the previous night's snow, the sun's light glinting off the white peaks of the Dyuglebai. A tower rose from the castle's center, stairs snaking around its form.

Aebakhmë led Brenn to the tower's top, where the view was most impressive. Brenn could see for miles, the brisk wind tousling his hair, his cloak pulled tight against his throat.

"We are close to the border of Len Khalayu," Aebakhmë said. "Thou canst see their scouting towers from here. We could walk to the nearest one within a day, but the way has become dangerous of late. My father built this tower. It was his personal tradition to climb up here at midnight before each new year and look out on his land, and he would say farewell to what had been, and welcome what would come."

Brenn, his curiosity piqued, asked, "Who is thy lord-father?"

"Aeboli. He was a great warrior."

"Is he not now?"

Aebakhmë, his voice tinged with sorrow, replied, "Alas, he is dead these many years."

"Accept my dearest sympathies, my lord," Brenn said, his words a balm for the lordling's grief.

"Wouldst thou hear the story of how fate took him?" Aebakhmë asked.

Brenn, eager to learn more, nodded. "I would, if thou wouldst tell me."

And so, atop the tower, with the world stretched out before them, Aebakhmë began his tale. "Very well, Brenn. I will tell thee the story of Aeboli of Jub Khewi. Almost thirty years ago, my father was twenty-two years old and the son of a wadhestor, and a great warrior besides. By the time he was of age to marry, he had seen a dozen battles. His own father, the wadhestor Tethter, was a man of great faith, keeping to the teachings of Rilun, but that did not stop him from being a man of war as well. The wadhestor was not the sort of man to wait for enemies to attack, and he was known for taking his private army into battle several times each year. He never returned without spoils of conquest."

Aebakhmë's voice grew somber as he continued, "Tethter became old, and he was ready to retire as leader of his company of soldiers—but a new threat came to the land. The Hudas tribe invaded the lands of Len Khalayu to the west, and the wadhestor knew that the savages would soon be at Jub Khewi. Tethter gathered his army and attacked when the Hudas expected it least. He killed their warrior-king Hwadhor, and the victory was swift. But when Tethter and his soldiers returned to Jub Khewi, they found the city burning.

"The Hudas had been joined by the Derwali, another wild tribe from Pellen. The wadhestor's army charged against the barbarians, and it is said that Tethter fought like a lion, but the enemy was too great. They overpowered the wadhestor's army, and my grandfather was killed in battle. My father and the surviving soldiers fought bravely, and when things seemed their blackest, the Six intervened. The Hudas and Derwali turned on each other, and the Derwali retreated back to Pellen. Father and his men found new strength and drove the Hudas back. They cut the barbarians down to a single man, whom they captured and executed on the steps of the Temple of Rilun. It was a complete victory, and the army returned to their great city to find it still smoking from the fires of the savages. The villages outside the city walls had suffered as well, with many homes and farms burned."

Aebakhmë paused, his gaze distant, as if seeing the past unfold before him. "Father was yet young and wanted nothing of the responsibility of being a wadhestor, and so he turned Jub Khewi over to his brother Regoboli. My father marched to war once more, taking with him the remnants of Tethter's forces. They traveled to Markhlen and killed the rest of the Hudas tribe, then found the Derwali on their islands and put their villages to the torch, their men to the sword, and their women to bed.

"He returned from his war and took his place as leader of the army of Jub Khewi and began an armory to stockpile weapons lest any other people try to take the shining city. He raised an army of two thousand men, keeping a hundred with him at all times as his personal regiment. Everyone remembered for years afterward how the Hudas and Derwali had destroyed the crops and laid waste to the lands around Jub Khewi; Regoboli therefore ordered that all villages give to Father their firstborn sons and one part in a hundred of their crops. Soon Father had a formidable host, and his sword-hand itched for battle once more. He took his army and went west, crossing through the Dyuglebai and settling where we now stand. He married and had two sons…"

Aebakhmë's tale trailed off, his eyes meeting Brenn's. "I think, dear Brenn, that is all I am willing to tell until the time is right to finish the tale."

Brenn nodded, his mind awhirl with the details of Aeboli's life. "It is a good story as thou hast told it. Thou didst speak last night of thy father, that he was betrayed by his brothers, yet thou didst mention only Regoboli. Were there not other sons of Tethter?"

Aebakhmë, his face a mask of secrets, replied, "I

will say no more today. Perhaps I shall finish the tale as we travel. It is a long ride to the windport in Beridh-Ostaith."

"A windport, sayest thou?" Brenn asked, his interest piqued.

"Hast thou not seen it? Then thou shalt be surprised when we arrive, I deem. If thou art ready, we should return to the yard. Suthai and Husin will be wanting me at practice, and we will discuss our journey to Jub Khewi."

With that, Aebakhmë turned, making his way down the tower's winding stairs, Brenn following close behind, his mind alight with the promise of the journey to come and the secrets yet to be revealed in the tale of Aeboli, the great warrior of Jub Khewi.

That afternoon, as the Sun's gentle rays caressed the castle's walls, Brenn made his way to the stables, his thoughts lingering on Boriwar, his faithful steed. He hoped that the night's chill had not been too harsh on his equine friend. A stable boy, eager to assist, directed Brenn to the stall where Boriwar resided, and there, amidst the sweet scent of hay, he found his horse, contentedly munching on straw. The stable hands, diligent in their duties, had washed the saddle and bridle, beating the dust from the blanket, which now sat neatly by the gate of Boriwar's stall.

"Hello, my friend," Brenn said, his hand outstretched to pet the horse's neck. Boriwar's coat, clean and glossy, spoke of the care he had received, and his eyes, bright and alert, met Brenn's gaze.

Boriwar, sniffing Brenn's hand, spoke in his equine tongue, "This is a good place."

Brenn, a gentle warning in his voice, replied, "Aye, but be not too comfortable. We leave tomorrow."

"Whither do we go?" Boriwar asked, curiosity piqued.

"To Jub Khewi," Brenn said, and then, sensing his steed's confusion, he sent images to Boriwar's mind—a harsh Sun beating down upon a desert landscape, hills of dry sand stretching as far as the eye could see. Brenn, having never witnessed the desert firsthand, relied on the tales Deugwer had shared, hoping to convey the essence of their destination.

Boriwar, puzzled, asked, "Is it snow?"

Brenn, shaking his head, explained, "Sand. Dirt. Dust. So much of it that it forms hills that change with the wind."

"Strange," Boriwar mused, before adding, "I shall be ready." With that, he returned to his meal of straw, content in the knowledge of their impending journey.

"Glad I am that thou art taking this news so well," Brenn said, a smile playing on his lips.

Suddenly, a voice rang out, "Speakest thou to thine horse?"

Brenn turned, his eyes falling upon Husin, who stood in the doorway, dressed in fine riding clothes, a great green cloak draped over her shoulders. Her brown eyes sparkled with mirth, a bright smile adorning her face.

"In truth, I was," Brenn admitted. "When one has been alone as long as I, one speaks to whomever will listen."

Husin laughed, a melodious sound that filled the stable. "Horses are good listeners, 'tis true. I tried asking mine own for advice once, but he said he cared not for politics." She laughed again, and Brenn joined her, doing his best to hide the discomfort that threatened to show on his face. "Well, Brenn," Husin continued, "I was looking for thee. I have a message from our dear Baiwieth."

At the mention of Baiwieth's name, blood rushed to Brenn's face, a telltale sign of his interest. "What says the message? What does she want of me?"

"Only to know if thou wilt speak with her, now or later, at thy leisure. She awaits thee in thy chamber," Husin said, her smile widening.

"Then I will see to her now," Brenn declared, his heart quickening at the prospect of meeting with the enigmatic servant.

Husin, clapping him on the back, offered a word of caution, "Baiwieth is a beautiful woman, Brenn, but she is trouble. I have known her since she came into our service, and she is frightful when one crosses her."

"Then I shall not cross her," Brenn said, his resolve firm.

As he made his way through the great hall, Brenn felt the eyes of the castle's inhabitants upon him—servants, soldiers, and workers alike. He caught many of their gazes before they turned away, but not before he sensed a mixture of surprise and hope in their eyes, as if they expected him to be someone else.

Entering his room, Brenn's heart fluttered at the sight of Baiwieth, who stood beside the bed, her hands clasped behind her back. She wore the same servant's clothing as the night before, yet somehow, she seemed even more beautiful. Her black hair, braided and hung over her left shoulder, framed her face, and her green eyes sparkled as they met Brenn's. He stepped inside, closing the door behind him.

"Good day, Brenn," Baiwieth said, her voice like moonlight, soft and enchanting.

"And to thee," Brenn replied, his own voice nearly catching in his throat.

"I am sorry for intruding," she said, a hint of uncertainty in her tone.

"Thou art not," Brenn assured her. "This is the house of Aebakhmë. Nevertheless, I am glad to see thee. Didst thou need to speak with me?"

Baiwieth nodded, her eyes filled with a longing that Brenn could not quite place. "I had hoped thou wouldst do me a kindness and tell me of mine homeland."

"Dol-Nopthelen?" Brenn frowned, a twinge of regret in his heart. "I am sorry, but I have never been to that beautiful country, though I have heard much about it. Panaikh Polekheft was of that land; it was he who led the settlers to my country, Keulen."

"Then thou knowest some things," Baiwieth said, her voice filled with hope. "Oh, please tell me even a little history! I was yet a small girl when my father took me from that land, and he told me little before he died."

"I did not know he was dead," Brenn said, bowing his head in sympathy. "Thou hast my sympathy. My brother and father are dead; the wound of my loss is deep and pains me still. Perhaps I can tell thee a story I read from a Dol-Noptheleno book, which I bought from a traveler who came from that land; but it is only a legend, and I know not whether it is true."

Baiwieth smiled, settling herself on the edge of the bed, her eyes fixed on Brenn with rapt attention. Brenn, taking a seat in the chair by the hearth, breathed deeply, collecting his thoughts as he prepared to share the tale. And so, with the Sun's gentle light streaming through the window, and the crackling of the fire in the hearth, Brenn began his story, his voice weaving a tapestry of words, a legend from a land he had never seen, but one that had captured his imagination and now, he hoped, would bring a measure of comfort and connection to the beautiful and mysterious Baiwieth.

It is said that before humankind came to Edorath, there lived an Elder race created by the gods to tend the earth in preparation for our coming. For countless years, the Elders lived, and they seldom died for they did not age, and were hale and not prone to sickness. But they could be slain, and their hearts were akin to our own, so that they were envious of one another and vied for power.

Many wars they fought, and the old songs told that the ancient gods of the Elders joined in their battles, and the tumult thereof shook the earth and reshaped the land and seas many times. When mortal humans crossed the Aikhwë and found the verdant expanse of Edorath, the Elders had already marred and affected much of it with their conquests.

But the First Folk were wary of the Elders, and though the Elders were for the most part friendly to the newcomers, the Folk chose rather to keep to their own company. And so for many centuries the Folk and the Elders sundered themselves one from the other, and the Folk journeyed ever westward to seek a land which the Elders and gods had not yet scarred with their wars and machines. Thus the Folk discovered Annath, which means Realm to the West, for it lay westward of all known lands in Edorath, lying within the Gwelio Sea.

Now there was one of the Elder race called Lwamëa who loved a woman of the Folk called Therfwima, and to them were born twin sons: Therkoër and Edhlofwima. The lives of these brothers have been recounted in other tales, and in this one they serve small roles. Here it may suffice to say that Edhlofwima lived with his father in Mithoër, before Lwamëa was transfigured by his gods and now appears to us as the brightest of wandering stars. Therkoër lived with his mother and her people.

Therkoër and Therfwima came to Annath, and Therkoër was brought up in the ways of the Folk, growing and learning much until he was a man of great stature both of body and of mind. The Folk of Annath then chose Therkoër as their first king, and he ruled the Annathu for many centuries in peace. (Long life he had inherited from his father, though agelessness he did not receive; he grew old and died as other mortal Folk, though slower.)

Therkoër begat many sons and daughters, and many grandchildren they gave him, and all of his bloodline received as their birthright the health and long life of their forebear. Nine generations passed, and Therkoër lived to be five hundred years old, having ruled Annath for more than four hundred, and at last he died. His first-born daughter Deudiryag then took the Annatho crown.

Deudiryag bore four pairs of twins, each pair being a brother and sister. Now the Annatho law at that time declared that the eldest child should inherit the crown, and though the girl was born moments before the boy, Queen Deudiryag said to her people:

"These two shall rule after mine own time; yea, both shall rule Annath as king and queen, and the island will be divided—the northern part for my son and his wife, and the southern part for my daughter and her husband. And these parts will further be divided unto mine other children, so that there will be two kings, two queens, eight lords, and eight ladies to govern Annath."

And she named her eldest daughter Kliëdho, and her eldest son she named Adalkhë. The names of the four younger brothers were Probwi, Gwelyel, Menoflen, and Kersurwidas. The names of the four younger sisters were Probeher, Soleno, Eneluyel, and Redhas. The northern part of Annath, which was called Norlen, Deudiryag divided for Probwi, Probeher, Gwelyel, Soleno, and their spouses. The southern part of Annath, which was called Gavlen, Deudiryag divided for Menoflen, Eneluyel, Kersurwidas, Redhas, and their spouses.

Now the capital city of Annath lay in its very center, and the people called it Thirubol, City of Stars, named for their first king Therkoër, whose name signified Star-foam. When Adalkhë and

Kliëdho ascended the twin thrones of Annath, the city Thirubol was divided therefore, and Adalkhë ruled the northern part while Kliëdho ruled the southern. Thus the people of southern Annath and the people of northern Annath began to see themselves as two peoples, rather than a united kingdom. And because the lands were further divided unto each sibling, the people of Annath likewise were as divided.

And it came to pass that three hundred and forty years passed since the beginning of the rule of the Twins. The Annathu grew to be a great people, learned in shipbuilding and statecraft, warfare and architecture, art and science. They built monuments to their kings and queens, their lords and ladies, and buildings and statues rose high above the island-nation so that it is said they could be seen from the western shore of Gavwer in Edorath, hundreds of miles away.

And they wrote books on all subjects, as well as poetry that surpassed all that came before or after, and in metalworking they were unmatched by any other people. Wood, also, they built with and shaped, and glass, stone, and clay. The stars they mapped, and the courses of the Wanderers they charted through the sky and could predict.

It was the people of Annath who first divided the year into four parts, one for each Season; and they divided the days and nights into equal hours, the reckoning of which is still used today. They counted their years from the day of the coronation of Therkoër, their first king.

The Annathu grew to be numerous, and their

mortal blood was mixed with that of the Elders so that each Annatho lived many hundreds of years, and each begat many dozens of children. Then the houses and buildings of Annath reached to the heavens, for there were so many who lived on the island.

Now it came to pass, in the one thousandth year of Annath, there was a man called Lwisnaser who spread rumors, saying, "Behold, our people are too numerous, and our buildings rise too high so that the gods will become jealous of their place above us. I have dreamed a dream; yea, even a vision I have had. The gods did come to me and said, 'Lwisnaser, thou good and faithful servant: Lead thy people from Annath and sail eastward in your ships, and land on the shores of Edorath. For thy people are too numerous, and your sky-reaching buildings offend the gods. Therefore, go and find new land on which to live, lest we strike down your buildings and lay waste to your island.'"

And when Lwisnaser said these things, many of the Annathu were afraid, and many were angry, and they said one to another, "This man speaks true; we must journey eastward over the sea and make homes in Edorath, lest we offend the gods and they destroy us."

And others yet said, "This man fancies himself a prophet! But who can speak with the voice of the gods, except the gods themselves? We are content here in our tall buildings, with our great monuments, and our fine things. Are we not the greatest people on Earth? Yea, our art and our clothing, our buildings and our books, they are finer than any of their kind elsewhere in the world. Why should we have such talent unless the gods look upon us with favor? For surely the gods give talent unto mortals, but only those whom they love."

But the words of Lwisnaser touched many, and soon he gathered a great host of many thousands, and they boarded and said into the east. Then those who followed him declared Lwisnaser their king, forsaking those who ruled them on Annath.

Whether it was the wrath of the gods or an impersonal force of nature, I know not; but the tale holds thus—the people of Lwisnaser recorded thereafter that from their vantage on the western shore of Gavwer, they beheld great storms in the west with lightning and rain and howling winds. And though they saw it not, Annath met her end in that storm. Lo! there was a great earthquake, and the sea was torn asunder, and great waves washed over Annath, and the island fell beneath the waters. There exists today no trace of that great island-nation, nor the countless people who perished there.

Now there was, at this time in Mithoër, a certain powerful man whom the people called Addinnas, meaning Noble Giver; and Lwoëras, meaning Bright Lord. Who and what Addinnas was, none knew for certain. Some held that he came from the stars, others that he emerged from beneath the earth, and others still that he was a spawn of the ancient gods, perhaps a demigod or demon. But this all agreed upon: Addinnas was a cunning sorcerer, for he used magic and built devices never seen before or since in all the world; and with his knowledge of the workings of nature he ruled over his people who worshiped and feared him.

Addinnas resided in the land which today we call Skegyo, in a tall tower which he devised and made his servants build for him. The Folk in Skegyo feared him, aye, but they also revered him and held a respect for him akin to a god. Indeed, there were many who did the bidding of Addinnas out of fear of punishment, but there were more still who loved him and believed in his leadership.

In the area in the southwest of the Gwithu mountains, there stood a city of the Elders called Wilo, in which the Elders had resided for thousands of years. A learned man lived there called Telfekhthis, wise and accomplished in all manner of craft. It is said that he was descended of the goddess Thirikh, who crafted the very stars, and the light of the stars shone through his eyes. Many cities he had built, and many monuments he had designed in reverence to the kings and queens of the Elders, as well as their gods.

In matters of science Telfekhthis was unmatched, even by those who lived on Annath. He devised figures for calculation, and also the methods of calculation, and using these he determined the relationships between numbers, music, colors, and shapes that are pleasing to the mind and functional for architecture. It is said that during a storm in his youth he caught lightning in a stone, and with this he produced all manner of strange devices.

It happened one day that Addinnas sent a messenger to Telfekhthis, bidding the man visit him in his tower in Skegyo. Addinnas promised not only riches in exchange for his aid, but also knowledge unimagined. Knowledge was more precious to Telfekhthis than any treasure, and so he traveled to Skegyo with the messenger and came to the tall tower of Addinnas.

"Happy indeed I am to have thee as my guest," said the Bright Lord to Telfekhthis. "I require the help of a cunning mind of thy talent, and if thou wouldst, I shall give thee knowledge of the earth, the sea, the heavens, the stars and Wanderers, the inner workings of the soul, and the secrets of the gods themselves."

"What aid might I give thee, Lord?" asked Telfekhthis. "I will not say that I have not desired these things which thou dost offer, and I will gladly give what aid I am able."

Thus it was that Telfekhthis came into the service of Addinnas and helped him construct the Entroïr, which have been called the Gates, or the Rings—for rings they were in shape and construction, set upright like rounded gateways, and large enough for ten men to walk through abreast. These Rings connected locations one with another, so that one passing through one in a certain place would emerge through another many miles away.

These Rings Addinnas gave freely as gifts to kings and queens of Mithoër and using them the sovereigns held tighter dominion over their realms, for messages could be sent in shorter time, and goods were delivered quickly over vast distances. For many years, the Rings were the symbols of power in Mithoër, and the common folk both hated and loved the Rings, for they had brought an age of prosperity to Mithoër never before seen; but in the same way the people could now live not without them, and the Rings were as an addiction that the kings and queens would not and could not relinquish.

Now it happened that Addinnas in secret built in Skegyo his own Entroër, and none knew of its construction, not even his apprentice Telfekhthis. Then one day in the city Wilo, the queen there, who was called Gwenim, saw that her Ring came to life of its own accord, and she looked through and saw there Addinnas in his tall tower in Skegyo.

"What is this treachery?" she asked, for to her it seemed that the Bright Lord had built a Master Ring to control all others, and in his hands would rest the fate of all Mithoër, for he could extinguish the Rings at his own whim, and therefore hold it ransom to his malice.

But Addinnas professed innocence, saying, "Queen Gwenim, think not that I have deceived thee; this Entroër is for mine own use, which is my right as its creator. I hold no ill will against thee, thy realm, or those of other sovereigns."

"Pray, what is the purpose of thy secret Ring?" asked the queen of Wilo.

"That is not for thee to know," said the Bright Lord, "for even were I to tell thee its purpose, thou wouldst understand it not."

At this the queen took offense, and she ordered her Ring destroyed, and sent word to the other lands of the betrayal she had discovered. And it came to pass that the Rings were for the most part destroyed, and Mithoër was cast into a time of chaos and strife. But some Rings were maintained and held in secret, and many tales have been told of those king and queens who turned not away from the malice of Addinnas, but I shall not recount them here. But war spread over Mithoër, and Addinnas was named the Enemy.

It also happened that when Telfekhthis learned of this betrayal, he said to himself, "I am also to blame, for I helped in the construction of these Rings. And though I did not have a hand in making the Master Entroër, I will forever live with the shame of not seeing the true intent of my teacher. Alas, that I should be cursed to be of the Elder race and live forever! This I cannot abide." And Telfekhthis threw himself from the tall tower in which he lived with Addinnas, and he died, and the world has not known a wiser mind.

Upon the sandy shores of Gavwer did Lwisnaser and his people disembark, their eyes beholding a realm torn asunder by discord and ruin. The once proud lands of Mithoër lay before them, a testament to strife and the folly of unchecked ambition. The air was thick with the scent of turmoil, and the ground beneath their feet whispered tales of a world in upheaval.

It was not long ere Lwisnaser, wise and discerning, came to learn of the dark shadow that loomed over this fractured land. The Rings, creations most wondrous and terrible, had been misused, their power turned to the service of greed and dominion. At the heart of this maelstrom stood Addinnas, the Bright Lord, once revered, now feared and hated, whose sorcery had birthed these Rings. Though given under the guise of tools that would knit the fabric of Mithoër into a tapestry of unity and strength, in the wrong hands they proved tools of tyranny, capable of subjugating realms and enslaving the free.

His gaze turned eastward, Lwisnaser resolved to act, lest the chaos of the Rings consume all. He envisioned a Mithoër united, a land where the disparate threads of Folk and Elders might be woven into a singular and harmonious design. Thus, with a heart steadfast and unyielding, Lwisnaser began to forge a new destiny for Mithoër. The journey would be fraught with peril, but in his breast burned hope, a beacon to guide him in these dark hours. For he believed, with the fervor of one who has seen the depths of despair and the heights of potential, that the most fractured of worlds could be mended under a banner of unity and purpose.

In the days that followed, Lwisnaser journeyed across the breadth of Mithoër. His words, like the gentle fall of life-giving ran to a scorched plain, began to mend the fractures of a broken land. He traveled to the courts of kings, the halls of lords, all places where the cries of war had long echoed.

With each sovereign, Lwisnaser spoke of unity, his voice resonating with the conviction of one who had seen the rise and fall of a great nation. He offered them a bond of alliance, a promise of mutual support. From the wisdom and knowledge of the survivors of Annath, he brought forth technological marvels, sharing secrets that could give new life to the land and fortify cities. The rulers, once full of doubt, now saw Lwisnaser not just as a leader from a fallen realm, but a harbinger of hope and renewal.

In the hamlets and villages marred by the Rings'

misuse, Lwisnaser's presence became a beacon of peace. He walked among the people, his words soothing the wounds that fear and suspicion had wrought. With wisdom and compassion he mediated disputes, unraveled misunderstandings, and rekindled a sense of community among those who had been driven apart.

His efforts bore fruit, and the lands that had once bristled with the specter of conflict now blossomed with the prospects of peace. The people, who had viewed each other as adversaries, now shared tales and broke bread together under the banner of newfound harmony.

In every corner of Mithoër where Lwisnaser's influence touched, trust was sown. The people, once weary of the chaos the Rings had brought, now looked to Lwisnaser with reverence and loyalty. They saw in him not only the wisdom of Annath but also the heart of Mithoër itself.

Thus through strategic alliances and the healing of divided communities, Lwisnaser began to stitch together the torn fabric of Mithoër, its threads strengthened by the shared resolve to stands against the shadows of the past and embrace a future bright with promise.

As the dawn of unity broke over the lands of Mithoër, Lwisnaser turned his gaze towards an allegiance of kingdoms and beheld the gathering forces. From the frosty mountains of the north to the sun-drenched fields of the south thousands heeded his call: warriors, knights, sages, cavalry, archers, mystics, and scholars.

Gathered now in Keglas, near the Kenë

mountains that separated Skegyo from Mithoër, Lwisnaser convened with his council of war. Around tables laden with maps and scrolls, they devised a strategy to confront Addinnas. Lwisnaser, drawing upon the knowledge of Annath, introduced tactics and machines of war that were marvels to the leaders of Mithoër: catapults that could hurl projectiles farther and with greater precision, shields imbued with alloys unknown to Mithoër, and swords that remained sharp through many days of use.

The council saw the need to counter the sorcery of Addinnas. To this end, Lwisnaser turned to the mystics and scholars. They delved into ancient tomes and forgotten lore, seeking spells and wards that might shield against the Bright Lord's dark magic. In secret chambers they worked to blend the arcane with the mechanical, creating artifacts that harnessed both the ethereal essence of magic and the tangible genius of technology.

A war unlike any other began to unfold, a storm of steel and spell, of cannon and conjuration. The army of Lwisnaser advanced with purpose, each battalion an embodiment of Mithoër's newfound unity. The clashing of swords was accompanied by the chanting of spells, and the air was filled with the thunder of cannons and the crackle of magical barriers.

The strategic brilliance of Lwisnaser, coupled with the combined might of magic and technology, brought a new age to the art of warfare. It was a conflict that would determine the fate of Mithoër, a battle not just for the land, but for the soul of its people. In this crucible of war, the hopes and dreams of an entire realm were forged, ready to confront the shadow of Addinnas and reclaim the destiny of their world.

The siege of the Tall Tower came as a tempest. Lwisnaser's united armies, a formidable host drawn from all corners of Mithoër, encircled the bastion where Addinnas, the architect of discord, had ensconced himself. The city, with its towering spires and labyrinthine streets, stood defiant, a fortress of ancient magic and modern machination.

Addinnas, from his tower, watched the encroaching armies with eyes that burned like embers in the night. With a wave of his hand, he unleashed his countermeasures. From his tower's battlements, arcane turrets erupted in a symphony of destruction, hurling bolts of eldritch energy that tore through the ranks of the besieging army.

The ground itself shook as Addinnas summoned golems of stone and iron, made in the fiery belly of his sorcerous forges. These behemoths strode forth, their steps thunderous, their arms swinging like wrecking balls against the siege engines of Lwisnaser's forces.

Yet, Lwisnaser, steadfast and undeterred, had prepared for such eventualities. He brought forth a device, a relic created by the artificers and sages. A crystal, it was, pulsing with an inner light, crafted to harmonize with the very essence of magic itself.

As the battle raged, Lwisnaser, under the volley of eldritch fire, advanced to the forefront. Raising the crystal high, he invoked its power. A wave of serene light emanated from the jewel, weaving through the chaos of battle. Where the light touched, the sorcery of Addinnas began to unravel. The golems, those monoliths of destruction, crumbled to dust. The magical turrets, their fury so recently unleashed, fell silent, their energies dissipating harmlessly into the air.

With the Bright Lord's defenses failing, the united armies surged forward. Warriors, mages, and scholars alike, all fought as one, their resolve unbroken by the sight of the city's now vulnerable walls. The city, which had once seemed impregnable, now echoed with the sounds of gates being breached and walls being scaled.

In the heart of the city, within his tall tower, Addinnas awaited his fate. He watched as his empire of magic and machinery, once unassailable, crumbled under the indomitable spirit of a united and free people. There, amidst the sound of failed tyranny, Lwisnaser confronted Addinnas, not with the blade of vengeance, but with the weight of truth.

"Behold the fruits of thine unchecked ambition," Lwisnaser proclaimed, his voice resounding through the stone and metal chamber. "Thou hast sought dominion over all, and in thy quest thou has sown the seeds of thine own downfall."

Addinnas, his sorcerous might waned, gazed upon the resolve in the eyes of those who stood against him. In that moment, the realization of his folly came to him—the peril of power wielded without wisdom, the tragedy of a vision marred by vanity.

With solemn determination, Lwisnaser approached the dais where lay the Master Ring, the source of the Bright Lord's dominion. He took his sword, and in a singular act of finality, pried it from its foundation and pushed it through the window, whence it fell to the ground and was destroyed. As the Ring shattered, a wave of liberation swept throughout the city, breaking the last chains of the Bright Lord's reign.

In the aftermath of Addinnas's defeat, the kingdoms of Mithoër, once fragmented by suspicion and strife, began the task of rebuilding. Together, they forged a new path forward, one built on the foundation of cooperation. The scars of war and division slowly faded, and in their place grew a society that valued the strength of unity. The Rings, once symbols of control, were remembered as cautionary tales of the perils of power untempered by humility and the common good.

Lwisnaser's legacy endured long after his time. He was heralded not merely as a conqueror, but as a visionary who saw beyond the squabbles of realms and races. He was remembered as the Unifier, the one who, in the face of overwhelming adversity, brought together a world on the brink of ruin. Statues were raised and songs were sung in his honor, but the greatest monument to Lwisnaser was the enduring peace and prosperity of Mithoër. Under the starlit skies, the people of that land lived and thrived, their hearts and hopes entwined in the legacy of a man who had turned the tide of history, not merely through the might of army, but through his desire to see his land freed from bondage.

Baiwieth sighed and closed her eyes. "I have never heard such a tale. But what has it to do with Dol-

Nopthelen?"

"The same King Lwisnaser," said Brenn, "after he overthrew the Bright Lord, took the last of the Annathu to a land northward, where the Elder race had built many cities in ancient times. At the time of Lwisnaser, these Elder cities had fallen into a shadow of their former glory. He rebuilt these cities with the help of the surviving Elders and his own people, and he made his home in Thunyab beside the Lolkhwed Sea. From there to the Pellë mountains in the north, the Kweberos river to the west, and the city Pedhirthi to the east on the border of Markhlen, that realm was known thereafter as Dol-Nopthelen—the land of the long night—for part of the year the Sun does not rise, yet in the other part of the year the Sun does not set. Why then is it not then called Dol-Dyeulen, I wonder?"

Baiwieth laughed, and although she appeared tired, she looked at Brenn with gratitude. "That was a fine story, Brenn. I am glad thou didst tell it to me."

"I am glad to have told thee," he said.

"Wouldst thou walk with me?" she asked. "I have no duties for the remainder of the day, until the evening meal."

He nodded, and she arose and took his hand, and together they walked down the stairs and through the halls of Aebakhmë's house, then through the large wooden doors. They went through the yard, to the castle walls and portcullis, then along the wall until they came to a small copse of trees and bushes on an outcropping of stone some distance from the castle. They sat there a long while, listening to the birds sing, looking out over the dale, and watching Aebakhmë's serfs in the village go about their day.

It seemed to Brenn that they sat there for many hours, feeling the Sun on their faces, hearing the breeze rustling through the trees, speaking of nothing of importance, until Baiwieth said, "Brenn?"

"Yes?"

"When hither thou goest," she asked, "wouldst thou take me with thee?"

Brenn drew back in surprise and asked, "What meanest thou?"

She turned to him, and he saw that she watched him with hope and trepidation. "I would go with thee, to be near unto thee. I would go whither thou goest, to see things through thine eyes."

He looked upon her without understanding. "Thou wishest to leave this place, leave thy family and friends, all that thou knowest?"

"I do," she said, "more than anything. I have been thinking about it since I met thee yestereve, following thee, watching thee. I want to leave this place, but I fear I shall not be happy if I go alone."

Brenn shook his head. "I know not whether I can give what thou dost ask. I have no home, Baiwieth, no place of mine own, nothing to offer thee." He reached out and took her hand. "I think thou art beautiful and kind, but I would not ask thee to be my wife because of the life I have chosen, and I would not ask thee to sleep in a tent or in the open field."

She returned his stare, and in her gaze Brenn saw she was hurt by his words. "Thou hast nothing?"

"Nay," said he. "Nothing save mine horse and

the scant items in his saddlebags."

She looked away from him, down the path, over the few huts where the masons who worked on the castle stayed. "And yet I wish to go with thee," she said.

Brenn sighed. "Then come with me," he said, taking both her hands in his. "Come with me, and we will see where life takes us. I will take thee to the ends of the earth and sea, to the peak of the tallest mountain and the depths of the darkest cave, into the wildest forest and across the widest river. Thou shalt see what I see, and thou shalt not regret having departed this place."

Baiwieth smiled, her green eyes showing the stars what it means to shine. "Nay, I shall not regret it, Brenn, for I will be with thee."

Brenn stood, pulling her up with him, and he kissed her. She returned his kiss, and for a moment they were lost within one another, their surroundings forgotten.

A voice interrupted them. "Brenn?"

They broke apart, and Brenn turned to see Husin standing there, looking at the two of them.

"Yes?" said Brenn.

Husin gave a smirk. "I was searching for thee."

Brenn looked to Baiwieth, who blushed. "I had gone for a walk," he told Husin.

"I do apologize for intruding." She looked at Baiwieth. "Please return to the servants' quarters."

Baiwieth nodded, and she held onto Brenn's hand until she was too far to reach, and Brenn watched her go until she was out of sight.

Husin cleared her throat. "Wouldst thou walk

with me, Brenn? I have not had opportunity to spend time with thee, and we have things to discuss."

The two of them walked down the path and turned to walk along the castle wall a short distance, until they came to a cleft in the hills where a small stream flowed into the dale below. There they stopped and sat beside the bank.

"What wouldst thou discuss, Husin?" asked Brenn.

"For one," said the soldier, "I would know about thee and Baiwieth."

Brenn looked away from Husin, instead casting his eyes at the stream. "What about us?"

"I see how thou dost look upon her, and how she dost look upon thee. And that's to say nothing of how I caught thy lips on hers."

Brenn cleared his throat. "If I have offended thee or Aebakhmë—"

"Carest thou for her?"

"I know not," said Brenn, for it was the truth. "I have known her for only a day."

"But thou couldst care for her, and she for thee?"

"Aye, it could be so."

"Thou canst not deny thy feeling for her."

"Nay, I cannot."

Husin leaned back and looked up to the Sun. "This is why I desired to speak with thee. Know that if thou wantest her for thine own, thou mayest have her. Neither I nor Aebakhmë would stop thee from taking her."

A smile teased at Brenn's mouth. "Ye would not?"

"Nay. But also know that she is costly."

Brenn's smile fell. "She is no slave to be bought and sold as cattle."

"Baiwieth is not a slave, 'tis true, but her father owed a great debt to Lord Aeboli and gave Baiwieth as payment. She is indentured, and her service has some years yet before the debt is paid. To shorten her time with us would be to take on the unpaid balance of her father's debt."

"And I would have to pay this in order to release her," said Brenn.

"Aye, you grasp it."

Brenn was silent for a moment. "What is the sum?"

Husin smiled and said, "More than one thousand ethi."

Brenn's heart fell, and he glared at Husin. "Dost thou jest?"

"Nay. Hast thou the money?"

He did not but was reluctant to admit it. There was but one method of making such a vast sum so quickly, and that was something he was loathe to do. "I shall have it," he said, "if I need it."

Husin sat back and looked at Brenn, her eyes curious. "How?"

"There is aught I can do." Something in his voice betrayed his hesitation to do what needed to be done, and he caught Husin's concerned expression. Brenn nodded at her, reassuring her that he was sincere.

She nodded in return and said, "Then I will speak to Aebakhmë of thine intent. Now, about the true reason for my visit—thou art coming with us to Jub Khewi, yes?"

"I told Aebakhmë I would," said Brenn, "for I owe him a great debt, though I wish he knew what business he had there."

"Hast thou not guessed his purpose?" Husin's smile reminded Brenn of a venomous snake about to strike. "We are taking back the lord's birthright."

Brenn asked, "An heirloom of some kind within the city?"

Husin's laughter reached her eyes before passing her lips, and then the sound was like the cracking of ribs. "It is the city herself! Aebakhmë is the rightful heir of all of Len Khalayu, and Jub Khewi is the heart." She sat quietly, watching Brenn react to her words.

Brenn looked down into the water, the shape of his reflection wavering and distorting as the water flowed over the rocks. What could he do? He owed Aebakhmë a debt for saving his life, for he surely would have frozen that night if the lordling had not offered a warm meal and bed. Brenn had run from home to avoid war only to fly into another of which he had no part. He considered the possibility of running again when Husin's voice cut into his thoughts.

"Brenn, what is the matter?"

He looked at Husin and said the first thought that came to him: "I do not want to go to war."

Husin looked down at her folded hands, then into their shared reflection in the stream. "I noticed the sword that thou carriest. It is a fine blade. Is it thine?"

"It was my brother's," the man told her.

"Such a fine blade has not been seen in this country since the Easterlings joined Mitho Gorikhwa in driving out Khesi Addeu." She looked sidelong at Brenn. "Aebakhmë fought in that war, didst thou know?"

"I did not," said Brenn.

"Aye. Most of the men from these lands joined in the war against Khesi." Husin slid a knife from her belt and cleaned her nails with it. "That was after the Mad Prophet betrayed Aebakhmë and drove us from the land of our forebears. I remember there was a man who had defected from Khesi's army, then swore allegiance to Aeboli, presenting his sword at our lord's feet, saying he would do anything the lord asked of him. Now, this man owed Aeboli a debt after the lord helped his family escape Len Khalayu. Aeboli took the man's sword and service, asking that he join the vanguard during their next attack. But when the time came, the man broke his oath and fled into the mountains. Aeboli tracked him down, clasped him in irons...and then, knowest thou what he did?"

Brenn's voice caught in his dry throat, so he shook his head rather than speak.

"Aeboli delivered the man to Addeu." Husin laughed, the sound more putrid than the last one. She slapped Brenn on the back before rising to her feet with a grunt. "I am glad thou didst promise Aebakhmë thy service, Brenn; we will need thee and thy...talents in the coming conflict. And worry not, for Aebakhmë is generous to those who aid him, as was his father. Indeed, Aebakhmë is like unto his father in many ways."

With that, Husin stood and walked away. Brenn sat alone and pondered her words for a long while, feeling the chill of what he had heard in Husin's voice, feeling fear lurking in the depths of his soul like Death itself waiting to steal away his life with a withered hand.

But Brenn would not allow fear to rule him; fear was something he had left behind in Keulen. He had come to this place to be free, and to fight for himself, not for others. He would go with Aebakhmë to Jub Khewi long enough to repay his debt, and then he would go his own way.

For now, one thing occupied Brenn's mind: how to get the money needed to free Baiwieth. There was but one option left to him for such a sum and he hated even the thought of it. Boriwar had traveled with him over many miles and had been a faithful friend, but Brenn could not let sentimentality cloud his judgment; the freedom of Baiwieth was worth more than Boriwar's companionship, and so Brenn would have to sell him. He fought tears as he walked the path to the castle and through the portcullis as the men on the walls shouted at him.

"Take heed, there is a curfew!" one said. "We close the gate at sunset." This Brenn ignored and continued into the castle, wither he knew Aebakhmë would be sitting down for the evening meal.

Brenn strode down the halls, passing the nobles and servants who stared as if he were an invader; soon he found the dining hall. Several servants, men and women, set the table for the meal and attended the lordling and his household. Brenn went to Aebakhmë, who stood at the hearth with a drink in his hand, speaking with a squat bald man. The lord saw Brenn and waved.

"Thou art yet early for the meal," he said. "I will send for thee when the food is laid out."

Brenn thanked him and turned for the stairs that led up to his room. He opened the door and entered, finding Baiwieth sitting on a stool beside the bed, staring through the window at the evening sky with the light of the setting sun shining through the rippling cotton of her skirts. She turned when Brenn entered, her face solemn. Brenn knelt beside her and took her hand, and she rested her head on his shoulder. A moment of peace passed between them as they held each other, and then Brenn spoke.

"I will give thee mine horse," he said.

Baiwieth's face twisted as she looked up at him. "Why wouldst thou do such a thing?"

"To buy thy freedom."

She pulled her head from his shoulder, and Brenn looked into her emerald eyes. So full of pain they were that he thought they glowed. Baiwieth began to speak, but Brenn pressed a finger to her lips.

"Say not that I have acted wrongly," he said, "for I cannot bear to hear unhappiness in thy voice. I will do what I must, Baiwieth, for I have promised to free thee. Now it is done; I have made my choice. Boriwar is thine horse; I will surely ride into battle and wish not to take him—I have made my own promise to him. Therefore take Boriwar and trade him for thy freedom. Husin told me of thy debt, or rather that of thy father. It is a hefty sum, but Boriwar is bred of the finest warhorses in Keulen and will bring thee enough to buy thy freedom and more besides."

Baiwieth's eyes were fixed on Brenn's as he spoke, and he felt her hand tremble on his chest, but she did not flinch as he said these things. Her face was still, and a single tear escaped the corner of her eye and trailed down her cheek.

"Never has any soul done me such kindness," she said. "Even were I to live a thousand years I would not forget thee, nor cease honoring thy memory. But what of my life after the debt is paid? Wouldst thou not have me beside thee?"

Brenn said, "I have told thee that I own no land and hold no titles, and there is little money in my purse. I possess only this sword that my brother wielded, and I shall wander Edorath with it for the rest of my days. Such is the life I have chosen, and I would not force it upon thee."

"And I have said," replied Baiwieth, "that such things matter little to me. Of all the excuses thou hast given for me not to remain at thy side, never once hast thou said that thou lovest me not. Perhaps it is my lot that I should say those words before thou dost find the courage to do so; and so I say that I love thee. I ask not that thou shouldst return my words so quickly; I know that love may come softly before it comes at all. But I do ask thee for a promise: whether thou lovest me or not, swear that thou shalt return to me after thine own debt to Aebakhmë is paid, when the war in Jub Khewi is over and thou art as free as thou hast made me—return to me and we shall ride together on Boriwar. Swear it, Brenn.

These words stunned him, and he pulled her in and kissed her, and she returned it, pressing her body against his, and he felt her heart beating against his chest. At length, their lips parted, and she rested her head on his shoulder once more, and he held her in silence for a time. Then he said, "I do swear it."

A servant's voice interrupted their embrace, announcing the evening meal. Brenn descended to the dining hall, where Husin, engrossed in discourse with Aebakhmë, and several others sat about the grand table. As Brenn took his seat, a goblet of wine was given him, which he drank with haste. The meal unfolded, and Brenn, seizing a momentary lull, declared, "Noble Aebakhmë, I beseech thee, lend thine ear to a matter I wish to convey."

The lordling Aebakhmë, with wine's crimson hue reflecting in his chalice, arched an inquisitive brow. Upon drinking, he asked, "What weighs upon thee, Brenn—One Touched by Flame?"

Brenn proclaimed, "Unto Baiwieth I have bestowed by steed."

The mirth that once danced in Aebakhmë's eyes then dimmed, and he gently placed his goblet upon the table. "The serving maiden? Pray, what compels such generosity?"

"In mine heart, I am resolved to rid her of the debt she owes thee," said Brenn.

Aebakhmë, with a gaze that sought clarity amidst the assembled guests, replied, "Such magnanimity is rare, yet the burden is not thine to bear. The girl, though beautiful, hath rendered thee no service; tis not just that thou shouldst assume her father's obligations."

"Yet my will remains unyielding," Brenn said.

A look of astonishment graced Aebakhmë's face. "Such sacrifice, Brenn, is beyond expectation. In the sands of Len Khalayu thou shalt require thy steed. How dost thou intend to journey with us?"

"From thine own stables my lord shall have to lend me a mount," Brenn responded with conviction, "for Boriwar, once mine, now belongs to Baiwieth. Should it be thy desire that I accompany thee, provision must be made. My decision stands, unswayed by bonds of camaraderie."

Aebakhmë, with eyes that bore into Brenn's soul, leaned back, contemplative. "So be it," he conceded with a hearty chuckle, then gestured to his friends. "Behold Brenn, with a spirit unyielding and a heart ablaze! Some might deem his rash, yet I find valor in his ways." Raising a goblet in salute, he drank deep.

Merriment ensued, yet Brenn, lost in introspection, partook of the meal in silence. His thoughts wandered through the recent events: the promises given, souls encountered, the pull between himself and Baiwieth, and the impending clash of steel in the desert.

As night's embrace took hold, he sought peace in slumber, though his rest was plagued by dreams.

Come the morn, Brenn, dressed for the day, ventured to the stables amidst a hive of activity. Aebakhmë's soldiers and banner-men, a formidable force, prepared for the expedition to Jub Khewi; the castle's environs teemed with life.

"Seekest thou something, Brenn?" inquired the master of the stables, observing him amidst the horses.

"A mount," said Brenn, "for I am bereft of one."

"Ah, word was passed to me of thy noble deed," said the man with a smile. "For thee, the good horse Theg awaits. A creature of war, swift and fierce, akin to the noble steeds of our lord. Upon thy return from the morning meal, she will be readied for thy journey."

Brenn thanked the man and approached the distant stall where Boriwar, his trusted horse, resided. He had no stomach for breakfast and would better use his time here. The noble creature, sensing the impending change, greeted Brenn with knowing gaze. Brenn, with a carrot fetched from the castle's kitchens, approached the horse, his heart heavy with the weight of parting.

"Forgive me, faithful friend," Brenn began, his voice laden with emotion. "Our paths diverge this day. In thy strength, a fair maiden shall find her liberty. Though mine heart aches, I trust that she shall care for thee as I have. I beg that thou rememberest our shared journey, for thou shalt ever dwell in my memories." As tears threatened to spill, Brenn continued with quavering voice. "Our bond, Boriwar, shall forever remain etched in time."

The wise Boriwar, lifting his majestic head, replied, "Fear not, valiant Gwennotir. Thy deeds, twice shielding me from the horrors of war, are not lost on me. In thine actions I find solace. Our memories shall remain, and in another time perhaps our paths shall intertwine once more."

With heavy heart Brenn departed from Boriwar's side, moving towards Theg, a magnificent, dappled mare, her coat a tapestry of grey with a radiant white star upon her brow. As Brenn acquainted himself with Theg, the stable master in his duties presented a saddle for the journey.

"Gwennotir, I am named," Brenn whispered to her.

They, with a hint of surprise, asked, "Thou dost possess the gift of speech? Why do others of thy kind remain silent?"

Brenn with gentle smile replied, "Many speak, though not in the manner I do. A divine gift allows me communion with all sentient beings. Alas, our shared path leads to the battlefield."

Their silent discourse was interrupted as the stable master returned. Now equipped, Theg allowed Brenn to lead her from the stable into the castle yard. There they joined the throng of warriors preparing for the journey ahead.

Theg, seasoned by previous battles, sought to assuage Brenn's apprehensions, speaking of the nature of war and the exhilaration of the open field. The prospect of venturing into the vast desert seemed less formidable with Theg by his side.

Aebakhmë, the esteemed lordling, beheld Brenn and Theg amidst his soldiers. With a nod of approval he remarked, "A fine choice in Theg, dear Brenn. As the sands of time shift, art thou prepared for our voyage to Beridh-Ostaith? There, sakhnoë await to carry us to the heart of Len Khalayu. Hast thou gathered all that binds thee to this place?"

With solemn countenance Brenn declared, "Yea, I stand prepared. To Baiwieth I have given Boriwar, my noble steed and closest friend. May none obstruct her path as she employs this gift to absolve her father's debt unto thee."

Aebakhmë with regal nod replied, "Upon mine honor, thine act shall remain unchallenged. Rare is the man who would sacrifice so for one scarcely known. Mount thine horse, for the hour of departure is upon us!" With grace the lordling ascended his majestic chestnut steed, its tail and mane intricately braided. Brenn mounted Theg, and the assembly of warriors followed suit. A rousing cheer erupted from the gathered men, echoed by the jubilant voices of the populace as they crossed the portcullis. "Ride close, dear Brenn," commanded Aebakhmë, and Brenn, guiding Theg, maintained pace.

As the silhouette of the castle began to fade, Brenn's gaze drew to a figure on a balcony, her raven tresses flowing freely, dancing in the morning wind, her azure gown billowing about her. Baiwieth, with a gesture of fond parting, raised her hand, to which Brenn responded in kind. As she vanished from sight, Brenn's focus shifted to the looming mountains and the distant realm of Len Khalayu.

Theg, sensing Brenn's turmoil, inquired, "What troubles thee, Brenn?"

With heavy heart Brenn confided, "The parting from Boriwar weighs upon me, as does the impending absence of Baiwieth. Yet, solace I find in their union, though silent it may be." Sharing his thoughts with Theg, her understanding met him.

"Thine actions are noble," she conveyed, "and the path of love is oft a meandering one."

Brenn, with a hint of crimson on his cheeks, said, "She professed her love, yet of mine own heart I remain uncertain. Tell me, do horses understand the intricacies of love?"

Theg, amused, replied, "Ah, love, a profound enigma," and left the topic to hand in the ethereal space between them.

They rode out the day, through the dale that led to the Dyuglebai mountain range, its ridges cloaked in snow, the higher peaks lost in white clouds. The wind from the north, cold and carrying the tease of winter, whispered of the journey's trials to come. At the base of the mountains, a small town clung to the slopes like lichen on a pine trunk, and the small army followed the road to this haven for a night's rest.

Most of the soldiers remained without the town, making camp beneath the open sky, while a select few, chosen by Aebakhmë, rode with him the rest of the way into the town to stay at a lodge beside the road. A simple affair it was, with a stable and small kitchen, where Theg was provided a stall and a bag of oats, and Brenn ate dinner with Aebakhmë, Suthai, Husin, and a few other men whom he had not yet met.

As they ate a simple dinner of goat stew and bread, Aebakhmë spoke, his voice a beacon of guidance in the gathering night: "We will be in Beridh-Ostaith tomorrow. The pass through the mountains will be the worst part of the journey, and I hope neither man nor horse suffers much from the ride."

Brenn, his curiosity piqued, asked, "Who is it that rules Len Khalayu, now that the Mad Prophet is dead?"

"No one in the usual sense," said Aebakhmë, "but there are men who have been given the task of maintaining order. They are few and far between, but they are sufficient for the task. Mostly the people follow the word and example of their local wadhestorë, who themselves claim to speak for their... lone god." He spat the words, disdain dripping from his tongue. "I think that it is better that the land is ungoverned, or at least not united; our task will be simpler because of it."

Husin, her words muffled by a mouthful of bread, inquired, "What do we do when we arrive in Beridh-Ostaith? Are we to meet the Badhë there?"

The lordling shook his head. "The Badhë seldom travel outside the Sakhdo Mor. They will meet us after we cross the border, though we may meet a few in Beridh-Ostaith. Once we are within the Sakhdo Mor, the Badhë will join us."

Brenn, his interest kindled, said, "I have never sailed on a sakhnau. What are they like?"

"Akin to the ships built to cross the seas," Aebakhmë explained, "though the sakhnawë take advantage of the high winds of the Sakhdo Mor to glide upon skiffs and wheels. The trip will be swift; two days, perhaps three, and we will be there."

Suthai, a note of caution in his voice, interjected, "First we must make it through the pass." The others nodded, their faces grim with understanding.

"What of this pass?" Brenn asked. "Thou hast spoken of it, but no one has described it to me."

Aebakhmë, his voice heavy with the weight of experience, replied, "It is a difficult ride. The pass is narrow and the sides high, with little room to maneuver, hazardous ledges... I have lost two men and several horses in my years of leading soldiers through the mountains, but there is no alternative other than to ride around the mountains altogether. That would take several months, at least."

Brenn, his spirit undaunted, declared, "It sounds like a challenge, but I look forward to testing myself."

After he finished his stew and bread, Brenn lay down in the simple cot given to him, but sleep eluded him, his mind awhirl with thoughts of the journey ahead. The next morning, they awoke before dawn for a light breakfast of bread and fried ham.

"Thou dost look nervous, Brenn," said Aebakhmë, a hint of reassurance in his tone. "There is nothing to worry about."

When the time came, they left the mountain town at a brisk pace. The road within the pass was empty, the wind cold and biting. The surrounding peaks scraped the sky, as their name suggested, and the army rode in the shadow of the range for a time until the sun rose high enough to shine down through the ravine, its light fleeting, lasting only a few precious hours.

The road was steep in many places, its condition varying from passable to awful. Holes and rocks strewn about the ground forced the soldiers to lead their horses at many of these spots. In a few places, a small glacial stream ran alongside the road, and a few squat trees grew there, their presence a small comfort in the harsh landscape.

The sun rose in the sky, then slipped behind the peaks with little time to shine down on the soldiers, and they continued riding into the night. When the light began to fail, Brenn thought they would stop, but Aebakhmë pushed them on.

"We are only a few hours away, and the road is clear," the lordling said, his voice filled with determination. "If we push on, we can be at Beridh-Ostaith by midnight, and we will cross the border in the morning."

Brenn thought it not a good idea, but he held his tongue. The road was terrible and the mountains steep, and he imagined many of the horses would be too tired to make it through in one night. But he said nothing and kept riding.

Theg walked without a sound, but Brenn felt her tension. Her only protection against the cold was the blanket beneath her saddle, and Brenn sensed how cold she felt. They both longed for the warm sun on their faces.

As the moon shone in the sky, the mountains were stark and black, and then the night was lit by a flash of lightning, followed by an incredible boom of thunder. The strike had been close, and Brenn looked around to see if a storm was approaching. The sky was clear and there was no sign of wind; then a few raindrops fell, followed by a few more, and then the rain fell in a steady stream. The road became wet and the horses slipped in the mud and on the slick rocks, forcing the soldiers to slow to less than a walk. Brenn felt the tension rise in Theg, and he tried to calm her.

"We must take shelter!" Husin called to Aebakhmë, her voice barely audible above the deluge.

The lordling nodded and waved behind him, motioning for the company to halt. They had brought along a few tarpaulins to keep the rain off, and a few men hung them from the cliff-side. There was hardly any room to move, and the men sat beneath the tarpaulins shoulder-to-shoulder. The rain pelted down upon the makeshift roofs, making it impossible to build a fire. The men passed the time in silence, and Brenn worried about Theg standing alone in the torrent with the other horses.

"This storm was brought by the Six," said Husin, her voice tinged with foreboding. "It is an ill omen."

Suthai, ever the pragmatist, countered, "It is an omen of a wet night, nothing more."

Aebakhmë, his voice rising above the rain, sought to reassure his men: "Worry not. We are sheltered well enough, and there is no danger in getting wet. We will continue in the morning and reach Beridh-Ostaith before noon."

And so, amidst the fury of the storm, the company huddled together, their spirits tested by the trials of the journey, yet bolstered by the steadfast leadership of Aebakhmë and the promise of their destination. Through the long, wet night, they endured, their resolve as unyielding as the mountains that surrounded them, their hearts set on the path ahead, and the challenges that lay in wait beyond the borders of Len Khalayu.

The rain continued all night, and by morning's light the ground was drenched, the road a veritable river. Every man was wet and cold, but naught could be done. They broke camp, mounted their steeds, and pressed on through the pass, though many horses slid and slipped on the wet road, their hooves making sucking noises as they trudged through mud, through which the small river flowed freely, their damp backs steaming in the morning air. Slower they were than usual, but the road was not impassable.

"Art thou well, Theg?" Brenn asked as they rode.

"Of course," she said, though he felt her discomfort in his own heart.

Eventually they reached the western mouth of the pass and found themselves on a hillside overlooking a valley 'tween the mountains. Wide it was with few rocks or trees, the land like an empty plain. A river ran through, swollen with rain from the storm.

"We are but a day's ride from Beridh-Ostaith," Aebakhmë said. "The road is easy, weather fair. The pass is behind us; there's no need to worry."

After they overcame the first steepness of the western mouth, the valley shallowed, and they rode down without trouble. The muddy road turned to grassy plain, though ground was soft. At the bottom, the valley leveled out and going was easier than thus far, the company made good time.

The valley was dotted with short trees, yellow-green grass stretched to horizon. Air was damp and cool, sun high and bright, the soldiers dried. Ground soft and wet, rain began to fall again; this time light and not as cold as the previous night. Brenn tired, for they had ridden two days and camped in rain, so he was glad to be out of the pass and in the wide valley.

"This is a beautiful place," he said.

"It is," Aebakhmë replied. "These are the hinterlands of the Badhë. They keep the land in good order, never shortage of game or water. They are good people. Beridh-Ostaith just a few hours' ride ahead, we'll cross the river at the city gates. For now we follow it south."

They rode across the valley 'neath night sky, sun warm and pleasant on their heads. Brenn thought of the pass, how cold it had been, and he was glad for warmth and light. Mood of company lightened, Aebakhmë in good spirits, laughing, smiling, joking with the men. Brenn imagined how wonderful it would be to ride here in summer with sun overhead and water running high.

Aebakhmë pushed the men and horses faster, for 'twas important to arrive at town before nightfall. Light rain came and went, sometimes falling in drizzle, sometimes stopping altogether. River flowed on their left, snaking its way through valley, then widened as it neared town.

Before sun set, army came upon the town at bend in river where it changed course from south to east, Beridh-Ostaith on southern shore. Some Badhë could be seen, living in large tents dotting riverside. Tall watchtower stood at city gate, men with spears and bows atop. In distance to south-west, Brenn saw what seemed enormous, sailed ships sitting in the valley.

"Is this Beridh-Ostaith?" Brenn asked Husin, who rode beside him.

"Yes," she said. "Smaller than thou didst guess, eh? I thought same, my first time here. But there is brisk trade, for it's on border of Maikhethlen and Len Khalayu, many boats come through this port."

"Are those ships in distance the sakhnawë?"

"Not quite, for we're still in a green valley."

Husin laughed. "But they are of a kind, built and steered by Badhë who wander these lands. Those ships are rather called goranawë."

In grey of morn, when chill did pierce the air, and rain of yestereve had ceased its fall, the town, still wrapped in slumber's gentle shroud, beheld the army mount the creaking docks. Brave Brenn and comrades crossed the gangplank's span to board the grandest ship of Aebakhmë's fleet.

The deck, alive with bustling sailors toil, some twenty souls prepared for voyage long. Two sister ships, their berths at neighboring piers, swelled with the weight of steeds and sundry stores.

From distant decks, commanders' voices rang: "All souls accounted, lord!"

Then Aebakhmë, with regal mien, declared: "Let us begin this journey, fraught with fate." The captain, hearing thus his lord's command, bid crew to cast off lines and set their course.

The great sails rose, unfurling to the sky, as mighty wheels, released from earthly bonds, began their turn with groan of timber strained. Slow motion grew to swift and steady pace, as Beridh-Ostaith faded from their view.

Upon the watchtower's lofty height, flags of vibrant hue did dance and wave, their message guiding pilot's hand. Young Brenn, entranced by sights so strange and new, gazed down upon the waking townsfolk's throng.

The ship lurched forth, embraced by damp, cool air, and Brenn, his heart a-thrill with mingled awe and trepidation, breathed the bracing wind. He marveled at the snapping of the sails, this first adventure on a ship of land.

"O wondrous craft!" he cried in joyous tone, "that bears us forth on wheels instead of waves! What sorcery of science guides our path across the verdant sea of swaying grass?"

The dale stretched wide, a green and boundless plain, as southwest bound they sailed with steady aim. To north and east, the Dyuglebai stood proud, their snowy peaks diminishing with time.

The Sun, ascending o'er the mountain's brow, cast shadows long and turned the slopes to ink, while bathing lowland meadows gold and bright. The undulating grass, like ocean swells, danced in the breeze that bore them on their way.

Then Brenn, his thoughts turned inward for a space, recalled the wolf in the house of Ker, and of his mother, left without farewell. A pang of guilt did pierce his youthful breast, as hope for her forgiveness stirred within.

"O mother mine," he whispered to the wind, "forgive thy son for leaving without word. This journey calls me to a destiny unknown, yet fraught with purpose grand and true. May fortune guide me home to thee again, with tales of deeds to make thine heart swell proud."

Thus Brenn and company sailed forth that morn, their hearts set firm on quests and glories new, as Beridh-Ostaith faded in their wake, and unknown lands stretched endless 'fore their prow.

Beridh-Ostaith faded, a speck upon the vast horizon's edge. The army, borne on wheels through shifting sands, had crossed the bounds of fair Len

Khalayu. Where once green meadows swayed in gentle breeze, now stretched the infamous desert, vast and gold.

Oft Badhë bands, with tents and beasts of burden, appeared like mirages upon the dunes. They hailed the ships that sailed on land's dry sea, and Brenn, with kindness, returned each salute. Though stomach churned with each rise and fall, he soon grew used to this strange vessel's gait.

On fourth day's morn, when heat did parch the air, came Peryost, the Badhë first mate, to call: "Lord Aebakhmë requests thy presence, Brenn."

Upon the deck, 'neath blazing desert Sun, stood lordling proud, with Suthai at his side, and Husin fair, their eyes fixed on the east.

"Behold, dear Brenn," quoth Aebakhmë with pride, "yon wall of red amid the golden waste? 'Tis Jub Khewi, our journey's fated end."

Brenn strained his eyes against the blinding glare, to spy the distant city, squat and low. "How far?" he asked, for distance here deceived.

"A day, no more," the lordling swift replied, "yet we shall not sail straight to yonder gates. My army waits beyond Borheno Gwega, where we shall meet and plan our bold assault." He spoke of Badhë warriors, fierce and true, their desert blood a weapon sharp and keen.

"How won thou to our cause?" Brenn asked.

Said Aebakhmë, "I promised to bring back the ways of their forebears; that in overthrowing the wadhestor and ending the line of the Mad Prophet, I shall rebuild their dying culture atop the ruins of Jub Khewi."

"End the line of the Prophet?" asked Brenn. "But he is Mover! Ending his line would sever all folk from the gods—surely thou canst not mean to end his line completely."

Aebakhmë laughed. "Didst thou not know, Brenn? Surely thou hast guessed it. Khesi Addeu betrayed my father—the same Khesi whom thy father, Deugwer Ker, drove across the Terunthleu." The lordling grinned, and Brenn felt his blood chill despite the heat of the desert.

"Knowest thou who I am?" he asked.

"I am no fool, Brenn," said the lordling. "From the moment I found thee alone in the dale I suspected that thou wouldst not be honest about thine identity. My suspicions were confirmed when I heard thee talk to that horse of thine. True, many speak to their mounts when there is none other to speak with, but I have never met someone who held an entire conversation with his horse. Besides that, thou art clearly a Keuleno as thine hair and skin and eyes betray, yet thou speakest our small dialect as if born to it. By the time I found thee, word had reached even mine ears of the son of Deugwer, now a fugitive from his own king."

"Why not deliver me to Gwalo's hands?" Asked Brenn, his heart now racing with dismay.

"I say unto thee again, I am no fool. Wherefore would I send away such an asset when I could use thee to mine own end, and also help thee achieve thine own goal?"

"Mine own goal?" asked Brenn. "What is my goal, and how knowest thou of it when even I do not?"

"Oh, Brenn, it is as plain as the sword thou dost carry; yea, the sword Pukhso is renowned in Len Khalayu, for it is the blade that struck down my father, Aeboli, while in the hands of thy brother Kolewa Ker. I saw it with mine own eyes, Brenn: thy brother struck down my father in the battle of Gwelulo Pass, whereupon the Prophet fell upon thy brother and smote him in the shallows of the river. I know that sword, as I knew thy brother and father; verily do I know thee."

But Brenn, though tempted by revenge's call, Stood firm against the lordling's wicked scheme: "I'll not be slave nor pawn in thy designs," He cried, and drew his blade. "Release me now, or by mine own hand I shall fall, and risk the world's unmaking with my death."

Aebakhmë laughed, though reached for his own sword, while Husin stepped forth, her hands raised in peace: "Oh, Brenn," she pleaded, "let me explain all—"

But he rebuffed her words with blazing eyes: "If friend thou art, then stand against thy lord, and say I would not die to thwart his plans."

The crew looked on, their breath held in suspense, as Brenn, surrounded, weighed his desperate choice. His thoughts turned to Kolewa, fallen brother, and Deugwer, father lost beyond the sea. With voice that cracked like parched and barren earth, he spoke: "Thou shalt not take me as thy thrall."

At last, the lordling, with a mocking smile, did offer Brenn three paths to choose between: "Stay, fight, and conquer Jub Khewi with me; or leap, and face the desert's cruel embrace; or seek our camp beyond Borheno's gorge, where welcome and forgiveness thou mayest find."

Young Brenn, his heart resolved, his spirit strong, declared, "I am no weapon for thy use." With that, he climbed the ship's high side and fell upon the shifting sands, his fate unknown. His bag was tossed, a final gesture made, as Husin waved farewell with saddened mien.

Thus Brenn set forth alone in desert vast, the Sun-scorched land stretched endless 'fore his feet. Behind, the ship sailed on, a fading speck, while Jub Khewi loomed distant in the haze. What path he'd choose, what perils he might face, lay hidden in the shimmering desert air.

Beneath the blazing Sun, over sands that burned through boots of leather thick, did Brenn stand fast and gaze upon the ship receding swift, its sails the last to fade on desert's edge. With naught but sword Pukhso and meager things in bag that Husin cast to him (and coin from Gwalo's coffers pilfered), he took stock: no food nor water, map nor steed had he, nor knowledge of the barren wilds ahead. Two paths lay fore: to trek to fair Jub Khewi, or seek Aebakhmë's camp past Borheno Gwega, whatever that be. Amid the gusts of sand astir, Brenn pondered his escape.

"Have I come far to fall in snares anew, like unto those in Keulen that I fled? Am I consigned to perish in a war not mine to wage, no matter course I choose? What fate awaits, now freed from would-be kings?"

He sank upon the sands, Pukhso across his lap,

and shut his eyes. The winds fell still; the Sun beat fierce upon his reddening skin. His sack's sparse contents spilled before him there: a rag of cloth, a coil of sturdy rope, a purse with meager coin, some meat long dried, a shirt to spare. He mused on his ill lot as Sun blazed on. One path could save his life: to trek with haste unto the gates of Jub Khewi.

Long leagues lay twixt him and that distant town, and hotter waxed the day with each drawn breath. The rope he rent and with the rag he bound a shield against the Sun around his brow and neck, though naught could spare his eyes the blinding glare. Then to his feet he rose, Pukhso secured upon his hip, his bag slung across his back.

With every step his feet like lead did sink into the yielding sand. For hours until he pressed ahead, til Sun reached zenith's height and thirst overcame him. Bag cast down, he lay his weary head and veiled his face in cloth, then shut his eyes in slumber's uncomfortable embrace.

"Hail, and well met!" a voice did call. Brenn woke, the Sun far lower than he recalled. A figure stood, with camel laden near, in loose robes clad, a hood and veil to turn the searing heat and ever-shifting sands. From what was seen of dark, uncovered face, Brenn knew him as a native of these parts. "Ah, praise God, thou livest still," said he. "Hast thou need of succor in thy plight?"

The stranger's tongue was odd to Brenn's ear, but in a thrice he knew it as a dialect of Kalayo. He grasped the meaning. "I am lost," said Brenn, "and parched with thirst. Hast thou water to slake my sand-dry throat?"

"Come hither, friend," the man said, reaching for the bladder at his hip. So Brenn drew nigh, feet plunging deep in dune with every stride. The skin he took with thanks and drank his fill. "Lost, sayest thou?" asked the man. "Yet there ahead Jub Khewi stands within our very sight."

Brenn nodded, skin returned, but bade to drink again; then said, "Aye, yon city I spy, but I was parted from my caravan and know little of this wild terrain."

"I see," the man replied, then sipped himself and bowed. "I am called Ettor. Who art thou?"

"My name is Brenn," he said, returning bow.

"Art thou a man of northern climes?" asked Ettor. "For few of thy kind have we seen since war's surcease."

Brenn shook his head. "Nay, Dol-Nopthelen is my far home, but twixt my folk and those of Keulen flows a common ancestry, as our pale hair and skin doth plain attest."

"Hm," mused Ettor, then to his beast repaired to seek among its packs. He thence withdrew a bale of cloth and to his newfound friend presented it. "I pray thee, don these robes. They shall avail thee more than thine attire."

"Thou layest me in debt," said Brenn, and pulled the azure gown over his head near to the ground. At once he felt the searing heat subside.

"Nay, 'tis but duty owed to all who fare across Sakhdo Mor's unforgiving waste, lest we prove cruel when faced with others' need. Let me instruct thee how to wrap thy garb, for thou art new to our Kalayo dress."

He chortled soft as Brenn allowed his aid: "This gwarnyemeth," said he, "wards off the heat and stinging sands. Oft beneath its folds we wear the small-clothes for the air to waft between. And this, a kirven." Round Brenn's head he wrapped a cloth far larger than the rag he'd used. "Upon thy crown and neck it turns the Sun. Now draw this part across thy face but leave thine eyes unshaded." With a cord he bound it fast. "How fares it now? An improvement, no?"

"Far better than my former wraps," said Brenn. "My thanks for thy most generous soul, Ettor."

"Now let us hasten ere the Sun doth sink! For bitter cold the desert nights become. Come, walk beside me, friend, and pass the miles."

Relieved to have a kind companion's aid, Brenn fell in step as they strode toward the town. "Canst thou describe Jub Khewi fair to me?—for little do I know of that famed place."

"Ah, yes!" said Ettor. "Jub Khewi, grandest city of Len Khalayu, its seat of power and jewel of Sakhdo Mor. There meet folks from all towns and lands afar, nomads and traders of the sands, the Badhë tribe, and wayfarers from realms across Edorath. Since war hath ceased, commerce and faith and peace hold sway. Jub Khewi was the first king's throne in triumph over the pagans who long dwelt in this domain. Beneath God's guiding hand, it grew into a hub of trade, a font of art and learning for the region around."

"Thou speakest as one whose pride runs deep," marked Brenn.

"Aye, pride I bear," affirmed Ettor, "for 'tis a

wondrous home, and daily I lament my frequent absences, for business draws me far afield through much of each long year. The rilŷn whose roots in fair Jub Khewi lie anchored can their lineage trace unto the Kelai's noble stock of old."

"I've heard tale of a great academy in thy fair city," Brenn remarked. "Do they admit even those whose blood is not of pure Kala descent into their learned ranks?

With hearty mirth did Ettor laugh, and his camel groaned behind in rude reply. "An apt query, my friend!—for never would is claim rank as first among Edorath's schools if every door were barred to those not born into our ancient ways. Dost thou aspire to imbibe of its font of wisdom deep?"

"In altered circumstance, perchance I might," said Brenn. "But other tasks compel me now. Pray tell, who sits upon Jub Khewi's mayoral seat?"

Again Ettor's guffaws rang out. "Good sir! Our city hath no need of lord or king, no mayor upon a throne to make decree—for by the Kanakh-ri's sage and holy writ the rilŷn live, and thus are ruled by naught save their own rectitude of heart. If any could be called the town's high seat, 'twould be our wadhestor, the one most near to God, who shepherds folk of lesser faith. Dannwi Asakhdo is that righteous man. Though never I've stood before his noble self, his sermons oft I've heard, and can avow his virtue and his wisdom heaven-blest."

He paused, then said, "Of course, the Prophet too some reckon…"

Brenn broke in, "Dost thou refer to Khesi Addeu? I thought him lost when war's tide turned and his defeat was sealed."

"Mm, yes," said Ettor, stroking his beard. "The Mad Prophet is gone, though none can say if he be dead or if he wanders still. But no, I speak now of his son and heir, the new Prophet, imbued by birthright with the Power of Space, as tradition holds."

Brenn nodded, musing, "Yet this younger seer, he too holds no command over town affairs?"

"Nay, friend. If any could assert such claim, his reach would encompass all Len Khalayu and every rilŷn soul, yea, even those beyond our borders. Young in years is the son, and sooth, we rilŷn brook no rule save our own conscience beneath the Almighty's eye. Dannwi Asakhdo is the sole true voice the folk of fair Jub Khewi heed and trust."

"Thy wisdom runs both broad and deep," said Brenn. He yearned to loose his tongue, so sound alarm of dire threat lurking past Borheno Gwega, but prudence counseled waiting to impart his fears unto a more empowered ear. "Whence dost thou hail?" he inquired instead.

"Jub Khewi is my birthplace," Ettor said, "though most my days I've dwelt in Ëogor, that city far to south and west, night to the shores of great Pel Khalas. Never a man of desert sands was I, but of the sea, for might Maikhethlen Mor's lucrative ports Pel Khalas doth unlock for trade and chance. To hawk my wares I journey far and wide, else my roving soul would pine away, confined to but one place overlong. Such is my lot. In Ëogor bides my wife, belly now all swollen ripe with child. When I conclude my traffic in Jub Khewi, I'll to her fly swift, to greet our new babe, new gift from God."

"Upon thee I bid all blessings rain," said Brenn. "A child's birth ever deserves great joy."

"And thou, hast thou offspring at home?" asked he.

Brenn shook his head. "For fatherhood, I am as yet too green in years."

But Ettor scoffed. "Fie! Age holds no dominion over such things. If thou canst meet a babe's most pressing needs and lavish it with love, thou art full fit to wear the mantle of paternity."

Thus conversing, the unlikely pair traversed the shifty dunes, as Borheno Gwega's arid breath beset them round. Yet steadfast strode they on, the spires of great Jub Khewi looming nigh, while cloaked Aebakhmë's menace in the west still lay unseen beyond the shimmering haze.

Of sundry matters light they spoke to while the passing time, til lo! the gates appeared. The Sun had fled, and Brenn felt night's chill breath upon his back. He turned his gaze westward and spied a dark line, Borheno Gwega, though closer view would more assurance yield. Had light availed, he fancied he might glimpse Aebakhmë's ships on yon far oasis, where massed his force with Badhë allies, poised to strike a blow against fair Jub Khewi unaware.

This secret dire weighed heavy on Brenn's heart; he needed to seek Dannwi Asakhdo out, the wadhestor, to sound the dread alarm.

Carved as from living stone the high walls rose in grandeur vast, no join of block to block discernible. The dying Sun's last rays set them aglow in hues of flame, as if some inner fire burned, stretching out of sight, sheer faces smooth, impregnable redoubts. One portal sole Brenn saw, a gate of iron full wide enough for ten horsed men abreast, its bands more thick than his own brawny arm. Though now flung wide, into the city's heart admitting Ettor with his beast in tow, his step assured by long familiarity.

Less certain, Brenn clutched tight his kirven's folds, knowing his eyes' blue-green hue and pale complexion could not stay hid for long, yet shadows deep within the walls might briefly cloak his race and foreign mien til his grave task was done. Before him, grand Jub Khewi sprawled immense, all ornament and beauty, soaring high in stone and cedar, doors and casements graced with tracery fine. The avenues swept broad and clean, to Brenn's surprise by lush groves lined despite the desert's arid tyranny. Unto a plaza vast their path did wend, its bustling commerce stilled by fading day, a few souls yet abroad in raiment bright, their speech like music, fair Kalayo-tongue, by Brenn's Power rendered plain as if they native speakers were of his own land.

Amid the square a marble wonder stood, a woman's form, all smiles, with arms outspread, her gown's stone folds the semblance of true drape and motion by the sculptor's cunning wrought.

"Behold, the Lady of Flowers fair," said Ettor. "She, the conquest-king's own child, her heart all charity, who raised Jub Khewi to learning's peak and culture's cynosure."

"Great beauty here I see," Brenn marveled soft. "The craftsfolk of thy city know their trade."

"Aye, none surpass them," Ettor said, and signed toward a dwelling nigh. "At yon street's end a house thou wilt find, its gwirnit unsurpassed, and beds to let. Tell thou Doroidho that I sent thee; she will trim thy lodging's cost. As for myself, I must away. God grant our paths may cross again, and fare thee well!"

With thanks for aid so unstinting, Brenn bade the merchant kind goodbye, and watched him fade into the gloaming with his plodding beast. Brenn gazed about, to fix his bearings new. Not distant stood the inn of which he'd heard; down shadowed ways he passed, the town's maze-like profusion of dim paths and structures tall misdirecting not, for all streams to one great river ran, and he knew he'd not stray.

The house surprised him with its modest size and homely air, more domicile than inn, as its small placard over the door proclaimed. He knocked, unsure of fit propriety, and soon a crone appeared, stooped low with years, her arms mere wands, in gwarnyemeth plain clad, no kirven to conceal her time-grooved face. "Good even, sir; seekest thou a room this night?"

"I do, grandmother," said Brenn, the words unknowing from his lips, by Power placed as one to this land born, though such address in Keulen never would fall. "Ettor did say to mention that he sent me to thy door."

"Ah, Ettor, bless him!" cried the bedlam kind. "He is a pearl, my friend of old, to whom I owe so much. But any soul in need is here full welcome, come they self-commended or no. I am Doroidho; pray come in!"

The chamber small yet comfort promised, graced with cushioned chairs and sturdy table plain, three doors the further disposition showed. As Brenn looked on, the goodwife bustled spry, a lamp to light against night's gathering murk.

"The leftmost door leads to thy room; the right doth open to the washing place; the third, to kitchen and mine own snug chamber too. My cookery wants for size yet serves as well for hungry mouth as any grand cuisine. And hungry sure thou art! I'll fetch thee food—but stay, what unmannerly hostess I, to pry of rooms and board, yet fail to ask the name of him who shelters beneath my roof!"

"Brenn I am called," said he. "A sup and bed would be sore welcome, and my thanks to thee."

"Kalayo thou hast mastered," she observed, "though thy fair hue bespeaks a distant shore. Whence camest thou by thy flawless parlance of our tongue, as a native born and bred?"

A tale to serve both then and later too Brenn quickly spun. "From Dol-Nopthelen far I hail, and with a caravan I ride—kith, kin, and boon companions, our small band. One fellow traveler, a man from Ëogor, tutored me in Kalayo from tender youth, and ceaseless practice over the leagues hath left me nigh untraced by foreign tone. But I am flattered thou shouldst deem my speech so pure." With such half-truths, he thought, all tales should chime, lest contradictions sly his ruse betray.

Into the kitchen snug Doroidho led, the lamps and stove to life swift kindled there, a kettle placed to boil.

"Ettor did praise thy gwirnit to the very skies," said Brenn. "I know not what it is, yet fain would try."

"O, wag thy tongue, thy silver fool!" she cried. "Mine humble fare no better is than all the other goodwives' in this town, I swear, though kindly 'tis of him to claim mine best, and I care not if flattery or truth guide his opinion." From a cupboard nigh she drew a bowl close-capped and platter heaped with savory bread fried crisp. "Never tried is, sayest thou? Then fall to straight!" She whipped the cover off to bare a white mash within the bowl, whose scent of garlic, herbs, and fragrant oil provoked in Brenn a keen hunger's pangs.

A shred of bread he seized and plunged it deep into the ivory heap, then crammed the lot into his watering mouth. No potatoes, these, though like in texture, rich with spice and all most toothsome. "What are these?" he mumbled out around a second bite. "The Immortal's food and Idhuthi's apples would not have tasted thus!"

The goodwife beamed. "Again, such praise. I vow, if all my guests were so easy to please, this humble inn into a great repast I'd turn, and never stint for custom. Nay, dear lad, 'tis not but white peas mashed fine with oil and savory seasoning.—but I'm right glad it sits well with thee. Now eat thy fill whilst I fetch thee a plate of roast pork from last night. Go wash thyself the while; within the room thou wilt find fresh clothes laid out for thee to don whilst I launder the ones thou wearest—for I deem they need it, as thou dost."

Her words rang true, for grit of road and field, in hair and clothes and very joints ingrained, cried out to be assuaged. The bath, though small, boasted a basin, tap for water clear, and clean, soft toweling upon the wall, while in a mirrored cabinet he found sundry absolutionary aids. That folk in this fair land such clever plumbing knew, beyond the ken of folk in Keulen, struck him as passing strange, yet welcome.

His road stains scoured away and body clad in clean, cool robes of linen fair, he felt renewed in every sinew as he stepped once more into the fragrant kitchen, where Doroidho deftly placed his meal. The savory scent drew him like lodestone, and he fell upon it with a traveler's zeal, while in the parlor, with swift hands grown sure through years of practice, his hostess plied her knitting needles with a soothing click. Her thread and victuals done, she rose and bore the empty dishes thence.

"Now get thee to thy rest, dear boy," she urged. "And if thou shouldst have need of aught to mar my nighttime peace, come rouse me straight. My sleep is light, and I must often stir ere dawn; 'twill be no trial. An innkeeper must such demands expect!"

Once more his thanks he made, and sought his bed, the first since Beridh-Ostaith's luxury to cradle him in comfort. Gratefully surrendered he to slumber's waiting arms.

The morn arrived, and Brenn woke to the scent of eggs and vegetables sizzling in the pan. His visage washed and body proper clad, he sought Doroidho in her snug kitchen, where she, at table set for two, did place the savory food. Brenn sat down and helped himself to bread and gwirnit, then addressed his hostess kind: "I slept full well, and give thee thanks, but I must soon be on my way. Pray tell, what do I owe thee for thy pains?"

The goodwife waved a hand. "A score of segi will

more than compensate. I need no more."

But Brenn pressed on, "For two good meals and bed, a score alone? I'll give a full othë and wish I could give more."

She shook her head. "Thou wilt do no such thing! When I name my price, 'tis fair and final. Thou art always welcome beneath my roof, for never have I played the host to one so courteous. 'Tis plain thy mother reared thee well, my gentle guest."

Thus chided, Brenn forbore to argue more, and bent him to his breakfast with good will. When every scrap was gone, and he had taken a third portion at Doroidho's behest, he pushed back from his board and rose. "Dear dame, I must be on my way, but ere I go, I wonder if thou might assist my quest. I seek Dannwi Asakhdo. I am told he is the wadhestor of this goodly town."

"Aye, that he is," she said with nod. "To his words the people flock in droves, and if thou wouldst attend his sermon, thou must come betimes—two hours ere the start, or else content thee to sit without, and strain to catch his voice."

"My business brooks no delay," said Brenn, "and bears upon the fate of all—this town, its folk, the rilŷn faithful, yea, all Len Khalayu. If not the wadhestor, to whom should I address mine urgent plea? Who holds the reins of power in Jub Khewi's teeming streets?"

Doroidho laughed. "Ah, Ettor! Ever he attributes all dominion unto God and deems His spokesmen here the fount of rule. But if thy matter touches faith, or all the rilŷn people, then perhaps thou art wise to bend thy steps toward Dannwi. Hie thee hence to the deukis with all speed; his service starts anon. Thou mayest not find a seat within, but if thou art fleet of foot when he concludes, thou mayest contrive to catch his ear withal."

"And wilt thou not attend the service, too?" Brenn asked.

The goodwife smiled. "Nay, I am quite content to worship in the quiet of mine home, sans all the pomp and babble of the crowd. But go thou, Brenn, and when thy task is done, come back to sup with me, and lodge the night."

The youth clasped her worn hand in his. "I shall, and once more thank thee, grandmother."

She waved him on. "One small thing more—the garb thou didst wear beneath thy gwarnyemeth, and the robe itself, were sadly soiled. If thou wilt not take offense, I'll launder them while thou art about thy rounds, that thou mayest fetch them fresh and clean anon." Brenn ventured a demurral, but the dame forestalled him. "Nay, I will not be denied. Go thou about thy tasks and fetch the lot on thy return."

He smiled and bowed assent, then took his leave, Doroidho's helpful map to the deukis fixed within his mind. The sacred seat, he learned, stood not far-flung from his kind hostess's abode, indeed amidmost of the town, its seed and core, from which the lanes and byways radiated like petals of some vast, stone-carven bloom.

Beneath the savage Sun's unblinking eye, amid the dust and din of thronging streets, where tides of change and strife roiled just beneath the bright mosaic of the city's life, Brenn strode, a stranger borne on errand grave, to seek the ear of those who held the reins of governance, and sound a warning knell of war and woe, calamity to come.

But as he pressed on through the clamorous souk where merchants vied in hawking wares and griefs, a scene of rank injustice smote his eye: a mob, a roiling mass of rage inflame by righteous wrath, ringed round a slender girl, a child enisled in a sea of hate. Their raucous cries, a hellish antiphon, proclaimed her guilt of crimes as yet unnamed, and vowed to mete out judgment swift and fell in blows and blood, to crush her tender life on fury's altar.

And in that instant, Brenn's reluctant heart, averse to discord and contention's roar, knew torment's very crucible, as each sinew and fiber of his being cried in stark negation of the grim scene, the cruelty unmasked, the wrong unvarnished flaunted in righteousness's mocking guise.

With leaden steps, he cleaved the sullenly resisting press, his voice a reed in tempest's teeth. "For love and mercy, hold your hands! What madness goads you to this cruel extreme? How hath this poor maid earned such foul redress, to forfeit life beneath obdurate hatred's heel?"

At first perplexed, the throng, their ire provoked by challenge unforeseen to their design, turned baleful eyes on Brenn, who dared presume to thwart their grim prerogative. Then spake one brawny knave, eyes glinting flinty scorn: "Stand clear, thou meddling fool! This girl hath sinner and brought our godly town to disrepute. Now must she wash away trespass with blood, a crimson libation to our wounded pride!"

But Brenn, his heart now girded round with

right, would not be turned aside, nor brook this vile perversion of true equity's intent, this grim burlesque of law. With shoulders squared and voice a-thrum with passion's armature, he faced the ravening pack and gave full throat to reason's poignancy and pity's plea:

"O people of Jub Khewi, stay your hands! I do entreat you, ponder well your course, and mark the cruelty, the twisted logic of what ye undertake in justice's name. What crime, I ask again, hath this poor child committed, to deserve such brutal doom?"

Chastened a whit by Brenn's audacious stand and stirring exhortation, the raw edges of their murderous intent now blunted by uncertainty's dull strop, the rabble stirred uneasily, their fixed resolve now touched by flecks of doubt, compunction's creeping rust.

Yet their fell chief, his vaulting pride up-stung by bold defiance of his stern command, his palm now primed with retribution's tool, a jagged blade of adamant, bore down upon the youth whose words had blocked his will. In that tense instant, poised on danger's brink, Brenn's sinews, galvanized by primal dread, uncoiled in reflex born of stark despair.

His hand shot forth to seize the ruffian's wrist in grip of steel, then with a supple twist he sent the man sprawling, his weapon's threat reft from his grasp to clatter on the stones. For one charged heartbeat, silence reigned supreme, disbelief and awe now writ on every face.

Sensing reprieve's frail window, Brenn moved swift to press his sole advantage. With the girl ensconced within his reach, he clove a path through their stunned ranks, his strident voice raised high in plea for aid, for succor from their rage. And as they fled the howling pack's pursuit, her small form sheltered in his strong embrace, he felt a groundswell of conviction surge within his breast—a new-forged creed to stand against cruelty, oppression's yoke, to be a voice for those bereft of power, a shield and shelter for the dispossessed—though all the world should rise to cast him down.

Doroidho's hearth was a refuge sweet from chaos, fury, and the mob's fell roar. The stove's soft radiance limned the careworn faces of Brenn and the poor girl ensconced within his sheltering arms, her whimpers soft and low amidst the distant din of anger's cries.

With tenderness, he laid her on the bed, his voice a balm to soothe her fears and pain: "Be still, dear child, thou art safe here, and none shall bring thee harm within these sturdy walls."

Doroidho, her visage graven with concern, turned to Brenn. "She is with child, and grievous hurt. We must salve her wound and bruises and tend the babe beneath her heart. But first, we need clean water, linens fresh to cleanse and heal, restore her shattered frame."

With urgent mien, she gestured to the door. "Brenn, my Gwerkyo, friend and neighbor, a healer of renown, hath skills to mend both flesh and spirit. Haste thee to her now, convey our need, and bring her to this place to lend her aid and comfort to this child."

Brenn wavered, torn betwixt the compelling pull to stay and guard the girl, ensure her weal, and the fell exigence of the goodwife's plea. At last, with heavy sigh, he yielded to the press of grim necessity. "I shall return anon, with Gwerkyo at my side and all that thou requirest, to heal this girl and knit her raveled sleeve of care once more."

One backward glance he cast upon the child, her tortured mien now gentles by the fire's benignant glow, then slipped into the glare of day, his steps a martial cadence against the cobbles as he clove the winding ways toward Gwerkyo's house, his thoughts awhirl with musings on the contrarieties of conscience, duty, and compassion's call.

As on he pressed, he pondered the dire stakes of his resolve to intervene, to save the waif from brutish fury, bear her to this sanctuary of succor and repose, knowing it well might complicate the warp and weft of his grand purpose, his chief charge to rouse Jub Khewi to the imminent threat, the gathering tempest of Aebakhmë's wrath.

Yet in his marrow he knew he could not spurn the cry of one in anguish, could not quell the summons of his very soul to stand for right against might, for justice against brute force, even though it meant a steeper, craggier road toward his great aim of shielding the walled town from depredations of a tyrant's lust for conquest and dominion absolute.

With wry grimace at his own foiled designs, his cross allegiances, he hasted on to Gwerkyo's door, hand upraised to knock, to bid the sage doctor to her work of mercy, her vocation to bind up the wounds of flesh and psyche, stanch the flow of anguish from the fountainhead of pain.

Apace they sped to Doroidho's abode, Gwerkyo's satchel full and close to hand with philters, poultices, and opiate draughts, her mien composed and purposeful, a match for Brenn's stalwart air, his urgent need to render aid, to offer comfort unto the broken bird they sought to mend.

As they overpassed the threshold, the girl stirred and hummed, a piteous keen of raw despair that pierced him to the quick, roused with full spate of his vast store of adamant resolve to offer refuge from the predator, the grim marauder, ravin and despair that preyed upon the helpless and alone.

With unpracticed yet gentle hand he sought to plump the pillows, smooth the coverlet, extend what meager easement that he could to her, so frail, so lost in pain's fell throes, so needful of a bulwark against the tide of suffering and abjection, fear and woe.

Doroidho, lips a-twitch with tempered mirth at his inept yet sincere ministrations, reproved him with affection, guiding him to tend with deft yet delicate address the girl's immediate afflictions, her most keen and pressing wants of body and of mind.

"Nay, Brenn," she said, "attend: with light, unhurried touch, with patience limitless and love unfeigned, arrange the pillows thus, the blankets so, and offer sips of water, murmurs soft of reassurance and fidelity to her, so fragile, wounded in her flesh and spirit, needful of our strength, our calm, our steadfast presence to draw her back from the pain's enshrouding miasma to health's clear air."

The boy, abashed yet grateful for her aid, her sapient tutelage in healing's art, essayed a wan smile, meeting her kind eyes in mute acknowledgment of all that passed between them, fellow feeling, firm respect that blossomed in extremity, in the face of dire compulsion to mend and restore.

As the two wise women plied their craft, with Brenn attendant on their each behest, a shared, fell sense of purpose charged the room, a force nigh tangible in its dread weight that spurred them to redoubled efforts bent upon the preservation of one life, one innocent enmeshed in fate's cruel skein as dark strife gathered, poised to smite the town and rend its moorings, sow fear's crop in blood.

In the bustling heart of Jub Khewi's streets, as morning's light dispelled the lingering shadows and the town awakened to the whispered tales of the previous day's tumultuous events, Brenn found himself adrift, a stranger in a sea of hostile glares and accusations. The marketplace, once a place of refuge and anonymity, had transformed into a stage, a crucible of public scrutiny and mistrust, of anger and resentment directed at the one who had dared to disrupt the fragile peace and delicate balance of the city's life.

With heavy steps, he made his way among the stalls and vendors, the jostling crowds, his mind intent on resuming his initial quest, his mission to warn the city's leaders of the impending war and the gathering storm that threatened to engulf them, to sweep away the very foundations of their world. But as he walked, he found his path impeded, his progress blocked by the hostility and open animosity of those who once had paid him no regard, had spared no thought for the stranger in their midst, the outsider who moved among them like a ghost, unseen and unnoticed in the bustle of their lives.

Now, as he passed, their eyes bore into him, their whispers followed in his wake, their words a hissing chorus of blame and accusation: "Look, there goes he, the one who spat upon our ways and thought himself greater than us who know ourselves. Behold the one who placed himself within the path of fate and took upon himself the mantle of a savior, foregoing all tradition and teachings from the Kanakh-ri; an Easterner, one who would see our city burn, our lives destroyed by the actions of his people, his kin, the Keulenu."

Brenn sought to press on, to ignore the barbs and taunts, the whispered condemnations that assailed him from every side, his mind fixed on the need to reach the city's leaders, to convey the urgent message and warning that he bore of Aebakhmë's army and the coming war. But as he neared the center of the market, the heart of Jub Khewi's bustling life, he found his way blocked by a group of angry men, their faces twisted with contempt, their eyes alight with a fierce and bitter flame, their words a snarling accusation, a demand for answers, for retribution for the wrongs they claimed he and his people had inflicted upon their city, their way of life, their fragile, cherished peace.

"Outsider," the leader of the group called out, his voice a harsh and grating rasp, "what brings thee to our city, to our streets, thou who bringest memory of war, of doom? What right hast thou to walk among us, disrupt our lives, our livelihoods, with thy meddling and thy troublemaking, thy defense of those who would defy our laws, our customs?"

Brenn, his heart pounding in his chest, his mind racing with the need to find a way, a means to extricate himself, to press on with his mission, sought to calm the men, to reason with their anger. "Please, I mean no harm, no disrespect to you, or to your city, to your way of life. I come with a warning, a message of the danger that approaches, the army that even now marches on your gates, intent on conquest, on destruction and on death."

But his words fell on deaf ears, on hearts too full of anger and resentment, of fear and hate, to hear the truth, to heed the warning that he sought to bring, the urgent plea for action, for preparation and for unity in the face of the coming storm, the threat that loomed on the horizon, dark and vast.

"Lies!" the leader of the group spat out, his face contorted with contempt, his hand clenched into a fist, a threat of violence barely held in check by the thinnest thread of civility, of restraint and reason's sway. "Thou speakest of danger, of an army at our gates, but we know the truth, we see through thy deception, thine attempts to sow discord, to undermine the peace and stability of our city that we have made in thy kin's despite, to weaken us for thine own nefarious ends."

Brenn, his heart sinking with the realization that his efforts, his attempts to warn, to help, were being met with only anger, only scorn, sought to press on, to find another way to reach the city's ears, to convey the message that burned within his heart, his mind, the knowledge of the danger that approached, the urgent need for action, for defense. But as he turned to go, to seek another path, another means to reach his goal, his purpose, he found his way blocked once again, this time by a wall of hostile faces, of angry eyes and clenched fists, of voices raised in accusation, in condemnation and bitter hate.

And in that moment, as he stood there, trapped between the angry mob and his own sense of duty, of the need to warn, to help, he felt despair, hopelessness, wash over him, a wave of bitter gall that threatened to engulf him, to drown his spirit in a sea of anger, of resentment and of fear. For he knew that his efforts, his attempts to influence events, to shape the course of Jub Khewi's fate, were met with naught but hostile mien, with mistrust and suspicion, with a wall of anger and of prejudice insurmountable, blocking his way at every turn, thwarting his every move.

What could he do but return to Doroidho's home, a haven in this sea of hate? What can one do against such blinding ignorance and fear, but retreat and live to fight for those beloved to oneself?

The night lay heavy with the weight of impending war, a shadow on the hearts and minds of those who stayed in Doroidho's house. In her home, a somber mood prevailed, as Brenn and Gwerkyo, united in their grief, kept vigil over the girl they'd saved from harm, their thoughts awhirl with all that had transpired. The day's events, the violence and the rage, the cruelty of the mob, the bitter price exacted on the innocent and weak, weighed heavy on their spirits, their very souls. And now, amidst the silence of the night, a new tragedy, a fresh wound to bear, as the girl, her body racked with pain and fear, went into labor, far too soon, too young, to bring a new life forth into the world.

Brenn, his heart aching, held the girl's hand, attempting in his voice to show the calm he did not feel himself. "Be strong, young one, thou art safe here, with us now. We'll see thee through this, no matter what may come." But even as he spoke, he knew the truth, the bitter reality that lay ahead; for the child, born too early, too fragile, and too small, stood little chance against the odds arrayed.

Amidst the sorrow and the pain, the girl, her face a mask of anguish and despair, delivered forth a tiny, silent form, a life that flickered briefly, then was gone, snuffed out before it ever had a chance to know the joys and wonders of the world. In the aftermath, the girl held her babe, her young heart breaking for the loss endured, and Brenn slipped away, his mind rent with painful thoughts, with questions that demanded answers and truth.

Searching for the chance to speed along the healing of the poor ill-fated girl, Brenn found himself in search within the bag of Gwerkyo's tools. With furtive hands, he took a small worn book, the leather cover weathered, its pages rich with ink. And as he read, his heart began to race, his mind to reel with all that was revealed. For there, amidst the healer's careful script, a secret lay, a truth long hidden from his ken, a connection that would change the course of all.

Aebakhmë, the lord who sought to conquer and subdue, to bend Len Khalayu to his ambitious will, was kin to Khesi Addeu, the tyrant Prophet, whose cruelty and viciousness placed a blade between the ribs of Kolewa, good Kolewa. Aeboli, Aebakhmë's father, was the Prophet's brother, a younger son of a dynasty of Movers—they who Hold the Power of Space, of power and oppression, blood-soaked and vile.

The revelation hit Brenn like a blow, a punch to the gut that left him reeling, stunned. With this new knowledge, this bitter truth, he saw the world in a different light, a harsher glare that stripped away the veils of illusion and deception, laid bare the rot that festered at the heart of Power's game. What but fate and destiny would have led Brenn through that cursed blizzard, which led him to the service of that lord Aebakhmë? What odds were there that he should find the kin of that same monster who drove his brother to a bitter end before his youth was spent?

"Forces there are, connecting Form to Shatter," Brenn murmured to himself, "that conspire to drive my life toward predetermined ends. Alas, what cruel and twisted fate is this, that I, a mere mortal, should be bound by forces vast and inscrutable, beyond the ken of human understanding or control! O, how I rail against this tyranny, this yoke of destiny that doth constrain mine every step, mine every choice and deed, directing me along a path unseen, towards ends that I can neither know nor change.

"What use is free will, that vaunted gift, when all around, the currents of the cosmos conspire to shape my course, to bend my will to purposes I cannot discern? I am a leaf upon the wind, a mote adrift in the vast ocean of the universe, tossed hither and yon by tides invisible, powerless to resist or to defy the inexorable pull of fate's decree.

"And yet, though I may rage and storm and curse against this bitter draught, this cup of gall, what choice have I but to endure, to bear the weight of this unwanted destiny? For all my struggles, all my fierce defiance, I am but a pawn in a game whose rules I cannot comprehend, whose end I cannot see.

"O, would that I could break these bonds, could shatter the chains that bind me to this narrow path, and chart mine own course, mine own way in the world, free from the tyranny of forces unseen! But alas, 'tis not to be, for I am caught in a spider's web that will not let me go, a puppet dancing on the strings of chance, helpless to resist the pull of fate.

"And so, I must endure, must bear this burden of a life not wholly mine, and find what solace I can in the knowledge that even in my struggles, even in my pain, I am part of something greater still, a thread of the vast tapestry of life, woven by hands unseen, by powers beyond my mortal ken. Though I may rail against it, though I may hate this fate that doth constrain and bind me fast, I must accept my place, my role to play, in the grand drama of the universe, and trust that in the end, all shall be well, and all manner of thing shall be well, though I may never know the reason why."

Brenn took his repose upon the sofa that night, while with the morn, Doroidho did prepare a simple fare, which he partook more out of wont than hunger's keen demand. And on the second day, Gwerkyo emerged from where the ailing maid lay, and surprise writ plain upon her face to see him still.

"I thought thou wouldst have gone by now," she spoke, to which he said, "I feel a bond of duty unto the girl. Doth she now wake?"

A nod from the elder dame—"Thou mayst knock, yet expect but few words in return."

So Brenn approached and gently rapped upon the door. No sound came from within. The latch left free, he pushed it wide a hand-breadth and peered past the jamb. There lay the maid, her gaze fixed on the beams above, at first her features veiled by gloom and her own earth-hued tresses. As his sight adjusted to the dim, he spied beside her right eye, near the temple, a clean gash, healing apace, no bandage to require.

"May I come in?" he asked, all soft and low. She shifted slightly, which he took to mean assent. The door ajar, he ventured close unto the bed, where stood a waiting chair, yet he remained afoot. "My name," he said, "is Gw…" A swallow. "Brenn. My name is Brenn."

A puff of air escaped her, like unto a mirthless laugh. "Thou seemest unsure," she whispered.

"In these strange days," said he, "that is most true." A still beat passed. "And what art thou called?"

She pondered ere she spoke. "Deubmeni."

"Thou soundest quite certain." He essayed a smile, but wan, and she returned it, meeting his gaze briefly ere her own sought heaven once more.

"Pray, sit," she bade him. "Do not hover so." Obedient, he sank into the chair.

"I am in grief," said Brenn. "I should have moved with greater dispatch 'twixt thee and thy foes."

"Thou didst far more than any other would here, where thy foreign mien marks thee a stranger. For those who spurn the teachings of Rilun, the mob's cruel justice swiftly falls."

"This faith, these customs of Jub Khewi, pass my ken. I had heard tell the rilŷn were a folk of gentle ways."

Now she did laugh outright, then clutched her ribs in pain. "I owe thee thanks, and more besides—the very breath of life."

"Nay," he demurred, "thou owest naught. The fault is mine entire that thou... that thy..."

"No more," she pleaded, and reached out to him. He clasped her proffered hand, and once more she smiled. "What moved thee to defy the crowd, to bear me from their wrath? A stranger to thee, I, and thou hadst no just cause to hazard all."

He groped for words, the face of her fell people emblazoned still in memory—the eyes alight with vicious glee, the voice raised high in vengeful cries as blows rained on her form, prostrate and weeping while her unborn babe perished within. His own travails, he knew, to hers were as a mote to blazing sun, yet well he knew the murky fount of hate whence such rage springs, the selfsame bleak abyss wherein he'd locked a measure of his own ire smoldering, since sire and brother fell, since Gwalo pressed a sword into his hand, and he that nameless knight in fury slew lest he once more in fetters be compelled to slay at some enthroned tyrant's behest.

"I... I cannot explain," he fumbled. "I... I know not what to say."

Her fingers tightened round his. "Whatever the cause," she murmured, "still I thank thee."

Silence reigned once more as Brenn observed her youth in finer grain, her native hue like rich, new-turned loam, her eyes a deep, beguiling umber, limbs and features black and blue with cruel abuse, yet in her level gaze and steadfast clasp he read a bedrock strength, a spirit steeled to rise above all wounds of flesh and heart.

"Wilt thou take thy leave soon?" she ventured then.

"Aye, this day or the next," he answered her.

She made to speak again, but in that breath Gwerkyo entered, said, "I must needs tend that gash." The girl inclined her head, and bore the examiner's touch stoic, save a wince. "It knits up fast," the healer soon pronounced. "'Tis shallow but shall leave its signature. Thou hast a lion's courage, little one."

"'Twas fortune's grace alone," the girl demurred, as Brenn inquired, "How many years hast thou?" "Nigh unto fifteen, come the harvest moon," she said, and smiled to see his plain surprise. "Doth that confound thee so?"

"Is it the wont in these parts for a maid to bear a child so young?" he blurted, and at once could have bitten his tongue in half. Deubmeni frowned, face downcast. "I entreat thee to forget," Brenn swiftly said, "I spoke in errant haste."

Gwerkyo, her task complete, quit the room, leaving a weighted silence in her wake, til finally the girl said, voice pitched low, "Thou knowest what I am."

"I know no such thing," Brenn countered, and leaned close, intent. "Thou art a newcomer to me, 'tis true. But I would name thee friend withal. What I overheard outside the market from that rabble's lips, 'twas naught to me. I only saw a soul in desperate straits and moved to lend my aid. My past is pocked with stains I dare not voice, yet this much I hold true—we all may strive to chart a nobler course, reshape the clay of our own destinies. If thou desirest to break the chains of what was and begin anew, thou wilt find no stauncher advocate than I."

Her gaze still lowered, but a smile played round her mouth. "Gladly would I embrace that vision bright. But in this rigid town, my life's shape is not mine to freely mold. Change comes not at a handmaid's merest whim."

"Then quit this stifling realm entire!" urged Brenn, "and seek thine higher calling far afield." A beat, then, haltingly, "I have to tell thee, sweet Jub Khewi may not long endure if this moon sees its course."

Her eyes flew wide. "What meanest thou?"

"Across Borheno Gwega," he said, "some leagues beyond the city wall, there lurks an armed host, by one Aebakhmë commanded, who makes bold to claim descent from Khesi Addeu, the Mad Prophet. The path that brought me to his ranks is long and winding, but the nub is this—I joined, then soon forswore allegiance to his cause, which bodes naught but ill will to this fair land and its good folk. I sought to treat with him, Dannwi Asakhdo, wadhestor revered—'twas with that aim I neared the deukis' gates when thou wert so beset. But now I fear the foe's advance outstrips my best attempt to raise alarm. Belike their forces mass even now beneath the very walls. Therefore I beg thee, all three, fly this place with speed, lest that dread wave break over thee and bear all away in ruin."

He ceased, and marked their aspects as his message sank home—mute stoic reserve from the two elders, but Deubmeni's eyes stretched round with kindling dread. Doroidho spoke the first. "What wouldst thou have us do? Snatch up our meager goods and go to die of thirst in yon unwatered waste? I have seen many winters, and this burgh is all of home I've known. Come fire, come sword, I shall abide to meet what fate decrees."

"And I," chimed in Gwerkyo, "have walked this globe a goodly span, and feel no driving need to draw my days out past their natural reach. My truest heart-friend here has pledged to bide, and hand-in-hand we'll face the coming storm, that each might to the other comfort give should that dread summoner at last hold sway."

Though this resolve Brenn had in part foreseen, to hear it voiced aloud still smote his breast with leaden weight. He fixed imploring eyes on young Deubmeni, said, "Where standest thou? The bloom of youth mantles thy cheek; a score of years and more of promise stretch ahead. Say not thou wilt tarry here to be mown down ere thy true course has even yet begun!"

"What wouldst thou have me do?" she echoed back Doroidho's plaint. "I have nor coin nor mount, nor any kith or kin to grant me aid."

"Come, then, with me!" Brenn urged, and seized her hand in his, as though that clasp alone might anchor her against fate's impending blast. "My purse is full enough to see us far, and I speak tongues enough to open our way wherever our path may turn. I have one aim—to seek a peaceful life, if that's to be—but e'en that yields to this, my chief concern, that thou mightst escape the doom now gathering here. Say thou wilt share the road with me and find that true autonomy that comes of free self-governance in all things. Let thy will, not blind caprice of birth or fate's decree, shape thy tomorrows from this moment hence!"

The goodwives traded glances, fond, astute, as 'twixt the two youth silence reigned once more.

At last, Deubmeni spoke, tone hesitant, "Thou wouldst have my company on thy strange road, knowing full well what shame adheres to me, what taint of scandal colors my renown?"

Brenn shook his head, firm-jawed. "In wandering days now sped," he said, "I've marked humanity in every shade and guise; one truth gleaned thence is, never are we wholly the mere sum of our worst acts. Something ineffable, some unquenchable spark of life divine, doth animate these fragile tenements and raise our strivings far above the mire of our misfortunes and most grievous faults. Thou mayest not escape thy past entire, but nor must it alone define thee. Trust in this—there's more, far more to thy complex spirit than what overweening fools outside this room have dared to name thee, or to understand."

Deubmeni, wan but resolute, inquired of the elder woman, "When might I remove from thy kind care, and set my feet to his proposed adventure?"

Gwerkyo pursed her lips. "One further night of rest should thee suffice; yet mark me, sir," (this stern admonishment to Brenn), "she'll bear no fast or far-flung pace for some days yet. My meaning takest thou?"

He nodded, mute, as beneath his fingers twined Deubmeni's heartfelt press spoke full assent.

"With all mine heart," she said, tone low but clear, "I shall be glad to tread my path with thee, come what may, for good or ill or aught between. In thy resolve to see me free, unshackled from a past not all my own, I read the stirrings of a kindred fire, a shared compulsion to no more be blown by fickle winds of fate or fell mischance, but captain of my soul and days at last. Whithersoever our way shall wend, in thee I know I'll find a faithful friend, a steadfast guide, and in the simple knowing of that truth, I feel the first faint flux of hope reborn."

And as she spoke, within her lambent gaze, Brenn marked the kindling of a brighter flame, a light to pierce the shadows of despair that had so long enshrouded her—a dawn, though frail, of new possibilities vast, horizons of the spirit that even now began to limn themselves in gold and rose against the dimming purple of her pain.

In the still watches of the night, ere dawn's first blush had tinged the eastern sky with light, when fair Jub Khewi, wrapped in silence deep, lay like a city of the dead, a pause before the day's tumultuous dance began, sat Brenn, his heart and mind overwhelmed with doubt and nameless dread, the fruit of long, dark hours of contemplation on the city's plight.

Long had he striven, with all his might and main, to bend the arc of fate, to turn aside the tide of war and chaos, grim and fell, that threatened to engulf the embattled town, to sweep away its ancient walls and towers, and lay its beauty waste, a smoking ruin. But now, amidst the hush of night, a truth stark and unsparing, like a blade of ice, pierced through his breast, a reality too dire to be gainsaid or cast aside—his efforts, though born of love and noblest intent, were all in vain, like candle's guttering flame against the raging fury of the storm.

The engines of destruction, gears of war and politics and base, unbridled greed, were too entrenched, too potent far for one frail mortal to oppose, however he fought with valor and resolve. In that bleak hour, as black despair threatened to overwhelm his spirit's light and quench all hope within, a sudden clarity, serene and sure, dawned like a beacon in his troubled mind, illuming plain the true path he must tread.

Not on the grand, heroic stage of strife, where blood and steel held sway, lay his true call, but in the humbler, yet more vital task of sheltering those he cherished most from harm, from war's red ruin and fell fortune's blast. Deubmeni, this innocent and wounded girl to whom life had been so cruel, was laid upon his charge, and he would keep her safe from peril, come what may betide, no matter what the cost or sacrifice.

With gentle words, he roused her from her sleep,

his voice soft-pitched yet urgent in her ear. "Deubmeni, sweet friend, the hour has come for us to quit this place, to flee the strife and chaos that engulfs this fated town, and seek a path to peace and refuge sure, however far-flung the journey, steep the road."

The girl, her lids still heavy, limned with grief, yet in her eyes a light of trust unfeigned, assented with a nod, her hand in his, a silent pledge to brave what trials might come, and find a way together through the dark.

To southward of Jub Khewi, stark and drear, reared craggy hills, where Brenn and his fair charge made their spare camp beneath an overhang of weathered stone that looked out over the waste. Still halting from her hurts, her lip cleft deep, her gentle eyes enshadowed, purple-bruised, Deubmeni had sore travailed to win thus far from the embattled city's clamorous din.

Hard by their rude redoubt, a wadi dry cleft through the barren land, its stony bed gaping and parched, yet destined, come the rains, to run brimful with winter's bounty clear, a precious draught to slake Borheno Gwega's thirst. Amidst swirling dust and grit by soldiers raised as they marched grimly past, intent on war, the twain sat close, muffled against the choke and sting of billows thick that draped the stones in shroud of pallid gold.

Beyond, the desert's face, flat and austere, stretched to the encompassing horizon's brink, against which walled Jub Khewi stood incongruous, a strange, proud diadem on nature's brow, at once an aberration and a jewel whose beauty, born of art and ancient toil, shone all the more amidst such stark barrenness. By light of day, the crash and clang of arms, of engines dire and sword on ringing shield, smote the besieged walls, a hellish fugue faintly conveyed to the observers' ears when fickle winds conspired to bear the din.

By night, chill airs bit deep, and Deubmeni sought what scant warmth she could in Brenn's embrace, he long inured to cold's remorseless nip. Oft with the dawn, supply wains rumbled by, escorted by a motley host of foot, mainly the fierce Badhë who'd cast their lot with proud Aebakhmë's cause, while mounted high on steed or camel, swarthy lords held sway, the short-necked, broad-hoofed mounts of Kelai. More beasts of burden bore the precious stores of provender and water for the troops, while groaning carts hauled arms and raiment too, lashed 'twixt the straining backs of man and beast.

On two dread dawns, titanic engines passed, twelve straining teams to each, their timber wheels raising a fearful creak and groan of toil as with slow majesty they trundled by.

Once in the compass of the Sun's brief arc, the clash of battle stilled, and through the hills echoed the massed devotions of the hosts, one faction calling on the Six to speed the city's fall, while those within implored The Lone God's aid against their relentless foes. On both sides of the battle lines, too many already slept the long, cold sleep of death, while those yet spared, combatant and civilian, in town and field, raised anguished prayers alike that this new scourge of bloodshed might abate.

At last, when thirty days had waxed and waned, the two adventurers resolved to quit that land of strife, Deubmeni's strength restored enough to brave the rigors of the road. Eastward they set their course, their backs to war, for naught but grief and ruin lay out west, in Len Khalayu and realms yet more remote. Three thousand souls had perished in the time they'd tarried near, mere drops in sorrow's flood that would engulf unnumbered more ere peace returned to that fair clime. And as the pair mounted the long and weary road to exile, from proud Jub Khewi's heart a black plume rose, smoke from a city's funeral pyre.

Canto 3

Ten years had passed since Brenn and Deubmeni had fled the chaos and the strife of war, seeking a haven from the world's harsh cares in fair Sarheud Forest's tranquil heart. Here, by a lake of crystal clarity, whose placid face gave back the vault of heaven, they made their camp, a rustic sanctuary where towering trees stood sentinel and proud.

In this green oasis, far removed from all the tumult and the pain of lands beyond, three souls, by love and shared adversity forged into bonds unbreakable and true, lived out the simple rituals of life, the homely tasks that knit the ties of kin.

Brenn, once a wanderer in search of truth, now bent his mind to cookery's humble art, tending the savory stew whose fragrant steam promised a feast to come. Close by the shore, Deubmeni, refugee from hate's pursuits, found blessed ease, her spirit soothed and healed by nature's balm, the sense of safety won.

And young Laidho, his heart ablaze with joy,

explored the wonders of this woodland realm, his laughter pure and bright amidst the calls of birds and susurrant whispers of the leaves. This scene idyllic, like a waking dream, belied the trials and the pains endured that bound these three, through fire and adversity, into a family, steadfast and complete.

Deubmeni, brow furrowed with gentle care, called out to Laidho, "Venture not too far, dear child, for even in this peaceful glade, dangers unseen may lurk. Stay close and let thy roamings be confined to where our watch may guard thee from all harm."

But Brenn, his hand a consolation, spoke, "Fear not, my friend, for Laidho's heart is true, his wisdom deep beyond his tender years. He knows the bounds of safety's compass and will not transgress."

Deubmeni sighed, "I know, and yet the world is vast, and fraught with perils manifold. I would enfold you both, all I hold dear, in love's embrace, and shield you from the grasp of sorrow and mischance."

Brenn's fingers twined with hers, a bond of perfect unity. "And so thou hast, and shall, mine heart's true home. But life, for all its dangers and its snares must still be seized with joy, embraced in full, else we are thralls, though no physical chains constrain our limbs." Their converse, soft and low, blended with the merry sounds of Laidho's play, a counterpoint of solemnity and mirth.

But in a trice, all changed, as Laidho burst into the clearing, face alight with awe, a stranger stumbling in his wake, a boy of age with him, half-starved and scantily clad, his wrists and ankles bearing cruel traces of galling chains.

"Brenn, Deubmeni!" he cried, "this child, Gwidhotir, seeks our aid and comfort, alone and sore oppressed. Is it not right, our sacred charge, to succor the forlorn, the weak and friendless?"

Deubmeni stood mute, her heart in anguished turmoil, torn between the call of conscience and the primal need to shield her loved ones from all threat and harm.

But Brenn, his eyes aflame with righteous wrath, stepped forth and spoke, his voice a clarion, "Yea, we shall extend our help and grant him refuge, for were we not once outcasts too, in flight from spite and malice? Did not others' grace see us to sanctuary and respite? The debt we owe, we shall in turn repay."

Gwidhotir quavered, eyes by horror haunted, "I beg your mercy, for I've nowhere else to turn for solace in this pitiless world. I bring you peril, this I know full well, but desperation drives me to your door."

Brenn, though beset by doubt and nameless dread, held out his hand in fellowship and said, "Here thou art safe among devoted friends. We'll strive to heal thy wounds of body and of soul, and guide thee to a life of dignity, for in this task, we find our own salvation."

And thus into their circle, warm and close, was welcomed one more wounded, weary soul, a child by cruelty's caprice ill-used, but here, in love's embrace, vouchsafed the chance to mend, to dream anew of brighter days. As Brenn and Deubmeni lent their ears to his heartrending tale of woe and wrong, their hearts grew heavy with the burden of such pain endured by one so innocent.

Gwidhotir, scarcely more than babe in arms when first misfortune marked him for her own, recounted, voice a-quaver, how his mother, shipwrecked and sold into captivity, had perished 'neath the yoke of slavery, while he, bereft of parents and of hope, had known no moment's respite from the lash of fear and anguish, til his faithful friend, dear Lorem, braving all to set him free, had thrust into his hand the precious key that opened the way to liberty and life.

"Yet ere we reached the gate to sweet release," the child recalled, tears trembling on his lash, "our cruel pursuers overtook us. Then brave Lorem hid me safe and led them off, yielding his life for mine. With his last gift, the key, I found the door and made my flight, til, drawn by scent of food, I chanced upon your camp and sanctuary."

Brenn, his heart pierced by the pathos of that tragic tale, spoke gently, eyes alight with fierce resolve, "No innocent should ever endure such wrong, such undeserved affliction. With us, thou art safe, and we shall strive with utmost might to grant thee what all children sure deserve: love, joy, and freedom from oppression's yoke."

But prudent Deubmeni demurred, "Dear heart, I share thy outrage and thy zeal to aid, but we must ponder well the risks and perils of harboring this child. His cruel masters, brooking no loss of what they deem their chattel, will stop at naught to hunt him down, and we, by granting refuge, may incur their wrath."

Brenn's jaw set firm, his gaze unwavering. "I know thy fears, but can we live with our own conscience if we fail to lend our strength to one so vulnerable and sore in need, yet still claim virtue? Nay, my friend, we must do what we know is right and good and true, though all the world may rise against our choice."

To Gwidhotir he turned, hand clasping hand. "Child, thou art part of us now, one of our small fellowship of dreamers and outcasts. For thee we'll strive and sacrifice, that thou mayest know at last the blessings of a life of peace and dignity too long withheld. This is my sacred vow, and from it I shall not be swayed by danger or duress."

As night's dark mantle wrapped the glade in hush, and Laidho and Gwidhotir, lost in sleep, wore on their faces innocence serene, untouched by cares that weighed on older minds, on Brenn and Deubmeni, who bore the charge of their small band's security and fate in a fell world fraught with uncertainty, with strife and peril, Brenn in urgent tones, low-pitched and grave, to Deubmeni spoke: "We must not tarry long in this green bower, this transient oasis of repose, for even now, the minions of ill will, of cruelty and spite, may gather strength and dark resolve to track us to our lair, to seize again what they, in arrogance, deem but their chattel, theirs to bind and rule."

Deubmeni, her eyes reflecting deep the selfsame burden, the identical weight of duty and foreboding, thus replied: "Thou speakest sooth, my friend; we must prepare to flee at any instant, leave behind this brief respite, this momentary peace, and venture forth anew into the vast uncharted wild, to seek another home, a sanctuary where we may draw breath free from pursuit, from threat of servitude."

Brenn nodded, and his hand already sought their scant supplies, their precious, meager store of goods and tools to serve them on their road, their flight from those who fain would drag them back to chains and bondage. "Let us gather up only what we must bear, what we can take upon our journey, and abandon all the rest, a trifling forfeit to ensure the preservation of our cherished kin."

As they made haste, their motions deft and swift, their minds intent upon their solemn task, a sound intruded on their fixed resolve, a distant howling, an uncanny cry that pierced night's bosom, chilled their very blood with dire presentiment of lurking threat, of imminent calamity and woe.

Brenn's eyes grew keen, his whisper taut with dread: "Hark, how the wolves raise their alarum fierce, how from the trackless wild that hems us round they send a portent, an admonishment of hunters drawing nigh, of danger's advent hard on our trail. We must be vigilant, be one in purpose, steadfast in our bond."

Just then did young Gwidhotir stir and wake, his small form trembling, eyes wide-stretched with fear, the old, familiar specter of his pain: "Draw they so near? Will they overtake us now and hale me back unto that lightless pit, that hell of bondage, that unending bane I thought escaped? Must I endure again the crushing of my soul beneath sorrow's weight?"

Brenn, his heart rent by the child's distress, yet in his tone the bedrock of resolve, the adamant of courage undismayed, made answer: "Nay, sweet boy, they'll not prevail, they'll not lay hand on thee or work thee harm, for we, thy sworn protectors, thy true kin, will stand as shield and bulwark 'twixt thy form and all that menace thee, be it shade or substance, memory or present threat. While we draw breath, thou shalt know sanctuary, solace, peace."

Then did Gwidhotir sink once more to rest beside his new companion, faithful Laidho, as Brenn and Deubmeni plied their task with speed and stealth, til all was made prepared. And as dawn's blush paled the horizon's verge, as rose and gold bled softly through night's veil, the little band stole from their place of refuge, muted in tread, yet stalwart in their hearts, while round them still, in counterpoint bittersweet, the wolves' sonorous anthem marked their flight towards fortune unknown, horizons vast, where hope, though frail, might yet spring forth anew beneath the boundless vault of heaven's wide blue.

As twilight's mantle draped the hallowed ground of that forsaken church, where Brenn's small band sought fleeting sanctuary from their trek through darkling woods, a pall of nameless dread, of imminent calamity, hung low upon their spirits, a nigh-tangible weight that pressed on mind and heart with leaden touch.

Yet Brenn, his visage set in grim resolve, hand clenched on sword-hilt like a vise of steel, spoke words of reassurance to his friends: "Let fear not cow thee, though night's ebon wings may cloak unknown perils, dangers dire; for we stand unified, our sacred bond of fellowship a bulwark against all foes that dare assail our concord and repose."

Deubmeni, her dark eyes mirroring the sun's last aureate rays, in dulcet tones gave answer to the mounting tide of doubt: "In thee, brave Brenn, we trust implicitly—thy valor, thy devotion to our weal, thy steadfast ward against all adversities. Yet still, my soul lies freighted with unease at what unseen malevolence may lurk beyond the circle of our waning fire."

Then Laidho, his young mien creased with concern, small hand entwined with Gwidhotir's a-tremble, in quavering accents ventured forth his plea: "Will they overtake us, Brenn? Will they here find our hidden bastion, drag poor Gwidhotir back unto that pit of endless, sunless woe wherefrom he so intrepidly broke free?"

Brenn, heartsick at their innocent dismay, their unalloyed, uncomprehending fright, knelt down to meet their eyes and soothly swore: "Nay, little brothers, they'll not claim thee back or lay one hand in anger on thine heads, for I shall stand as thy unblenching shield, pitting my every faculty and nerve against any who would dare imperil thee."

And then, as if in mocking counterpoint to all their hopes and whispered supplications, the stillness shattered like a crystal pane: a thrashing, over-eager, through the brush, disgorging from the wood a lone male form, cruel calculation graven on his face, rapacity alight in piggy eyes.

"What ho, thou varlet!" he exclaimed with glee,

"I, Dannwi Asakhdo, would have words with thee! Charged by the Godhead's self to track and take the whelp I know thou harborest from my grasp. Yield up the boy, that portion of my chattel, (nay, more than mine, the very property of heaven's omnipotence) that thou hast filched and dost conceal, and I may grant thee leave to skulk away, to nurse regret and rue that e'er thou didst thwart my august decree!"

Brenn, blade leaping to hand, in thunderous voice made answer to this rude, imperious charge: "Thou shalt not touch a single hair of his, for he is not thy thrall or thing possessed, but a free soul, a child inviolate; and I shall fight unto my final breath his liberty and person to ensure!"

With those defiant words, the die was cast: a score of Dannwi's minions now came on, eyes lit with malice, naked blades a-thirst for blood and vengeance against their bold-faced foe. But Brenn, a whirlwind of lethality, met their advance with flashing sword and fury, matching each stroke with parry, thrust, and cut, his peerless skill and adamant resolve a rampart against the breaking tide of hate.

And at his side, the wolves, those untamed spirits, guardians of vert and vale, now sprang to join the carnage, tooth and claw a blinding storm, ripping and savaging the encircling foes til all the ground lay soaked with reeking gore, the air a-rent with anguished cries and screams for mercy or surcease from the fell might of Brenn and his lupine confederates.

At last, the ragged remnant turned to flee, maimed, and dismayed by their sound thrashing, while vile Dannwi too slunk off to lick his wounds and plot revenge with new-stoked, smoldering rage. Then Brenn, erect and proud in victory, raised his ensanguined blade and loudly cried:

"I'll see thee dead, thou loathsome fiend, if e'er again thou seekest to lay thy claim on him I now hold dear as any brother born! For I shall be his constant guard and ward, and thou hast seen how even the forest's hunters do fight with fang and fury at my side!"

Then, gathering young Gwidhotir to his breast, heart brimming with relief and boundless joy, Brenn soft conveyed this promise, solemn, true: "Dear friend, thou art safe, forever shielded by my love, my might, my all-consuming will that thou shouldst thrive, shouldst grow in grace and light untouched by cruelty or blighting fear. This I avow by my name, my father's, and that of my lost brother. Thou art free."

At this, Gwidhotir, overcome with feeling, made no reply but pressed his tear-drenched face hard into Brenn's broad shoulder, and his sobs of pure, cathartic gladness gently shook that sylvan bower, that temporary home, remote and still beneath the vault of stars.

As dawn's first light suffused the firmament, gilding the tranquil scene with lambent light, Brenn, ever the faithful sentinel, arose to ply his craft, provision to secure for those within his charge, his chosen kin. O'er crackling flame he bent, with practiced hand stirring the savory brew, its fragrance rich with herbs and wholesome grain, a promise sweet of strength renewed to meet the day's demands.

Round him, his fellowship, by love's ties bound, moved to their wonted tasks, their faces soft with ease of slumber yet, but in their eyes the lively glint of shared purpose, the calm and joy that only true communion brings.

But in that halcyon moment, darkness fell, dread and destruction its grim heralds—from the tangled fringe of wilderness there burst a form of primal might and savagery, a bear, by hunger's cruel pangs enraged, its eyes alight with madness, desperate from hibernation's fast too-early broken. With roar like thunder's voice, it challenged all, bent on the rending, on the crimson feast.

Brenn, swift as thought, Pukhso in hand agleam, leapt forth to meet the threat, crying aloud to those he loved, "Away! Seek refuge in the trees! I shall its baleful gaze hold fast!"—then hurled himself upon the ravening beast, his blade a meteor, a flashing wheel of deadly grace, of grim determination to shield, defend, protect unto his last.

The bear, by pain enraged, by Brenn's strike stung, its hide now glistening with scarlet sheen, reared high, its claws like scythes, a deadly arc seeking to crush, unmake the audacious foe, the man who dared contest its dominance. But Brenn, ablaze with valor's purest flame, undaunted, met the brute assault head-on, his sword a thunderbolt that pierced its bulk, drawing a gout of steam, a howling cry that shook the very roots of Earth.

In whirling blur of blade against fang, they strove, this man and beast, the hero against the bear, a dance macabre of lash and parry, thrust and snarling riposte, will to live full-matched against hunger's frenzied ire, red in tooth and claw. The glade resounded with the clash, and Brenn, battered, torn, yet still unbowed, his sword now dark with ursine life, stood tall at last, victorious o'er his foe's now still, prone form, its fury quelled, its mortal thread cut short.

Even as his comrades dear made haste to him, faces white with dread and gratitude commingled, Brenn felt the world careen, his senses swim, as wounds untallied took their grievous toll, his lifeblood fleeing fast from rent flesh and bone. He fell, as from slack grasp his weapon tumbled, crumpling onto the sod all incarnadined, sight dimming, pulse ebbing with each breath.

Deubmeni, wail of anguish on her lips, cradled his head, her tears like sorrow's rain flowing unheeded o'er his pallid cheek. Young Laidho and Gwidhotir, stricken mute, agape in numb despair too deep for speech, watched helpless as their guardian's light waned.

But then, as death's grey shroud stole o'er his mind, Brenn felt a wrenching shift, a cord unbound, his inmost essence soaring high and free from fleshly fetters into realms unknown—a sea of orange light, a fragrant haze redolent almonds burnt he swift traversed, towards a Presence vast, at once both strange and wondrous intimate, that to him called with soundless voice from Time's abyssal deep.

"Brenn, my dear man, to greet thee once again here past the Mortal Veil brings me great joy, where truth unshrouded and Creation's tides may be perceived by spirit unconfined by the narrow compass of a world of dust."

Brenn, heart afire with cryptic revelation, with yearning ache to fathom, understand this place, this moment charged with import dire, found trembling voice to frame his anxious plea: "Who art thou, that so gently speaks my name with power and tenderness in single breath? What realm is this of light and scent that thrums with unearthly energies beyond my ken? Why am I called to this uncanny borne in darkest hour of need, when all I cherish trembles upon a knife-edge poised 'twixt life and unrelenting doom?"

The Voice made answer soft: "Peace, Brenn, for thou art called to destiny more vast than thou conceivest, a path decreed by Agency far deeper than the roots of ancient peaks, outlasting tide and time. Thou art not friendless in thy striving—nay, but guided, guarded, succored from on high, part of a Cosmic Song that cannot die."

At this, the Voice grew hushed, the orange sea diffusing into shadow, leaving Brenn once more descending, falling like a stone through layers liminal of vision, dream, and solemn revelation, to rejoin the realm of clay, the plane of Mortal breath, of love and loss, of beauty and of death, the bittersweet mosaic of Life.

Within a healer's sanctum, clean and bright, where golden rays poured through expansive panes, illuming shelves and tables amply stocked with herbs and draughts, the tools of healing arts, lay Brenn upon a cot, his form so still, his breath the merest whisper, visage wan as if dread Techutet's hand already clasped his shoulder, poised to guide him past the veil.

Close gathered round, scarce daring to draw breath, his faithful comrades held their anxious watch—Deubmeni, Laidho, and Gwidhotir young, his tiny hand in theirs, their faces graved with deep concern, eyes red-rimmed, hollow, spent from countless tears and vigils through the night, hoping against hope for some small sign of life returned unto the breast of their felled friend.

Then all at once, a shriek, a sound so raw, so primal, tore from Brenn's constricted throat, his body bowed up rigid, as if wrenched back from death's yawning brink by unseen force. Wide flew his eyes, unfocused, wild with dread, as he sucked air in great, convulsive gasps, hands scrabbling at the coverlet, the air, aught that might serve as anchor, prove him yet among the quick, the realm of mortal breath.

Deubmeni, voice a-catch with joy and awe, reached out to stroke his fever-beaded brow. "Be tranquil, Brenn, thou art safe, in healing's halls of fair Kebowadhor. Recallest the bear? Thy valor vanquished it, preserved our lives, but at nigh-mortal cost—thy wounds so dire, we scarcely dared to hope... but lo! thou wakest, returned to us, as by a providence!"

Brenn, mind yet clouded, grasped at memory's threads—the fray, the pain, the stygian abyss that swallowed him, then spewed him forth into that amber realm, strange voice accosting him. He strove to rise, words rasping in his gorge: "The leech I must thank for my salvaging, for snatching me from death's cold, lightless sill."

The healer, venerable and kind of mien, stepped forth, a gentle smile upon his lips. "Nay, valiant Brenn, 'twas not my skill alone restored thee, knit thy flesh, and mended bone. Gaikhud, a sorcerer of mighty gifts, his power lent to raise thee from the brink, a feat surpassing far mine humble craft."

At mention of enchantments, Brenn's eyes flew wide, a frisson palpable of doubt and dread across his pallid features. "Sorcery? Invoked on my behalf? In mine own land, such arts forbidden are, accounted dark, transmuting those who truck with eldritch force to grendekith, the stuff of blackest dreams to fright the young and innocent of heart. I deemed them fables mere, til once I spied..." He shuddered, calling up that horror past, their grim encounter near the very town where they had found young Laidho, lost and lone. "What if this magic, bent to heal and save, somehow pollutes, transmutes me, renders me a twisted thing, a mockery of man, in spirit marred as grievously as flesh?"

The sage, perceiving Brenn's soul-deep unease, made gentle bid to soothe, to turn his mind to gentler thoughts, and fixed his kindly gaze on silent Laidho, still and watchful by. "Ho there, young master! Thou puttest me in mind of mine own brother, lost this many a year. He too was... different, solace oft would find in music's realm, in dulcet melody. I am informed thou yearnest to play, to mold thy skill to rival Stennas, minstrel famed, whose lays could stir the very hearts of gods."

With tender touch, he reached past vial and jar to draw forth an instrument of rarest craft, of burnished wood and bright, well-tempered keys—a gurdy, thing of beauty and potential. "Here, gentle boy, a gift to help thee find thy voice unique amidst this troubled world. Let music be thy lodestar and thy strength, a bulwark against the trials yet to come."

Young Laidho, features rapt with purest awe, took up the gurdy with near-reverent hands, cradling it like a fragile, precious babe, a smile so rare upon his somber lips as questing fingers brushed the gleaming keys, coaxing to life a halting, poignant air, whose magic seemed to set the very light, the lambent motes, to dancing, soul-enthralled.

The leech, well-pleased, turned back to his rapt guests. "Good friends, full much ye've borne, privations dire and perils far beyond your tender years, but now, ye must seek rest, a chance to heal, not just in sinew, but in heart and mind. Hard by there lies a tavern, snug and warm, where ye may bide, your strength and spirit mend, and chart your course, in safety and in peace, far from the menace of untamed wilds."

Brenn, feeble still, yet brimming thanks, renewed in purpose and resolve, reached out to clasp the healer's hand in his. "All gratitude I render thee, for my deliverance, for granting Laidho too this taste of joy, amidst the shadows of our perilous path. We shall, in sooth, thy wise direction heed, to rest, restore ourselves in flesh and soul, ere sallying forth to meet what fate awaits."

Amidst the cozy bustle of the inn, where savory scents of hearty provender commingled with the cheerful din of talk, sat Brenn and his companions, basking in a fleeting interval of hard-won peace, a transient balm to soothe the chafing wounds of their long, weary pilgrimage. Just then, a courier appeared, in hand a package wrapped in homespun cloth and twine, inscribed to Brenn, a riddle and surprise. With curious touch, he loosed the bindings to reveal a cloak of sumptuous heft and sheen, its substance wrought from pelt of that selfsame bear whose fury nigh had claimed his mortal breath, transformed his thread.

Secreted in its folds, a missive lay, disclosing the identity of him who'd sent this offering: Gaikhud, mage of puissant skill, whose arcane ministrations had snatched brave Brenn from death's ungentle grip. In wonderment, he pondered this strange gift, this totem grim yet apt, which spoke to him of destiny transmuted, a design recast by agencies beyond his ken.

As Brenn stood rapt in contemplation deep, a voice, at once familiar and long lost amid the echoing corridors of time, pierced through the clamor of the common room: "Gwennotir, can it be? By all the gods, I scarce dared dream I'd find thee in this place, of all the far-flung corners of the world!"

'Twas Leubkherth the Younger, son of the man who once stood fast beside Brenn's noble father, his staunchest friend and sworn companion true—though Leubkherth the Elder, to his lasting shame, by foul betrayal sent Kolewa down to death's dark portal, a dread secret Brenn believed the son knew not. This welcome shade, this emissary from a life foresworn, from duty's yoke and sorrow's cumbering pall, stirred in Brenn's breast a maelstrom of regret, of loss and longing for the sundered ties that bound him once to kith and kin and home.

"What wind of chance or fortune, Leubkherth, blows thee to this haven far from all we knew? What word hast thou of those I once held dear, the realm whose claim upon my soul I fled?"

Then Leubkherth spake, his visage a relief of light and shadow, gladness tempered by the solemn burden of his grim dispatch. "Know this, Gwennotir—mighty Gwalo hath quit this mortal sphere, to join the shades of long-dead ancestors. His scepter now hath passed to Gwalo the Younger, and his writ hath sent forth knights to every point of compass, to seek thee out, restore thee to thy place, thy birthright as the Baithas of thy people."

A pall descended on Brenn's turbid brow, the gravity of grief and obligation pressing like millstones on his weighted heart, the ghosts of immemorial loss and pain ascending in a flood of memory. Yet resolutely did he shake his head, averring, "Nay, I cannot, will not go, not now, not ever. My rightful place is here, among these faithful souls who most have need of my protection, succor, and my love. I'll not desert them, not for any crown or duty undesired, a destiny I've striven mightily to overcome."

Sudden commotion nigh the tavern bar drew their attention, an unseemly din that roused misgivings. Some sot, emboldened by the false courage of the cup, advanced with clumsy blandishments on Deubmeni, that fierce and peerless maid, as if to win her favor through persistence. With a flash of righteous ire, she drew her blade and dealt the rogue a lesson memorable and apt, dispatching him in howling disarray.

This display moved Leubkherth to mirth. Remarking on it, he observed to Brenn, "It seems thy friend hath scant need of a knight to fight her battles—she acquits herself with deadly grace, surpassing many men!"

Suffused with mingled pride and warm regard, Brenn made reply, "In sooth, my Deubmeni is to herself a host and law entire. When first we crossed paths in Jub Khewi's streets, ringed by a ravening mob inflamed by hate, who sought to stone her for the precious life she nurtured 'neath her heart, I could not let such beauty be despoiled by ignorance and malice. So I interposed myself between their wrath and her, and in that act, I sealed a covenant, a deathless bond, which trial and adversity have forged to adamant strength."

Then Leubkherth asked of Laidho, that uncanny, silent boy whose still, watchful demeanor yet betrayed some glimmer of a high, unfolding fate. "Whence came this foundling to thy motley band, thy chosen family knit by love's strong cords?"

With gaze grown distant, memory-enchanted, Brenn spake of that dread day when he came on the child abandoned, doomed to fall as prey to grondeketh, that twisted jungle-fiend. "Mine heart forbade me leave him to a fate so cruel and senseless. Nay, I snatched him thence to be a part of something new and true, a sacred compact amongst like wounded souls. And now Gwidhotir, that poor chattel-boy I liberated from his life of thrall, hath too annexed himself unto our fold, we vagabonds who seek a nobler path."

Stirred to the quick by all that he had gleaned, Leubkherth lapsed into a brown study, chin cradled pensively 'twixt thumb and finger. At length he mused, "Gwennotir, brother mine, I see with newfound clarity the course that thou hast fixed upon, thy north star true. Though fraught with hazard, still 'tis rightly aimed at all we hold most sacrosanct, those pearls of great price which redeem our mortal lot from futile vanity. I must reflect on all that thou hast shown me, all that I this night have heard and marked. With morning's light, I shall return, and we shall speak again."

As Sun peeped o'er the sill, to gild the snug hostelry's panes with lambent light, Brenn shook off sleep's chains, and ventured forth to seek repast and converse with his friends. But at table sat young Leubkherth, ringed by Deubmeni, Laidho, and Gwidhotir, their features rapt, attending to a tale of heroes bold from days long sped, whose deeds still kindled hearts and minds with valor's flame:

Hark, now, a tale of two souls—stout Kopeg, he of flocks and fields the lord, and great Bolikhwi, dragon fell and mighty, whose destinies by chance and choice entwined, impelled them on a quest perilous and strange to heal the wyrm of dire, consuming blight.

From far Dol-Nopthelen came Kopeg, blessed with kine and fowl, a man of means content, until Bolikhwi, sore beset by pains unfathomed, in his pasture made her bed, her frame once terrible now gaunt and wan. With pity moved, the farmer, all undaunted by her dread form, drew near, and succor lent of watering, and solace of his voice, whereat the dragon marveled, that a man should offer aid and comfort to her ilk.

When Kopeg asked how best her ills to assuage, Bolikhwi spake: "A poison gnaws mine heart, against which, in distant realms, some antidote is rumored to exist, though fruitless yet my long, despairing search. Legend avers a lake lies in the west, the Pool of Secrets, wherein abides the omniscient Naga sage, who haply might disclose the cure I seek."

To which bold Kopeg pledged, "That fabled mere, though strange to me, I'll strive alongside thee to find, and ne'er forsake thee to thy doom!" The dragon, touched by his devotion pure, her strength renewed with viands from his herd, upon her back the stalwart farmer set, then winged their course to lands beyond the dawn.

Ere long, they spied the Pool, its mirrored face limned by the glister of the Naga's scales, refulgent blue like lambent summer skies. To her they put their plea for wisdom's light, but grim her fateful words: "No earthly salve can purge the dire corruption from thy veins." Yet as Bolikhwi sank beneath despair, quick-witted Kopeg a shrewd question posed: "If on this plane, no remedy may be, what of those realms and spheres beyond our ken?"

The Naga paused in deep reflection, then vouchsafed: "In far-off mountains lies a cave wherein a stone-wrought arch, a threshold stands 'twixt this world and the next. Mayhap therein thine answer dwells." Resolved anew, the twain, their spirits steeled by friendship's adamant, set forth upon a journey fraught and fell across unmapped and unforgiving wilds, until at last, through toil and travail sore, they gained that portal writ with runes of yore in tongues draconic, from an age remote ere humankind first trod this mortal sphere.

"I contain that which never ceases," read the dragon. "Mawayu keeps me— cryptic words betokening passage to a realm beyond, once held by beings strange, now lost to time."

"Then let us dare to cross that liminal bound," cried Kopeg, all aflame with yearning bold, and headlong plunged into that numinous arch. Yet on its marches, dread Bolikhwi balked, overawed by whispers from the sentient air, of voids abyssal, stacked in endless planes like infinite regress, past mortal grasp.

But at her friend's exhortings sage and kind, the wyrm took heart, and amidst that world sublime of light and voice, they wandered, rapt and amazed, til from the luminous ether boomed a Voice. "'Tis I, Mawayu, guardian of this gate, and all who pass its beam in spirit pure. Speak now thine heart's desire, and if I may, I shall see it granted, full and free."

Then Bolikhwi, in accents meek, replied: "O puissant shade, my life ebbs slow away, gnawed by a poison dire no physic stems, for which I've sought, in vain, a healing touch. Wilt thou, if 'tis within thy cosmic scope, release me from my body's lingering bane?"

At this, the Voice a glad assent pronounced, and bade the travelers, dragon and stout man, to step beyond the circle of the known, and feast their awestruck eyes on vistas grand of Truth, and Being, in their naked form— the warp and weft of all creation's loom, from birth of stars to final entropy, each mote and world, each life and death entwined in one stupendous, mind-confounding whole.

They saw the secret language of the spheres, the arcane dance of wind and tide and flame, the vastness of the cosmic all laid bare, its patterns intricate of joy and pain, the eons-long unfolding of a world, with all its wonders, woes, and denizens, from dawn of thought to far-posterity, as civilizations blossomed, warred, and dreamed, then faded to a whisper on time's breath, their echoes ringing out in starry lays.

They saw the birth of the world, its pains and its first steps. They saw the world tower over the small beings on its surface, saw them struggle and grow, venture out into the world, build great civilizations, live and die, wonder, argue with the world and with one another, wage war, make peace, raise families and continue on, grow old, then young again; saw them struggle with their understanding, struggle with their nature and their gods, struggle to understand and to survive, and struggle to die.

And when the world trembled and the seas receded and the mountains cracked and the skies fell and many of the small beings died, and then many more, they saw the rest flee in their ships, into the sky and beyond. They watched them go, watched the skies grow quiet again, watched the dust settle, watched the healed world be born anew. They witnessed it take its first step, then the next, and the next, and the next; saw it grow green and bear flowers and fruit and tall trees, and the trees bore fruit and the fruit grew fat and heavy, and the fat heavy fruit dropped to the ground and broke, and the seeds inside scattered and bore fruit of their own.

Ten thousand years passed while Kopeg and Bolikhwi watched the people of the world, strong and weak in their faith, wise and foolish and cruel and kind. The people took joy in their strengths and sorrow in their weaknesses, and they passed into death and into the world beyond in a great wave of color and light and song.

Bolikhwi and Kopeg saw it all and began to sing with joy and sorrow, with wonder and fear, with the voices of the people of the Earth and the Earth itself as they passed into the great wave of time, and they sang and they sang until they had sung themselves into oblivion.

So rapt and humbled by these visions vast, their finite minds overfraught with Utter Light, that Kopeg begged surcease, to be returned to life's snug limits, though transformed for aye. Yet as he turned to take his leave, the Voice once more detained him: "But a single face of being's boundless gem I've shown to thee; thy journey's compass hath not reached its term!"

But Kopeg, all undone, demurred: "'No more! What I've beheld's already past my strength, so far beyond a mortal's crib and scope!"

Then to Bolikhwi turned sage Mawayu: "Thy grievous malady forever cured, 'tis thine to linger here in this bright realm if so thou wilt." But she, true comrade still, would not abide while yet her friend remained affrighted by his glimpse of Truth unveiled, and for his sake, forsook those gleaming shores.

Emerging from that crucible of awe, like divers surfacing from deep-sea gulfs, they stood once more before that graven door, their minds awhirl with all that they had seen. Kopeg, in faltering accents, scarce could frame the numinous immensities they'd grasped, the sweep and grandeur of the Form beheld, the terror and the splendor of the Shatter.

But Bolikhwi, possessed of larger view, urged him: "Though words may fail, we must essay to share these marvels with our kith and kin, and all who'll hearken to our stumbling tale, that they too may be enlarged in thought and spirit by meditations on the All's design, its pattern, beauty, and its mystery!"

Thus did they vow, the man and dragon sage, to chronicle and spread, as best they could, the wisdom won through their transfiguring trek beyond the pale of customary life, that those unnumbered yet to come might glimpse the strangeness and the glory they'd been shown, those points of light that wheel beyond the veil, the weft of worlds all bound in skein of Love that hath no end.

As Brenn drew nigh, young Leubkherth's visage lit with warmth and welcome, balm to the wanderer's soul. "Friend Brenn, come join our circle, break thy fast, and hear the tidings that I bear, the fruit of sober cogitation through the night. I'll not compel thine homeward journey, not deliver thee to Gwalo's grasping hand, the life thou hast fled, the yoke thou hast cast off. Nay, here's thy rightful place, amongst these thy loves, who lean upon thine arm and counsel wise."

Then from his scrip he plucked a missive sealed with sign and signet of Brenn's mother, Segwi. "She sent this, one of many, by the knights charged to restore thee to thy native seat. But I'll have no part in that stern pursuit, that bid to bind thee to unwelcome fate. Instead, I'll bear thy words, thine heart's true voice, unto her hands who waits with bated breath, a mother's love that spans the yearning leagues."

Ere Brenn could express his thanks, his full-brimmed heart, the doors flew wide, disgorging violent men with cruel Dannwi at their head, their eyes ablaze with malice, bent on Gwidhotir's frail, quaking form, ensconced in the embrace of fierce, protective Deubmeni. Then snarled their chief, in tones of avarice and threat: "Yield up the whelp, ye meddling, witless fools, who dare to thwart my will! He's chattel, naught but goods and property, to sell or rent or break, as I see fit. Gainsay me not!"

But Brenn, his hand a-thrum on Pukhso's hilt, his heart a-kindle with righteous ire, stood forth, a bulwark against that tide of greed. "Thou shalt not have him, fiend! Not while I draw breath, and command the sinews of mine arm to strive, to shield, to counter force with force, and with my body dam that raging flood of cruelty thou fain wouldst loose on him!"

In but a trice, vile Dannwi raised and loosed a bolt that sped, a harbinger of doom, straight to the breast of faithful Leubkherth, who sank lifeless, eyes wide with shock and pain, to the ale-soaked floor, his thread of fate full-spun. Then Brenn gave tongue to grief's unabated rage, a rallying cry to arms against infamy: "To cover, quick, my charges! Seek ye out what refuge may be found, the while I deal with these unleashed hellhounds, who dare to bay and snap at all I cherish and protect!"

As his companions scattered to their hides, a rising clamor smote the sultry air, a choir of howls and growls and snarls uncouth—the roofless strays, the village curs, now drawn as by a lodestone to that place of blood, summoned by scent of violence and the Power of Brenn, the Baithas, Focus of their kind.

A storm of hide and fang, they burst within, rending and savaging with slavering jaws the soldiers of base Dannwi, whose screams and abject terror-shrieks now split the din in descant harsh and horrific to the ear. Amidst that maelstrom of brute, red-fanged chaos, Brenn stood unbowed, crossed swords with the most fell and puissant of his foes, whose skill at arms and flashing blade met his in stridence shrill of clashing steel, a deadly, dazzling dance of cut and thrust, of parry and riposte. The battle surged, now this way and now that, as each sought vantage, pressed attack, or feigned subtle withdrawal, testing for the breach in guard or balance that would spell undoing.

At last, Brenn's point found home, through bone and flesh driving, unstoppable, til the severed head of his dread adversary lolled and rolled upon the gory stones, forever stilled. In that taut span of hue and cry and strife, Dannwi took flight, eluding both the jaws of his canine pursuers and the wrath of Brenn's keen blade, escaping to fight on. Til, amidst the shambles of that common room, Brenn stood alone, a-drench with sweat and gore, victorious, yet sore forspent, at last rejoined by his companions, who with eyes admiring, anxious, looked upon their friend, battered and weary, but defiant still.

Yet even as they gloried in his triumph, their hearts were shadowed by the loss, so swift and tragical, of noble Leubkherth, who with his life's blood had asserted his soul's truth. Gently did Brenn reach out, in wordless grief and fellowship, to touch that cooling brow, knowing the toll, the perilous price of love in a world rife with evil's darkling sway.

Upon the shore, where gentle waves caress the sands, the assembled group with heavy hearts bid farewell to Leubkherth, brave and noble, their fallen friend, whose loss weighed on their souls. With reverent hands they did prepare the boat, and on the pyre they placed Leubkherth's form, serene and still, as if in gentle slumber, his spirit free to roam the realms beyond.

Then Brenn, his voice thick with emotion's weight, spoke to his friends, his family in grief: "We gather here in sorrow's darkened shade, to honor one who gave his life for us. Leubkherth Morhwa, steadfast, loyal, brave, stood with us true, for this I am most grateful."

Deubmeni, her hand in Brenn's clasped tight, in solidarity, spoke soft yet strong: "May thy gods be with thee, kind Leubkherth, who showed such grace and kindness to us all."

As setting Sun suffused the shore and sea in golden splendor, Brenn and company heaved forth the pyre unto the waiting waves. Within, Brenn placed a burning torch aflame, and with a final gesture set adrift the fallen Leubkherth to his final rest. The flames consumed the wood, the mortal flesh, releasing spirit to the vast Beyond.

In silence stood the group, heads bowed in grief, their hearts overfilled with sorrow and with thanks. Then Brenn, his gaze fixed on horizon's edge, where sea and sky converged in distant haze, spoke once again: "My friends, the time has come to leave this place, to face what lies ahead. The noose of fate, of those who wish us ill, draws ever tighter with each passing hour. We must embark, seek shores and allies new, and break the chains of cruelty's despair." Thus Brenn addressed his stalwart company, and turned their backs upon the Sauleno Sea, where Leubkherth's pyre vanished beneath the waves.

On the bustling deck of the ferry that crossed the inland Sauleno Sea, passengers from all walks and stations mingled and milled about, some lost in thought, others engaged in lively conversation, while some attended to the tasks at hand, the daily rituals of shipboard life.

Amidst the colorful tapestry of souls, Brenn stood, his eyes fixed on the distant western shore, his mind awhirl with thoughts of what lay ahead, the challenges, the dangers, the unknown, that he and his companions must soon face. Then a voice, unknown and unexpected, broke through his contemplation: "Brenn, is it thou? Well met upon this voyage!"

He turned to see a man with yellow hair and blue

eyes, yet robed in the style of Len Khalayu. "Forgive me, friend," he told the man, "but I remember not where I've seen thy face."

The man laughed, coming closer. "Thou hast not seen it, I should think, for thou wast aswoon with loss of blood. I brought thee back with mine arts, though the doctor, my good friend Paresh, did all he could."

With realization, Brenn smiled—this was Gaikhud, the sorcerer, whose magic, whose arcane and potent skills, had saved his life, had brought him back from death's dark threshold, when all hope had seemed but lost. With gratitude and warmth, Brenn clasped his hand, his words sincere, heartfelt, and deeply moved. "Gaikhud, wise and generous, I owe thee more than words can say, more than I can ever hope to repay, for the gift of life, of breath, that thou has bestowed upon me, in mine hour of direst need, of pain and desperation."

Gaikhud, his smile strange yet kind, replied, "Think nothing of it, Brenn, for it is my calling, my sacred duty, to use my skills for the good of all." He paused, his eyes alight with a sudden spark of excitement, of the thrill of new discovery. "But let us speak of other things, my friend, of the marvels, the wonders, that the mind, the hand of humanfolk, can conjure and create! I have, of late, been working on a new invention, a substance of such power, such potential, that it could transform the very fabric of our world."

Brenn, intrigued, but also troubled by the sorcerer's words, the implications of such a claim, leaned closer, his voice low, saying, "What is this substance, Gaikhud, of which thou dost speak? What properties, what forces, doth it harness, that could so dramatically alter the course of human history, of the lives of all who dwell upon this earth?"

Gaikhud, his voice a whisper, a conspiratorial murmur, as he drew from his robes a small, innocuous pouch, replied, "Behold, the fruit of my labors, the culmination of years of study, experimentation, and ceaseless toil, in the pursuit of knowledge, of the mastery of the primal elements that shape and govern all of nature's realms. I call it fire powder, for its essence, its very nature, is that of the flame, the spark, the conflagration that can rend the very earth asunder, can shatter stone and metal, can unleash such devastating force, as to beggar the imagination."

He paused, his eyes meeting Brenn's, a glimmer of excitement, of the thrill of discovery, mingled with a hint of trepidation, of the weight of responsibility, of power. "Its uses, Brenn, are manifold and varied, from the mining of precious ores and gems, to the creation of dazzling spectacles, of entertainment, wonder, and delight."

To illustrate his point, Gaikhud gestured to a secluded corner of the deck, whither the two men went. With a flick of his wrist, a whispered word of power, he ignited the tiny charge, and in an instant, a blinding flash and a pop of small thunder rent the air, sending a plume of smoke and flame skyward, a miniature eruption, a taste of the unimaginable forces that the powder, in greater quantities, could unleash.

Brenn, startled, awestruck, and perhaps unnerved

by the display, the implications of such a substance, in a world already riven by conflict, by the clash of arms and ideologies, of the lust for power and dominion, over land and sea alike, spoke, his voice a mix of admiration and apprehension, of the wonder and dread that such an invention, such a discovery, could not help but evoke, in any mind attuned to the complexities, the perils, of the human condition, the human heart.

"Gaikhud, I am amazed, and deeply troubled, by what thou hast shown me, by the power and potential, both for good and ill, that thy fire powder represents, embodies. In the right hands, in the service of the noble, the enlightened, the humane, it could indeed be a boon, a blessing, to the progress, the advancement, of our kind. But in the grip of the malicious, the cruel, the ruthlessly ambitious, it could also be a curse, a scourge, a bringer of such devastation, such unmitigated horror, as to make the wars, the conflicts, of our past seem but a pale and trifling shadow, in comparison to the cataclysmic storm that such a weapon, such a force unleashed, could bring down upon the heads of all who dwell within this fragile, mortal coil."

He paused, his gaze intense, his words a plea, a warning, a challenge, all in one. "I urge thee, Gaikhud, to use this power, this knowledge, that thou hast gained, with utmost care, with the wisdom, the compassion, and the foresight that thy years, thy learning, thine experience, have surely granted thee in ample measure. For the fate of nations, of generations yet unborn, may well rest upon the choices, the actions, that thou takest, in the days and years to come, as the custodian, the guardian, of this terrible, this wondrous, this awe-inspiring secret, that thou hast brought into the world."

Gaikhud, his expression grave, his eyes alight with a profound and solemn understanding of the weight, the magnitude, of his creation, replied, "I hear thee, Brenn, and I share thy fears, thy doubts, thine apprehensions, about the use, the potential misuse, of this discovery, this invention, that I have brought to light. I swear to thee, upon my life, mine honor, that I shall guard this secret, this knowledge, with all the vigilance, the care, the wisdom that I can muster, from the depths of mine experience, my learning, and my love for all that is good, and true, and beautiful in this world, that we both cherish and defend."

He placed a hand upon Brenn's shoulder, a gesture of reassurance, of solidarity, and trust. "I give thee my word, my friend, that I shall be a steward, a guardian, of this power, this potential, that I have unleashed into a world already rife with strife and conflict. I shall use it only for the benefit, the betterment, of all humankind, and never for the purposes of greed, of conquest, or of wanton destruction, that would make a mockery of all that we, as thinking, feeling being, hold dear and sacred in this life, this world."

And with those words, a promise, a sacred vow, Gaikhud and Brenn stood silent, side by side, their gazes fixed upon the distant horizon, where sky and sea converged in a blaze of light and color.

In Goreuhwo's bustling streets, where life pulsed

strong in vibrant hues, and voices raised in song and trade, the weary travelers sought respite from burdens of their long and arduous journey. Deubmeni, kind and practical of heart, took on the task of seeking out a meal, a simple fare to sate their hunger's ache. With purpose in her step, she made her way towards a vendor's stall, where savory scents of roasted meats and spices filled the air.

"Good sir," she spoke, her voice a gentle lilt, "I seek a hazra wrapped in fragrant bread, to share among my friends, my family dear. Name thou thy price, and I shall gladly pay."

The vendor, sour of mien and gaze, looked up, his eyes narrowed with disdain, as he beheld Deubmeni's features, exotic and unique. With cruel sneer, he spat upon the ground, his words a hiss of venom and of hate: "I'll not serve thee, thy kind from tainted soil. Thou art not welcome here, in our fair city. Take thy foreign ways, thine heathen tongue, and begone, lest I summon the city guard."

Deubmeni, stunned, her eyes wide with shock, stood mute, her hand a-tremble, spirit bruised by casual cruelty and rejection's sting. Brenn, witness to this display of spite, felt righteous anger surge within his breast. With purposeful strides, he crossed the space, his voice a call of challenge and defiance: "How darest thou, sir, speak with such contempt, to judge and cast aspersions on their worth, whose only crime is hailing from lands not thine?"

He drew himself up tall, his eyes alight with fierce, unyielding fire, as he met the vendor's gaze, unflinching and bold. Reaching out, he grasped Deubmeni's hand, a shield and shelter from the storm of hate. "We shall not be cowed or shamed," he declared, "by thy words, actions, or dismissal of our worth." With that, he turned, his arm around Deubmeni, and led her and their companions from the stall, their heads held high, their spirits undimmed.

As they walked in silence through the streets, each lost in thought, in tumult of emotions, Laidho spoke, his voice a whisper clear: "Wherefore do they hate us, Brenn? What have we done to earn such scorn, such bitter enmity?"

Brenn sighed, piecing together words to convey an answer to his friend's perplexity: "Many years ago, when thou wast but a babe, a great war drove a rift 'tween Edorath's folk. Khesi Addeu, Mewas and Prophet to his people, though mad with dark delusion, led a charge from ancient desert nation of the Kelai, Deubmeni's homeland. With his forces, he sacked cities, burned farms, wrought death and flame.

"An alliance formed to rise against the power of the Mad Prophet, to establish peace where chaos reigned. My father, Deugwer, fought, as did Kolewa, my elder brother. Westward they chased Khesi, to Gwelulo's shore, where Prophet drove a blade 'tween my brother's ribs, his blood spilled in the river, ending in Albovor.

"Goreuhwo and its homeland, Mitho Gorikhwa, suffered greatly at the Taf-Waikht's cruel hands. My father brought his forces south to aid their fight, and chased Khesi to Endless Sea, where he and crew perished, fate unknown. Such sorrow hath my father's end wrought in my life!

"And so, dear Laidho, thou perchance may see wherefore these folk look upon Deubmeni thus, for though she played no part in Khesi's crimes, those who suffered cannot see beyond the surface of those different from themselves, their pain too raw."—thus Brenn unto his friends, and Laidho looked in wonder at the depths of ignorance, yet glint of understanding at their grief; Gwidhotir, ever quiet, held Laidho's hand; Deubmeni, silent, blinked away her tears, of anger or of sorrow, even she knew not.

Brenn wandered, mind intent upon the task of gathering supplies, provisions for the journey that lay ahead, the winding road that would, he hoped, lead them to peace and safety, a new beginning, far from haunted pasts. His friends, his chosen family, did wait at nearby inn, a moment's brief respite from burdens of their long and weary travails.

As Brenn moved through the crowded marketplace, alert for wares most useful, came a voice, familiar yet tinged with hesitation: "Brenn? Is it thou? Forgive me, I am Den. I saw thee in Kebowadhor."

Brenn turned, his gaze falling upon the drunkard's face who had accosted fair Deubmeni ere Leubkherth's blood was spilled. With wary air, Brenn spoke, his voice a measured, even tone: "Surprise indeed to see thee here. What brings thee to Goreuhwo, far from thine home? And what desirest thou with me, with us?"

Den, face a mix of shame and earnest light, replied with fumbling, halting plea: "I wished to apologize for my transgression against thy friend, the lady fair, Deubmeni, whose beauty, grace, and strength I did offend. I have no excuse, save mine own weakness, folly, and despair." A pause, eyes searching Brenn's, a glimmer of hope within their depths. "I also hoped to learn of her welfare, her journey, since that night of blood and sorrow. She made a mark upon mine heart, my soul, that time nor tide could wash away."

Brenn, brow furrowed, mind awhirl with thoughts of caution and a strange, unsettling kinship with this lost and broken soul, replied: "Deubmeni is well, Den, and safe among friends who value her for all she is and all that she has overcome. As for her path, her destiny, 'tis her own tale, not mine to share without her knowledge, consent."

Den nodded, eyes downcast, shoulders slumped with disappointment and familiar despair. With sigh and gentle smile, Brenn reached out, his hand upon Den's shoulder, offering compassion. "Take heart, Den, know thou art not alone in thy regrets, thy pain. We all have demons, battles, wars we must fight each day to be the best, most noble versions of ourselves."

But ere he could say more, Brenn's ear caught snippet of a sinister exchange drifting from nearby alley, dark and narrow: "The Taf-Waikht here, in Goreuhwo, thou sayest? Seeking for a boy escaped their keep? This news is valuable indeed to those who know the right ears, palms to grease…"

Brenn's heart seized, blood running cold, mind racing with dire implications. Gwidhotir, the innocent, was still pursued, still hunted by those who saw him as their property.

With muttered curse and prayer, Brenn turned, mind awhirl with plans, the urgent need to warn his friends of peril imminent, the threat that loomed unseen o'er bustling streets. Heedless of startled cries, he ran, heart pounding, desperate to reach the inn, gather his companions, find some way to elude the closing jaws of their relentless foes.

Bursting through inn's door, face a mask of urgency, Brenn called out: "My friends, we must leave now, without delay! The Taf-Waikht, slavers, hunters are here, seeking Gwidhotir. We are not safe, even in this vast, anonymous city. Our enemies are cunning, ruthless in their quest to re-enslave, to crush the spirit of those they see as mere expendable cogs in their engine of power, greed, and lust."

A sudden commotion near young Laidho broke, the boy whose gentle heart found solace in his cherished gurdy's music. In the brawl, a stray blow shattered the fragile instrument, and with it, fragile peace. Laidho's anguished cry pierced through the din, a sound of deepest wound.

Brenn rushed to the boy's side, his own heart breaking, gathering the child into his arms with comfort and unwavering love. "Laidho, my brave, sweet boy," he softly spoke, "I know the gurdy meant so much to thee, a source of joy in times of darkness, doubt. Its loss is cruel, but let not despair consume thine heart. The music, light thou didst bring lives on within thee and us, in thy gentle soul, thy spirit bright. No loss can dim that gift."

Laidho looked up, eyes brimming tears, yet with a flicker of hope kindled by Brenn's words. "But what shall I do now?" the boy asked, voice a trembling whisper. "Without my gurdy, how can I find joy, make music that I love?"

Brenn smiled, warm and understanding. "There are many paths to joy, little brother, wonders in this wide world to lift the heart and mind. Tomorrow, we shall visit the gwerfegi, where dragon-slayers perform feats of skill, a spectacle to take the breath away and fill the mind with thrilling tales and dreams."

Laidho's eyes grew wide, a tentative smile tugging at his mouth's corners. "Dragon-slayers? But I thought thou disapprovest of their blood-sport, seeing it as reckless, dangerous, offensive."

Brenn chuckled, ruffling Laidho's hair. "Thou hast the right, I do not much admire their deeds for glory, gold, and fleeting fame. But for thee, I'd set aside a thousand disapprovals, a thousand doubts, to see that joyous light return to thy dear face, chase shadows of this day's misfortunes dark."

Laidho embraced Brenn tightly, fiercely, shaking with a mix of gratitude and love. "I thank thee," he whispered, "dearest Brenn, for always knowing what I need most, for being truest friend."

Brenn held the boy close, heart full to bursting with deep, abiding love for this brave child, this precious soul entrusted to his care. "Always," he murmured. "I'm with thee til the end."

In the gwerfegi's grand arena, where crowds had gathered, keen to witness valor's feats, the dragon-slayers' dance with death and glory, Brenn and his companions took their seats, hearts filled with anticipation, awe, and in Brenn's case, a touch of grim unease.

Beside him, Laidho's eyes shone bright with wonder, yestereve's misfortune now eclipsed by promise of a spectacle to lift his spirits, chase the shadows from his heart.

As fanfare grand announced the event's start, the dragon-slayers, brave and proud, strode forth, their armor gleaming, weapons sharp and ready. But sudden cries rang out, shouts filled with hate, as scattered figures in the crowd stood tall, their voices raised in dreadful unison: "In name of the Lone God!"

And chaos reigned supreme, as fire, smoke, and shattering debris filled the arena, maelstrom of destruction, panic, and unimaginable fear. Brenn, caught in blast, felt his world spin, senses overwhelmed, body battered, thrown through air, to land unconscious amidst the rubble and broken, bleeding bodies of the fallen.

Time passed, eternity of darkness deep, before he woke, head throbbing mass of pain, eyes blurred with dust and acrid, choking smoke. Around him, devastation spread, a hellish landscape of twisted metal, stone, and mangled remains of those who, moments past, were full of life, of laughter, joyful anticipation.

Brenn struggled to his feet, left knee ablaze with agony, throat raw and scorched, voice rasping as he called out, desperate, for his friends, for those he loved more than the world itself. But silence answered him, a void of emptiness, despair, broken by distant screams and moans.

Limping, stumbling, Brenn made his way through debris, heart laden with dread and sorrow deep, searching in vain for any sign or trace of those he sought. And then, amidst the carnage, his eyes fell on a sight that froze his blood, sent spike of terror through his very breast.

For there, across the broken, burning floor, strode Dannwi Asakhdo, cruel face alight with triumph and with malice, as he dragged a small, struggling figure by his side. Gwidhotir, the boy Brenn had sworn to shield from cruelties of the world, now helpless in the grasp of his worst nightmare, cries of fear and anguish failing to pierce through the din.

Heart tempest-tossed with despair, fury, and bitter impotence, Brenn tried to surge forward, to close the distance, save the boy, but injured knee buckled, sending him sprawling, gasping, to the ground, outstretched hand grasping only air, as Dannwi and his captive disappeared into the swirling crowd, lost to sight, to hope, to chance of rescue.

And Brenn, spirit crushed beneath the weight of his own failure, weakness, could only watch, could only weep, curse the Derevai that brought such tragedy, such horror, to this day that had begun with promise bright and wonder.

For in the space of a few heartbeats, all had changed, turned to ash and bitter gall, as forces of hate and cruelty struck with savage fury at the heart of all he held most dear. Amidst the wreckage, broken bodies, shattered lives, Brenn knew a pain, a grief, a sense of loss profound, as he confronted harsh and bitter truth of his own helplessness, inability to protect, to save, to shield from harm those who depended on him, looked to him for strength, for guidance, and for hope.

But even in this darkest hour, this moment of deepest anguish and despair, Brenn knew he could not, would not, let this be the end, the closing chapter in the tale of his and Gwidhotir's intertwined fates.

"I will find thee," Brenn croaked, his voice a ragged whisper, promise sealed in blood and tears and will unyielding. "Though I must crawl, drag myself through every circle of this hell, I will not stop, will not rest, until I hold thee in mine arms once more, until I know that thou art safe, and loved, and free from clutches of those who seek to harm thee."

Brenn limped forward, passing a woman, body broken, eyes wide with pain and terror. She reached out, her voice a desperate plea: "Please, help me, I beg thee, do not let me die alone, forgotten here."

Brenn, heart wrenched by her suffering, could not ignore her need, her anguished call, despite the urgency of his own mission, drive to find and rescue Gwidhotir. With groan of pain, he lifted her, cradling battered form against his chest, as he carried her to safety.

But no sooner had he set her down, his own injury flaring with each step, each move, than another voice, another desperate plea rang out, a man, face masked with blood, reaching, begging for aid, salvation from the wreckage.

And so it went, seemingly endless stream of suffering, of need, of human anguish, as Brenn, his own pain and exhaustion growing, carried one victim after another, heart torn with conflicting demands of urgent quest and unrelenting call to help, to heal, to offer comfort in this darkest hour.

At last, strength all but spent, leg throbbing mass of agony, Brenn came upon Deubmeni, face streaked with dust and tears, cradling limp and lifeless form of Laidho in her arms.

With cry of anguish, Brenn fell beside them, hands trembling as he reached out, touched the boy's pale, still face, heart shattering with realization he had come too late, that Laidho, gentle soul who brought such light, such joy, into his life, was gone, beyond the reach of any mortal aid.

Deubmeni, choked with grief, with pain, looked up at Brenn, her eyes a well of sorrow deep, and said nothing, words inadequate to express the depth of loss, the yawning void within.

Brenn bowed his head, tears flowing freely now, as he gently, tenderly, brushed stray lock of hair from Laidho's brow, his touch a final gesture of love and farewell to the boy whose light had been extinguished far too soon, a candle snuffed by cruelty's brutal hand.

Canto 4

In a tranquil, sun-dappled orchard, where the gentle morning light, in golden shafts, filtered through the boughs of apple trees, casting patterns on the dew-kissed grass, Brenn and Deubmeni, their hearts heavy with sorrow, loss, and grim resolve, gathered to perform a solemn, painful task.

Beneath the spreading canopy of one ancient, gnarled tree, they carefully, reverently laid to rest the earthly form of Laidho, their dear friend, companion, and adopted kin, whose life had been so cruelly, senselessly cut short by hatred's blind and vicious stroke.

With gentle hands and tear-filled eyes, they dug the grave, a narrow, simple resting place, yet one imbued with all the love, the care, the tender reverence and deep respect that Laidho's bright and shining spirit deserved.

As they lowered him, wrapped in a white shroud, into the welcoming, consoling earth, Brenn spoke, his voice a hushed and trembling whisper, thick with emotion, grief, and bittersweet remembrance of the joys, the laughter, the countless small, yet infinitely precious moments Laidho had brought into their lives.

"Farewell, dear Laidho, child of mine heart, though thy time with us was far too brief, thy spirit, thy light, thy gentle, loving soul will live forever in our memories."

Deubmeni, her own voice choked with tears, laid a hand upon the freshly-turned earth, a final, tender gesture of farewell, as she spoke, her words soft, yet fervent: "I pray thou findest peace, sweet Laidho, in the arms of whatever gods or powers watch over the innocent, the pure, the true of heart."

Together, Brenn and Deubmeni carefully arranged a circle of smooth, rounded stones around the base of the simple, unmarked grave, a humble, yet heartfelt tribute to the boy who had meant so much to them.

In the bustling common room of the inn, where chaos reigned and panic filled the air, as the survivors of the fell attack upon the gwerfegi sought refuge, aid, and some small amount of security amidst the aftermath of violence, Brenn and Deubmeni found themselves once more caught up in the maelstrom, the swirling tide of fear, confusion, and the desperate need for order, for direction, for a clear and steady hand to guide them through the storm.

The contrast could not have been starker, more profound, between the tranquil, solemn peace of the orchard, where they had laid to rest their fallen comrade, and the frenzied scene that now surrounded them, the cries, the shouts, the urgent pleas for help, for information, for some small shred of hope, clarity, in a world turned upside down, a life forever altered by the brutal, senseless act.

As Brenn and Deubmeni sought to navigate the throng, to find some quiet corner where they might regroup, assess, and plan their next uncertain steps upon the treacherous path that lay ahead, a sudden commotion, a parting of the crowd, announced the arrival of soldiers, armed and grim-faced, their eyes scanning the room with cold, appraising gaze.

A hush fell over the assembled mass, as one, a man of bearing, rank, and clear authority, stepped forward, his voice ringing clear and strong above the murmured din. "We seek the one called Brenn, the hero who, amidst the carnage and the smoke, the blood and horror of the gwerfegi's fall, stood tall and led the charge to save the innocent, the helpless, and the wounded from the jaws of death, of ruin, and of utter devastation."

Brenn, his heart sinking with a sense of dread, of foreboding, and the heavy weight of all that had transpired, all that he had done, and all that he had failed to do, stepped forward, his voice a weary, hesitant reply: "I am Brenn, though 'hero' is a title I do not claim, nor feel I have earned, through my actions, my failures, on this day of sorrow, loss, and bitter consequence."

The soldier, his gaze appraising, keen, fixed upon Brenn with an intensity that seemed to pierce the very soul, the heart, as he spoke, his words a mix of awe and grim resolve, of admiration and the weight of duty, obligation, and the call to service, sacrifice, and higher purpose. "The Chancellor himself has heard of thy brave deeds, thy selfless acts of courage, strength, and the unwavering, indomitable will to stand against the tide of evil, the onslaught of terror, chaos, and despair, and he would have thee brought before him, now, to receive the honor, the recognition, that thine actions, thine heroism, have earned."

Brenn, his mind awhirl with implications, the potential consequences, of this sudden, unexpected turn of fate, of circumstance, nodded slowly, his voice a quiet, firm acknowledgment of the summons, the command. "I will go with thee, will stand before the Chancellor, and hear what he would say, what he would ask of me, in the wake of this dark, tragic day."

With a gesture and nod, the soldier turned, and Brenn followed, leaving Deubmeni behind, his steps heavy with uncertainty, the weight of the unknown, the path that lay ahead, the twists and turns of fate that had brought him to this moment, this strange, surreal, and unexpected juncture in the long and winding, perilous road that was his life, his struggle, and his quest.

As he was led through the winding streets, past throngs of survivors, mourners, and the grim and haunted faces of a city, a people, reeling from the blow, the brutal, vicious strike against the very heart, the soul, of all they held most dear, most sacred, and most true, Brenn's thoughts were a churning sea of doubts, fears, of the heavy burden of responsibility, of the countless lives that had been lost, been shattered, been forever changed by the events, the horrors, of this day.

At last the reached the Chancellor's hall, a grand and imposing edifice of stone and soaring arches, a symbol of the power, the authority, and the unyielding will of those who held the reins of state, of law, and the fate of nations, peoples, in their hands.

As he entered with the soldier at his side, the Chancellor, a man of years, of gravitas, and the weight of office, rank, and the mantle of leadership, rose from his gilded seat, his voice a rich and sonorous command: "Approach, Brenn Ragnir, hero of the gwerfegi, and kneel before me, in the sight of all assembled here, to receive the honor, the recognition, and the solemn charge that thy brave deeds, thy selfless acts, have rightly earned."

Brenn, his heart pounding with a mix of awe, of trepidation, and the sense of fate, of destiny, and the inescapable, inexorable hand of higher powers, moving him, shaping him, guiding his steps upon a path he had not sought, not chosen, knelt before the Chancellor, his head bowed low, as the man spoke, his words a ringing call to duty, service, and the sacred trust of those who hold the fate of others, the lives and hopes of innocents, in their hands. "Brenn Ragnir, by the power vested in me by the people of Mitho Gorikhwa, witnessed by my ancestor the High God Uë, by the laws, the customs, and the ancient rites of our people, our nation, and our way of life, I hereby dub thee knight, champion of the realm, a defender of the weak, the helpless, and the innocent, a shield against the dark, the chaos, and the forces that would seek to tear asunder all we hold most dear, most sacred, and most true."

He laid his sword, a gleaming blade of steel and gold, upon Brenn's shoulder, a symbol of the weight, the burden, and the solemn charge that came with this new title, this new role, as he continued, his voice a grave and stern reminder of the duties, the obligations, that came with such an honor, such a rank: "But know, Sir Brenn, that with this title, this elevation, comes a price, a toll, a duty and a service that cannot, must not, be shirked or cast aside, no matter what the cost, the sacrifice, may be."

Brenn, his heart sinking with a sense of dread, of foreboding, and the weight of all he had feared, had suspected, from the moment he had been called before the Chancellor, raised his head, his voice a quiet, firm, yet resigned acknowledgment of the truth, the reality, that he had long sought to avoid, to escape, to cast aside in the pursuit of a higher, nobler calling, free from the chains, the bonds, of rank, of station, and the grim machinery of war, strife, and the endless, bitter cycle of violence:

"I understand, my lord, and I accept the charge, the duty, and the solemn trust that thou hast placed upon me, though mine heart, my conscience, and my very soul, recoil at the thought of taking up arms, of shedding blood, in the name of causes, conflicts, that I do not understand, do not believe, and cannot, in good faith, support or serve,"

The Chancellor, his gaze stern, unyielding, yet not without a glimmer, a faint spark, of understanding, empathy, and the weight of his own burdens, his own painful choices, replied with a voice a mix of steel and sorrow, of the harsh realities, the grim demands, of power, leadership, and the heavy mantle of those who must make decisions, take the steps, that shape the fate of nations, peoples, worlds: "I know, Sir Brenn, that this is not the path that thou wouldst choose for thyself, the road thou wouldst willingly, gladly, have trodden; but in times such as these, when darkness, chaos, and the forces of destruction, of the grim and unrelenting march of war, strife, and the clash of nations, peoples, faiths, threaten all we hold most dear, most sacred, we must all take up the burden, the grim duty, of standing firm against the tide, the storm, and doing what must be done, what fate, what circumstance, what the unyielding hand of history, demands of us, as men, as leaders, and as guardians of the flame, the light, the hope, that guides us through the dark."

Amidst the clamor of the crowded space, Brenn stood, the weight of unexpected chains now clasped upon his heart. His visage paled, the realization of this forced conscription striking deep, like venom coursing through his veins, his path forever altered by the Chancellor's hand.

Within, Brenn spoke so none could hear: "What cruel jest is this, that acts of brave design should chain me thus to endless strife, to bear the sword against my solemn will, and fight a war that tramples on my creed?" A silence fell within his storm-tossed mind, as anger, helplessness, his spirit flooded. His fate now sealed by honors undesired, he looked upon the faces blurred by fear, and knew the course set forth would test his soul beyond the limits of his mortal frame.

Brenn said, "How heavy lies the crown of forced acclaim! What honor is in servitude to war, to bear the sword for peace, yet peace abjure?"

Thus replied the Chancellor: "Thou speakest of peace? The world knows not such luxury. Thy bravery at the gwerfegi's fall has marked thee as a leader amongst men. 'Tis not for thee to shirk the call of duty, but to embrace the mantle fate bestows."

"Embrace?" said Brenn. "Nay, sir, 'tis but a yoke I wear. This knighthood, though it glitters like the stars, is black as night, where war's dogs howl. I am conscripted, not by choice, but force, to fields of battle whither my soul doth fear to tread."

The room, once loud with the clamor of the crowd, now hushed, awaited the echo of his plight—a man of peace, now a pawn in games of power, his will oppressed by titles undesired.

Brenn said, "What choice remains? To flee or face the fire? To live in shadows or die in light? If honor binds me to this wretched fate, then honor is not worth its pain."

As soldiers circled around, the Chancellor stepped close, his voice a whisper veiled in threat and guile. Brenn, encircled now by fate and foe, stood firm, his eyes like flint against the storm.

"We speak in circles, Brenn," the Chancellor then said, "or should I say, Gwennotir Ker, Baithas? Aye, the tales of thine escapades have reached even royal ears. Such secrets as thou keepest are currency in realms of power and strife."

Incredulous, Brenn asked, "How camest thou by

this name, this title worn in shadows cast by my former life?"

"The world is smaller than thou mightest presume, filled with eyes and ears that miss naught. Thine acts at the gwerfegi—brave, no doubt—did more than save lives; they peeled back the mask thou wearest. What is a hero, if not a beacon drawing gaze and intrigue?" Thus said the Chancellor.

Then Brenn: "And what wouldst thou with this knowledge, Chancellor? To what end is my name employed?"

"'Tis simple," said the Chancellor; "a lever to move thee whither the realm doth need thee most. On battlefields afar, where valor and Power such as thine can turn the tides of war. Think not of it as blackmail, but as a summons to greater glory, a chance to serve as only thou canst."

"Blackmail by any other name would weigh as heavy," said Brenn. "Thou wieldest my past as a blade to my throat."

"Wouldst thou rather I proclaim thine identity aloud?" the Chancellor asked. "Consider the chaos, the claims to thy life and fate, the feud set ablaze 'twixt my country and thine, ending in further bloodshed in thy name. Nay, I think it better kept between us, a secret bond that ties thee to thy duty."

"A bond," asked Brenn, "or a shackle? I am no fool, Chancellor. I see the chains thou d with words of duty and honor."

"Call them what thou wilt. In the end, we both know that thou wilt march, for the alternative bears consequences too grave for thy contemplation. Thine heroism hath ensnared thee as much as any secret.

Embrace it, Sir Brenn, and let us see what mettle truly lies beneath that calm exterior."

The Chancellor's words hung heavy in the air, a fog of inevitability that shrouded the room. Brenn, caught in a web of his own making, felt the weight of his true name now a burden too great to bear alone. With a nod, resigned to the path laid before him, he stepped forward, a knight propelled by destiny and design, into the fray that awaited beyond the country's confining borders.

The Chancellor, unmoved, his gaze as steel, spoke not but signaled with a solemn nod. The soldiers closed around, their duty clear, to take this knight, this Baithas, to war.

As Brenn departed, the heavy door swung, shutting behind, a chapter closed within, and Brenn, alone, must walk the path ordained, a journey fraught with peril, pain, and strife, his heart a battleground no less than war's.

Within the inn, bags lay heaped, a testament to a journey's end and new begun. The air hung thick with the weight of imminent parting, as Brenn and Deubmeni, companions forged in adversity, confront the painful separation of their paths.

Deubmeni said, "Brenn, the time draws near, and mine heart weighs heavy with the sorrow of our parting. I am torn, for though my place is by thy side, the echoes of home call me back—to seek my brother lost in time, a child's memory now a woman's quest."

"Deubmeni," said Brenn, "thou hast been my rock amidst the tempest; thy strength hath bolstered mine own. That thou must leave is a sorrow deep and wide, yet in seeking thine own blood, thou honorest the bonds that tie us not just to the living, but to our pasts, our histories."

"The decision rends mine heart," she said, "for every step towards my kin is a step away from thee. How cruel, that fate should grant us comrades in such trials, only to sever the ties in our triumph. Yet I hold to hope, that what is parted may in time be joined again."

"In thy journey west," said Brenn, "let not thy purse be light. Take this, my share of our scant earning; let it guard thee well and bring thee safely to thy kin." He handed her the purse, heavy with the coin of their shared endeavors.

"Thy generosity knows no bounds," Deubmeni said with tear-filled eyes. "Yet, how can I accept this, knowing the road thou must travel bears its own need of sustenance and safeguard?"

"It is thine," said Brenn, "no less than mine own breath; for what sustenance needs a body if the heart is starved of affection? Keep it, and let it be a tether between us, however distant our sojourns may lead."

Their hands met in clasp, a silent covenant of shared pasts and hope for reunion, and they embraced within each other's arms. Eyes gleamed with unshed tears, reflecting the sorrow of separation.

"Then let it be so," Deubmeni said. "Thy will is mine own, and with this gift I carry a part of thee with me. Yet, 'tis not just in coin but in spirit that thou art with me, Brenn. Til paths cross once more, hold fast to the light."

Brenn said, "Farewell, Deubmeni. May thy roads be safe, thy burdens light. Remember our time, the struggles we overcame, and let those memories be a beacon in darker times."

With a final embrace, they departed, the door closing softly behind her. Brenn stood alone, the silence in their room a stark contrast to the warmth of their closeness. In the quiet, memories flickered like candle flames—bright, then dimming, as he turned to face his own path, marked by duty and the looming specter of war.

The chill of dawn wrapped its cold embrace around the fields of the training camp, north of the strife-torn city Goreuhwo. Thither Brenn arrived, clad not just in armor, but the weighty mantle of a knight's title, thrust upon him in moments not of choice but chance. As conscripts mustered, roused by bugle's call, Brenn stepped among them, a knight, yet still a stranger to the rank and file whose lives and dreams now marched with his.

He thought to himself, "Here lies the field where futures are forged or broken. I, though clad in knight's esteem, stand no less a novice than any soul here gathered."

In this frost-touched morning wandered Den, once briefly acquainted to Brenn, now joined again in purpose as much as place. Den, seeking a life's calling, found in Brenn a familiar face, a beacon in the uncertain dawn of military toll.

"Brenn is it?" asked Den. "Clothed now in knight's regalia, yet I see the man beneath remains. What winds have blown thee back to such a novice's field?"

Despite himself, Brenn smiled. "Den, thy sight is a comfort here amidst the chill of unknown fates, though in our last encounter I held thee of little esteem—of this I apologize. Fortune's hand has dealt me this garb and duty. Let's walk this path together, for shared burdens lighten the heaviest load."

As they trod the camp's worn paths, the gap wrought by Brenn's title began to close, bridged by tales of past and dreams of what may lie beyond the war's grim shadow.

"Thou knighted," said Den, "art thou yet the Brenn thou wast? What hopes drive thee forward on this war-tossed road?"

Thus Brenn answered, "To live a life that mine own heart can honor. And thee, Den, what seekest thou in this muster of souls?"

"A purpose," said Den, "something to shape a life too long adrift. Perhaps together, we might steer a truer course."

As they spoke, a harsh voice cut through the chilly morning air, and a group of soldiers approached, their intent clear in their sneering faces.

"What's this?" asked their leader, a man of stout build and violent mien. "The knight fraternizes with the like that know not their own nature. A strange alliance, this."

Den frowned, all too used to such comments. "My nature needs no counsel from such as thee. Leave us, please."

The soldiers, not deterred, advanced, malice gleaming in their eyes. Brenn stepped forward, his stature a barrier between them and Den.

"Hold friends. We are all blades of the same

forge here, tempered by battle, not by brawls amongst ourselves."

"This one's nature offends us," said the stout soldier. "Stand aside, let us teach them the order of things."

Brenn answered, "The order I defend gives no room for base assaults on any under this banner. Stand down, lest ye seek quarrel with me."

As words escalated quickly to shoves, the soldiers tried to push past Brenn. With a swift motion, Brenn deflected a blow meant for Den.

"I am sworn to protect," said Brenn, "and under this oath, none shall harm another within my sight. Stand back! Den has earned their place no less than any person here; and yet perhaps they rank above thee in spirit, as Den came of their own accord and free will, and ye were forced to join, as I."

The scuffle grew heated; Brenn shielded Den, though one strike found its mark, and Den fell to the damp ground. With one last swift motion, Brenn grabbed the stout man's wrist, twisting until the man cried out in pain.

"Shall I break thy sword arm?" asked Brenn, forcing the man to the ground, squeezing ever tighter.

"Leave me be," he said, "and we shall do the same. Never will ye see us come to harm you."

Brenn released his grip, and the soldiers retreated, muttering threats under their breath. Den, shaken, looked to Brenn with newfound respect.

Brenn helped Den to their feet and said, "Den, thy courage in face of this storm speaks more of thy character than any the world might write for thee."

"Nay," said Den, wiping tears from their eyes, "I am but a coward, too afraid and ashamed to stand up for myself and what I believe to be right. Mine own uncle, who raised me, oft beat me until I fell. Then saying, Stand still, he would drag me to my feet and continue in his tirade. This I endured for ten long years, and thus I came hither, a person of no identity or skill. But thou, my friend, hast shown thyself a true knight not by title, but by deed. In this camp of trials, let us vow to bear together whatever may come, with hearts unyielding."

Brenn and Den clasped hands, and thus their friendship took root.

Upon the dusty grounds of the training camp, where the noon Sun's harsh scrutiny bore down on the backs of toiling conscripts, the day wore on with the weight of an anvil. The air, thick with the dust of exertion, carried the sharp commands of Falo, the commanding officer, whose voice cut deeper than the Sun's heat.

"Mark well my words, ye sons of the soil! The enemy cloaks in guises most foul, bearing ill will and corruption. It is our sacred duty to cleanse the land of such filth, to restore purity where darkness seeks to dwell."—thus Falo to his soldiers.

Brenn, amidst the ranks, his brow knitted beneath the weight of Falo's words, could hold not his tongue. His voice, firm and clear, rose above the clatter of arms.

"Sir, I must protest. Thy words paint with a brush too broad; not all our foes wish us harm from birth. Might we not seek paths to peace and understanding rather than rush to meet blood with blood?"

A murmur rippled through the ranks, some heads turned, eyes wide with disbelief. Falo's face, once merely stern, now darkened like a storm-swollen sky.

"Peace?" said he. "With vermin who threaten our homes? Thou dost speak folly, Sir Brenn. A knight, thou sayest thou art? Thy words betray a softness ill-befitting the title or task at hand."

Said Brenn, "'Tis not softness but strength to seek peace. Courage lies not only in the wielding of swords but in sheathing them ere bloodshed stains our souls. Violence is but the easy path; any man can bring another to harm. Pity and mercy lie on the path more difficult to tread, and oft upon this path is found the greater destination."

The air thickened with tension, the soldiers' breaths held tight in their chests. Falo, with a sneer curling his lip, stepped closer, his authority challenged before his command.

"Such insolence," he hissed. "Shall we let pleas for peace deter our duty? Nay—if thou lovest thine enemy so, thou shalt share their fate. Guards! To the lash!"

Dragged forth to the center of the assembled troops, Brenn's arms were bound to a post. The leather whip cracked in the air, a sinister promise of pain. Yet, as the first stroke fell, Brenn's jaw set firm, and no cry escaped his lips.

With each lash, Falo cried, "Let each strike remind thee of thy place!"

But Brenn, steadfast, endured silently, each lash a testament to his resolve. The soldiers watched, a complex brew of respect and fear mingling in their eyes. Here stood a man who, even in pain, swayed not from his convictions.

As the punishment ceased, Brenn, his back marred but his spirit unbroken, was released. His gaze, though pained, met each soldier's eye, a silent challenge and an invitation: to question, to think, to choose.

Whispers fluttered like disturbed sparrows as he walked back through the ranks, his every step a pain. Some averted their gaze, unable to meet the accusation in his silence; others nodded in quiet respect, their hearts stirred by the courage of his dissent.

As the first light of dawn breached the horizon, casting long shadows across the training camp, Brenn awoke. Where pain should have dwelt, an absence thereof filled its stead. He rose, probing the wounds that yesterday's discipline had etched into his flesh. No signs of the whips fury his skin did show, the scars erased by some benevolent hand unseen.

Brenn sat alone, wondering at his turn of fortune. The memory of Gaikhud, the enigmatic sorcerer whose abilities had skirted the edges of miracle, surfaced in his thoughts. Brenn mused aloud, his voice a soft murmur against the stirring of the camp: "Could it be that Gaikhud's magic yet lingers upon me, that his sorcery works still in my blood, healing as I rest?"

The notion stirred within him a mix of relief and unease. That such power could reach across distances and days to mend his wounds spoke of a magic potent and profound. "What bond have I to this magic, unwitnessed yet palpable in its effects? And what debt might such healing exact upon its beneficiary?" No answers could he find.

Weeks later, the soldiers deployed to Saulen, Brenn found himself within the grim confines of a war prison, in the familiar town of Kebowadhor, beneath the oppressive glare of the midday Sun. Brenn stood, yoked to his sorrowful duty. The walls, stark mirrors of the occupation's cruel heart, enclose the captives and their watchful guard alike.

"How harsh this duty that upon me lies, to guard these souls in misery confined. What honor can there be in such a charge, that asks of me mine empathy to starve?"—thus Brenn aloud to himself.

Within the throng of desolate faces. a young girl's plea struck his ear. Her voice, though faint, carries the weight of parched despair.

"Good sir," she said, "I pray thee, a drop of water grant. For mercy's sake, I beg, relieve this thirst."

Brenn cast a wary glance about, then made decision swift to break the law. With canteen drawn, he stepped within the bars that caged the weak and offered solace small in water's form.

"Here, child," said Brenn, "drink and let it ease thy pain. And thou, and thou—none shall this day go parched whilst I can serve."

But no good deed in shadows long remained; his actions caught the watchful eye of one who favored rule above the cries of folk.

Commander Falo, stepping near, said, "Brenn, what madness prompts thee to such folly? Knowest thou not the law that governs here?"

"Sir," said Brenn, "the law of Man may rule these walls, but higher yet the law of mercy reigns. What threat be these, the weakened and the worn, that we should see them suffer beneath our gaze?" His words, though bold, fell like stones in water deep, provoking waves of ire from his commander.

"Thou hast overstepped thy bounds," said Falo, "and shalt behold the weight thy softness brings upon their heads."

His punishment, grim and severe, was thus: Brenn witnessed the cruel fate of those he sought to aid; the scaffold raised, the nooses tied, a somber march unto the shadow of death.

Crying aloud, held back by his peers, Brenn wept. "O bitter cup that I, by mine own hand, have pressed to the lips of those I wished to spare! At what cost, my soul, this kindness have I shown?"

With heart encased in leaden dread, he watched as the innocent met an end unjust. Each snap of the cruel rope etched deep lines of conflict fierce betwixt duty bound and conscience clear.

As Sun withdrew its light from day's long end, Brenn stood alone, his thoughts as dark as night. His act of kindness paid in blood and tears, a lesson harsh in the merciless course of war. Where once stood certainties, now doubts arose, and Brenn, with heavy heart, weighed the cost of living true to principles held dear against the harsh demands of martial law.

The Form and The Shatter

In their census duty through Kebowadhor's roads, Brenn and Den ventured near a house, outwardly plain. Yet keen Den, whose eye for subtlety never failed, discerned a draft where none should blow, a sign that secrets veiled behind the mundane walls might hide a tale untold.

"Hark, Brenn," said they, "attend this soft air that speaks of hollow spaces cloaked beyond yon wall. Perchance some hidden chamber here awaits our curious gaze."

Brenn, bound by duty, gave assent to probe the depths. Their hands, though unskilled in such craft, by fortune found the latch that sprung the door, revealing thus a cramped and dimly lit retreat, where faces worn by fear and toil stared back in mute appeal.

Among them sat an elder, his age-lined face crowned with silver hair, from whose neck hung a chain, bearing a pendant well known to Brenn—the selfsame his father oft adorned.

"Sir," said Brenn, "whence came the necklace that upon thy breast doth hang? It mirrors one my father, lost Deugwer, held dear to heart, for my mother Segwi gifted it to him on their wedding day."

The old man's voice, though frail, carried the weight of years and secrets long borne. "Long past," he said, "a stranger crossed the sea, bearing yon token as her own. She spoke of distant shores, of lands rich and mysterious, and of her husband who found refuge there. 'Twas from him she had this necklace, then to me she payment made for offering shelter to her and her suckling babe."

Struck by the tale, Brenn felt the past and present merge into one, his role within this larger drama now painfully clear. "And this man, her husband, what fate befell him?"

The old man shook his head. "Left behind, beset with illness, too weak to sail, said the woman. Perhaps he lives there still."

Brenn said to Den, "Seest thou, my friend? The fabric of our fate is woven far beyond this war's confines. This chain that binds me to my father's past pulls also towards an unseen shore, where secrets of his heart and ours may lie."

With the elder's tale still echoing, they left the hidden sanctum, allowing its occupants their shadowed peace. Brenn's spirit, laden with the gravity of his heritage, now saw his commission in this war as twofold: a servant of the present fray and a seeker of the truths veiled by time and ocean's expanse.

"Let us depart," said he to Den, "with minds enlightened and hearts heavy. For our path is set not just by war's design but by the quest to seek out whither my story winds, and perchance to close the circle left by his mysterious steps."

Thus Brenn and Den, with the day waning, resumed their course, the weight of many worlds upon their shoulders, their journey now as much inward into the realm of familial bonds as it was outward into the fray of mortal conflict.

In the muted aftermath of their grave discovery, Brenn and Den withdrew to the quietude of a secluded space, where the burden of their knowledge lay heavy between them. Their duty as soldier called for report, yet humanity urged silence to shield the rilŷns' fragile secrecy.

"We stand at a crossroads," Brenn said to Den. "To speak is but to summon death upon those poor souls, whose only sin is clinging to forbidden faith."

"Yet silence," said Den, "though it shields, may brand us traitors. The weight of this secret could yoke us to doom if ever it were unveiled by eyes less merciful than our own."

"True, the risk is great," said Brenn. "But greater still the cost of lives if we betray their trust. How could we serve as heralds of their destruction?"

"It is a heavy mantle, Brenn, to decide whose lives weigh more in the balance of our actions."

The decision, once spoken, became their pact: a silent vow to protect the hidden rilŷn, though shadows of consequence began to gather darkly around them.

Time, ever a relentless stream, soon bore upon them the inevitable discovery. Other forces, less lenient and more suspicious, unearthed the sanctuary of the rilŷn. Swift on discovery followed accusation: Brenn and Den, once soldiers, now stood branded as conspirators, their loyalty impugned.

Led to confinement, the iron bars of their cell a stark reminder of their chosen path, Brenn and Den faced the grim reality of their plight.

Brenn said, "Our choice, it seemed, has led us

here, to cold iron and colder prospects. Did we, in our hope to protect, merely delay the inevitable at too dear a cost?"

"Perhaps," said Den. "Yet had we chosen otherwise, the cost would have been to our souls, weighted down by the guilt of betrayal. This, at least, is a burden we bear together, and in knowing the cause was just, mayhap there's some comfort yet."

"Comfort in chains is cold comfort," said Brenn, "yet I concur. Better to suffer for doing right than thrive by wrong. Yet, see how our silence has purchased but brief safety for those we shielded, and at what cost to ourselves!"

Den said, "The wheels of fate grind slow but exceeding small; our actions are but cogs therein. We chose a path less trod by folk of war, and though it leads us to this sorry state, the integrity of our intent remains untarnished."

Brenn and Den sat cloistered from the world, yet not from its sorrows. The walls, thick and unyielding, yet permitted the faint cries of chaos and despair to seep through, a dismal chorus to their confinement. The air hung heavy, laden with the weight of impending doom, as outside their meager sanctuary, the cruel hand of Falo meted out death to the rilŷn they had sought to protect.

Brenn, falling to his knees, cried out, his voice breaking, "O powers that govern this vast cosmos, if thou art just, if mercy yet resides in thy celestial realm, cast down thine eye upon these wretched souls! Mine heart doth break with each cry that pierces this stony barrier. Hear me, I beseech thee!

Intervene, lest innocence once more be swallowed by the voracious appetite of unjust war!"

Den, with knees against their chest, sat in a corner of the room, and mumbled, "Thy plea, though noble, may fall on ears that cannot hear, or, hearing, choose not to heed…"

Brenn, clenching his fists, his eyes shut against the tears, continued, "Yet I must call upon them! For what are we if stripped of faith in justice, in powers greater than the tyranny of Man? I am confined, helpless to wield aught but words, yet wield them I shall, though they echo back in vain."

As his voice faded, a raven, black as the cell's shadowed corners, alighted upon the narrow window ledge, its eyes a piercing contrast to the dimness of their prison. It cocked its head, as if listening to Brenn's lamentations, a silent witness to his despair.

Brenn, his voice now hushed, said to Den, "Look, the raven—it heeds my call, or so it seems. Can it be that we are not forsaken? That some watchful guardian marks this hour and offers sign of hope?"

Den, eyeing the raven, skeptical yet intrigued, said, "Or perchance it is but a bird, drawn by the scent of captivity. Yet, it is strange to see such a creature here, at such a time."

The raven, undeterred by their doubts, fluttered its wings and dropped a small, glinting object through the bars. It clattered to the stone floor—a piece of wire.

Picking it up, Brenn asked the raven, "Who art thou, little messenger? What puzzle dost thou bear? This wire—could it be a tool for our escape, or merely a trinket dropped by chance? Wherefore thou answerest me not, dear friend? I am Baithas, yet I do not hear thy voice."

"Nay, Brenn," said Den, "do not dismiss the means of our deliverance, however slight. This raven, whether divine agent or mere beast, brings potential to our plight."

With renewed resolve, Brenn stood, the wire form in his grasp. Though the darkness of their cell remained, the appearance of the raven instilled a sliver of light—a beacon of possibility in the grim night of their circumstances.

"Then let us use what gifts are granted us, and trust that fate has not yet closed its book on our endeavor. This raven, this wire—small keys to unlock the door of hope."

Within the darkened jail that fate had cast as both their cell and crucible of chance, Brenn and Den stood poised on fortune's knife. The wire, a slim herald of hope delivered by the cryptic raven, now served as their slender key to freedom's gate.

As they worked the lock, Den whispered, "This wire, thin and unassuming, may yet bear us through these confining walls. Hold thy breath and lend me silence, for every click and clack is thunder in this cursed abyss."

Then, lo! the lock yielded with a soft, telling click, a sound both terrifying and sublime. With great stealth and the grace of shadows, Brenn and Den stepped beyond their cell, each movement fraught with the pulse of peril.

As they advanced, Brenn murmured, "Every step is a step towards liberty, yet each may also be the step that leads us back to chains, or worse, to death. We must needs find Pukhso and escape this den of vipers."

Their path led them near the guards' quarters, where Brenn's heart caught at the sight of his old sword—his strength, his birthright—lying upon Falo's table, a symbol of Kolewa's memory kept within his heart, now within his desperate grasp.

Reaching for it, Brenn whispered, "At last, my faithful steel, we meet again. Thou art a sight for sore spirit, a reminder of the man I must continue to be."

With sword in hand, Brenn's resolve solidified like tempered iron. Yet, as he turned to leave, a soft moan drew his gaze to a corner dimly lit, where lay a young girl, chained and abandoned to squalor and despair—the very one Brenn had shown a small kindness to amidst the harshness of his duties.

Brenn, his voice a mix of wrath and sorrow, cried out, "What hell is this that innocence should suffer so under the guise of order? Fear not, child, I will not leave thee in this vile place."

Quickly, he moved to her side, his hands now working to free her from her bonds, his mind racing against the tick of time that might bring their captors down upon them.

With voice as weak as rain in a drought, the child whispered, "Sir, I knew thee kind. Thou art mine angel or my ghost; it matters not which, for both are sent from beyond."

"No angel, I," said Brenn, "but merely a man who cannot abide the suffering of others. Come, we must make haste."

With the girl now in their care, Brenn and Den navigated the jail, a maze now doubly dangerous. Each corner turned could spell recapture; each stair ascended, a step deeper into jeopardy.

"We are close now," said Den. "Hold fast to thy courage, for the night is yet dark, and full of terrors yet unseen."

Then, in the shadowed hall of the war-torn jail, the very symbol of the war's relentless cruelty, Commander Falo, stepped forth, weapon in hand, his eyes alight with the cold fire of battle. The air thickened with tension, a precursor to the clash that must ensue, a storm long brewing now ready to burst.

"At last," sneered Falo, "the errant knight, the traitor to his own, comes before me. Hast thou come to plead mercy, Brenn, or to play at revolution?"

Brenn, his grip tightening on Pukhso, replied, "Neither plea nor play brings me before thee, Falo. I come for justice—for the rilŷn whose cries echo still in these streets, for the girl thou hast chained in filth, and for all those oppressed by thy tyranny."

With no further words to waste, Falo lunged, his blade a flash of silver in the dim light, meeting Brenn's with a clang that stung of metal tested by fire. The duel ensued, fierce and fraught with peril, as each man proved his skill and resolve in the dance of death.

Brenn parried a vicious thrust and said, "Thou art skilled, Falo, but thy skill is marred by malice, thy strength by oppression."

Laughing, Falo answered, "A pity words do not win wars, knight! Thy sentimentality is thy weakness."

The battle raged, each blow struck with the force of conviction, each maneuver a testament to their opposing creeds. Brenn, fueled by righteous anger and a burgeoning sense of duty that transcended his own survival, found within himself a reservoir of untapped power.

Brenn saw his chance—an opening in Falo's guard, a fleeting moment but enough. With a cry that was both a lament and a battle cry, he drove his blade forward, striking true. Falo's eyes widened in shock, the realization of defeat etching his features even as he fell.

His breath heaving, Brenn stood over Falo. "Let this end thy reign of terror. Thy tyranny dies with thee."

With Falo vanquished, the air trembled with the weight of the moment. Brenn, pausing to regain his breath, turned to the prisoners, their faces ghostly in the half-light, watching him not just as a liberator but as a leader forged in the furnace of conflict.

Turning to them, Brenn cried out, "Rise, ye who have suffered under the yoke of oppression!" Finding the key to the cells on Falo's corpse, Brenn opened wide the barred cages. "The key to your freedom lies with the quartermaster. Arm yourselves, claim your liberty, and let no one hold dominion over your souls henceforth!"

The prisoners, stirred by his words, rallied with newfound hope, their spirits kindled with the prospect of freedom. As they moved to arm themselves, Brenn stood amid the chaos, a figure transformed by his trials endured and choices made.

———

At the dark and somber docks of Kebowadhor, where shadows blended with the night, Brenn and Den, now branded as fugitives, made their silent approach. The waters, black as pitch, lapped quietly against the hulls of moored vessels, the only witnesses to their covert endeavor.

"Here lies our vessel," whispered Brenn, "small yet seaworthy enough to bear us hence from this accursed place. Let us make haste, ere the night wanes and our absence is marked."

Den, nodding, said, "Aye, let us be swift and silent as the night itself. Our freedom lies yonder, upon these humble waves."

Together, with careful hands and watchful eyes, they loosed the moorings of a small fishing boat, its timbers creaking softly under their weight. Each movement was deliberate, a quiet dance with danger, as they stole away into the obscurity of the sea's embrace.

Pushing off from the dock, Brenn said, "Pray, let these waters be kinder than the land has been."

Then Den: "And let us hope the soldiers find no cause to gaze too keenly upon these lonely docks until we are but a memory."

The boat drifted out, carried by a gentle current, and they unfurled the sail with hands that, though untrained, were guided by the urgency of freedom. The sail caught the breeze, and the small craft began to cut a path through the waters, heading south toward the uncertain country of Kebkhelin.

As the shoreline receded, Brenn cast a lingering look back at the fading lights of Kebowadhor, the town's dim glow a stark reminder of the ordeals they left behind.

"Look how the lights of Saulen shrink away," he said, "like hopes into the heart's recesses. There lie both our deepest sorrows and our bravest deeds, forever entwined in the city's shadowed streets."

"Aye," said Den, "but look ahead. The sea stretches wide before us, a tapestry of starlit waters. Herein lies our path to new endeavors, new battles that await our tempered steel."

"True, Den. We forge not merely an escape, but a quest anew. For the peace that has eluded us thus far. Let us then sail into this darkness not as fugitives fleeing from their past, but as seekers of a brighter dawn."

Their words, carried on the wind, mingled with the sounds of the sea, a symphony of the free and the boundless. Together, Brenn and Den faced the vast, open waters, their spirits buoyed by the promise of new horizons and the steadfast resolve to fight for a future forged by their own hands.

Canto 5

Upon the desolate, storm-beaten shores of Kebkhelin, where the sky, heavy and sullen, hung low, and the sea, enraged, hurled itself against the land, Brenn and Den staggered forth from their small, battered vessel. Their limbs, weary from the ordeal at sea, trembled as they set foot upon the uncertain sands, the ocean's roar a constant ache in their ears.

Brenn, surveying the grim surroundings, said, "Here at last, firm ground beneath our feet, yet little respite it offers, with the sky so full of threat and the land stretching barren before us."

Den pointed toward a narrow path leading from the shore. "Yet there lies a path, Brenn, cutting through the jungle's heart. It promises no comfort, but perhaps a passage to more hopeful lands beyond this harsh embrace."

Their relief at landfall was soon tempered by the realities of their plight. With provisions spent and strength dwindling, each step became a testament to their resilience. Together, they pressed on, the path a winding serpent through dense foliage that seemed almost to resist their passage.

As they struggled through the undergrowth, Den muttered, "Each step's a victory hard won. How much further can this path wend before it yields some sign of human hand?"

Brenn, his voice gritty with fatigue, replied, "Onward still, my friend. For now, the sea lies behind, and before us, unknown trials. We've naught but forward to press, and hope our course leads us to kinder fate."

As they navigated the inhospitable terrain, their bodies taxed by hunger and weariness, the forest around them teemed with the unseen and the unknown. Every rustle in the underbrush spoke of potential peril; every distant cry that pierced the air sharpened their sense of vulnerability.

Brenn paused, placing his hand on Den's arm. "Hark, Den," he whispered. "Beyond those final trees, thin smoke rises to greet the sky. Signs of life, of civilization—perhaps our journey's end or another's beginning."

The sight of a small village, glimpsed through a break in the trees, rekindled a flame of hope within their beleaguered hearts. With renewed purpose, they pushed forward, each step drawing them nearer to the promise of shelter, of sustenance, and of new challenged that awaited in this uncharted domain.

With a weary smile, Den sighed. "A village! At last, a chance to rest our bones and fill our bellies, to mingle once more with kindred souls, though strangers they may be. Tell me, friend, speakest thou the language of Kebkhelin?"

Brenn nodded, his gaze fixed on the village. "Aye, let us find welcome among them, for our tales are rich with trials, and our needs are simple: peace, a meal, and a place to ponder our next course under a less hostile sky."

Beneath the pall of night, the quiet village lay, its inhabitants enshrouded in the deep embrace of slumber, unaware of the strangers who trod softly upon their land. Brenn and Den, driven by the gnawing pangs of hunger, prowled the edges of this peaceful hamlet, their desperation sharp as a blade.

"We must needs find sustenance," Brenn whispered to Den, "lest we not see the morn. Let us try yonder house, where perhaps we may discover some small store to ease our want."

"Aye," said Den, reluctance in his voice, "though it sits ill with me to play the thief, our need presses hard. Let us be swift and silent as the night's own shadow."

Their approach was clumsy, born of inexperience and dire need. The breaking of a latch, a sound minute yet monstrous in the stillness of the night, quickly roused the household. Before Brenn and Den could lay hands on even the meanest morsel, the villagers did seize them, all robust and quick despite their sleepy state.

"What deviltry is this?" demanded a villager, holding Brenn's arm firmly behind the back. "To break into our homes like common rogues! Speak—why would ye steal from us who harbor no ill will, who would have freely given of our stores to the needy?"

Brenn, his voice dripping with regret, repented thus: "Forgive us, good sir. We are but weary travelers, far from our own shores, and driven by hunger. We knew not whether ye would extend your hospitality or drive us hence like dogs."

Den murmured their apology. "We did not know ye would give it freely. Fear of refusal drove us to this folly."

The realization of their rash act settled heavy upon them as they stood restrained, the villagers' faces a mix of bewilderment and indignation. A woman, her countenance marked by the soft traces of compassion, addressed them, her tone a blend of reproof and puzzlement:

"Had ye but asked, freely would we have given. What poor fortune, that your first act here should be one of theft, and not of trust. What brought you to such desperate straits?"

Brenn answered, "We are adrift from a land torn by strife, seeking only a place of respite. Our judgment, clouded by hunger and despair, led us astray. We meant no harm, nor sought to bring trouble upon your peaceful village."

Bound and led away, the taste of their misstep bitter upon their tongues, Brenn and Den deeply repented of their plight. As they were ushered into confinement, the night air carried with it a whisper of what might have been, had fear and need not clouded their better natures. In the quiet that followed, both pondered the fragile thread of trust, now severed by their own hands, and how they might in time mend what had been broken.

In a building humble, north of the market square, they brought them to a basement dark and damp, where men already languished in a cell. Untied and locked within, Brenn called out: "What happens now? What fate awaits us here?"

The jailer answered, "We wait upon the magistrate's arrival; a week or more may pass ere he appears."

"Kind sir," said Brenn, "I pray thee, fetch my pack and sword, dropped in the house we robbed, for they hold great import."

"I shall retrieve them," said the man, "but they must remain locked in the bailiff's office, safe from harm."

Brenn thanked the man, who departed with a wave.

Three Kalayu men, who shared the cell, stood up as Brenn and Den entered their midst. "Saham sahaal inum," said Brenn to them, greeting them in their own tongue: My soul greets your souls.

The three men grinned, and the smaller of the three replied, "Hello, friend! Thou speakest our language? Whence hailest thou?"

Brenn said, "In Keulen I drew first breath, but I have wandered far. Brenn is my name, and this is Den, whose Kalayo is yet sparse—a help it would be if ye spoke some Jongwo."

"I do, at that," replied the man. "I am Erwo. This is Fehi and Rilun. Well met! What brings you to this gloomy cell?"

"Alas," said Brenn, "hunger drove us to a desperate act; we sought to steal some food to stay alive."

"I judge thee not," said Erwo, "for I too have transgressed when need outweighed the law's command. But our own tale is long and convoluted. I daresay ye have heard tell of the gwerfegi's fate in Goreuhwo?"

Brenn's face fell in darkness, recalling dear Laidho's smiling face. "In truth, I was there. I lost a friend in that destruction. Two, in fact, and then a third parted ways from me soon after."

"My sympathy," Erwo said with a frown. "The three of us were in that city on that day, guests at the university there, with plans to meet an inventor of great acclaim. His newly discovered tool was to help us in our profession, but the attack happened ere we could meet. Seeing the city then fall to prejudice and hate against our people, we fled, only to end up here as word of the attack spread south to Kebkhelin, and with it the bigotry." He laughed. "Our only crime is being born in the wrong part of the world, it seems."

"Ye three are from Len Khalayu," said Brenn, "that much is evident in thy speech and look. I have been to that fair country. From which part do ye hail?"

"From Jub Khewi's bustling streets, born and raised," said Erwo. "Hast thou seen it?"

"What fate connects us thus," mused Brenn. "I too passed through thy great city, and claim a friend who calls it home as well. Deubmeni, she is called."

Chuckling, Erwo asked, "But what is her true name? For Deubmeni is no name I have ever heard, and means merely 'my dove,' such as an endearing moniker a father may call his child. What is her family name? Perhaps I know her people."

"I know not," said Brenn. "But thou didst mention thy profession—what is it? Is thy trade connected to the great universities in Goreuhwo or Jub Khewi?"

Here Fehi interrupted. "Brenn, beware of Erwo's school-bound talk, a rabbit hole from which you'll never escape."

"Unless," said Erwo in defense, "thou fanciest tales of ancient kings and tombs buried in the sands of time."

Brenn smiled. "Now in these things I have great interest. Pray tell me more."

"We study history," said Erwo, returning Brenn's smile, "of ancient times and civilizations lost, pursuing knowledge in the field and teaching in the classroom."

Now excited, Brenn said, "History captivates me—tell me all thou knowest!"—here Fehi and Rilun groaned.

In days that followed, kindness marked their stay. The jailers brought them meals and blankets warm, yet Brenn was vexed by this strange paradox: such gentle souls, yet quick to judge by race. In that dark cell, where time seemed to stand still, Brenn found in Erwo a kindred spirit, whose passion for the past knew no bounds. With eager words, Erwo wove tales of yore, of battles fierce and figures long revered.

"Since I could read," Erwo said, "mine heart has been ensnared by stories true, not tales of fancy spun. In Jub Khewi's halls of learning I did thrive, outpacing all my peers in wit and skill. The university welcomed me, though young, and there I delved into the sands of time, unearthing secrets of the desert lands.

"Three tongues long dead I studied with great zeal, but Keshic claimed mine heart and mind alike, the common tongue of its golden age, the language of law, trade, and pacts. My mentor, wise Agwayabo, did unearth a stone beneath the desert's shifting sands, inscribed with words in tongues both known and lost. With Old Kalayo's aid, he did unravel the mysteries of Keshic, long obscured."

Erwo then drew with a finger in the dust on the floor. "Attend, dear Brenn, and I shall teach thee now the intricacies of Keshic's ancient script."

Brenn listened and watched, grinning with pride of knowledge. "Thy words ignite a flame within my breast, a love for history and tongues long past. Pray, teach me more, for I would gladly learn."

Beside them, Den played a game with Fehi and Rilun, knocking stones and practicing their speech.

Three weeks did pass in that confining space, yet Brenn and Erwo's bond grew strong and true, united by their passion for the past. But lo, the lawmen came with horses swift, to bear the Kalayu to their destiny.

Grasping Brenn's hand, Erwo said, "Dear friend, it was a joy to share this time, to find a kindred soul in this dark place. May fate decree that we shall meet again, in this life or the next, let friendship reign."

They shook hands, while Den said farewell to Fehi and Rilun, who clapped them on the arm.

And thus the trio left that gloomy cell, while Brenn and Den remained, their fate unknown, yet richer for the bonds they forged within, a glimmer of light amidst the darkness grown.

The magistrate, with girth that spoke of ease, regarded Brenn and Den with curious gaze, his voice through phlegm did query make: "Do ye speak Kebkhelinu, or will ye be mute?"

Brenn said, "I speak it well, but my companions lacks the knowledge of thy tongue, so I shall be his voice, if it doth please thine Honor so."

"Then let them speak their name," said the magistrate. "I wish to hear it from their lips, not thine, though thou shalt be the bridge between our words, a task I loathe."

Den, with nervous voice, spoke their name.

The magistrate asked, "No kin, no family, neither one of you? A tale that strains belief, but I digress. What brings you vagabonds to Kebkhelin's shores?"

"We wander, sir," said Brenn, "with no aim but to see the world's great wonders, taste its varies fare, and meet the folk who call each land their home."

"Spare me thy fancies," said the magistrate, "I'll have none of it. Who shall come to claim you, wayward souls? A month has passed, yet none have sought you out."

"Alas," said Brenn, "we are alone, no ties to bind us to the world beyond our own two hearts."

"So be it, then. Your fates are now decreed: To Milridh, to toil in mines of gold, until your debt to Kebkhelin be paid."

Brenn, in shock, relayed this to Den, who in

Jongwo exclaimed, "Thou canst not do this! It is not right, it is not just, I say!"

But their words fell on ears that understood no Jongwo, nor would have cared; the guards then led the two friends to a waiting wagon without the magistrate's hall.

A cage, its metal maw, did swallow them, along with four Kebkhelinu, cramped and soiled. Den, gripping the bars with white-knuckled rage, cried out, "Ye cannot do this thing! Let us free!"

"Peace, friend," said Brenn, "we shall find a way, I swear. Though now it seems our path is dark and grim, we'll navigate this trial, our wits our guide."

The wagon lurched forward, bearing them to the western coast. And thus their fate was sealed, a cruel twist that tore them from the world they thought they knew, to labor in the depths where gold doth gleam against the dimness of despair.

In a ship's hold, a fetid prison, dark and grim, the slaves like chattel chained and left to rot, no mercy shown, no comfort to be found—for days they languished thus, hungry, parched, and spent, their bodies racked with cramps, their spirits crushed.

At last, their ship made port, a bustling scene, where commerce reigned, and human lives were sold. The slaves, led out, squinted in the Sun, their eyes unused to light, their limbs to movement. In Maikhethlen they stood, a wretched sight, awaiting fate's decree, their future grim.

A fat man came, with painted face and fan, his manner soft, yet cold as winter's heart. He questioned each, appraising worth and skill, til

Brenn, with tongue well-versed, did catch his eye. Reading the sign that Brenn bore upon his neck, the man asked, "A tutor, thou? In tongues and histories? Impressive, I must say. Any thy small friend?"

"From Skegyo, they were born," said Brenn, "but raised in Saulen—thence they hail, a student once, now refugee, like me, from war's cruel grasp."

The fat man smiled. "And now ye find yourselves in bondage here." He inspected the others, then paid the slaver's fee.

The slaves, now bought and paid for, joined the train, a caravan of beasts and goods and folk, all bound for destinations yet unknown. They marched, in heat and dust, for hours on end, til sunset brought a brief respite from toil.

A meager meal, a bowl of watery soup, is all they got to fill their aching guts, while their new master feasted on roasted fowl, his appetite as vast as his girth.

Beneath the stars, they slept, still chained and bound, no guard in sight, no hope of swift escape—for where would they, in this strange land, find aid? No, better to bide time, and wait for chance, than risk the lash, the brand, the axe.

And so, in mud and filth, they rested the heads, dreaming of freedom, home, and better days, while all around, the night's dark mantle spread, a cloak of sorrow, beneath the distant stars.

In Milridh, a cursed peninsula in southern Maikhethlen, a pit of toil, a goldmine, vast and deep, its steps descended, where all folk were bound, to dig and carry, sift and wash the earth, in search of precious flecks, their lives the cost.

Amidst this scene of misery and woe, a fat man rode, Mihindu, overseer; beside him, Kananat, the master stern, whose word was law, whose whip was ever near.

With voice loud and firm, Kananat spoke: "I am your lord and master—heed my words. This mine, your home; these slaves, your kin, your life. Obey Mihindu, as you would obey myself, for we are father and children, now, and he is your brother."

Kananat inspected the slaves, assigning each to their place. "To dog, to carry, or to sift, your fate is sealed, by my decree, my judgment swift." To Brenn he said, "A carrier, thou wilt be, thy strength put to use." Then to Den: "And thou, so slight, a sifter, thy new role." Then conferred he with Mihindu as the guards led slaves to mine.

In cramped and squalid huts, the slaves found rest, four to a room, save Brenn and Den, who shared a meager bedroll, friendship their sole comfort.

Thegikh and Perangorai, cousins dear, from Kebkhelin hailed, their tale one of woe, of capture, bondage, and a grandmother lost. Yet still they smiled, their spirits undefeated.

And Tobëa, tall and strong, from lands unknown, a decade spent in chains, yet still unbowed; his tongue, a mystery, to Brenn's quick ear, a challenge met, a friendship forged.

Brenn said to Den, "We shall not let this fate define our lives. We'll find a way to break these chains, escape. Though now it seemed our path is dark, we'll keep our wits, our hope, our bond of fellowship."

Song of the Crickets

And so, in that bleak place, where gold was king, and human lives, mere grist for fortune's mill, Brenn and his fellow slaves did toil and strive, til chance or gods deliverance did bring.

In throes of toil beneath the Sun's scorching gaze, two figures labored, yoked by fate's decree. Their baskets, laden with the stony fruits of ceaseless drudgery, pressed down like lead upon the wearers' frames. Yet in this wasteland of sweat and grime, a bond took root and grew.

Tobëa, ever stoic with words few and far between, nevertheless spoke to Brenn—for his own tongue, that of his homeland, he had heard not on another's lips for nigh on ten years; therefore he spoke with Brenn as a fast friend.

"Whilst toiling under the weight of rocks and soil," said he, "I turn my thoughts to lands beyond this place. Brenn, speak to me of that which birthed thy soul, the distant shores that shaped thy face."

"The Valk," said Brenn, "a province of fair Keulen, lies far to the north, amidst chill and frosty breath. Yet beauty reigns in snowy peaks so tall, in rolling summer plains of green, and lakes of blue. I dwelt beside the sea, salt upon my tongue."

As Brenn recalled his homeland's wild expanse, Tobëa too felt the tug of memory's thread. "I too once lived beside the boundless deep, and rowed for leagues to gather cod and more, or simply behold the blackfish swim."

"What manner of creature is this blackfish?" Brenn asked.

With reverent hand, Tobëa drew back the veil of

tattered cloth that hid his dark thigh, revealing there an image etched in ink. "A sacred being," said he, "revered by my folk. Behold upon my flesh its likeness inked: a monstrous fish with eye of ghostly white, sharp teeth, and tail of mighty breadth and length."

Brenn asked, "How vast in size doth grow this holy fish?"

"It dwarfs the boats of men in its domain. Those fool enough to abandon craft and oar are dragged beneath, never to draw breath again."

"These gods in creature's form," said Brenn, "thou wouldst not eat, surely?"

"Nay!" said Tobëa. "No more than I would sup upon my mother's corpse. But tell me, Brenn, is thine own native soil akin to this strange land we now tread?"

With baskets emptied, lightened of their load, the pair retraced their steps to gather more, their words a balm against the gritty sting of dust and rock that clung to sweat-slicked skin.

"Nay, friend," said Brenn, "but in thy words of thine home I do hear the same of mine own. Mine home too knows the bite of winter's chill, the slopes and meadows green in Summer's glow. My people trawl the shores for daily catch, and hunt for elk and stag in the Polgwelë Wood."

"A moose, thou meanest?" asked Tobëa. "Like to a hart but grander, with antlers wider than a standing man, whose hooves could cradle thy prodigious head?"

At this, their laughter rang like temple bells, a fleeting sanctuary in black terrain—for Brenn saw on

Song of the Crickets

Tobëa a kindred soul, whose gentle heart gleamed bright amidst their gloom.

Brenn said, "I cede, my crown is large, and larger still the mirth we share, despite our present lot. For even amidst the dark, thy spirit gleams with gentle light unbowed by cruelty. In times of dearth, when flesh is far and few, thou spurnest the beef, and sup on naught but fish and venison from beasts whose end thou didst witness."

"Aye," said Tobëa. "If we must take a life to sate our need, we owe our prey the grace of company as it traverseth from this realm to next. To perish is a frightful thing indeed, but loneliness compounds the pangs of death." This spoke Tobëa, his words solemn.

Amidst the toil, a question rose unbidden, as Tobëa sought to know his fellow's roots: "What name hath the village of thy birth?"

Brenn said, "In Albogorwë first I drew mine infant breath, the city over which my father Deugwer was lord, and my mother Segwi is yet lady. And thou, what place did shape thine early path?"

Tobëa, his visage shadowed by the weight of baskets borne upon his shoulders broad, fixed Brenn with eyes that seemed to penetrate the veil of time itself, as memories stirred within. "My native soil is Yenmiskelanë. But Albogorwë...that name strikes a chord within, a distant echo of a tale long past."

"What tale is this?" asked Brenn. "Pray, speak of this memory."

They reached the summit of their labor's mine, and there discharged their burdens, stone by stone. Then, as they trod the downward path once more,

Tobëa gave voice to secrets long concealed.

"In days gone by," he said, "ere fate's capricious hand did tear me from mine home and kin alike, a ship, borne swift upon the wind's embrace, crossed over the sacred sea to grace our shores. From its dark hull emerged a band of men, their skin as pale as thine, with hair like flax, a hue unseen by any gathered there. Their chief, a man of stern and noble mien, did lead them forth to dwell amongst our tribe.

"For once full cycle of the seasons' dance, they shared our hearths, our bounty, and our lives. But as the year drew to its fated close, some men grew weary of our simple ways, and longed for hearths and kin beyond the waves. The chief, he hailed from Albogorwë's distant vale, and like thyself, did master our tongue with speed uncanny, in mere moments, as thou hast done."

At this, Tobëa did pause, his gaze intent, as if he saw in Brenn some specter past. "Thou bearest his likeness, etched in every line, a mirror of that man."

Brenn asked, "Where bides he now, this man of mysterious origin?"

"He tarried in our land, with some pale kin, while others sailed for lands beyond the foam. Some of my people, drawn by tales of wonder, did join them on their voyage over the deep, in hopes of seeing realms beyond our ken."

A shadow passed over Tobëa's weathered brow, as memories dark and painful surged anew. With baskets filled, he lent his strength to Brenn, then shouldered his own load beneath the Sun, whose searing gaze beat down without remorse. He said:

"But fate did not smile on that bold endeavor. The ship, beset by tempests fierce and wild, never reached the shores of that far-distant land. Full many perished in the raging sea, while those who lived fell prey to other folk, who bound us fast and bore us far away. Since first I trod this bleak and barren ground, no word have I gotten of those I once called friends, nor know I what dark fate befell their lot."

Thus spoke Tobëa, his tale a mournful dirge, a testament to lives and dreams undone, while Brenn, transfixed by echoes of his past, beheld in his a mirror of his own uncertain path through fortune's shifting sands.

In that grim place, where hope itself lay chained, the turning of the seasons marked the span of lives enslaved, their fates by others claimed, until at last, their time on Earth was done. The masters of that bleak and barren mine, with cruel cunning and malicious will, gathered thralls from lands far-flung and wide, each tongue a stranger to its neighbor's ear.

Those wretched, culled from every distant shore, toiled in isolation, mute and dumb, their thoughts and dreams forever locked within, unable to conspire or rise as one. Yea, they did labor in silent Hell, no comfort found in shared experience, no bonds of friendship forged in common pain, until their sentences at last concluded.

And so, amidst the clamor of the mine, where pick and shovel rang in ceaseless rhythm, the slaves, divided by the walls of speech, did bend their back to unrelenting toil. But even there, where mercy held no sway, the sands of time ran out for some poor souls, whose fates were sealed the moment they set foot upon that cursed and unforgiving ground.

Before the crowd, the master Kananat spoke: "Bring forth the condemned, whose debts are paid in full, with sweat and blood and broken stone. Their time is up, their usefulness expired, and now, their thread of life must needs be cut."

The chosen few were dragged before the throng, their eyes devoid of light, their spirits crushed beneath the weight of years in servitude, no hope of freedom or redemption left.

Brenn heard the first slave, a woman with grey eyes and olive skin, call out in a dialect from Greulas: "Is this the end, then? After all this time, to die alone, unmourned and far from home? What cruel jest is this, that I should fall so far from all I knew and held most dear?"

Then an ebon man, speaking words of far-off Aunlen, cried out, "I cannot even beg for mercy now, or plead my case to those who stand beside me. We suffer here together, yet apart, each locked within the prison of our speech."

With brutal swiftness, then, the deed was done, the slaves dispatched, their mortal frames broken, while those who yet survived could only watched in mute despair, their own fates known. And so the cycle turned, as new slaves came to take the place of those whose race was run, each one a stranger to the next, alone amidst a sea of misery and stone.

Thus order reigned, and none should ever rise to challenge the master's dominion over that place—for even if they could, what words would serve to bridge the yawning chasms twixt their kind?

In slumber's depths, the slaves of gold and stone lay still, their dreams a fleeting respite from the ceaseless grip of harsh servitude. But Brenn did stir, his heart afire with newfound hope, and roused his comrade Den from sleep's embrace.

"What vexing cause doth bid thee wake me thus?" grumbled Den, sitting up.

"Come, friend," said Brenn, "and let the night air cool thy brow, for I have tidings that must needs be shared."

With murmuring mien and sleep-encumbered steps, Den followed Brenn beyond their humble shed, where secrets whispered beneath the starlit sky.

"Tobëa," said Brenn, "the one thou callest a pagan soul, hath been my font of knowledge and of lore. Didst thou know he hath labored here night on a decade?"

"Gods below, Brenn, such a fate I dread!" said Den. "To toil so long in this accursed mine…"

"Fear not, for we shall not share in his lot. Our path leads far beyond this bleak domain, to Tobëa's homeland, across the Terunthleu Sea."

Den asked, "What madness speakest thou? Naught lies beyond the Endless, hence its name."

A distant bark, a guard dog's lonely cry, pierced through the stillness of the night, as Brenn, with eyes alight, unveiled his plan.

"'Tis there, in that far land beyond the waves, that my dear father dwells, alive and well. Tobëa himself hath met him face to face, and now I mean to find him, come what may."

"But how, my friend?" asked Den. "What means hast thou to fly this place of stone and sorrow, and embark upon a journey fraught with perils dire?"

"First," said Brenn, "we must break the chains that bind us here, and then, with Tobëa's aid, we'll find a way to cross the vast expanse of briny deep."

"But why, I ask, did thy father not return with Tobëa and his comrades to thy side? What could compel him to remain apart from those he loved, in lands so far and strange?"

"The reasons matter not," Brenn said; "I know in mine heart's deepest core that I must undertake this quest and find the truth that lies concealed. Perhaps some duty binds him to that shore, or fate's capricious hand hath dealt a blow that keeps him from the ones he holds most dear."

"Thy words, though strange, do stir a chord within my breast, and I shall stand with thee, my friend, through calm and storm, til journey's end be reached. But by what means shall we this feat achieve? How break the bonds that hold us in this place?"

With gentle smile that spoke of playful guile, Brenn answered, "Thou dost forget, my beloved Den, a truth most plain: I am Baithas, and thus the chasms between tongues have now been bridged."

As dawn's first light crept over the eastern sky, its golden rays pierced through the veil of night, illuminating Milridh's grim domain, where slaves, in bonds of servitude, did toil. The shadows, long and deep, stretched across the land.

Amidst the throng of those who labored there,

stood Brenn, a spark of hope within his breast, who saw, in morning's light, a chance to strike against the chains that held them all in thrall. With furtive glance and whispered words of fire, he rallied those whose hearts yearned to be free: Thegikh, Perangorai, Tobëa, Den, and others still, united in their cause.

"My siblings," said Brenn, "bound by fate's cruel hand, the time has come to rise against our plight, to cast aside the shackles of our woe, and claim the freedom that is ours by right. With makeshift arms and courage in our hearts, we'll strike against the tyrants of this mine, and break the bonds that hold us in this hell."

Then said Thegikh, "But Brenn, the risk is great, the peril dire, for if we fail, our lives are surely lost, or worse, condemned to torments yet unknown. The guards are many, armed with steel and wrath. How can we hope to stand against their might?"

"'Tis true," said Brenn, "the path ahead is fraught with danger, but to remain in servitude is to condemn our souls to slow decay, a living death, bereft of hope or light. I say we choose to stand, to fight, to strive, for even in defeat, our spirits soar, unbound by fear, untamed by mortal chains."

With words of fire, Brenn ignited hearts, and soon, a murmur rose amongst the slaves, a whispered chorus, swelling to a roar, as one by one, they took up their tools as arms and stood, united in their purpose and resolve. The guards, at first, were slow to comprehend the rising tide of fury in their midst, but as the clamor grew, they sprang to act, their weapons drawn to quell the gathering storm.

"The die is cast," called out Perangorai, "the river is forded, there can be no retreat, no turning back, for we have staked our lives upon this cause, to break the chains that bind us to this rock."

Tobëa said, "Then let us fight with all our strength and will, and if we fall, we'll fall as free folk, true, our names remembered in songs, as those who dared to stand against their fate."

And so, with shouts of rage and clashing metal, the battle was enjoined, the slaves and guards engaged in deadly dance, where every blow held life and death in its unyielding grasp. Brenn, with the Power of Speech, did rally all, his words a beacon in the midst of strife, inspiring those who faltered, urging on the brave to greater feats of strength and will.

The mine became a scene of chaos, wild, as slaves and guards alike fell to the ground, their blood commingling in the dust and gravel, a testament to freedom's bitter price. The outcome hung upon a blade's keen edge, as fate itself did tremble in the balance, uncertain if the day would end in triumph, or see the dreams of liberty undone.

Brenn called out, "Stand fast, my friends, for we are almost through, the guards' resolve doth crumble beneath our onslaught, victory is within our grasp at last! Now let us press the attack with all our might, and break the final chains that hold us down, for freedom's light awaits us, shining bright, beyond the darkness of this heinous pit."

With one last surge, the slaves overwhelmed their foes, the guards surrendering or fleeing fast, as shouts of joy and triumph filled the air, proclaiming liberty's hard-fought success. The mine, once symbol of their servitude, lay shattered, broken, like the chains they wore, a monument to courage and to hope, that even in the darkest pits of Hell, the human spirit, indomitable, could rise above its bonds and dare to dream of brighter days and futures yet to come. And so, the slaves of surrendering tasted freedom, their hearts alight with newfound hope and purpose, as they embarked to forge their destinies with their own hands and leave behind the sorrows of the past.

In the rebellion's wake, a scene of chaos unfolded in the storerooms of the mine, where once the tools of bondage had been kept, now turned to instruments of liberty. The freed slaves, moved by urgency and hope, did hurry to and fro, their purpose clear, to gather what provisions they might need for the uncertain journey that lay ahead.

"My friends," said Brenn, "we must be swift in our endeavors—for time, that fickle mistress, works against us. Let us divide our labors, each to each, and see that all are well-equipped and fed, for the road we travel will be long and hard."

Den said, "I'll oversee the weapons, ensure that all who wish to bear arms in defense of freedom are granted blade and shield to guard their lives. We must be ready to defend ourselves, should those who seek to chain us come again."

"Well spoken," said Brenn. "And I shall take the lead in securing food and water for our band, that none may falter from hunger or thirst as we make our way to brighter shores."

With tasks assigned and purpose firmly set, the

freed slaves worked with diligence and speed, their hearts afire with hope and grim resolve, to seize the chance that fate had granted them. As they toiled, word of their uprising spread like wildfire through the countryside beyond, and soon, the specter of retribution loomed, as those still loyal to their former masters gathered their forces to reclaim what was lost.

"Brenn," said Den, "we must make haste to quit this place—for even now, our enemies draw near, determined to extinguish freedom's flame and drag us back to servitude's embrace."

"Then let us to the port with all due speed," spoke Brenn for all to hear, "and there commandeer a vessel swift and sure, to bear us far from this accursed land, and set our course for brighter destinies."

With provisions gathered and their path made clear, the freed slaves made their way to the water's edge, where ships lay moored, their sailed furled and waiting, like slumbering giants yearning to be roused. Brenn, with a leader's grace and steady hand, did guide his people to the finest craft, a symbol of their newfound liberty, and bid them all embark without delay.

As dusk descended on the bustling port, the stolen ship, now crewed by those once bound, slipped from its berth and ventured out to sea, a daring escape from tyranny's dark grasp. Brenn stood upon the helm, his visage grim, the weight of leadership upon his brow, his bear cloak billowing in the evening breeze, a token of the trials he'd overcome.

"My siblings," he called out, "we have won the day; but still, the road ahead is more dangerous than I can put to thought. We must be vigilant and united in purpose, to see our hopes to fruition and claim the lives we've dreamt of for so long."

Then Perangorai shouted for all to hear, "We stand beside thee, Brenn, our hearts as one, ready to face what challenges may come—for in thy strength and wisdom, we find courage to brave the unknown waters that lie ahead!"

And so, with hearts emboldened by their triumph, the freed slaves set their course for distant shores, guided by hope and dreams of brighter futures, free from the chains that once had held them fast. The ship, a tiny speck upon the vast expanse of ocean, bore them ever onward, toward horizons yet unseen and lands unknown, where they might forge their destinies anew.

Three cycles of the Moon had waxed and waned since Brenn and his companions, bound by fate, had cast off from the shores of tyranny to seek their fortunes on the boundless sea. And now, at last, their ship did chance upon a sight that filled their hearts with hope renewed: the verdant coast of fair Yenmiskelanë, where azure skies and rolling hills did meet.

As they drew near, a village came to view, its thatched roofs nestled against the emerald green, a haven of tranquility and peace, that called to them like sirens' sweet refrain. With eager hearts and eyes alight with joy, they guided their vessel to the waiting shore, where longboats, manned by Tobëa's long-lost friends, did row out to embrace him with open arms.

Tobëa, smiling, said, "Behold, my brothers, how the Raven hath smiled upon our journey's end, to bring us here, to this fair land, where once mine heart did dwell. These shores, these skies, they whisper welcome home, and in the faces of my dearest kin, I see the love that time could not erase."

Brenn answered, "Thy joy is palpable, dear Tobëa, and rightly so—for to be reunited thus, after such trials and tribulations borne, is a gift beyond all measure or compare. Let us embrace this moment, share in mirth and laughter, as old friends and new do meet."

With great elation and hearts full-brimming, the crew disembarked, their feet upon the shore, greeted by warm embraces and by tears of happiness that flowed like cleansing rain. Gifts were exchanged, tokens of friendship true, as bonds were forged anew twixt distant kin, a symbol of the hope and unity that marked this joyous moment in their tale.

Yet even as they reveled in their welcome, the weight of all they'd braved hung heavy still, upon their weary shoulders and their souls. The journey's toll, both physical and deep within their hearts, could not soon be forgotten, and mingled with the happiness they felt was a sense of longing, bittersweet and keen, for respite and solace, hard-earned and won.

"My friends," said Brenn, "though we have cause to celebrate, I cannot forget the purpose that did drive me to these shores, across the raging main. For I, like Tobëa, seek a homecoming, but of a different kind, one that may yield the answers to the questions that have haunted my every waking moment and my dreams for nigh on ten years: my father's fate, long shrouded in mystery, lies somewhere in this land, waiting to be found."

Tobëa replied, "And we shall stand beside thee, Brenn, steadfast in our resolve to see thy quest fulfilled. For just as thou hast been our strength and guide, through perils faced and obstacles overcome, so shall we be thy beacon in the dark, thy stalwart companions on this path thou dost tread."

And so, with heavy steps but hearts alight with hope and determination's fiery glow, they ventured forth into the great unknown, ready to face what trials may yet await. For Brenn, the weight of leadership, once more, sat heavy on his brow, a mantle borne with grace and grit, as he led his faithful crew toward the truth that beckoned from afar.

As day gave way to evening's gentle embrace, the village stirred with life and energy, as old and young alike did gather around the crackling fires, their faces aglow with warmth and friendship, a sight to soothe the weary souls of Brenn and his brave crew. Tales were told and news was shared, as friends and families reunited, bound by love and common history, a tapestry of lives entwined, as roots beneath the soil.

"Mine heart is full," Tobëa said, "to be among my kin once more, to hear their voices and to share in their joys and sorrows, as I did in long days past, when youth still coursed through my veins. But tell me, friends, what of my family? My mother, father, do they still draw breath? And what of those brave strangers from Keulen, who sought to forge a bond between our two lands?"

A hush fell over the gathering throng, as eyes grew dark with sorrow, and with pain untold. The elder of the village, by name of Denë, wise and grey, stepped forward, her countenance grave and somber, as she prepared to speak the heavy truth that weighed upon the hearts of all who knew.

"Dear Tobëa," she said, "thy return is a balm to our wounded spirits, a light in the dark that has too long enshrouded our fair home. But I must bear sad tidings, news that will strike at thy soul, and test thy fortitude. A plague, most vicious and unrelenting, swept through our village, like a scythe through greening grass, claiming the lives of many, young and old, including those most dear to thine own heart. Thy parents, may their spirits find peace eternal, were among the fallen, as were the men from distant Keulen, who had come to forge a bond of friendship, strong and true."

The weight of grief, like a physical blow, fell heavy on Tobëa and the crew as they absorbed the news, their hearts overfilled with sorrow and with pain, raw and unrelenting. Silence reigned, a tribute to the fallen, as each did grapple with the loss, so keen and unexpected, a reminder harsh of life's capricious nature, and the fate that oft befalls the best and brightest souls.

"Tobëa," spoke Brenn, his voice a gentle calm, "words can scarce express the depth of mine own sorrow, and the ache I feel for thy loss, so profound and intimate. Thy pain is ours, as we are bound by ties that go beyond mere friendship or alliance, but rather, forged in the fires of adversity and shared experience, a bond unbreakable."

Tobëa answered, whispering, "Thy kindness and thine empathy, dear Brenn, are a balm to my wounded spirit, a light in this dark moment, where despair would seek to overwhelm me, body, mind, and soul. Though I grieve for those I've lost, I know that I am not alone, for I have thee, and all our brave companions, by my side, to weather this storm, and find the strength to carry on, in the face of such great sorrow."

So in the gathering dark, they mourned, united in their grief. But for Brenn, the news of plague and death struck a deeper chord, a resonance with his own quest, still unfulfilled and shrouded in mystery and doubt, the fate of his father a question, looming large and unresolved. The weight of leadership once more did press upon his shoulders as he grappled with the knowledge that his journey was not yet done, that answers long-sought still lay ahead, waiting to be uncovered, like gems within the earth.

"My friends," he said, "though we have cause to grieve and mourn, I cannot forget the purpose that did bring me to these shores, across the vast expanse of ocean and of time, to seek the truth of mine own father's fate, still yet unknown."

Within the chief's abode, a place imbued with history's weight and artifacts of yore, Brenn sat, his heart afire with questions, yearning for answers long denied, yet ever-sought. The chief, a woman of years and wisdom, gazed upon the man's face, perceiving there the hunger for truth, the need to know the fate of one held dear, though long removed from life's embrace, by time and circumstance.

"Young Brenn," said Denë, "thy father's tale is one that spans the years and distances, a story writ in courage, strength, and sacrifice, a life lived fully, in the face of adversity. When first he came to us, a stranger, cast upon our shores by tempest's rage, we knew not what to make of him, this man of foreign tongue and mien, yet possessed of a spirit indomitable and true."

Brenn said, "My father, Deugwer, I have long sought words of his survival, and the path he trod, after that fateful voyage, so long ago. To hear thee speak of him with such regard brings comfort to my weary soul, a balm to the ache of absence, keenly felt. Yet still, I must know more, to understand the choices he did make, the life he lived, so far from those who love him, and who mourned his loss as one would mourn the setting Sun."

The chief, with eyes that sparkled with the weight of memories, both joyous and bittersweet, did then recount the tale of Deugwer among the Raven Clan. She spoke of how the man, through strength of will and heart, did earn the trust and love of all, becoming not just friend, but family, a part of the weave, rich and varied, that made up the Clan's beating heart.

"Thy father, Brenn, was a man of many talents, a skilled hunter, a crafter of fine tools, a teacher, a leader, an interpreter, all in one. He shared his knowledge freely, and in turn, learned from us the ways of land and sea, becoming one with the rhythm of our life, as though he had always been a part of it. Yet still, there was a sadness in his eyes, a longing for the home and kin he'd left behind, across the vast expanse of ocean blue."

"But why, then," asked Brenn, "did he not return, to those who loved him, and who waited, all those years? What kept him here, so far from all he knew, a stranger in a strange land, though beloved? I cannot fathom it, the choice he made, to stay, when every fiber of his being bust have cried out for home and hearth and kin."

Denë, with heavy heart, did then reveal the truth, long hidden, of Deugwer's fate, and the ties that bound him, inexorably, to the land and people of the Ravens.

"Thy father, Brenn, did not stay by choice alone, but rather, by the dictates of his heart, and the bonds of love, unbreakable and true. For in his time among us, he did find a love, a woman, strong and fair, who captured his soul, and carried his unborn child. Though he longed for Keulen, and for thee, he could not bear to leave his new-found joy, this family, that he had come to cherish so."

His eyes wide, his mouth a-tremble, Brenn murmured, "A sibling...I have a sibling, here, in this place, a part of my father, living, breathing still?"

"Alas," said Denë, "thy father never met his unborn child, for Sarkhangwena—the mother—departed on that same ship that took so many of our own away, Tobëa as well. What became of them, we shall never know. But thy father remained behind, fearing that the plague had come upon him; he wished not to infect his family or new friends."

"Where is he?" Brenn asked, wiping a tear from his stinging eye. "Where is my father now?"

Denë pointed northeast. "Thy father resides at the top of the hill, overlooking the village, with the mountain to his back. Go to him on the morrow, and thou shalt find thine answers."

As dawn's first light crept over the horizon's edge, casting a pallid glow on the sleeping village, Brenn stirred from slumber, his heart heavy with the weight of what lay ahead, the final leg of his long journey, to the father lost. With steps determined, yet burdened by the mix of hope and dread, anticipation and fear, he set forth from the warmth of hearth and bed, toward the hill that rose, majestic and stark, against the backdrop of the snow-kissed mountain.

The landscape, once lush and green, now lay concealed beneath a blanket of pristine, untouched snow, a world transformed by Winter's icy touch. The silence, broken only by the crunch of Brenn's footsteps, as he forged ahead, a solitary figure, small against the vast expanse of white that stretched out before him, like a blank page waiting to be filled with the story of his father's final plight.

As Brenn crested the hill, his breath a cloud of vapor in the chill, crisp air, his eyes fell upon a sight that stopped his heart, and stole the breath from his lungs, in a rush of grief, and loss, and pain, so sharp and keen. There, stark against the snow, a simple marker, weathered by the elements, yet standing tall, a testament to the life that he had lived and lost upon these distant, foreign shores. "Here lieth Deugwer Ker, called Albobeder by the Raven Clan. Husband of Sarkhangwena, father to her child. Killed by Paidh of the Frog Clan."

Freezing in his steps, Brenn stared long upon the grave, then finally spoke with broken voice: "Father...at last, I find thee, here, alone, beneath this cold, unyielding ground, thy story etched in stone, a final chapter, writ in sorrow, and in longing, for the home and kin thou didst leave behind so long ago. The weight of all the years, the missed embraces, the words unspoken and the love unshared, crashes over me like a wave unyielding, dragging me down into the depths of grief!"

And there, before the grave, Brenn fell to his knees, the snow seeping through his garments, chilling him to the bone, yet unnoticed, in the face of the torrent of emotion that engulfed him. Tears, hot and stinging, coursed down his cheeks, as he reached out with trembling hand to trace the letters of his father's name carved deep into the stone, a tangible connection to the man he had loved and lost.

"O Father, I came to find thee, to unlock the secrets of thy life and of thine heart, to understand the choices that thou didst make, and the paths that thou didst tread, so far from all that thou didst hold dear in days gone by. And though I find thee silent and at rest, I feel thy presence here in this sacred place, a part of thee, forever woven into the fabric of this land, and of my soul."

For long moments Brenn remained, head bowed, lost in the tide of grief and of remembrance, for the father he had lost, and found at last. The wind, a mournful whisper through the trees, carried with it the echoes of a life lived fully and with purpose, though far from home, a legacy etched in stone and in the hearts of those who knew and loved him in this place, and in the son who had journeyed far to find the missing pieces of his own identity.

As day's last light faded from the sky, and night, with her dark mantle, did descend upon the hillside where Brenn knelt, alone, beside the grave of Deugwer, father lost, the snow began to fall in gentle flakes, blanketing the world in a shroud of white, ethereal and surreal, a dreamlike scene, where reality and vision intertwined.

"Father, I am undone by grief and pain, the weight of all that might have been but never was crushing my spirit like a millstone, heavy upon mine heart, my soul, my very being. In this moment, I am lost, adrift, alone..."

And there, as a tree overcome by rot and insects will lose its will and collapse, so too did Brenn fall amidst the swirling snow. His cries, muffled by the blanket of white, echoed across the hillside, a lament for all that had been lost, and all that lay ahead, uncertain, unseen.

"Brenn," came a voice—whence he knew not, "rise from thy grief, and hear the words I bring to thee in this dark hour. Though sorrow, like a river, swift and deep, doth threaten to engulf thee, thou must not succumb to its embrace—for destiny, with all its weight and grandeur, doth await thy steady hand, thy courage, and thy strength."

It was the voice of Yog, like soft thunder in the night, blended with the whisper of the wind and the gentle fall of snow upon the earth, a presence all too real yet made of the stuff of dreams, bridging the gulf between the Form and the Shatter, life and death.

"Yog?" said Brenn, though his voice did not leave his lips, but passed through his mind. "Where hast thou been? When last we spoke, I was but a boy, naive about the world, in need of thy guidance. Now I am a man, and thine help has come too late, if help indeed thou offerest. My father is dead, and now I shall die upon his grave, as I should have died in Polgwelë all those years ago, reunited with Kolewa."

"Fear not," said Yog, "for always I've been with thee, a silent watcher, guiding thy path. And now I bring thee a gift, a boon, to aid thee in the trials that lie ahead. Behold, the Dorovagwer—Godsword—that holds within its blade the Powers four, a weapon forged in destiny's own fire, to be wielded by thine hand alone, in service to the world."

And there before Brenn's eyes, a blade appeared, shimmering like starlight in the swirling snow: Pukhso, his companion, transformed anew into a weapon terrible and grand, imbued with all the Powers of the Shatter.

"Yog," said Brenn, "I fear the weight of such responsibility, the power to shape the very course of fate, to wield a blade that could, with but a stroke, unmake the world and all that dwells therein."

"Thou art wise to fear the sword's great might," said Yog, "for in the hands of one unworthy or untested by the fires of adversity, it could bring ruin to the land and all who call it home, a destroyer uncontrolled. But thou, dear Brenn, art chosen to bear this burden and to wield this power, in service to the greater good, a champion of justice, truth, and honor in a world that teeters on the brink of chaos and despair."

Brenn said naught, and Yog then departed, and beneath the silent falling snow, Brenn fell asleep.

The Sun rose, casting a sad light upon the world, still and silent but for the gentle whisper of the wind through evergreen trees, and over the grave of Deugwer Ker, his son still lay, wrapped in sleep and sorrow deep.

"What warmth is this," thought Brenn, "that stirs me from my slumber? What comfort, in this bleak and frozen waste, where I had thought to perish, lost and lone?"

There beside him lay the form of Den, his friend, a source of heat and solace in the night, that had with its dark mantle near consumed the grieving son, leaving him cold and lifeless upon his father's final resting place.

Then a memory came to Brenn of a night and morning ten years thence, and his eyes did mist as he recalled to Den: "Alas, that bitter night, that endless dark, when cruel fate did tear my world apart, and news of brother's fall in distant war did pierce mine heart, like cold and ruthless blade. Kolewa, my light, my guide, my guardian true, snuffed out like a candle flame, forever lost to savage battle's senseless, brutal game, where kings and tyrants play with lives like pawns.

"The grief, the rage, the pain beyond all bearing, did fill my soul, til mortal frame did threaten to shatter, break, like glass beneath hammer's blow.

And so I fled into the frozen night, seeking solace, numbness, aught to dull the razor's edge of my despair's keen bite.

"I ran til lungs did burn, til legs gave way, and I did fall, exhausted, drained of all save bitter dregs of sorrow's poisoned cup, into the deep and drifting snow's embrace. There I lay, tears frozen on my cheeks, breath fading, waiting for death's sweet release.

"But fate, capricious mistress, had other plans—for I awoke, stiff, chilled to very bone, yet alive, my faithful wolf Wind wrapped around me, tether to this mortal coil. And in that moment, as I lay there, face buried in his grey fur, a flicker of doubt did rise, as it riseth now: Would it have been better, kinder, to slip away, to join my brother in our ancestors' halls, free from sorrow's weight, from life's cruel slings?"—thus Brenn to his friend.

Den smiled and said, "Brenn, my dearest friend, I could not leave thee to the mercy of the elements, to face alone the chill of Winter's breath and sorrow's icy touch. I love thee, Brenn, and would not see thee freeze."

Brenn answered, "Den, I am humbled by thy loyalty and love, and by the depth of feeling that binds us one to the other. Come, let us descend and seek the warmth of hearth and friendship."

With heavy steps and hearts yet full of grief, the pair did make their way down from the hill toward the village, where their crew awaited, anxious for their return. But as they entered, they found a scene of chaos and of disarray, the people in a state of agitation, their voices raised in anger and in fear.

Chief Denë came to Brenn and Den, saying, "We have ill tidings that do shake the very foundations of our Winter's store. The Frog Clan, in a raid most vile and bold, have struck against us, stealing that which we had gathered for the long and bitter months ahead."

"The Frog Clan?" said Brenn. "Those same villains who did take my father's life and leave me fatherless? This news doth stir within mine heart a fury hot and unrelenting that demands a reckoning, a balancing of scales, for all the wrongs that they have wrought upon us."

Den said, "Brenn, I share thine anger and thy thirst for vengeance against these cowards, who do strike against the innocent and steal away the very means of life in winter's thrall. But let us not be hasty in our wrath, and seek the counsel of the wise, the seasoned."

"Young Brenn," Chief Denë did say, "I see the fire in thine eyes, the rage that boils within thee, seeking release. But vengeance, blind and reckless, oft doth lead to greater sorrow and to deeper wounds than those which it doth seek to heal. In this hour, we must be prudent and take thought for all our people and their well-being."

"Your words, Denë, do give me pause," said Brenn, "and do stay the hand that yearns to strike in retribution. But how can we let this injustice stand? How can we face the Winter with the stores depleted by the actions of these thieves?"

"We shall find a way to weather this storm," said Denë, "and to rebuild what has been lost or taken. But first, we must secure our people's safety, and seek a path that leads to lasting peace, not further bloodshed and unending strife. Thy destiny, and thy father's legacy, do call thee to a higher purpose than the pursuit of vengeance or of personal gain."

In the depths of Brenn's heart, a storm did rage, a tempest born of grief and righteous anger, at the injustice wrought upon his kin by the hands of those who knew not mercy's touch. The loss of Deugwer, father, guide, and friend, did fuel the flames of vengeance in his breast, and drove him to a course of action, bold and fraught with peril, for his soul and all who followed him in this, his darkest hour.

"My loyal companions!" called Brenn. "The time has come to take up arms against the Frog Clan's might and visit upon them the wrath of those who have been wronged and seek redress in blood. With this sword, imbued with magic's power, we shall strike a blow for justice and for honor, and make them rue the day they dared to cross the path of Brenn, the son of fallen Deugwer!"

With hearts afire and weapons drawn, Brenn's companions followed him into the fray, their footsteps pounding on the frozen earth, a drumbeat heralding the coming storm. And they named themselves Erkhesgur—the Bear People—and lo, their coming was a bane to all who saw.

The Frog Clan, caught unawares and ill-prepared for the fury, the onslaught, that descended like a plague upon their village and their homes, could but watch in horror as their world was rent asunder by the power of that sword that Brenn did wield with deadly skill and purpose.

One man cried out with child in his sheltering

embrace, "What demon is this that comes upon us with fire and steel and magic's fearsome might? What have we done to merit such a fate, to see our lives and all we hold most dear destroyed in but a moment's savage blur?"

The battle, if indeed it could be called, such a one-sided contest 'twixt the strong and those who stood no chance against their might, raged on, with Brenn the eye of this fell storm, Pukhso a blur of motion in his hand, cutting down all those who dared to stand against the tide of his undying rage.

But as the village burned, and screams of pain and terror rent the air, a change did come upon the young warrior's heart and mind, a dawning horror at the scale of what his actions and his rage had wrought upon the innocent and guilty, both alike.

Falling to his knees, beholding the destruction before him, Brenn cried out, "What have I done? What monster have I become in pursuit of vengeance and retribution? This sword, a weapon of such fearsome power, has turned me into that which I despise, a bringer of destruction and of death, a scourge upon the land and all who dwell within its bounds. O Father, canst thou see the depths to which thy son has sunk in grief and anger at thy loss and at the world that took thee from my side too soon, too cruelly?"

Amidst the smoke and blood and ruin, Brenn stood, the sword now heavy in his hand, a symbol of the power he never sought, and of the price that he had paid to wield it. The Erkhesgur, their rage now spent and cooled by the sight of such wanton devastation, looked to their leader for a sign, a word, of guidance in this hour of doubt and horror.

"My friends," Brenn said, "what have we become? In seeking justice, we have wrought instead a great injustice on the innocent, and stained our hands with blood that cannot be washed clean by any means or any power. Let us lay down our arms and seek a path of peace and redemption, though no forgiveness will we find for this fell deed."

With heavy hearts and minds now clear of rage's blinding fog, the Erkhesgur did follow Brenn away from that dread place of carnage and of sorrow deep and lasting.

In the heart of the Raven Clan's domain, where once fires of welcome and of friendship burned bright for Brenn and for his loyal crew, a gathering of a different sort now loomed as villagers and elders, stern and grave, assembled to pass judgment on the deeds of those who had so rashly and so blindly unleashed the fury of a magic blade upon the unsuspecting and the innocent in a misguided quest for vengeance swift.

Standing before the throng, Chief Denë spoke: "Brenn, son of Deugwer, once we welcomed thee and thy companions to our hearths and homes as friends and as the kin of one we loved and lost to fate's unbinding, cruel decree. But now, thou standest before us not as friend, but as the perpetrator of a crime so heinous and so vile that it doth cry to heaven for redress and for the scales of justice to be balance against thy deeds. What sayest thou to this charge?"

Brenn said, "Chief Denë, elders of the Ravens,

and all gathered here, I stand before you humbled and ashamed of what my rage and despair have wrought upon the innocent and those who played no part in mine own father's fate. I let my grief and anger blind my judgment and lead me down a path of darkness and of ruin, for myself and for the land that had so generously taken us in and offered us a chance to start anew."

"Thy words," said Denë, "though true and spoken from the heart, cannot undo the damage that is done, nor wash away the stains of innocent blood that now do mar the honor of our clan, and of the memory of thy noble father. As chief, and as the voice of all our people, I have no choice but to decree thy banishment from this, our land, and from the fellowship of those who once did call thee friend."

Brenn and his companions stood stunned and silent beneath the weight of this consequence of their misdeeds, and of the failure of their leader to heed the wisdom of the elder's words, and temper the fire of his righteous wrath with understanding of the broader scope of leadership, and of the heavy burden that comes with wielding such power as his.

"I accept thy judgment," said Brenn, "and the price that I must pay for letting passion rule my actions and my thoughts in that dark hour. I only ask that thou, and all thy people, remember us not as bringers of destruction and sorrow, but as those who sought to do what's right, but lost their way amidst the labyrinth of grief and rage."

With heavy hearts and minds now burdened with the knowledge of their shortcomings, the Erkhesgur did gather their belongings and make their way toward the waiting ship that would bear them far from Yenmiskelanë, and from the chance of a new life, now lost to the consequences of their rash actions.

As Brenn, the last to board, did pause and gaze out toward the horizon, vast and empty, he felt the weight of leadership descend upon his shoulders, heavy, with the realization of the cost of vengeance. Looking up to the sky, he spoke so all might hear: "Yog, Derevai, gods, ye powers above who may listen—hear me now: never again will I wield this sword, for its power is too great, and I have wrought more destruction and death today than I imagined I was capable."

To the Erkhesgur, he said, "My friends, brothers, sisters, Den, we are truly, now, alone, without a home or sanctuary to call our own or offer us respite from the burdens of our own making and the echoes of the choices we have made. I take this blame, and I know that no apology would suffice to right the wrong I have done to you."

And as the ship did slowly pull away from the land that had once held such promise, Brenn stood upon the deck, his gaze fixed firm upon the distant horizon's edge, a symbol of the journey that lay ahead, and of the challenges that he and his companions must face with courage and humility, to find redemption, and to forge anew a destiny more worthy of the power that fate and magic had bestowed upon them.

Canto 6

In the once-thriving streets of Goreuhwo, where life and laughter flowed like gentle streams, a scene of devastation now unfolded, as rubble, smoke, and ash obscured the sky, and fear, like a miasma, thick and choking, hung heavy over the survivors, huddled, lost, amidst the ruins of their shattered lives.

Through winding alleys choked with debris, Pabelyo made her way, a lone figure, dwarfed by the immensity of this destruction, wrought by the hands of those who knew not mercy, nor the value of the lives they so carelessly and cruelly snuffed out in their misguided righteousness.

But in the heart of Pabelyo, beaten down yet undefeated by the weight of woe, a flicker of determination burned, an ember of resilience in the dark that drove her onward through the shattered streets, toward a future, uncertain yet alive with possibility and hope.

In this, the aftermath of horror and of prejudice

unleashed upon the innocent, Pabelyo became someone other than herself, a mask to hide behind, and to protect the truth of who she was and what she held most sacred, from the eyes of those who would seek to condemn her for her faith and blood. No longer Pabelyo, but Pabi now, a name to shield her from the storm of hate that raged all around and threatened to consume her if she did not stay concealed.

With identity now shrouded in a veil of secrecy and misdirection, Pabi made her way to a caravan that promised passage west, and to a land whither she might find a measure of safety and of peace denied her here in the ruins of Goreuhwo.

The caravan master, a short man named Saseg, asked her, "What brings thee to our humble caravan in times so troubled and so fraught with danger? Speak quickly, for the road ahead is long, and we must leave before the Sun climbs high."

"Good sir," said she, "I am Pabi, a traveler seeking passage to the lands beyond, where I might find my family, and a chance to start afresh, away from all the pain and sorrow of this place, now lost."

Saseg, with appraising eye, did look upon the young lady, so young and yet so burdened by the weight of history's cruel hand, and felt a stirring of compassion for her plight and for the journey she must undertake, alone and unprotected.

"Then join us, young Pabi," said he, "and may the road prove kinder than the fate thou leavest behind, in this, the cradle of thy shattered dreams, and memories now tinged with grief and loss."

With hope rekindled in her heart, and sorrow

mingled with relief, Pabi did take her place among the travelers, their faces etched with stories of their own, of lives uprooted and of futures sought in lands unknown and distant from the pain that drove them from their only homes they'd known.

As the caravan began to move, she did cast one final glance upon the city where her life and all she knew came to ruins. But even as she mourned for what was lost, she felt a glimmer of anticipation for the journey that awaited her.

And as the city faded into the distance, a speck upon the horizon's hazy edge, Pabi turned her gaze westward, whither she hoped she might find her long-estranged elder brother, Fehi, and a life begun anew.

Across the vast expanse of Mitho Gorikhwa, a winding trail of life and hope and dreams unfolded as the caravan, slow and steady, made its way through hills and vales and streams, a microcosm of a world in motion, where stories intertwine and fates collide, and where the journey is the destination, a crucible, in which the soul is tried.

Amidst the dust and sweat and toil of travel, Pabi found a measure of solace and of peace in the rhythm of the days and in the company of those who shared her path, and her release from the chains of a life now left behind in the ruins of the gwerfegi now lost to time.

One night, a young man approached Pabi. Euheth was his name, swaggering toward her with gleeful smirk upon his face. "Fair Pabi," he said, "let me help thee with thy tent, and share with thee the warmth of my campfire—for in this lonely journey, we must find solace in companionship, and desire to ease the burden of the road we travel, and to remind us of the joys of life that wait beyond the horizon's misty veil for those who dare to live and dare to strive."

"Thy kindness, Euheth," said Pabi, "is a welcome aid in times so wrought with uncertainty and fear. But in thine eyes I see a hunger, and in thy words a motive insincere that seeketh to claim me as a prize, unwilling, and to use my vulnerability as a tool to satisfy thy base and selfish longing revealed in every gesture, ever rule of courtesy now twisted to thy purpose, a trap disguised as friendship."

Pabi pulled away, her trust and heart guarded by a wall erected to protect her soul from the advances of a man so cynical and so consumed by his own selfish goal that he would use the guise of kindness as a means to satisfy his own base pass.

"Thou spurnest mine offer and my company?" he said. "How darest thou judge me with thine haughty gaze and thy cold demeanor, so unfeeling, when all I sought was to bring brighter days to thy life so burdened by the weight of sorrow and of loss that thou dost carry like a millstone around thy neck, a fate that I would ease if thou wouldst only tarry and give thyself to me in sweet surrender, a moment's pleasure for a lifetime's splendor."

"I see through thy facade," she said, "and thy deceit, the true intent behind thine honeyed words, and I will not be swayed by thy conceit, nor by the promise of a love unheard—for in thine eyes I am but a possession to be claimed, used, and discarded when thou hast had thy fill of my oppression, and my spirit by thy lust is martyred. I will not be a pawn in thy sick game, nor sacrifice my dignity."

With words so sharp and clear and full of fire, Pabi did cut through Euheth's web of lies, and in that moments set her spirit higher than the base desires that he implied, a choice so brave and so defining of the strength that lay within her heart and soul, to stand against the tide of his false love, and to claim her own self-worth and control over her destiny, and her decision to be more than just a man's possession.

But in the wake of her rejection, Euheth's anger and his wounded pride simmered beneath the surface, waiting to burn with a fury that he struggled to hide, a dangerous spark that threatened to ignite the tinder of his bruised and battered ego, and to set ablaze the fragile peace that the caravan had sought to grow between the disparate souls now bound together by the common thread of hope.

As the caravan wound its way through the tapestry of Mitho Gorikhwa's varied landscape, vast and unforgiving, yet alive with promise, two souls, once strangers, found a kinship born of shared experience and mutual understanding, a bond that blossomed like a desert flower amidst the hardships of the journey long.

In Baiwieth, Pabi found a kindred spirit, a woman whose sapphire eyes reflected the weight of stories left untold, and memories both sweet and bitter that shaped the contours of her inner world, a landscape as complex and rich as any that they traversed in their long, winding journey towards a future yet unknown.

And in Pabi, Baiwieth saw a strength that shone like a beacon through the fog of doubt and fear, a resilience born of trials overcome, and challenges met with grace, and courage, rare in a world that often seemed so cold, so cruel to those who dared to hope.

In the long hours of the journey shared, Pabi and Baiwieth found solace in each other's company, their stories intertwining like threads in the loom of life, tales of the struggles and joys that shaped them into the women they were now; and in their friendship they found warmth, a light, that guided them through the darkness of their doubts and gave them strength to carry a heart burdened with the weight of solitude.

"Let us ride together, thou and I," said Baiwieth, "and leave the pettiness of men like Euheth far behind—for in each other's company we'll find the courage and the will to forge ahead, towards a life rich with the joys that friendship true can bring to lives once shadowed by despair."

With hearts entwined and spirits high, Pabi and Baiwieth rode on, their bond a balm to broken hearts and contrite souls.

Beneath a canopy of stars, so vast and bright, the caravan like a weary beast came to rest, its members scatters around the campsite's glow, seeking solace in the quiet of the night, and in the murmurs of their fellow travelers a fleeting respite from the long and dusty road that wound like a serpent through the wilderness.

In this moment of tranquility, Pabi found a measure of peace for the soul so battered by the trials of her journey, and the weight of secrets carried like a stone within the depths of her own troubled heart. But even here, amidst the beauty of the night, a shadow lurked, a threat to her serenity.

For Euheth, like a wolf in human guise, stalked the edges of the campsite's light, his eyes agleam with a hunger dark and vile, fixed upon the form of gentle Pabi, as she sought the sanctuary of her tent, unaware of the danger that awaited in the form of a man consumed by his own lust.

"Pabi, my sweet," Euheth did say, "why fleest thou from mine embrace? Canst thou not see the depth of my devotion, the fire that burns within mine heart for thee? Come, let us put aside this foolish game, and give in to the passion that consumes us both—for in the darkness of this starlit night, who would dare to judge our sweet love?"

"Love?" said Pabi. "Thou speakest of love, when all I see is a twisted and perverse desire, born of thine own selfish and entitled heart? I have rejected thine advances, time and time again, and yet thou dost persist in thy delusion, blind to the fact that I am not some prize to be won, but a woman with a will and heart mine own."

With a roar of rage and wounded pride, Euheth lunged at the object of his dark obsession, his hands like claws, seeking to claim by force what he could not win through charm or guile. But Pabi, with a strength born of desperation, and a fierce, unyielding sense of self, fought back against her attacker with a fury that startled even her own brave heart.

"I will not be thy victim," shouted Pabi, "nor thy plaything, thou vile and loathsome excuse for a man! I am not some weak and helpless creature to be taken against my will and bent to thy desire. I am a woman, strong and proud and free, and I will fight with every breath within me to defend all that I am!"

The commotion of their struggle, fierce and loud, drew the attention of the caravan entire, as members roused from their slumber to behold the spectacle of Pabi locked in battle with the man who once had seemed so kind, but now revealed as a monster in disguise, a predator, unmasked by his own vile deeds.

"See how she attacks me," cried Euheth, "like a wildcat possessed! This woman is no victim, but a temptress sly who seeks to lure me with her wiles, and then cry foul when I respond to her own base desires! It is she who should be judged and censured for her shameless and unseemly conduct, here before the eyes of all our fellow travelers!"

Pabi said, "How darest thou twist the truth to suit thine own end, and paint thyself as the injured party here? It is thou who have pursued me relentlessly, despite my clear and firm rejections of thine unwanted and offensive overtures. I am not the one who should be judged, but thou, for thine actions speak far louder than thy lies!"

Saseg, the caravan leader, roused by the commotion, stepped forward to assess the situation grave, his eyes taking in the disheveled state of both Pabi and Euheth, and the tension thick and palpable that hung like a cloud above the gathered throng. With a heavy heart and a sense of weighty responsibility, he prepared to hear both sides of this sordid tale, and to render judgment fair and true upon the actions of the accused and the accuser, for the fragile peace of their community.

"Pabi," he said, "thou standest accused by Euheth, here, of conduct most unseemly and unbecoming of a member of our company, a charge that carries with it grave implications for thy standing, and thy place, among us all. What sayest thou in thy defense against these claims?"

"I say only this," said Pabi, "that I am innocent of the crimes that Euheth lays upon my feet. It is he who has pursued me relentlessly, despite my constant refusals. I have done nothing save defend myself against a man who would not take no for an answer."

"Lies!" cried Euheth. "All lies from a woman who would seek to besmirch my character and paint herself as the victim, when it is she who has led me on with her wiles and her temptations. I am a man of influence, and standing here I will not be slandered by this harlot's tongue!"

Saseg, swayed by Euheth's words, and the weight of his position in their hierarchy, felt the pressure of the moment bearing down upon his shoulders as he wrestled with the decision that would shape the fate of the accused and accuser in this trial of honor and truth.

"Pabi," said he, "I have heard the testimony of both sides, and I must render judgment based upon the evidence before me and the needs of this caravan, and all its members here. Though it pains me to take such drastic action, I am left with no choice but to expel thee from our company, effective immediately."

"No!" Pabi cried. "Thou canst not do this; I am innocent! I have done nothing wrong, save stand my ground against a man who would not respect my wishes! Please, I beg of thee, reconsider this decision—for it will leave me vulnerable and alone in a world that cares not for me and my kind."

But the caravan leader, his mind made up, stood firm in his resolve to cast her out into the wilderness of the Satin Road, where dangers untold awaited the lone traveler.

"Wait," said Baiwieth. "I cannot stand idly by and watch as my friend is cast out into the darkness alone! Pabi is innocent, I know this in mine heart, and I will not abandon her to face the perils of this road without the comfort of a friend and the strength of a companion by her side."

Saseg said, "Baiwieth, thou wouldst throw thy lot in with this woman and risk thine own life in expulsion from this company? Think carefully before thou makest this choice, for there will be no turning back once it is made."

"I have thought," said she, "and my decision stands. I will not leave Pabi to face this trial alone—for in her I have found a dear friend whose worth is beyond measure or compare. If thou wilt cast her out, then I will go with her, and together we will face whatever lies ahead."

And so, as the dawn came, with heavy hearts and meager supplies, Pabi and Baiwieth watched as the caravan slowly disappeared into the distance, leaving them alone and exposed on the vast empty road, their isolation and their fear living things, coiled in the pit of their stomachs as they contemplated the long and dangerous journey that lay ahead.

"Baiwieth," said Pabi, "I cannot thank thee enough for thy loyalty, and thy willingness to stand by me in this dark hour. I know the risks thou hast taken on my behalf, and I swear that I will do everything in my power to prove myself worthy of thy friendship and trust."

"There is no need for thanks," said Baiwieth, "or for oath's, dear Pabi—for in thee I have found a true companion, whose strength and courage give me the same, and whose heart is as true as the light from the stars above. Together we will face whatever challenges may come, and together we will find a way to overcome this lot that fate has placed before us."

Beneath the canopy of the Satin Road's dense underbrush, Pabi and Baiwieth, two women lost and weary, sought sustenance amidst the unfamiliar flora, their hunger a gnawing beast that drove them on to forage in a landscape strange and wild, where every leaf and berry held the potential for nourishment or danger in equal measure.

"Pabi," said Baiwieth, "be careful in thy search for food, for not all that grows within this tangled wood is safe for human consumption or digestion. We must be cautious in our choices here, and not let desperation cloud our judgment's call."

"I hear thy words, dear friend," said Pabi, "but hunger is a cruel and unrelenting taskmaster that drives me to the brink of recklessness in search of something, anything, to fill the aching void that gnaws within my belly. These berries, here, they look so ripe and sweet; surely, they cannot be harmful to the taste?"

With trembling hands and a heart full of hope, Pabi plucked the tempting fruit from its stem, and raised it to her lips with a prayer for sustenance and relief from the pangs that twisted and churned like a knife within her gut. But scarcely had the juice touched her tongue when a wave of nausea and dizziness washed over her like a tidal surge, leaving her retching and shaking on the ground.

"Pabi! What has happened? Art thou ill?" Baiwieth cried as she came to her friend's side. "Was it the berries thou didst eat, just now? Oh, curse my inattention and my lack of vigilance in watching over thee, in this our time of trial and of need! I must find help, and quickly, or I fear thy condition will only worsen with each passing hour."

"Nay," said Pabi, "please, do not leave me here alone and vulnerable in this wild place, where unseen dangers lurk in every shadow, and every rustle of the undergrowth holds the promise of some new, fearsome threat. I cannot bear the thought of facing this without the comfort of thy presence by my side."

But Baiwieth, torn between her love for Pabi and the urgency of the situation at hand, knew that she must act, and swiftly, if she hoped to save her friend from the clutches of this vile affliction that sapped her strength and clouded her mind with pain. With a heavy heart and a promise to return as soon as help could be found and brought to bear, she set off into the wilderness, alone, leaving Pabi to the mercy of the elements and the machinations of fate and circumstance.

Alone at last, and wracked with pain and fear, Pabi lie upon the forest floor, her body stricken with shivers and convulsions as the poison worked its wicked will upon her helpless frame.

"O Baiwieth," she prayed, "hurry back, I beg of thee—for I fear I cannot last much longer here without the strength of thy presence and thine aid."

But even as Pabi's thoughts turned to despair, a sound broke through the haze of her delirium, the tramp of heavy boots upon the earth, and the murmur of men's voices drawing near. With a surge of terror and adrenaline, Pabi dragged herself to the shelter of a nearby bush and huddled there in silence and in dread, as three figures came into view, their faces obscured by the shadows of the forest's gloom.

"Hold, my friends," said one, "for I hear the sound of water babbling nearby, a welcome respite from the dust and heat of the Satin Road's long march. Let us pause here and refill our skins before we press on toward our destination's end.

"Aye," said another, "a moment's rest and a cool drink will do us all a world of good, I think. But let us not tarry overlong in this place, for I dislike the feel of these woods and the way the shadows seem to watch us with malevolent intent."

Pabi, frozen in her hiding place, could only watch as the men drew closer to her position, her heart hammering in her chest like a captured bird as she prayed to whatever god may hear her plea, for deliverance from this new and unknown threat. The memory of Euheth's violence still fresh and raw within her mind, she dared not reveal herself or call out, for fear of what these strangers might intent towards a woman helpless and alone.

Silently, she thought, "O Baiwieth, where art thou in mine hour of need? I am lost without thy strength and thy protection, a lamb among the wolves of this dark wood, with no one to stand between me and the danger that lurks in every shadow and sound. I can only pray that thou returnest with aid before these men discover my presence here, and visit upon me some new and terrible fate, worse than the sickness that already gnaws at my vitals and my will to carry on."

And so, in silence and in fear, Pabi waited, as the men went about their business by the stream, their voices a murmur of potential threat that set her nerves to jangling and her pulse to racing, like a hunted creature's in the night. The minutes stretched into an eternity of dread anticipation and of desperate hope, as she clung to the slender thread of Baiwieth's promise to return with help and succor in her time of direst need and darkest desperation. But would that aid arrive in time to save the stricken girl from the perils that surrounded her?

As the Sun dipped low on the horizon's edge, and shadows, lengthening, embraced the land, the men, their purpose served, departed the glade, leaving Pabi weak and shivering in their wake, a small forgotten figure amidst the vastness of the forest's gloom and gathering dusk.

But with a rustling in the undergrowth, Baiwieth, faithful friend, returned at last, her arms laden with herbs of healing power to tend the stricken woman's most dire need.

"Oh Pabi," said she, "mine heart near broke to leave thee thus, alone and vulnerable in this wild place, but I have returned with hope and succor, too, to ease thy pain and lend thee strength anew. These herbs, though bitter on the tongue and strange, will work their subtle magic on thy frame, and banish the poison's grip from thy veins.

"Baiwieth," said Pabi, "thy presence is a balm to my tormented soul, a light in the darkness of my fear and my despair, amidst trials so great. I feared I'd never see thy face again or feel the comfort of thy steadfast love in this, mine hour of deepest, darkest need."

With gentle hands and whispered words of comfort, Baiwieth tended to Pabi's stricken form, coaxing the healing herbs past her lips and down to work their magic on her ravaged frame. And slowly, painfully, the girl revived, the color creeping back into her cheeks, as strength returned to limbs so long laid low.

"Come," said Baiwieth, "let us quit this place of fear and seek a refuge from the dark night's chill. I'll lift thee onto Boriwar's strong back, and together we'll ride to find a place of safety and of rest for weary souls."

Beneath the moon's pale, watchful eye, the pair set forth, their hearts both heavy and light with the weight of trials endured and overcome, and hope of sanctuary yet to be found. Through the long, dark hours of the night they rode, Baiwieth guiding Boriwar's steady steps, as Pabi clung to consciousness and hope, a fragile flame against the encroaching dark.

In the heart of the forest, a clearing lay, where stood a house with chimney tall and porch of sturdy wood, a haven in the wold. Upon a rocking chair, an old woman sat. Her fingers plucked at a lyre's strings, while at her feet two golden-haired dogs dozed, lulled by the gentle music of her song.

As Pabi and Baiwieth crossed the threshold of the trees, the dogs, alert, raised up their heads and sniffed, their noses pointing to the strangers' forms. The old woman, her song now at an end, set down her lyre and turned her gaze to meet the curious eyes of the two travelers.

"Hello there, children," she said. "With a smile upon my face I bid you welcome to mine humble home. Come inside, my dears, and rest a while, for ye have found safety here, and I will tend to you with all the skill I have. Though old I am, my strength is not yet gone."

With gentle words and gestures kind, the crone led the two women through the door of her home, where warmth and comfort waited to embrace the weary travelers, far from all they knew. Within, a world of wonder met their eyes, of furniture and art, so strange and fair, unlike the simple trappings of their lives.

The dogs, their tails a-wag, trotted inside to settle by the hearth, where crackling flames cast dancing shadows on the walls around. And from the kitchen, just beyond the door, the scene of something savory and sweet wafted to greet them, making Pabi's mouth water with hunger sharp and sudden-born.

"We thank thee, lady, for thy kindness shown," Baiwieth said, "to two poor wanderers, lost and far from home. My friend, Pabi, suffers from a handful of poison berries, and needs the healing touch of medicine to chase the fever from her brow."

"Of medicine, we have no lack," said the woman, "for in this house, all ills can be made well. Come, sit and eat; I had feared ye would not make it here in time to share the bounty of my table. A dish called lazanya waits for you, a recipe from lands I once called home, so long ago, in times now lost to memory."

With gentle hands and soothing words, the old woman led the travelers to the kitchen, where a feast fit for kings lay spread before them. With hunger's edge, they ate and drank their fill, of food so rich and strange, it seemed a dream, a vision of some far-off, fantastic land, where plenty reigned and want was but a shadow.

But as the meal drew to a close, a thought, like a dim spark, flared sudden in Pabi's mind, a nagging sense of something left undone. Looking around, she missed her friend, for Baiwieth had gone.

"What of Baiwieth, my dearest friend?" she asked. "Whither has she gone?"

"Fear not," the woman said, "for she is well and safe, resting in peace in chambers up above. Did I not say to leave thy cares behind, and trust in me to see to all thy needs?"

But Pabi's mind, now clouded as with fog, could scarce recall the words so lately spoken. The kitchen seemed to blur, its edges soft, as she sank deeper into a cushioned chair, the fire's warmth a blanket to her soul. With heavy lids, she fought the pull of sleep, her tongue grown thick and clumsy in her mouth.

"Where...where is she?" Pabi asked. "Where is my friend Baiwieth?"

"Asleep, my dear, in chambers above," came the reply, "her dreams untroubled. But hush thee now, and let thine own eyes close, for rest is what thou needest, more than aught."

As knitting needles clicked and clacked, a soothing rhythm like a lullaby, Pabi's last thoughts dissolved like a morning mist, and slumber claimed her, deep and dreamless-dark.

From slumber's depths, Pabi at last arose to greet a morn with sunlight warm and bright. The wooden floor beneath her feet was warm, a strange and pleasant contrast to the chill of early hours in her accustomed life. With steps uncertain, still half-lost in dreams, she made her way down to the kitchen's heart, where their hostess stood mixing batter, a homely scene of comfort and of peace.

"Ah, child," she said, "I fear I've quite forgot the milk, that ought to make these pancakes light and fluffy. But never fear, for in my well-stocked pantry, a worthy substitute I'm sure to find."

With deft and practiced hands, the old woman poured thick, white liquid from some hidden tin into the waiting bowl and stirred anew until the batter smoothed to glossy sheen. Then, with a smile, she turned to greet her guest, as Pabi, still dazed, sank into a chair, one faithful dog curled warmly at her feet.

"Good lady," she said, "pray forgive mine addled wits, but I must ask, though thou hast told me oft, what name hath thee?"

"I am Aweda, child, though once another name I bore, in lands now lost beyond the veil of time. But come, let us not dwell on what is past—for breakfast, hot and fragrant, soon will be a balm to chase away all shadows from thy mind."

In scenes repeated, as in dreams, the days passed by in Aweda's gentle care, each moment blurred and soft, the edges frayed by some strange magic woven in the air. Time stretched, twisted, pulled, until a week or more had passed unmarked, save in the healing of Pabi's weary soul, and in the bond that grew twixt her and Aweda, a friendship forged of comforts simple and of sorrows eased.

"Aweda," Pabi said, "thou seemest to live a life enchanted, with beasts and bounty far beyond the lot of those who wander on the wide world's roads."

"Enchanted?" asked Aweda. "Aye, perhaps, but also lonely, save for my faithful dogs, and gentle beasts that share my days in this my chosen home. But come, let us not dwell on what is lost, but rather on the joys that still remain, like knitting with its soothing, rhythmic song, and baking, sweet and savory in turn, to feed the body and soul alike."

And feed they did, on cakes and rich repasts, each bite a revelation to the tongue of Pabi who had never known such fare in all her wanderings on the dusty road. And as they ate and talked and laughed together, the bond between them deepened and grew strong, nurtured in the warmth of Aweda's hearth.

Yet still, as days and nights in turn went by, a nagging through like a persistent fly buzzed at the edges of Pabi's waking mind, a sense of something left too long undone, of purpose once held dear, now half-forgot in the soft haze of comfort and of ease.

"Aweda," said she, "thou hast been a friend so true, and given of thy bounty without stint, but still, I feel a call to wander on, to seek the answers to mine heart's unrest beyond the borders of this gentle place."

"I understand," said Aweda, "for I too, once, felt the same pull to roam and to explore the wide world's wonders, far beyond my door. But know that thou art always welcome here, a haven and a home whenever thou shouldst need a respite from the road's long miles. And as a token of our friendship true, I give to thee these scarves, so lately knit, to keep thee warm and to remind thee, always, of one who holds thee ever in her heart."

In the warmth of Aweda's sitting room, where comfort reigned and weariness found rest, Baiwieth sat, exhaustion on her face, her tangled hair a testament to sleep's deep hold upon her form, so lately roused. Beside her, Pabi sought the warmth of her companion's arms, a haven safe from all the trials that they had lately faced.

"Where are we, Pabi?" asked Baiwieth. "My mind is clouded still, as if a veil of dreams obscures my sight."

"We are at Aweda's, dost thou not recall?" Pabi said. "The kindly woman has taken us in and offered sanctuary in our time of need."

"Aweda, yes..." Baiwieth muttered. "Her name,

a distant chime, echoes within my thoughts, but faintly still. How long have we been here in this strange place? Time seems to blur, its edges soft and frayed."

"A strange question," Pabi said, "for truth be told, I find mine own sense of the passing hours strangely elusive, like a half-caught dream."

Into this scene of cozy domesticity, Aweda entered, needles in her hand, the steady rhythm of her knitting's click a soothing counterpoint to the crackling fire. One of her faithful dogs, Lor or Mora (identical save for their different sex), settled beneath her feet, content and still.

Aweda said, "Pabi, my dear, wouldst thou be so kind as to put on some tea? Its warmth would do us good."

But as the words left Aweda's smiling lips, Pabi became aware of a gentle heat emanating from the cup within her hands, the bittersweet aroma of spearmint and sage, laced with a hint of lemon, filled her nose, and on her tongue its flavor lingered still.

"But Aweda," she said, "we have our tea already; see how it steams, a fragrant offering to chase away the chill of weary bones."

"What was that, dear?" Aweda asked. "Here, let me tuck thee in, thee and Baiwieth both, snug beneath this quilt, that sleep may come and bring its healing touch."

With gentle words, Aweda lulled her guests to slumber deep, Baiwieth's soft snores a counterpoint to Pabi's slow and even breaths, as in the vast expanse of their shared bed, she curled her smaller form into the comfort of her friend's embrace.

"Rest now, children," Aweda whispered, "for tomorrow dawns bright with the promise of a new day's light, and challenges that will demand your strength."

The morning came, and with it strange delights, a breakfast feast of takos, filled with fare from lands unknown to Pabi and Baiwieth, but savory and satisfying nonetheless. The meal consumed, the dishes washed and dried, they gathered once more in the sitting room, where Lor and Mora lay content and still.

"Thou hast dogs!" exclaimed Pabi, noticing them seemingly for the first time. "How wonderful."

"I love dogs," said Baiwieth, "always have; their loyal hearts and gentle natures never fail to charm."

Aweda said, "Indeed, they are my constant companions, Lor and Mora, faithful and true friends."

But as they spoke, a flicker of unease stirred in Pabi's heart, a sense of something not quite right, a feeling of deja vu that nagged at the edges of her mind.

"Have I met these dogs before, Aweda?" she asked. "Their faces seem familiar, yet I can't quite place the memory."

"But of course thou hast, sweet Pabi," the woman said, "every time thou hast come to visit in mine humble home."

"And how many times have I come, Aweda? My mind is hazy, like a fogged-up glass."

Aweda answered, "Just the once, my dear, just once, and never more."

The day unfolded, filled with simple tasks, of tending to the creatures of the farm, the horses, chickens, and the placid cow, whose milk, so rich and creamy, graced their table. As they worked, Baiwieth's voice rang out in praise of this idyllic, peaceful life:

"This place, Pabi, is simply wonderful, a balm to soothe the weary, troubled soul."

Pabi said, "Thou has said that, Baiwieth, a dozen times since first we stepped beneath the morning Sun."

"But that can't be," said Baiwieth, "for we've just now come out, and yet...I find my thoughts are jumbled, strange. When did I loose my braid, that kept mine hair contained and tidy, ready for the day?"

"I can't recall," Pabi said, "for truth be told, I don't remember thee ever wearing such a style, at least not in the time we've spent here, lost in the soft haze of Aweda's gentle care."

With questions swirling in their minds, they turned to Aweda, seeking answers to the strange discrepancies that plagued their fractured memories like shards of glass reflecting different angles of the truth.

Baiwieth asked, "Aweda, when we first arrived, did I wear mine hair braided, neat and tidy-wise?"

"Perhaps, my dear," Aweda said, "but who can say? Such trivial details are lost in the grand scheme of things."

As she spoke, her needles clicked and clacked, the rhythm of her knitting soft and slow, a lullaby to soothe their troubled thoughts.

"But hush now, children," she said, "for the time

has come to gather up your things and set your course for lands beyond the borders of mine home. Your destinies await and will not be denied their dues by any force on Earth."

With heavy hearts and minds awhirl, Pabi and Baiwieth stood upon the porch, their possessions packed and ready for the journey that stretched out before them, vast an unknown, a blank page yet to be inscribed.

Boriwar then appeared, walking from the stables, his mane and coat shining and clean, his belly full, his hooves trimmed and shod. With a nuzzle to Baiwieth, he let the women know that he was ready to depart.

Baiwieth said to Aweda, "I wish that we could stay longer—for in thine home we've found a peace and joy that seems so rare in this harsh and troubled world."

"I wish it too, dears, with all mine heart," the woman said, "but fate is not a force to be denied, and ye must walk the path that lies ahead."

Pabi asked, "Canst thou not tell us, Aweda, what lies beyond the borders of thy gentle realm?"

"Alas, my child, such knowledge is not mine to give, for each soul must face its trials and triumphs in its own appointed time. To know the future is to rob the present of its power to shape and transform the clay of our lives into works of art."

With those words, Aweda drew them to her breast, enfolding them in one last, fierce embrace, the scent of cloves and myrrh a memory that they would carry always in their hearts. Around their necks, she draped the scarves that she had knit with loving hands, a talisman of warmth against the chill of loneliness and fear.

"We thank thee, Aweda," said Pabi, "for all that thou hast done, for taking us in and offering us rest when we were lost and weary and afraid."

Then Boriwar carried them away, as Aweda stood, her figure small and still, and waved her farewell, a smile upon her lips.

But as they looked back for one final glimpse of her kind face and the home that they had briefly known, a sudden breeze blew leaves across their sight, obscuring all for just a moment's span. And when the gust had passed, and they could see once more the clearing that had held such warmth, they found it empty, bare, devoid of live, as if the house, the woman, and her dogs had never been, but were a waking dream, a vision sent to guide them on their way.

The day that Pabi and Baiwieth set forth from Aweda's home, the sky above was grey, the air oppressive, laden with the weight of coming storms. They rode, undaunted, through the humid gloom, their hearts still warmed by memories of the peace they'd found within the shelter of her walls, but as the miles stretched out, the clouds grew dark, and ran began to fall, a steady beat upon the earth, the road, their weary forms.

"Look there," said Pabi, "a grove of trees ahead, where we might find some shelter from the rain and rest our bodies, sore from hours in the saddle."

"Agreed," said Baiwieth, "for I am weary to the bone, and long for nothing more than a dry place to lay mine head and let my troubles drift away on the soft currents of my dreams."

Beneath a canopy of leaves, they made their camp, a tent pitched with care, bedrolls spread out upon the dampened ground, a fire kindled to chase away the chill that seeped into their bones with every gust of wind that shook the branches overhead. A meager meal of bread and cheese sufficed to quell the gnawing hunger in their bellies but did little to lift the sense of gloom that settled like a shroud upon their hearts.

Pabi said, "I fear this storm, for it seems to grow in strength with every passing minute, as if the very heavens themselves conspire to thwart our progress and our hopes alike."

Baiwieth replied, "We've faced worse trials, I and thou, and come through stronger for the facing of them. This too shall pass, and we will find our way beyond the veil of rain to brighter skies."

But even as the words left Baiwieth's lips, the storm redoubled in its fury, sending sheets of driving rain to batter at the fragile shelter of their canvas tent, the water pooling around their huddled forms, a rising tide that threatened to engulf their meager refuge, and their courage, too.

"This is just perfect," Baiwieth said, "as if fate itself had marked us for its cruel jests to send such trials when we are at our lowest."

Pabi said, "It could be worse, my friend, for we at least have each other."

Scarcely had the words left Pabi's mouth when lightning split the sky, a blinding flash that seared the very air with its intensity, and thunder followed close upon its heels, a deafening crash that shook the very earth and set their teeth to rattling in their heads. Baiwieth, with a gasp of primal fear, drew close to Pabi, seeking comfort in the shelter of her friend's embrace, as if by clinging tight they might together weather the storm that raged without.

But nature's fury was not yet appeased, for in the next heart-stopping instant, lightning struck a towering tree just yards away, setting it ablaze with searing, sparkling flame that danced and flickered in the howling wind, before, with a groan of rending wood, it fell, toppling to earth with a deafening crash that sent both women screaming in terror, their ears ringing with the echoes of it, as if the very world itself shattered and left them stranded in a nightmare's grasp.

"Baiwieth!" cried Pabi. "Hold fast to me and let us pray to whatever gods may hear us in this maelstrom for strength and for deliverance from the storm's relentless, battering assault upon our souls!"

But even as they clung to one another, the wind like some great, howling beast unleashed, tore at the tent with savage, ripping claws, shredding the canvas like a flimsy veil, and sending it careening through the air, a tattered banner borne on tempest's wings, leaving them exposed and vulnerable to all the fury of the raging storm.

And Pabi, tumbling head over heels, felt the world spin madly as the wind and rain battered her body, blinding her with its relentless, stinging onslaught upon her face, her eyes, her mouth, until she knew not which direction was up or down, or where amid the chaos and the tumult she might find some shred of shelter or of solid ground on which to cling and ride out nature's wrath.

"Baiwieth!" she screamed. "Where art thou? Canst thou hear my voice above the roaring of the wind and rain? I fear I'm lost, adrift in this vast sea of churning water, earth, and splintered trees!"

But only the storm's fury answered her, drowning out her desperate, pleading cries with its relentless, deafening cacophony. Pabi, still beset by ringing in her ears, could scarcely hear her own voice as she called into the tempest, praying for a sign, a whisper of hope amidst the howling dark.

At last, the tumbling ceased, and she found herself sitting, dazed, in water deep, surrounded by the swaying, battered trees and churning skies that swirled like a typhoon. The rain pelted down in massive, pounding drops that stung her skin and blurred her fraught vision.

"Is this to be the end?" she thought. "Alone, afraid, battered by the elements, my strength spent in fighting against this overwhelming tide? Baiwieth, my friend, where hast thou gone? What fate hath torn thee from my side in this dark hour?"

And then, a sound rose, even over the storm, a roaring, rushing, like a thousand hooves thundering down from the hillside to her left. Pabi, with trembling limbs, stood, turning to face whatever new terror the tempest had now unleashed.

But 'twas no stampede that crested the hill's brow—a wall of water, towering and immense, arched over the summit, dwarfing all below, then bent and fell, a crushing liquid hammer slamming down toward the valley and the grove.

Pabi, transfixed by horror, could but watch as the flash flood, a roaring water-beast, careened down from the heights to swallow her. Then, with a crash, the deluge struck, and she was borne away like a leaf in rapids' grasp.

She surfaced, choking, gasping for each breath, fighting to stay afloat amid the surge that tossed her like a plaything in its midst. With flailing arms, she sought for something solid, a root, a branch, an isle of mud to cling to. But all was chaos, water, and the dark. Blind, for the clouds obscured all guiding light, the broken landscape offering no clue of here salvation might be hiding from the flood's all-consuming rampage, Pabi called out:

"Great Tuláhujut, messenger of God, hear my desperate plea amidst the raging torrent! Grant me the strength to swim, to fight, to live, and guide me to some fragment of thine earth where I might cling and weather out this hell!"

As if in answer to her prayer, her hand brushed against a floating root, a tenuous thread of hope amid the swirling, churning deluge. With burning limbs, she pulled herself along until her questing fingers found the mud, the blessed solidity of land, at last.

Dragging her weary, battered form ashore, she spied a boulder, rising from the mire, and crawled toward it, a small fragile figure dwarfed by the storm's titanic, raging might. There, curled into herself, she squeezed her eyes shut tight against the lashing wind and rain, praying for fortune's change, for fate's reprieve from this crucible of fear.

"Baiwieth," she croaked, "my voice is weak, mine

hope is failing... Canst thou have survived this fell, relentless tempest? I dare not hope for such a miracle. Even the trees are gone, uprooted in the rout. Oh, mine heart weeps at the thought that thou mayest be lost! Am I now alone, sole witness to this wrath? Bereft of friend and comfort, left to face this raging maelstrom that has shattered all the world I knew, and cast me once again unto the mercies of a road unknown..."

Upon a hill now barren stood Pabi, alone, the rains abated, the Sun now risen, its golden rays the flooded earth did warm. Exhausted, cold, and hungry was the woman, all signs of life and greenery now gone, the ground in muddy swirls from waters carved.

As far as the eye could see the land lay bare, to distant peaks and woods that once did thrive. Down from the hill Pabi began to trek, for Baiwieth calling out with strained voice. If yet alive her friend remained unknown, the landscape so transformed by the deluge great. Even the road familiar, Satin named, beneath the muck and debris now concealed.

With Sun as guide, the girl turned west and walked. Her garments soaked and torn, trousers stretched by water's weight, catching beneath her feet. The pant legs she rolled and chose a hill to make her destination and set forth. An eerie calm pervaded, life now fled. A tune did Pabi hum to pass the time.

Upon the hilltop a small spring she spied, descending down she bent to take a drink.

Then upwards climbed and once more called her

friend, but only silence greeted her alone.

Hunger pangs now struck as time wore on, and anger rose at fate's cruel turn of chance. "Will troubles never cease?" Pabi did cry. "With Aweda I should have remained behind!" Aweda surely knew what would transpire, thus giving food enough for just the day, and urging quick departure—but wherefore would she dispatch them into peril's midst?

In desperation Pabi then did pray to God for aid, deliverance to send, some help from her impending death. The prayer gave some comfort to her soul. Then she recalled the rituals of home, the daily prayer in rilyun-style made. Though not the hour appointed, still she knelt and bent her form unto the muddy ground, the sacred words unto the Messenger spoke, then stood, the prayer complete in proper form.

When she arose, behold! at hill's base stood a figure lay, a man in tattered cloak with eyes shut to the world.

"Art thou alive?" Pabi inquired with a nudge.

The stranger stirred and coughed up mud in streams, then rasped, "Hast thou some water for my thirst?"

In tongue of Len Khalayu then she asked, "What be thy name?"

The man in Kalayo spoke, "A fellow countrywoman! Erwo I am called. Say, wast thou caught in the tempest? Art thou hurt? Thy name, pray tell? And hast thou drink to spare?"

"None have I," said Pabi, "but over yon hill a spring doth run, its waters fresh and clear."

Then slowly rose the man with pained groan, bemoaned his ruined garb and missing shoe. With smile he asked, "What saidst thou of thy name?"

"I did not say," was Pabi's curt reply. "I must depart," she then informed the man.

"Alone?" asked Erwo with surprise. "No steed nor goods to aid thee on thy way?"

"I shall make do," Pabi assured him firm.

From cloak's wet folds the man some papers drew, now spoiled by rain, and cast them to the ground. "The effort of long years, dissolved like chaff!" At last, a package wrapped in waxen cloth he did extract, and offered salted meat to Pabi, who declined with shaking head. A morsel for himself Erwo consumed, then gave the rest. "Now 'tis fairly shared." With quiet thanks, she took the proffered food.

"And whither goest thou?" Erwo asked. "I only ask, for I search for friends whom the flood did cruelly separate. Perchance thou might have seen them on thy way?"

But Pabi encountered none save him. "And hast thou spied my companions tall, with mighty swords equipped?" she asked in turn.

Erwo shook his head. "Alas, I have not. It seems we both find ourselves quite alone."

At this remark, Pabi withdrew in haste, eager to be gone on her path.

"Forgive my foolish words!" Erwo exclaimed. "I meant no ill, and only to seek my friends. I wish thee well in thine own earnest quest. Now I'll away, yon stream to slake my thirst." As Pabi turned to leave, he called once more: "If to the same place we two make our way, 'twould make sense and survival's odds improve that we as fellow travelers should join..."

When no reply was given, from cloak he drew a blade for hunting, long and keenly hones. In fright Pabi took flight but turned when called. With hands upheld and posture meek, the knife Erwo did toss before her in the dirt.

"Take thou that," he said, "and use upon myself if I dare stray from honor's narrow path."

She retrieved the dagger, gripped it fast. "For now, we two may walk as one," said she, "until my friend—my friends—I find once more. The large ones, armed with swords of mighty size."

"Aye, thy companions girt with blades so grand, I do recall," Erwo with grin replied. "Now wilt thy name impart, so long withheld?"

A pause, and then, "Pabelyo," uttered soft.

With bow theatrical, the man rejoined, "Pabelyo, 'tis my pleasure and delight to make acquaintance on this flood-washed morn!"

And thus, uneasy allies now they stood amidst altered lands, their fates indefinite, to walk as one in westward track unknown, until Baiwieth at last Pabi regained.

Of age with Pabi, or perchance older by two years' span, stood Erwo, just few inches in height surpassing her, though she be small. His hair like hers was short and dark and curled but cropped more close. His eyes like coffee hued, with lines of laughter 'round the edges creased.

Together walked they, after some fashion, though Pabi kept her distance from the man. Had she her druthers, they'd not walk as one, but both in same direction being bound, and two surviving better than sole one, his presence she endured with bitter gall. She strove to pay him no regard nor mind, his voice to far-off reaches of her thoughts consigning, while she bent her focus whole on finding Baiwieth, that she might quit Erwo's unwanted company for good.

To present moment was she then recalled when Erwo laughed and said, "Dost take my point?"

"Oh," she replied, to him a backward glance directing, "Yea, I do."

With smile he asked, "Is that so? Pray, what was it I did say?"

A sigh escaped her. "Truth be told, I heard not."

"No matter, for myself was I addressing, in main," said he. "Accustomed am I to the presence of my comrades Fehi, Rilun. My tales, I think, to them are wearisome, but they unable are to stem the flow."

Quoth Pabi, "Less might their vexation be, if thou wouldst grant some seconds' peace each day."

With laughter Erwo said, "A marvelous thought! Pabelyo, thou dost please me mightily."

She blushed. "I pray thee, may we henceforth keep our discourse to a minimum?"

"'Tis doubtful," he frankly owned. "When nerves or solitude oppress my spirit, I am wont to talk at length. And since thou wilt not speak to me, 'tis as if I alone here wander now, no occupation for my mind but speech. "Thou needest not listen if thou hast no will, but 'tis my sole comfort in straits like these."

Through flaring nostrils Pabi sharply breathed,

her lips a thin line. "I feel not at ease."

"Forgive mine awkwardness, I thee entreat, but 'tis beyond my power to amend. Both nervous am I and a touch afraid."

"Of what?" asked she.

"Of losing my good friends, of starving in this waste, of wandering lost with one who shuns discourse," Erwo replied.

"I relish talk," said Pabi, "but not thine."

"Yet thou dost scarce know me," he pointed out.

"Just so. Nor do I thee an ounce of trust accord."

As Erwo walked, he downward looked, his feet with care 'mid rocks and riven branches placing, that strewed their path. Then with a sigh, "I understand," he said. "We strangers be, together lost, a plight we'd ne'er have picked if choice were ours. But here we are, conjoined by fate. I'd take it kindly if thou wouldst refrain from barbs and judgments personal toward my character, of which thou knowest naught.

"I own I am loquacious, but beyond that foible, I maintain I'm pleasant company, and never have I willfully caused harm, nor ever shall, so help me God. My worth I can't prove with mere words, but patience have, and trust I'll not destroy thee, nor thee hurt, if it be in my power to forbear. Thou needest not like me but pray judge me not."

Now Pabi wheeled on him and to his face drew near, her own a scant few inches off. "Thou idiot cur!" she spat. "No right hast thou to bid me anything. Thou knowest not what trials I have braved, what's me befallen, what deeds I've done. I'll judge thee as I please, for judging others is the lone defense that e'er has served me—"

"Wait, hush thee," broke in Erwo.

Agape, Pabi a step withdrew. "Didst thou just—"

"Quiet!" Erwo held up a hand, his gaze behind her scanning far afield.

Pabi a finger raised, her foot in wrath stamping. "Nay," she cried, "thou shalt not prattle on at such a length, then interrupt me when I start my own discourse—"

"But hark!" said he, "Dost thou not hear?"

Her protests Pabi curbed, and listened, but no sound her ears could catch. "Naught do I hear, thou churl," to him she said. No word Erwo returned, but swift took off behind her. "Whither goest thou?" she called.

"'Tis here!" his shout came back. No noise discerned, but still she grasped the dagger in her garb, and after him she went. Ahead she spied him crouched behind a thicket full of brambles, whence an awful shrieking din arose.

As Pabi closer stepped, a rabbit trapped she saw, its foot entangled, as it strove to pull itself to freedom. Blood ran down its limb, which Pabi guessed it had part gnawed in desperate attempt to loose the snare. "This poor soul is ensnared," Erwo observed. His hand to pocket moved, but empty found, and up to Pabi looked. "My blade, I pray thee, might I borrow brief? Or if thou list not that, then thou canst take the task." Unmoving, she upon him fixed her stare. "I care not which," he added. Pabi's cheek 'tween teeth was caught, but to his hand the knife at last she gave.

The rabbit Erwo freed with dexterous slice, but clasped it still, lest it should flee apace. "Thank Providence unbroken is the limb," he said, the creature's leg with care caressing. "Thou shalt mend well, my furry little friend." The hare then loosed he, and with bounding leaps it vanished from their sight. A joyful smile upon his face, Erwo the rabbit's flight observed. To Pabi back the blade he passed. "My thanks for thy forbearance and thy trust."

As in her cloak the knife once more she stowed, a frown her brow overcast. Then Erwo turned and onward strode. For long while after that, no further word did Pabi speak to him.

At midday's height, when sun aloft did ride, the twain their final morsels did divide—the salted beef that Erwo sole possessed, his pack and vittles claimed by raging flood. As they partook, Erwo a tale did tell of when his father at the college taught the discipline of numbers and their laws. But sudden ceased his yarn and north did point, where o'er a verdant hill a smoke plume rose. With quickened steps the pair the rise did scale, and there beheld, to their extremest joy, a cook-fire bright, round which two men and one fair maid reclined.

With shouts and flying feet Pabi to Baiwieth ran, her name on lips, and Baiwieth in turn to Pabi sped. Halfway they met in crush of tight embrace, as Baiwieth rained kisses on Pabi's cheeks, her eyes with welling tears of gladness brimmed. Nearby, with peals of laughter, hugs, and claps upon the back, Erwo with Rilun and with Fehi was rejoined.

"Ne'er leave my side again!" cried Pabi, voice

with passion rough.

"I meant not to," said Baiwieth, "but now all is set right. These gallants shall us tend."

Then Erwo, hand outstretched to Baiwieth, said: "Thou must be she of whom Pabi non-stop speaks, her treasured friend."

Baiwieth his hand did clasp. "Of me she really all the day discoursed?"

"Nay," answered he, "scarce ten words did she speak!" With grin he then his comrades introduced. "Lads, here before you stands fair Pabelyo. Pabelyo, meet my friends, Rilun, Fehi."

Rilun stood tall and lean, with hair uncurled, and as he Pabi's hand in greeting took, she marked his right eye brown, his left eye blue. Broad in the shoulders, Fehi, and full-bearded, but Pabi's hand took not, instead did bow.

Above the flames a rabbit slow revolved, its juices dripping on the coals below. When it was done, in fives they shared the meat, but scanty were the portions—yet all felt a keen thankfulness for what they had.

Quoth Rilun, on a rabbit bone engaged: "To Jub Khewi ye also make your way, so Baiwieth tells. As do we all, in time."

Pabi a glance at Baiwieth cast. "Ah, yes, 'tis so. How glad I am she thee informed!"

"My fault," mouthed Baiwieth with silent shrug.

"But first," said Erwo, "to a site we hie far northwest of the city. Have ye two in archaeology e'er interest shown?" Both women shook their heads to signify they had not. "Pity," Erwo then opined, "for history is a thing of wonder rare, and archaeology the past makes real. At university we students are of this fair discipline and apprenticed to the wise Professor Agwayabo for some years now. Know ye aught of ancient times, and Kollan ab-Kes?"

Anew the women gave negating signs. "The name I once or twice have heard," admitted Pabi.

Rilun broke in haste: "Pray do not boast we have unearthed the fabled city! 'Tis not yet assured. The sage Agwayabo bade us quell our premature delight."

But Erwo cried, "'Tis Kollan ab-Kes, I feel it in my bones! Have neither of ye perused the epic grand of Pervikhseryedhi?"

Pabi said, "In early schooling, yes. The king was he who immortality attained, was it not?"

Erwo demurred, "Not truly so. Ye ought to read afresh, or I the tale could tell, if ye so wish. 'Tis yarn of great import. But know that ancient Kollan ab-Kes was the very realm o'er which he held his sway. If it indeed be where we dig, we hope to find his tomb therein."

With wondering eyes, Baiwieth exclaimed, "Amazing! Of what age would he now be?"

"Above four millennia," said Rilun.

Baiwieth pressed, "On what grounds do ye deem this site the long-lost city is?"

Here Fehi chose to speak. "In annals old, whenever the place is named, 'tis ever called the City of the Cedar. Hard nearby our excavation lies a wood of trees, these selfsame cedars, ancient, proud, and tall. And there beneath the desert sands we find their forebears' forms in fossil state preserved. 'Twixt dig and forest, as a slender thread, an antique well or two the way connects. And yea, upon the site itself one spies shards of the fragrant wood, though spare and rare, for through the ages countless, most to dust and ruin have returned. But at the heart, a temple all of stone doth yet remain, and 'tis a sight... magnificent to see!" Here ceased he, and a dreamy smile he wore, his mind to bygone eons far removed.

With eagerness did Baiwieth inquire: "And what shall be if him ye do unearth?"

The trio shared a pregnant, mirthful look. "Our names," said Rilun, "shall the history books emblazon—though in sooth I seek as well both fame and fortune!" All burst out in glee.

"Nay," Erwo laughed, "Agwayabo taught the foremost lesson: that this trade doth not enrich its practitioners. But we aspire to have our names in time's vast sands indelibly inscribed, and Kollan ab-Kes with all its denizens in memory of Edorath revived and honored fair. To know we brought great Pervikhseryedhi forth from obscurity to bask at last in daylight's beams, after entombment long four thousand years... 'twould be a feat supreme!"

But Pabi mused, "Think ye he would not wish peaceful to bide beneath the sheltering earth?"

"He's dead," said Erwo, zeal somewhat abated. "Methinks he holds no strong desire either way."

"And when," asked Baiwieth, "shall we all behold this marvelous place?"

But Pabi interposed: "What, shall we wander to their far-flung site?"

"And why not so? 'Twould be adventure grand, and I for one find ancient things a joy! Forgot ye that at school I once engaged in studies of the distant past?"

To this Erwo with arched brow rejoined, "Coursework ye took in ancient history, yet ne'er chanced to hear of Pervikhseryedhi?"

Baiwieth shrugged. "That term my focus sadly was distracted... There was a boy, ye see..."

Declared Pabi then: "We go not to Jub Khewi with these men."

"But doth it not," asked Baiwieth, "lie betwixt our place and destination? 'Twere unwise to spurn the chance!"

With nod did Erwo say, "It lies indeed upon a roundabout yet still converging path. Your company we would esteem. And 'tis a day or two, perhaps, the land-ship port hence—doth any soul here gathered know our bearings and location?"

"Aye," Rilun japed, "I spy beside thy foot yon stone I recognize!" As peals of mirth the quip elicited, fair Pabi fumed.

Baiwieth gave nudge and urged, "Pabi, come! Embrace the moment, savor life a touch!"

"I, savor life?" cried Pabi. "O'er the breadth of Edorath I've roamed! Dost thou conceive this marks my first traverse of Satin Road? Hast thou forgot my roots in Jub Khewi, and that in Goreuhwo I did emerge? To journey from the one unto the next was my undoubted lot!"

Here Fehi chimed, "We too hail from Jub Khewi! Well, not Rilun..."

"At tender twelve thou didst abscond," ribbed Erwo. "Thou mayst not claim it as thy cradle true!"

"Shall we break camp and set our course?"

proposed Baiwieth. To Pabi flashed a smile, who yet with furrowed brow her discontent proclaimed.

The band their scanty goods did swift collect, the embers quenched, and westward set their course. Pabi apart did trail, in pensive mien, as fore the rest in mirth and converse joined. Baiwieth, solicitous, a backward glance cast oft, to mark her friend's well-being gauge.

When Sun 'neath horizon's rim did sink, a halt they called, their nightly camp to make. Erwo and Rilun forth did venture, keen to catch a hare for sup. Pabi remained with Baiwieth and Fehi, who regaled his tale of early days in Jub Khewi, and cause for flight from hearth at tender age.

Of Fehi's sire he spoke, a scribe for hire, retained by wealthy man to pen his scrolls, to balance keep of ledgers, and to guide his offspring's hand in sacred Kanakh-ri. This charge, thought Fehi, turned his father's mind to stern religious bent, til scarcely aught but prophet's imminent return he preached.

Quoth Baiwieth, "Yet truth he surely spake, for lo! the seer amongst us walks once more!"

A shrug from Fehi. "Whichsoever the case, no more could I abide beneath his roof. I yearned to roam, the wide world to behold, while he in joint enterprise me would bind. Thus fled I, tarried long in distant climes, Deulen and Mithoër. But when I learned my parents both had perished, I returned for studies to resume."

"Alas!" cried she, "You have my deepest sympathies for your loss."

"I scarce recall their faces or their ways, so long

from them estranged," confessed the youth.

"Thy plight I grasp," said Baiwieth, "for I too to Dol-Nopthelen make my way, to join kin all but lost to memory's fading hold. Now, sooth, I question inwardly my course, if to their hearth 'twere wise for me to fare."

"In Len Khalayu thou couldst e'er remain," Fehi proposed.

A frown her aspect clouded. "Of divers ills touching that land's fair sex I have heard tell—no slight to thee intended."

"And none is taken," he with haste replied. "No disrespect to womankind I show, and much hath changed since holy man assumed the reins of state. Progressive are his views regarding females—though I'll not pretend all meets with my approval. Cities razed, the multitudes expelled to wander far... Such tactics I deem misguided, if not worse."

With laugh, Baiwieth rejoined, "Mayhap I'll make thy domicile my own, if welcome there!" At this they both in merriment did smile, and she a wayward tress behind ear tucked. To Pabi's eye, her gaze on him seemed strange, his laugh and air him-like to her father.

An hour thence, the hunters back returned, a single hare their prize. This roasted they, and having dined, the three to prayer bent. They Pabi too invited to partake, but she demurred, which gracious they did take. When done, Erwo alone to southward trees himself betook. With curious eye Pabi his movements traced.

Quoth Rilun then, "Each morn and eve in solitary rite he speaks unto his Maker, such the bond they share."

Ere Erwo's coming, all save Pabi slept, and she in feigned repose still lay when he beside the waning fire himself composed. Some phrase below his breath he murmured low, but she its sense could not with straining catch.

They rose betimes, and westward pressed until the Satin Road they struck. In this far reach, where Maikhethlen and hinterlands of Keulen with Len Khalayu's bounds converge, the way with merchants and with travelers teemed. Branch roads in plenty from the main diverged, and one that south did tend, marked by a carven stone in scripts of Jongwo, Kalayo, Keuleno— "To Oyer Port, miles thirty," it proclaimed—the band, by Erwo led, did choose to tread.

Upon a wind-wagon capacious perched, dusk found them at the haven's bustling gate. Erwo a tavern sought, and viands hot with cleansing baths for all did there provide, his credit with the host their ticket proving. That night on proper beds their limbs they stretched, and Pabi, sinking deep in goose-down soft, of her exhaustion knew not til she slept.

Amidst night's watches she from slumber woke as Erwo from his prayers their chamber gained. With heavy, sniffling breath, he to his mat beside the bed where she and Baiwieth lay made labored way. Though murk his visage veiled, her ears caught sound suspiciously like sobs choked back, as though to stifle them he strove. Thus, minutes passed, the stifled weeping clear, til it to even cadence yielded place of sleep's oblivion. Pabi, wondering, heard.

Vaster by far than Baiwieth's wind-wagon the land-ships loomed, each one souls thirty holding, plus cargo in the hold. Their sails immense not only heavenward, but port and starboard spread. Though broad, the wheels were thin, for travel made on hinterlands' sparse-covered, yielding soil. Embarked, they forward seats did all prefer. Well-padded were they, and with belts endowed for safety's sake. The pilot and his crew down every aisle progressed, each rider's straps to test. Meanwhile, the ropes were hauled and plied, the knots inspected, and the sails unfurled. All being set, the hands gave lusty cry.

To Pabi Erwo leaned and smiling said, "If large thou deemest this craft, but wait until the desert port we gain!"

At captain's word, by pilot echoed, groundsmen blocks removed, the wheels' rotation freeing. Pilot then a lever threw, and straight the sails did drop from wagon's flanks, and taut with wind became. A lurch, a slow advance—but ere the strip of launch's greensward cleared, such speed attained that Pabi's eyes did water, and her hand to belt instinctive clung, lest she take flight!

By in a blur the scenery raced, and whoops of youthful glee arose. With joyous laugh, Erwo exclaimed, "The sensate rush of speed, akin to flight itself, I'll never tire!" She could but acquiesce. Once used to it, exhilaration came, and soon that force which aft had pressed her form did slacken, leave alone that heady feel of skimming earth swift as raptor's dive or hare's fleet dash. So close this seemed to gift of winged ones that fancy played she now a bird had turned.

To their left the Dyuglebai their snow-peaks reared, in frozen mantle never shed. How strange, thought Pabi, that this range's further face looked on her childhood realm, whose edge one might, but for the peaks' thin-aired and killing height, attain in footsore days. Yet round the mounts' far-stretching base, by north- and westward miles near countless, must the traveler wend to come unto that land beloved.

She had supposed the journey home, when by the wagon train abandoned in Mitho Gorikhwa, would consume of weeks a span—but this fleet ship, she saw, so rapid cleaved the leagues that border's brink they well might reach ere second sunset's glow. And meet her reckoning proved. On that day's close, the captain and the pilot, working levers, the sails updrawn, by crew secured, contrived. With slowing impetus, the craft advanced til halt she came. The brake engaged, groundsmen to wheels their chocks applied, and mooring lines to stony bollards fixed.

Pabi her belt unclasped, and down with others clambered, glad to feel unmoving ground beneath her feet. But earth and sky did reel as, sudden, balance deserted her, legs to the rhythm tuned of speeding craft. She stumbled, and his hand Erwo in steadying clasp about her laid, and to a quayside bench her guided safe. Beside her he sat down, the rest no less for stable footing grateful.

"Welcome back," he said, as her still-swimming head she raised.

"Thy meaning?" Pabi asked, intense vertigo and belly-curl assailing her.

He smiled. "We of late the border crossed. In Len Khalayu we have arrived."

Never before had Pabi seen this quarter northern

of her land. Beyond the great divide, sparse vegetation cloaked the sandy leagues that southward stretched afar toward Jub Khewi. And only now she marked the port's expanse, built up on stilted wharves above the powdery surface. 'Twixt the docks, like ocean vessels sized, the land-ships perched on wheels more vast than those their own had sported, by belt on belt conjoined. As Erwo told, the sand did belted wheels the best befit.

On stairways from their minor slip ascending, at such a height that, gained the top, beneath the forms of men had shrunk to merest specks, the fivesome climbed. The topside structures, thronged with folk who shouted, jostled, bales conveyed to waiting ships, ticket booth by booth displayed to service from each pier the outbound hordes. Far-off across the glittering plain were moored a score or more of craft their turn awaiting. From central tower commanding all the port, high-mounted watchmen did with flags of hue and pattern diverse to the ships below their signals send.

Through tumult and the press, on wooden streets with traffic humming, Erwo the party led, until the gate they neared whose legend "Beridh-Ostaith" proudly bore. Here passage for the five secured, they clambered aboard. But here no banks of seats Pabi found, bunks for repose instead, and tables where meals to consume. Like inn in motion planned, one deck for sleeping, one for company and viands, and below, for provender, for crew, and hygiene's needs, the vessel seemed. The mariners themselves the topmost tier did busy tread, to cast off making ready.

Departure's hour on point of striking, Erwo Pabi

below at table spied, and hied to her. "Come, lass, thou wouldst not this marvel miss!" He cried and took her hand. At touch of palm in belly strange a flutter stirred. He drew her up on deck in moment opportune to hear the first mate's clear command ring out to loose all bonds. Astern the steersman hauled on levers, brakes released, while forward hands drew ropes, and wide the major sails unfurled. With windy fingers tugged, they snapped and boomed. The ship, first slow, then fast, away did surge as foremast, mizzen, jigger, more canvas yet abeam let fall, til crowned she rode with vanes, a half-wheel's arc describing, swollen full with wind's aid, as though the bounding main, not wastes of sand, her natural element.

Before her face Pabi the sandy breeze felt, and o'er the side in wonder peered to see the shielded wheels on granules rise and fall. Once more that avian thrill her senses clad as the wide world rushed by, horizons vast their arms extending to engulf her round. She at the rail did lean, eyes blissful closed, a smile upon her lips. Then steadying hand her shoulder touched, and voice beside her spoke: "Have caution, Pabi!" Straight she stood, one palm the bulwark grasping as the pitching deck o'er dune and trough in swooping progress ran, as ships on rollers plow the furrowed brine.

To Erwo's kindly eyes she looked and caught her quickened breath. As gazed she on his face, that leaping in her core, unsettling, sweet, confusion bred. Its cause to ship ascribe, or to some deeper, unguessed power impute, lodged in the breast of him now smiling bright, she could not with conviction yet conclude.

Upon the second day, as Sun's orb toward western rim inclined, they disembarked at Beridh-Ostaith, town of breadth alike to that before, yet built on firmer ground, sans stilts, and docks of more restrained extent. Their vessel, though, all others there surpassed in grandeur. Round the square, the staples all of settlement—the shop, the inn, the stable with beasts for lease. Here Erwo purses loosed for five fair dromedaries, which they mounted and turned toward southwest.

Pabi's steed did plod in even pace with Erwo's, on whose face, as to the dig they neared, pure bliss suffused, which, spied, in Pabi sympathetic joy enkindled. "Much I long to thee impart," he said with grin unfeigned, "of all these wonders, yet fear my zeal, in thee no echo finding, will prove but dull. And more my thoughts defy the bonds of speech but crave the visual proof. Yet—ah!—one prize above the rest stands out, which to unveil I burn with scarce-pent haste! I pray it please thee…"

On and on he rhapsodized, as Pabi, rapt, each syllable drank in, and smiled to see him all with fervor glow—a passion she with secret envy marked, herself of such intensity devoid. Two hours thus sped, when sudden to his friends, engrossed with Baiwieth in colloquy, Erwo gave cry: "The site is well-nigh reached! Mark yonder rise—our goal lies just beyond!" This said, he spurred his camel to a run, Rilun and Fehi close behind. Pabi likewise bestirred her mount to brisker step, as Baiwieth pulled up abreast.

"I see," the latter smiled, with lip half-cocked in glee, "Erwo and thee a bond have forged apace."

Pabi, her face composed, rejoinder made: "Thy meaning is obscure."

"Come, think not I am blind!" the other pressed. At this a blush Pabi's cheek suffused; she kicked her beast anew, and up the slope it climbed, far from her friend, til crest was gained, and Kollan ab-Kes lay in prospect wide unfurled.

All preconception it mocked. No paltry hamlet-plot was this, with few sad timbers rotted, and some stones in ancient paths inset—nay, but a vast expanse, with Jub Khewi in scale matched, or e'en Goreuhwo's metropolitan sprawl. Posts without number did its bounds delimit, where dig concluded and the wild sands yawned. One quarter of the city limits, scooped from shrouding drifts, alone a township's scope encompassed. Sunken deep by ages' weight, in banded strata were the patient years here chronicled, since last this storied site the radiance of day caressed. From high upon the hill, a panoptic view was grasped. Square structures manifold of russet hue, in rock or petrified wood shaped, a grid of streets, flagged underfoot, interwove. All this did a massive stone pyramid command.

Upon the works, in gloves and wielding tools of fine-tipped edge and point, scores labored on, some armed with naught save stylus, ink, and leaf the unearthed treasures to depict. Like ants amid the excavations' grand extent they toiled—apt image of this seat of pride and power, o'er desert-sea once dominant, to puny band reduced, its majesty mere hollowed rugosities, by time defaced. Below, at footslope, Erwo and his friends stood clustered, and the women summoned down to join them. There, in hat broad-brimmed and garb of expedition-leader, stout of build, a figure did they greet—Agwayabo, the youths' preceptor. He, espying them, his hands on hips in stern-browed stance composed.

"By Heaven, my boys," he said, "I've been distraught nigh unto madness. Word but lately came of what in Goreuhwo passed, that fearsome brood, the gwerfegi—I feared the very worst! Why sent ye no assuring messenger?"

Then Erwo, light dismounting, clasped his hand, and round him threw a swift embrace. "Awhile no means we had; and then, such lack continued. But here we've won at last—and lo! what strides I mark since our departure! Holy Muse, sing glory unto sweet Tuláhujut!"

Here to the women turning, tilted hat in greeting, the Professor spoke: "Well met! Agwayabo I am called—these scamps' duenna and taskmaster." They in turn their names announced, as Erwo told the tale of their conjoined adventures.

"Have ye two," Agwayabo asked, "in matters ancient and interred a curious bent?"

"No," Pabi owned, "but sure, the spectacle doth compensate for prior disregard."

"For my part," said Baiwieth, "though history's charms I've long esteemed, they ne'er to vocational thoughts gave rise, much less did I the archaeologic arts with favor view."

"Ah," said the sage, "our field doth strangely

satisfy—and, mark you, bring rewards unforeseen..." Waving them to follow, he led them, five abreast, the dig to circle. "Most oft," he said, "our labor is but ink and vellum, or the shifting granular residues, for precious jots in quest. That last—the sifting process—Erwo here esteems above the rest. Odd duck, this lad!" Erwo to Pabi turned, eyes all alight. "The little things," he rhapsodized, "they draw my deepest reverence. Toys once clutched in hands of innocents, or combs through woman's hair drawn lovingly, or shards of earthen jar, or blades to hew and shape. They make it real, as naught else may—that flesh and blood, with hopes and cares as ours, once vivified these relics. When such I hold, mere specks, 'tis then I feel... How to define? The sense of transport, yea, the soaring of the spirit, as on wings invisible..."

In Erwo's eye a gleam not hitherto remarked by Pabi shone, and she in full reciprocation smiled. Agwayabo, grinning in his beard, some secret with his pupils seemed to share—marked straight by Fehi, who exclaimed, "Again, good doctor, thou that look assumest which saith more than thy tongue proclaims. I hate that look!"

"Indeed," chimed Erwo, "make us not to guess, for we are sore forspent."

In furtive tones, the Master whispered, "We a thing have found..."

At this did Erwo's eyes grow wide. "Some great discovery?"

"In very deed."

"Oh, say—is it Pervikhseryedhi's rest at last?"

The elder chuckled. "Peace, overeager youth!

Not that mighty—yet still a strike of note. Full glad I am thou art back; I scarce could bide until the secret shared. Though but of late—a few scant days—the treasure came to light."

"But what, O what?" cried Erwo, all aquiver. "To horse—or camel—and I'll lead the way!" Remounted all, Agwayabo afoot preceding, to the north he led. For miles, a tireless pace he struck, nor slacked until, 'twixt three low mesas, they at last arrived where busy excavators plied their trade. A woman, rapt, some large-scaled sketch limned, while round a void rectangular, just of size one form to pass, a dozen more made play with delicate-seeming tools. From this dark slot, cut in the baked substrate, a flickering glow of lamps escaped.

From saddle vaulting, Erwo exclaimed, "Ye gods! A tomb—why kept ye mum?" Then to the pit he flew, yet ere he plunged, to Pabi turned, and urged her to his side, that they as one the fated threshold cross. So down they went, the narrow stone-bound way, Agwayabo behind, all wreathed in smiles, in this his coup exulting. Lantern-lit, the passage ran, until it flared at last into a chamber spacious.

Pabi gasped. On every wall, in pigment rich and carving, one figure towered, of aspect grave, with beard full-flowing, and in stature all who round him were depicted overpeering. Strange glyphs beside each image stood, which Pabi took for Kollan's ancient script, to her opaque.

But Erwo to the frescoes strode, and palms in reverence o'er their contours passed, as he the archaic phrases voiced—that dusty tongue which long from living memory had lapsed. Some minutes thus immersed, he turned at last to Pabi, and in voice tear-choked exclaimed: "Stupendous! Nigh intact and limned with skill and grace surpassing—I'm overwhelmed, my friend!"

Now Fehi, Rilun to the task bent, the writings to decipher, as the rest the polychrome depictions, wrought with care meticulous, perused in silent awe. There too lay treasures—lo! a golden car, and kingly seat, and giant chest of stone whose amplitude might three inurn with ease, prone at the chamber's heart...

His shining eyes Erwo now dabbed, and of his guide inquired: "Whose is this sepulcher?"

"Why, yonder lord's," replied the sage, and pointed where the form heroic bulked upon the painted wall. "But here," he said, "the sarcophagus' reverse inspect with care."

"Is that the term for this?" asked Pabi, wondering. "Doth it him contain?"

"What else?" smiled Agwayabo. "To pry wide its seal, we did forbear til our bright stars—returned from wanderings—could partake. I ween young Erwo, left unwitnessed, would have slain me!"

"I would, upon my troth!" the scholar laughed. Then, indicating one tableau, where two male forms in portrait stood, unequal matched—the greater, and the less, with diadem adorned—beside an inscription placed, he mused aloud: "Is that who I divine?"

"Doth it spell out a name?" asked Pabi, curious. Erwo, near transport, read:

"Pervikhseryedhi!" And once more dashed the salt rheum from his cheek. "Whoever herein doth lie was to that king bound close. What man, Agwayabo, deemest thou this carved and frescoed crypt might memorize?"

The elder stroked his chin. "His core and thews, so lovingly anatomized, and sooth, adjacent to the very king he served, perforce bespeak a more than mortal strain. The demigod of whom the epics rhyme might well, I think, have earned such tribute rare."

"It cannot be!" cried Erwo, thunderstruck. "Then too, at last, his long-lost name we'll know!" So saying, to the painted cycles first he made recourse. "Come, Pabi—here's a thing I must to thee impart."

To wall she came, as he the alien characters and scenes expounded. "Note," he said, "this cartouche—see how round the glyphs a clear enclosure runs? So did they all designations mark nominal. But Keshic writing in this wise is flawed, that to their script the vowels they ne'er confide. Some few appellations—Pervikhseryedhi, to name the chief—from foreign pens we know, whence the gaps to bridge. But else, we must devise our own conventions—eh for all the lacunae. A labor, I'll confess, of years to master, and still incomplete. But behold!—'tis here writ plain, our hero's name: Erenkigwokh, brother to Pervikhseryedhi, the son of Meleg, deity revered." The scribe fell back a pace, a mighty sigh slow heaving, and in widest grin dissolved.

"That name thou recognizest not?" asked Pabi.

"In sooth, 'tis strange to me. But that he stood to Pervikhseryedhi so close in blood and heart, as brother e'en to be acclaimed—there's matter for conjecture! Meleg sired, it saith—a god his father. All my thought it shatters. The divine protagonist of lore we have, Agwayabo, exhumed!" So crying, to the floor he dropped, and there a quick press did; then, springing up, the air he boxed in pantomime pugilistic. Pabi his transport with a laugh indulged, as he, abashed, exclaimed, "Thy pardon, friend—the excitement whelms me sore. Since summers six this dream I've nourished, and now to see it approach fruition... But I babble. When may we prise wide this casket's treasured lid?"

"With all dispatch," Agwayabo said. "My brain I've racked, anticipating thee, nor can I wait this vault's hoard to disclose!"

Grasping his sense, Erwo cried, "Of course! This tomb, Kollan's own Valley of the Kings proclaims—the Epic tells Erenkigwokh by Pervikhseryedhi's side was laid in that most sacrosanct of hero-crypts! Somewhere adjacent, then, that greater king inurned awaits our spade—a mile, perhaps, or less..." Again that suspirant release, that swaying, as in swoon. Supporting him, lest he should totter, Pabi clasped his arm. "I'm well," he reassured, "but life til now about this moment's pole has turned—what shall my compass be, this longed-for goal attained? But to our task—come, let us breach the seal!"

Agwayabo now hied him forth to fetch all tools and aids of force the job required, while the three scholars at their ciphering toiled.

"For thee, my friend," to Erwo Baiwieth said, "mine heart overflows with gladness. How sublime, this privilege—to watch the event unfold!"

But Erwo scarce had leisure to return more than swift smile of thanks, so rapt was he. "When him we find—great Pervikhseryedhi—I know not how I shall with joy comport!"

Then Baiwieth, "To lend a hand above, they may have need. I'll to their aid repair."

Pabi's back she stroked and quit the space.

Fehi pursued her, saying, "Yea, for this unsealing, stout equipment must they bear down to this depth. Come, Rilun, let us too offer our sinews to convey the stuff."

"I'm with thee," Rilun said, and out they paced, Erwo and Pabi leaving sole within. A time passed, Erwo bent on the inscribed and colorific wonders.

"Canst thou read," asked Pabi, "all that here doth stand preserved?"

"Most, verily," he said. "So far, the tale doth but recite his provenance divine, and bond of soul to Pervikhseryedhi. No mention of a mother—Meleg's son, and that alone, 'twould seem. And yet, withal, as brother to the king he's hailed. Most strange—from chronicles we know that king but one male issue had, Lakaos his sire."

"Then might," Pabi proposed, "this paragon have shared a mother with the king—what was her name?"

"Ponnëagwerfor," Erwo supplied, but his brow he knit in negative. "That scarce doth fit the established facts. For had that queen an illicit passion nursed, both she and child misbegot had the extreme penalty paid with their lives. And sooth, had some less dame great Lakaos known, and male whelp sprung from such, our archives would that lineage record, for Kollan's scribes all patrilines set down, however irregular. Which sole conjecture admits—that no blood-tie, but amity alone, 'twixt Erenkigwokh and majesty the brother-bond created. Likeliest, the king's soul-mate and dearest boon companion."

Pabi absorbed all this, as deep in thought. Agwayabo now hied him back, with youths Rilun and Fehi, and Baiwieth, and a band of savants bearing levers shaped of iron. The five, new-armed, in ring the great stone chest surrounded, as spectators against the walls tiered themselves, keen to view the lid unsealed. With stakes at edge of closure placed, they poised.

"My fellows," said Agwayabo, "this capstone, rightly applied, should yield to forceful stroke. Is all in readiness? Asfer, thy bar an inch depress. Just so. My signal watch—to prying we'll as one our sinews bend. One, two, and... heave!"

With grunts and tremulous gasps they bore down, and a slab of three-inch thickness grudging did lift, affording half-inch chink all round. The Master cried, "Withhold! Withhold! Now Goa, Barthivo, and Ena, ye your stakes into the gap insert—well done! The rest, like action take. Attend anew—conjointly once again! One, two... and thrust!"

The massive lid yet further heaved, and now Agwayabo directed: "Ye that side, yet higher raise your purchase, while my flank doth ease the pressure, so..." The lid did tilt, then full aside with thunderous report crashed down, in twain asunder split, its edge sharp-fractured by the ungentle fall.

"Alas!" cried Pabi. "May that harm forever be mended?"

The sage but waved dismissive hand. "'Twas but the outer carapace for larger gem within. Come all, and marvel, as do I!"

What sight astounding! Huddled round, they peered forever into the opened vault, wherein a golden coffin shimmered, effigy of him whose form the walls did replicate in every part and member, down to dress and facial features—yea, with sapphire eyes to life reanimated, noble brow by gold locks wreathed, and beard of purest gold in many-plaited splendor worked! A robe the torso clad, half to the knee depending, yet chest Herculean bare to sight disclosed. Like carven oaks the stalwart legs did stand, in lapis-hued sandals terminating, while all along the gilded sarcophagus glyphs cryptic and chromatic gem-inlay—lazuli, bloodstone, alabaster pale—their fascination plied.

With digit trembling, Erwo reached out and touched the aurific sheen, then full-length shuddered, as at god's caress. "Ye might supernal," sighed he, "this bequest of ancient craft and reverence whelms my sense! The colors, and the fine-wrought sculpturing, millennia-sealed, yet glowing as when new—'tis nigh to see, and scarcely to believe!"

To Fehi, Rilun motioned. Both approached the legend-freighted flanks, and with hushed voice did the dead tongue articulate. But Pabi, as eke Baiwieth, could but stand enthralled, the myriad wonders—gold, and ornament, and costly stuff—imbibing.

Swabbed once more his trickling eyes, and to the elder turned, spake Erwo: "Whose, Agwayabo, deemest thou these relics of renown? Whose royal dust doth this most gorgeous receptacle hold?"

At this, to one graven panel pointing, where twin male forms—the taller, and the less, with carcanet becrowned—conjoint did stand, he asked, "Yon second figure—read I right?"

"Here," said Agwayabo, "close inspect the dedicative script."

To lettered group stepped Pabi. "Is that, as I think, his name?"

Scarce could he articulate for brimming joy: "Indeed—see, Pervikhseryedhi, just there!" Then, scanning the inscription, he went on: "Within this sanctum, Erenkigwokh is laid, Great Pervikhseryedhi's brother—his soul, with ancestress and forebears all conjoined, in realm of shades its domicile hath made. A goddess bore him, and the gods all bless. This coffer by high Peremet, priestess, is dedicate. The vault wherein it rests by Pervikhseryedhi, king, bestowed."

In chamber wrapped in silence of the tomb, the company as one deep reverence paid, with slow-inclined heads and sober mien, unto the kingly dead their homage due. Then one, Barthivo, on Erwo's shoulder a comrade's clasp bestowed, and softly said: "So close we are—dost thou not feel it, friend?"

"Yea, close as ne'er before," the scholar sighed, fresh tears unwiped. "Each rising Sun brings nearer bright advent of that day for which I've yearned!"

———

When Sun beneath the horizon dipped her lamp, the scholars young a mighty blaze did build, round which Agwayabo all the camp convened to break their bread, and tidings glad relate of treasure late unveiled by sweat and spade. With viands, melody, and nimble step the eve they passed, and converse blithe exchanged, til laughter reigned, and mirth held sovereign sway.

When vault of heaven with stars was stippled o'er, and Moon's orb on high her argent beam cast down, in knots more close the company drew, upon the cooling sand reclined, to share reflections intimate. Though first their talk round dig and artifact circled, soon it roamed to matters various, til each was stripped of wonted academic guise, and shone as individual sole, all roles forgot.

Pabi and Baiwieth with Erwo sat, Rilun and Fehi by their sides, and more of their collegium joined. The merriment of festal night so Pabi's sense absorbed, she scarce to jests or reminiscence attended, but when her eyes on Erwo lit, as oft they did, she with his every smile was moved accordant joy to feign. New aspects now of visage and of frame she marked—the bridge of nose by slight protuberance uneven, the lashes long that framed his lucent eyes... On these her gaze so fixed, he caught her full in act of rapt perusal. With a start, she looked away—and felt, with strange effect, his hand on hers descending, gentle, warm. A pulse-beat's space she lingered, seized with doubt, then drew back, rising with a murmured, "Pray, excuse me for a moment," and with arms about her drawn to fend the encroaching chill, into the empty desert night withdrew.

Erwo pursued, with hasty steps overtaking her form receding. "Pabi," he exclaimed, "if by my forwardness I did offend, or cause thee aught unease, I sorely rue my rash presumption. 'Twas not my intent twixt us to cast a shade, or mar what bond—"

She turned to him, but full eye-contact shunned, her glance fixed groundward by his feet. A sigh heaved from her breast. "Nay, thou art not at fault. 'Tis I... There's much thou dost not comprehend of my soul's history—more than e'en my friend Baiwieth hath been confided. Trials sore, and griefs unnumbered, have my steps pursued, whereof I dare not speak, nor yet endure to look upon..." She paused, and shook her head, as tears unbidden to her lids did start. "Forgive me," came her whisper strained.

With clasp consoling, Erwo on her arm his hand did lay, and gently pressed. "Nay, Pabi, 'tis I should beg thy pardon. For those wounds occult thou bearest, let none demand account, or bid thee convalescence feign ere thou art whole. Heal at thine own just pace—not when by some external voice enjoined, or sense of oughtness impelled."

Upon her now he smiled—no grin with wonted mirth suffused, but tender, grave, and luminous with sympathy sincere. She could but like expression kind return.

Then, half-averting mien, "Where shall our rest this night be found?" He pointed past the range of their encampment. "Yonder, nigh yon rise, pavilions manifold are pitched, to house gear and research. But these overpassed, thou shalt find more modest lodgings meant for traveler's ease. I craved the foremen space for thee to make, and for Baiwieth—tarry there as long as heart impels thee stay."

With grateful look, she bade him, "Gracious dreams!" as he the path back to the festal scene retraced. Inside the sleeping-tent she slipped, and on a cot untenanted sank down, deep night to embrace.

When next Aurora with her roseate hand the gates of orient morn flung wide, a day of toil yet more intense Erwo absorbed, with comrades studious and Agwayabo sage, deep in the sepulcher their skills to ply, recording all in chart and document. Pabi, to solitude that morn inclined, and shy from one whose presence now so moved her inmost core, from their endeavors stood aloof.

Baiwieth, marking her intent to keep sequestered, though full fain to join the learned crew, at Pabi's side remained. "No heart have I today," the latter owned, "to mingle in that press so animated."

Beneath awning broad she refuge sought, at bench for scribal tasks designed, and there reclined, the coolness savoring. When midday came, to her an instructress, Oma, refreshment bore in welcome bowl and cup. With gratitude avowed, Pabi partook of beans and tart-sweet nectar of the lime. Oma beside her sat on sheltering sand.

"Thou art Pabi, art thou not?" At nod affirmed, "My name is Oma," she in turn disclosed. "I thought this day thou wouldst by Erwo's side be found."

Pabi, in act to lift a spoonful, paused. "Why wouldst thou so conceive?"

Song of the Crickets

The other gave but shrug, nor pressed the inquiry sensitive. Instead she to the musing maid outlined with dreaming eye the glorious citadel, as once it proudly stood with cedar beams and templed stone adorned. Pabi her meal concluded, taciturn.

When Sun declined, the unwearied band led back, their chief-in-heart, Pabi despite herself with eager welcome tingled to perceive. Though tempted sore with query warm to haste unto him, and full circumstantial seek account of all his day's adventures held, that impulse she with rigor quelled, but watched at remove how, from group to group, he passed with genial cheer and ever-gracious mien. Such popularity, she mused, bespoke a spirit singular.

Whenever his peers, in labor's interludes, did him extol for skill and sapience, inly she agreed, recalling all his gest and port revealed of passion for his metier—how his smile beamed radiant, a potsherd worn in hand, or eyes and lips in joint amazement parsed some fragmentary graven rune—or how, in hark to others' reports, his head would tilt, giving each speaker sense he sole did merit regard so rapt, inspiring all who came within that aura cordial to lingering stay, fain to prolong the golden moment's charm with chat however desultory, but glad to claim his friendship's all-absolving balm.

Immersed in reverie, Pabi scarce kenned when Erwo, from an excavation clambered, toward her, dusting hands, his footsteps bent. Before her now he stood and proffered bold his open palm. "Come," he entreated, eyes alight, "what yestereve I pledged to share—dost thou recall?—e'en now I'd fain reveal!"

Assent unvoiced, she laid her hand in his, but, once arisen, loosed the electric clasp. With pace sedate, through Kollan's ruined ways, he led her to the temple vast of stone reared at the boreal extreme, hard by that palace-complex once of fragrant wood. Behind the fane he brought her, to a ledge of masonry where, 'twixt two mighty blocks, a print of human hand, in mortar pressed when wet and new, her startled glance transfixed.

Voice hushed with awe, said Erwo, "Here behold what doth entrance me most in all this place. See..." And her wrist with gentlest touch he grasped, guiding her stretched fingers to the groove. They nestled there, congruent, palm to palm with that dead artisan whose labors raised the soaring pile. "Reflect," he whispered on, "four thousand years ago, some nameless soul, devout and diligent, wrought here, amidst a host of fellow-toilers. As they strove to rear this fitting mansion for their gods—gods loved with passion, sought with earnest prayer—this one, this very mason, in the spot thou occupyest, indented this mute sign. He lived, as we—knew thirst and hunger, sneeze and cough, the glow of health, the pangs of flu, the spectrum of emotion—tears and glee, elation, wrath, and all that 'twixt them lies. Four millennia vanished—yet this trace remains, an unimpeachable attest to one real being, else to time's abyss surrendered, lost for aye."

As Erwo spoke, Pabi beheld him, utterly enthralled. However his rapt gaze on that print remained, seeming the imagined past to infiltrate, she only him could see. The inward surge, that flutter hitherto love's harbinger, now quite subsided, leaving in its place a deepening calm, a sweet complacency, as when two streams, long sundered, reunite, or familial wounds of old find sudden balm. Ne'er had she known such swift, complete repose in any mortal presence—yet that thought itself bred agitation. What if he, this paragon of kindness, intellect, and zeal emphatic, craved to know her past, that trail of woes which even to herself she dared not oft retrace? All, all would she to him disclose, did he but ask! The mere conception with unease her soul oppressed.

Fingers from antique matrix disengaged, "I must away," she gasped, and headlong fled, him leaving dumbstruck and dismayed. Hot tears blinding her course, she to her tent repaired, there on her pallet flung herself, and wept as if her very heart would break. Face pressed into the unfeeling pillow, sobs she muffled, unstanched til sinking day to gloaming turned, and stilled to silence, save where two—Baiwieth and some companion—entered, all absorbed in chat of matters trivial.

But soon, Baiwieth, quick-eyed, Pabi's prone form marked, and straight concern overcame her brow, as down she sat beside those feet in anguish writhed. Upon one shin her hand consoling fell. "O Pabi, what's amiss?" Her friend replied with naught save gusty, elaborated sigh. Gently Baiwieth shook the indicated limb. "Come, rouse thee, and attend me out of doors—I must some earnest words with thee exchange."

"Nowhere," came Pabi's smothered moan, "I'd go!"

"Now, now," her mate insisted, "or I'll hale thee

forth by ungentle duress!"

Pabi heaved again a mighty sough, but slow uprose, and out into the gloaming traced the steps of her so tender yet so stern a guide. Behind the hillock's sheltering bulk they paused.

"What are thy schemes?" asked Baiwieth, arms enfolded, "Touching Erwo?"

"My schemes?" the other parroted, throat taut with strangled feeling.

"Nay, I beg, affect not this dull ignorance! Thou knowest—and know I too—the crux of thy soul's care!"

Fresh tears astart, Pabi could scarce emit the syllables: "I cannot do it, cannot—"

"Do what, my sweet? Speak plain!"

"Why, anything pertaining to Erwo," the lady explained, voice cracking under passion's weight. "Thou hast no notion—nor has he—what trials, what griefs, have mired my path—shades which no sun can assuage, crimes even penitence can scarce unwrite! For him and me no happy end could be—best shun the dear temptation at the root!"

With sage and sober mien, Baiwieth nodded. "Some part I do surmise. Give ear, dear friend—a leaf from mine own history, seldom oped. When but a child, to bondage I was sold, my father's debts to acquit. As maid I served that household cruel, so exiled from mine own, til on a day arrived a stranger kind, with naught save horse and purse his name to establish. Some mere few days he tarried—yet in that span, such sweet discourse, such meeting of the minds, twixt him and me like golden thread was spun! Alas, our host—my master—forced his guest too soon to quit his hall. But ere he rode, that man of magnanimity supreme his mount, the noble Boriwar, bestowed to ransom me—my bondage to annul! Of love, no act more pure could e'er be writ. Yet brief his life thereafter—with his lord to death betrayed. I never did again his form or voice encounter. But that horse I kept, in testimonial eloquent to goodness, and to love unfeigned."

Pabi, arrested, interposed: "But thou—didst love him—thy deliverer?"

"In my mode," Baiwieth slowly said, "as he in his. But that our modes were sundered, time would prove. An almost-love it was—in speaking looks during some crowded feast exchanged, or smiles flashed back and forth as he some cherished tale from my far birthplace told; in tingling thrills at each fortuitous brush of sleeve or hip. Of loves, the almost-love's the worst by far—pregnant with ifs, heavy with vain regrets. To know joy might have burgeoned, but for chance malign, 'tis woe itself! Yet woe however excruciating, I would ne'er repent, were he alone the occasion and the cause."

She lapsed to silence, as these pondered things Pabi absorbed. At last, in accents faint, "I love not Erwo," she professed—but met Baiwieth's wry, assured smile.

"So thou sayest—yet some emotion grips thee, past thy ken. To probe its depth thou dreadst. Thy face betrays the war within: each day, each night, thou strivest, by force of will, by prayer, by distraction, him from thy mind and soul to exorcise, yet ne'er quite escapest his aura. At his name thy pulse doth leap—his merest step, his scent perceived, perturb thee, set thy wits awhirl!"

She broke off, and as listening Pabi marked the tone, its timbre, its impassioned lilt, suspicion dawned of loves yet unrevealed. "He's not a nullity to thee, I'll wage," Baiwieth pressed—but Pabi answer lacked.

Her throat, by wild emotion choked and swelled, no sound could utter, lest that sound extend into a storm of weeping uncontrolled. "Come hither," coaxed the other, arms outspread in comfort's offer. To that haven Pabi took eager flight, cheek laid to shoulders broad, as long, slow strokes her corded tresses smoothed. "No sin nor weakness 'tis, to hold one dear!"

Pabi clutched close this friend of all her friends. "I do love thee," she vowed, her vocals moist with salt rheum scarce restrained, "as sister of mine heart, my spirit's prop, my very soul! Thou only hast such empathy displayed."

Upon her brow Baiwieth kissed, and said, "I heard thee, when with Agwayabo late conversing, speak as if for Jub Khewi thou meanest erelong depart. Is this thy plan?"

Pabi but sniffed. "I know not—I must think!" From that embrace she wried herself, and toward her tent with laggard, pensive tread repaired. The night's cool stillness soon enclosed her round.

In hushed obscurity the camp was drowned, save where, from one pavilion's flap, did spill a beam of brightness, painting desert chill with its pellucid gold. That lamp revealed Erwo within, o'er some small object bent in studious scrutiny. Pabi paused, first raised to heaven one swift, beseeching glance, then with firm stride the glowing entrance sought. Alert to steps without, the immersed young sage his curly head reared up, face wreathed in warmth.

"What ho!" he greeted, "Thou, abroad so late? Come, see what treasure I inspect and judge!"

She ducked into the tent and leaned to peer at that he proffered 'twixt gentle palms. No more it was than humble figurine, of wood contrived, clad in a shift of cloth, its girlish features flecked with faded gold.

"This moves me to the quick," said Erwo soft, "these small mementos. Some dear child, long gone, once clasped this image to her guileless breast, with it held discourse, to it lent a name, lavished untold affection—until time decreed her too mature for so poor a proxy. Mislaid? Discarded? All her joy and woe, her secret hopes, her disappointments keen, lost in the insensate void... yet here survives her cherished plaything, to none other traced, mute witness to a fate beyond our ken."

At this most intimate splinter of surmise, Pabi averted eyes a-brim, and sighed. "Erwo, 'tis needful I commune with thee..."

Quick to her tone, he set his relic by. "Of course—what presses, friend?"

"Might we retire a pace beyond the camp, and there confer?" He doused his lamp and rose; together then under the moon's blanched aegis they progressed, til well apart from work and slumber's range. There Pabi faced him. "I would tell a tale—my tale—its darkest chapters hid before e'en from myself. Thou must my past explore, ere... ere between us…" But her voice here failed.

Stumbling at first, then with momentum gained from need's imperative, she poured her griefs, from parents' loss, through servitude and shame, a love and a child lost, then friends as well, to their first meeting beyond fate's cruel flood. As she spoke on, tears welled afresh—and then Erwo in strong, consoling arms her swept, there to his breast to sob her anguish out. With wordless murmur, soft caress, he soothed that storm, while she to resignation drooped.

At last he said, "For thy past woes and wrongs, I'd ne'er upbraid—nay, love more deep would spring from glimpse of all thy spirit's scars, which are no blight upon its beauty, but its gems. Thine history's the basis of thy self, as mine of me—whatever has scarred, has formed to highest, purest ends."

More words of grace thus showered he, til Pabi lapsed to calm. Still on his chest her brow reposed, as she his heartbeat timed, its rhythm hypnotizing. So full enfolded, so at one, she thought, ne'er had she been before, yet now she was where fate ordained, and rightly.

"Erwo, I…" Suspended, her avowal hung.

He prompted, "Yes?"

And she, all hesitation shed, exhaled in dulcet accents, "I do love thee."

Around her lissome figure his embrace constrictive grew, a pressure of pure bliss, as with brush-light kiss, he echoed back, "I, sweet Pabi, do love thee too."

At this, her soul, long cumbered and oppressed, soared free as lark at morn, on wings of joy. Against his frame, so stalwart yet so kind, she nestled close, nor recked of morrow's chance, but drank this timeless moment as elixir against all prior bane and future dread. Head pillowed thus, lids fluttered shut, a smile beak-like upon her mouth—so they remained as minutes trickled on, at peace, content, two hearts, two minds, two essences now fused in mutual passion and respect.

When thrice the Sun had blazed its daily arc, Rilun from Valley of the Kings returned, with summons for Erwo to join him there. On camel-back the trio made their way—Pabi and Erwo and their herald brave—to that sepulchral plot where late they'd found Erenkigwoth's eternal bed of stone.

Agwayabo greeted them with steaming cups of Kalayo's famed brew, rich and robust, though Day had scarcely her eye unclosed.

Pabi partook with relish, each hot draught savoring as nectar of the gods.

Then spake the sage: "Erwo, I deem we have divined the resting-place of sundry royal dead, but yet their portals seal inviolate. I crave thy practiced judgment, to assign each tomb its proper denizen."

Erwo, with alacrity, replied, "Lead on, and I shall strive thy trust to vindicate!"

A quarter-mile or less they rode, due east of that late-opened vault, til they drew rein where Fehi and his comrades plied their spades, flags marking bounds of promising terrain. One hollow they had delved, some few feet deep; thither Agwayabo led his guests.

"Behold," quoth he, "our foremost find! Note

there, above the entablature, an inscription rude, but pregnant with portent. Descend, my boy, and lend thine arts to its decipherment!"

Into the trench the eager scholar leapt, there stooping low to scrutinize the script half-hid by grit of ages. Loud he read: "'Here lies'... a name untraceable... 'queen of Kollan ab-Kes, and mother to...' Another lacuna! 'Wife of...' The residue hath crumbled past retrieval. Strange the glyphs that yet endure—to me, at least, occult. Pabi, attend—the dwellers in this vale oft chose to nominate themselves by signs and rebuses of individual cast, requiring prior cognizance to parse."

Thus saying, from the excavation climbed Erwo, and to a rough trestle table made his way, the rest close-following behind. There sat he, brow contracted, while his hand described the cryptic characters anew with stylus brisk. "Agwayabo," he asked, finger to page, "Doth this not strike thine eye as mes—behold the ibis-shape, and here, this element?"

His mentor peered. "Perhaps! I grant the likeness—and but two glyphs the name compose, guessing should pose slight toil. Pursue this line—assume the mes. What then make we of its companion?"

Erwo tapped his implement on chin, and slow replied: "A bloom it seems to figure, but its type evades me sore—not lem, nor het. I own my perfect blank! Withal, 'tis best we dig yet more, the while I ponder."

With a nod, the prof his crew led back to excavate, but Pabi, eyeing Erwo's sketched cartouche, observed, "That second glyph—a lotus bud?"

"Just so!" he cried, "But in our storied king's day and domain, no lotus ever grew."

"Mayhap," she ventured, "as thou didst explain, the queen herself this symbol chose, to mind some distant clime where that fair flower bloomed, and she had wandered once."

His visage glowed. "Thou reasonest like a sage! Yet that alone rips not the knot. Where in her age, now gone, did lotus rise?" Pensive, he lapsed, then said: "Deulen, perchance, or by the Pyaro's banks—then Aunlen yclept—in Bomba's fenny realm."

"Those tongues," asked Pabi, "hast thou conned a mite?"

"Some scraps and shards," he shrugged, but she pressed on: "The word for lotus in old Khemic—how would it in our script sound?" His eyes toward Heaven he cast, and sighed, "Gil, I believe, or near that strain."

"There," Pabi cried, "thou hast thy key. Align it with yon glyph, and mark if sense emerge!"

Bent to his task, Erwo all variations tried, as one who plays at tumblers til the lock gives way. "Kilmes—kelmes—gelmes—gilmes..." At this last he stopped and stared in sudden transport rapt.

"What quickens thee?" asked Pabi, "What result?"

But he, as if unhearing, scanned once more the entire legend, here and there a jot inserting... then afoot he sprang, and bade Agwayabo to him hie with utmost speed. The grey-beard sped to join him, while the twain ecstatic colloquy commenced, too low for Pabi's ears to apprehend distinct. At last she cried, "I pray thee, speak! What news?"

"Queen Somdhëo," said Erwo, voice a-throb with tense surmise, "was Gilmesh's royal dam, and great Pervikhseryedhi's consort sweet. That hero-monarch's wife (if I parse true) in yon dark cell forever lies embowered—which signifies her sometime lord and love hard by, perhaps straight underfoot, is laid! At least in one of those choice plots we've staked for imminent assault!"

Agwayabo mused: "The third sarcophagus I'd stake belongs to Gilmesh's own self—if so, we'll bare the full immediate household of our king of kings, vicegerent of high heaven!"

At this, Erwo turned ashen pale, then lobster-red. "Hot chills," he gasped, "along my limbs career, as if with fever caught—yet such a fever as goads to motion unrestrained. I could outpace the leopard, and the eagle's flight laugh to disdain!" But curbing that wild mood, he but embraced his Pabi with a kiss as chaste as irresistible, full on the brow bestowing that sweet seal—then off he flew to where his busy fellows toiled, there to resume his sapper's tool of trade, with thrice the verve of his first dig.

A smile, knowing yet tolerant, usurped the sage's wrinkled physiognomy. "He is a lad of passion and of parts, our Erwo, what? Mine heart, like thine, doth dance to witness thus his lifelong grail approach his yearning grasp. I've watched him, from a beardless boy, pursue this quarry with an agent all-consuming, brooking no rival, shunning each diversion, in converse, reverie, and dream alike questing his Pervikhseryedhi! And now, now that the prize looms palpable at last, I wonder... will his tongue find other tunes than this its monochord refrain? Or will discovery but lend new impetus to that obsession?"

Here the elder paused, as if in recollection wrapped. "We who the elusive past's enigmas would unriddle are wont to say—'From one conundrum solved, a brood of five new questions spring full-armed; two mysteries dispelled breed twenty more.' So may it prove with Erwo. His bright mind, and spirit ardent, are at once our field's hope and our fear. Such natures, once enmeshed in tasks of moment, oft their pith so spend in seizure of the prize, that this attained, they wither, lacking nutriment of new ambition. Somewhat in that wise I dread lest Erwo, having snared at last his hart, should languish, tied to the empty trophy's horns."

He lapsed to silence, shaded with concern avuncular, as Pabi pondered deep this character, more complex far than met the unschooled observer's hasty reckoning, who had (by fortune's book) become so dear, so bound by living cords unto her own. Below them in the trench, she watched him bend to labor, with redoubled pith, as if the exhumed tomb's narrow compass could confine not his slight mortal frame alone, but all the swelling infinities of his desire.

The toiling crew a cavity had hewn, of breadth sufficient for one man to pass, thrice five yards distant from where Gilmesh lay inurned in regal solitude. 'Twas here Erwo his rod of iron plied, to wrench the stony portal from its age-long clasp. This done, he foremost of that band advanced over a threshold by no foot profaned since first that monumental vault was sealed. A lamp they lowered to his reaching hand, and by its flickering radiance he beheld marvels undreamt, which from his throat unloosed a cry of jubilation. Hard upon his steps, two comrades pressed, to document with stylus swift the tomb's long-hoarded wealth. For one full hour they labored, while above the expectant throng kept vigil.

Then at last, his scrip with glyphs replete, Erwo emerged, and sought out Pabi's side. "O joy!" he breathed, "The splendors there enshrined beggar belief. Thou must behold them with thine own clear eyes! But here—see what mine hasty hand hath gleaned from that queen's chronicle, on wall and crypt in rainbow stain limned lovingly. Didst know she first drew breath in Valk—those distant hills which now like rampart guard the rising sun? Thence was she ravished in her flower of youth, to serve as slave in Pervikhseryedhi's bed. He, by her native graces captive taken, not only struck her fetters off, but raised her suppliant form to share his throne and heart. If this be not love's very avatar, then all faith is hollow!"

In this wise he gushed, while Pabi, all attent, each syllable drank deep, and pondered. Round them, student peers and grey-beard mentors craned to catch his tale, avid for each new crumb of lore disclosed. Erwo, perceiving how all eyes and ears upon him focused were, broke off, as one who fear to bare his bosom's treasured hoard to casual or inquisitive survey. But ere he turned his kindling gaze aside, Pabi from that bright mirror glimpsed a truth he dared not yet enunciate—a mute but eloquent assurance that the joy of this momentous hour but capped the tower of bliss which their two hearts' communion built.

That eve, as round the bonfire's ruddy glow the company in genial circle sat, a camel-rider, travel-stained and worn, into their midst abruptly thrust. At once, all converse ceased, all motion stilled, as if by some enchantment frozen. Erwo swift from his repose amid companions rose, and toward the stranger strode, hand outstretched to aid his sore-tried frame in its descent.

"Ho, bring this man some water!" he enjoined the staring throng. "Redhu, my friend, 'tis thou? What madness drives thee o'er the trackless waste beneath pale Moon's insubstantial beam? Dost tempt the jinn abroad?"

The weary wight, scarf-muffled features bared, at Erwo's voice a gratitude wordless by eyes expressed. Agwayabo, solicitous, drew nigh bearing a brimming bowl, which Redhu seized and quaffed in one great gulp, throat-parching dust and thirst at once assuaging. "My approach," he said, "seems most ill-timed—some festal cause hath doubtless drawn this gladsome gathering. What stroke of fortune doth such mirth inspire?"

"A tomb new-found," Erwo began—but his guest had turned to rummage in his pack, and thence a much-creased letter drew, which he in Erwo's hand thrust peremptorily.

"From Dannwi's self," he said, "a welcome word!"

"He lives?" cried Erwo, brow by joy surprised more than illumed. "How came this to thine hand?"

But Redhu merely shrugged, and with mute nod urged him the missive to peruse. At once, all animation from the scholar's face slow ebbed, as down the page his focused eye its burden traced. A frown, a troubled tic behind the ear bespoke some inward care. At last, the script laid by, he Redhu faced with look of mute inquiry. Once again, the messenger in silent gesture wrapped his sentiments.

Erwo a moment stood perplexed, then glanced to where his Pabi sat, her heart in wide eyes writ. To lifeless leaf of paper his regard returned—then, swift in resolution caught, he squared his form, and in the bonfire's heart the letter cast.

As up the fateful scrap in brief flame flared, fair Pabi ventured, "What doth message mean?"

"'Tis naught," he answered, "naught of good or gain." Then, voice to carry pitched, "My comrades all, I fear my lids grow heavy, and I must betimes to couch withdraw. Let us convene, when next Apollo's steeds have paced the east, at Valley of the Kings, our chief design with zeal redoubled to accomplish. Yon metropolis of stone a space must wait!" This proclamation made, to Pabi's hand he pressed a fervent kiss, bade all good night, and to his tent with pensive tread retired.

By his example moved, the dig's denizens their pallets sought; the glade, so late alive with quip and carol, lapsed to quietude. While o'er the embers Agwayabo strewed a stifling sand, Pabi to Redhu stole with query soft.

"The letter's news," she prayed, "Wilt thou

impart, for friendship's holy sake?"

But he, his gear unstrapping wearily, demurred with rueful smile. "Not mine to wag a tongue in Erwo's private sphere. Goodbye!"

When next Aurora's rosy fingers drew the curtain of the night, and ushered in the day's fair pageant, all that learned crew—preceptors sage and pupils keen alike—foregathered at the sepulchers' dark doors, impatient to resume their treasured toil.

Pabi, from circle of their congress, cleft her path to Erwo's side, and soft besought some gloss upon the mystery of that scroll which yestereve such perturbation wrought.

"'Tis but a trifle," he assured, and pressed a steaming cup into her anxious hand, aroma redolent of Dayadhath's hills. "Some slight affairs that call me home anon, mere dross of duty, naught to kindle fear."

"This Dannwi," she persisted, "what his tie to thee, that his bare name such power wields?"

Erwo, in sipping shrewdly long immersed, at length rejoined: "No friend, in meter strict, but more an adjutant, whose charge it is to oversee mine household in my stead. The head wadhestor of Jub Khewi, he, bound to my service by an ancient vow."

"On what design do ye in concert strive?" Pabi pressed on, unwilling to relent til all stood plain.

Erwo, with patient mien, thus satisfied her query: "'Tis his task to husband those domains and worldly goods which, when my parents to the shades retired, devolved to me, their sometime heedless heir. A plethora of chattels, lands, and rents, the least of which to manage or maintain doth tax my scant capacity! Yet all I must retain, in filial piety, and Dannwi in his husbandry confirm, lest I that precious heritage betrayed. So run my days—in silks to take my rest, from Mithoër's farthest reach my viands fetch... A jest," he swiftly added, marking how her eyes had widened at this proud display. "For Dannwi's chief concern—nay, call it fault—is that my fortune to my name adhere, the ambit of my kin not overpass. He to my father's blood belongs, thou seest, and holds our cousinship a holy trust. Whereas my own compunction bids me spill that copious store to ease my fellows' wants. God wot, my means could twenty ages last though not one obol to their sum accrue—yet dearth and indigence on all sides rage, now chiefly by this scourge of war increased, sad refugees in throngs my aid beseech... To hoard my pelf in such a pass were sin!"

Pabi, arrested by a sudden thought, broke in: "The prophet whom all tongues extol, he too in Jub Khewi his dwelling keeps. Hast thou his holy aura ever breathed, his puissance not alone of spirit, but of portent for our realm's convolute weal?"

Erwo in grave assent inclined his head. "Him have I seen, as all Jub Khewi's great perforce must rendering make—yet still occult his favor and his visage both remain, by veil and mystery impenetrable."

As one from reverie roused, the maiden spoke, half to herself: "That style, that Dannwi bore—some memory faint it stirs—but whence?"

"Small marvel," Erwo calmed her, "for that name in common frequency our country's ranks of nomenclature swells. But thou, my sweet, let no least shade of diffidence bedim thy new-blown rose of joy! All augurs boon, all stars benign upon our union wait, and Dannwi but a transient vapor proves before our bliss's sun!"

So saying, he her damask cheek caressed with bearded lips, and, eyes to eyes reflecting rapture, breathed: "I love thee, O my soul, with love past speech!"

"That know I," Pabi whispered, "as I thee, with all mine heart's unplumbed immensity!"

This tender episode to consummate, her swain, in accent brisk, rejoined: "Enough of mundane things—come, see what couch of fame invites our first enthralling glimpse!" With that, he led her light, to where, by Somdhëo's vault, a space new-cleared obtruded, bare of all save one broad stone, whose graven face appeared.

"Those characters—surmisest thou their sense?" Erwo inquired—then, as she silent shook her head, "I burn to hear thy guess express!"

"One word alone that legend doth comprise—Pervikhseryedhi, thine own monarch hist!" Pabi pronounced, with sudden thrill. At this, in wild surmise, she round him flung her arms, and cried: "Such joy for thee my soul transports! When shall this portal to thy gaze swing wide?"

"A few scant hours should to that end suffice, if to our shovels no reluctance tempt," he answered. "Not one moment more I'll bide til I that kingly sepulcher profane, though decencies of method and suspense cry out reproof. These years I've pined to view that sight, and now the climax stands at hand, mine heart, like courser at the trumpet's blare, leaps at the barrier, all constraint disdains!"

"Such transport nigh to malady reeks," the lady fondly chid. "Thy pulse doth throb in eyes dilated—'tis a parlous sign!"

As day wore on in desultory march, Pabi her station kept beneath the shade of yon provisional roof, where relics lay in neat array, and documentation thrived. Water with spearmint essence there she sipped, contemplating as Agwayabo conned fragments lithic to her untutored eye.

Sudden, from the excavation's living heart a cry exultant broke the studious hush. The sage looked up, then with spry step repaired to where the clamor's source its siren call broadcast. Erwo from deepened cavity his visage raised, Pabi by name to bid draw nigh. She hastened to comply and saw the portal freed sufficient for assault by Rilun and his stout-armed crew, who poised with levers braced that last defense to breach.

"Hold!" cried Agwayabo. "Hath any hand the frieze epigraphic o'er the lintel writ in facsimile exact? This door's unbarring may the original sore imperil—now our record must in fullness be secured!"

"I have them here," spake Erwo, "though their purport is scant and stark. List: 'Pervikhseryedhi, Kollan ab-Kes's king and cynosure. Whose feet this hallowed sepulcher profane, on him shall death descend with wings.'"

Rilun, his lever's haft in steady grip, rejoined in jest: "Naught there to shake resolve, or bid us pause!" His mates, in laughter strained, assent vouchsafed.

"Such dire anathemas but grave-robbers to fright are framed," said one.

"Are we not such," asked Rilun, "save alone in solemn title?"

More mirth bubbled up. Erwo, impatience in his tone, cried out: "Enough! Each moment's tardiness I rue as grievous wound! Set to and prize the door!"

On his command, the brawny engineers their engines plied—and with protesting groan, the age-clenched barrier parted, in a gust of trapped millennia, dense and redolent of mummial spice and majesty long pent. That antique exhalation Pabi sensed stir round her like a specter, thrilling all her flesh with transcendental horror. Then, suspended twixt relief and awe, the crew back from the cleared entryway withdrew—all save Erwo, whose form half-swallowed stood in shadow's maw, as one by fate compelled.

Agwayabo on his shoulder laid a palm, and gently spoke: "Go, Erwo—'tis thine hour, the crown and consummation of thy quest!"

The addressee nodded, features taut as if with tears unshed. Into the Chamber then he dropped, and through its narrowed access squirmed. A lamp to guide his path they offered—he received it mute and vanished from their sight. Seconds ticked by, with no least syllable from that dread orifice ejected.

Then Agwayabo called: "What doth thy witness bear? What meets thy gaze in that untrodden gloom?"

From vault's recess Erwo's hushed accents

welled, freighted with indefinable emotion: "All that I am, in one bright locus joined!" Faint sobs escaped him, which his comrades heard in silent sympathy.

For divers beats they kept mute vigil, honoring the awe and rapture of that longed-for revelation. At length, the sage proposed: "Our corps shall file in sequel, to assay the royal relics. What space affords this tomb for occupancy?"

Erwo through tears replied: "For six, I'd gauge, this room hath scope—the sarcophagus vast beyond compare outspreads its flanks!"

So briefed, Agwayabo turned to Pabi with a nod. "Thee first, sweet sister!" Her he helped descend to sepulcher's dark threshold, which she crossed with heart in mouth, and eyes wide wonderment.

No language could encompass or convey the strange, ambivalent beauty there enshrined, constellate in mute gorgeous galaxies of grave-gifts round the central cenotaph. From wall to wall rich tribute flowed, but chief, magnetic to her gaze, that coffin-hoard, like Russian doll of ever-lessening size in gold and gems contrived, until at last, in center of that gilded cosmic nest, the fleshly crucible of him they praised as god on earth, and light of Kollan, lay.

Pabi, in spirit amazed, picked halting path toward a still figure crouched against the wall. 'Twas Erwo, thralled in rapt contemplation of somewhat set before him, on a stand of cedar, silver-gilt, and lazuli. She to his side soft crept, and saw a cask of equal craft and cost, which now he took and in his lap with tender caution laid. She whispered, "Is not this past all belief? What transports, O my love, must thee possess at sight so long pursued, so dear achieved? But what contains that coffer?"

He nor moved nor raised his head, but with set lips and tense, the casket's lid threw back—and at its freight caught labored breath, one palm to mouth uplift as if in prayer. "My God," he stammered low, "For this fair consummation of my dreams, my thanks! Let all these wonders, as my soul, to thee revert, and own thy sovereignty!" So saying, from the chest a chain he drew, rude-wrought, yet more than regal in its freight: a tooth, in life some mighty beast's, now turned phylactery most sacrosanct.

Pabi gasped. "Canst put a name to that fell amulet?"

"Pervikhseryedhi's Power totem," he in tones of adoration murmured. "Here, as sacred writ avers, the fourfold might of heaven's supreme Powers once indwelt. Around his neck this pendent spur he bore and wielded thus untrammeled puissance!"

She, marveling, the uncouth relic eyed, so starkly plain amid that lavish hoard. No gold nor jewels graced it—just a cord, a tooth of cow or horse, and ties to clasp its circuit round some favored mortal's throat. In bantering mood she nudged him. "Try it on! Let's see our Erwo robed in royal power!"

He smiled, but waved dismissal. "On my frame, 'twould but a clumsy gaud appear." With care and sober mien, in cask he laid it by, then squeezed her fingers. "Come—along these walls, ten thousand tales their pregnant glyphs unfold. Fain would I trace our White-haired Hero's path from cradle unto kingdom, godhead, grave!"

That moment, at the tomb's mouth, Rilun winced, and swatted at his arm. "Ah... damned mosquito!" He chuckled, while the clustered company fond laughter at his small contretemps joined.

Canto 7

Sing I now of that cursed day when Ragnir's solitude did fail, when a band of Easterling soldiers led by Goraito Reu discovered in the hidden land Koraithlen the man whom Reu had chased for nigh on fifteen long years.

Who was it that sent Goraito on his quest?—Gwalo the Younger, king of Keulen, while at war in Len Khalayu saw that his need was great for the long lost Baithas; and so he sent Goraito with twelve knights to scour the world, seeking throughout all the myriad lands of Edorath for that man whose Power the king did lack and desire.

Goraito rode with his twelve knights; west from Len Khalayu to the islands of Pellen, where sea-folk sail and artists carve white marble; then north to Markhlen, home of horse-lords with their long black hair and fierce dark eyes; north again to Dol-Nopthelen, where the Sun shows not her face for more than half the year, whence come the forebears of the Easterlings; they went then south of Dol-

Nopthelen to Mithoër, that rolling land with white mountains and low grasslands, and haunted forests thick with groaning trees; south once more to Gavwer—there the people drink dark wine and use the wind to mill their grain; now o'er the inland sea that divides north from south, into the dry and dusty Deulen where giant cats prowl, and the giant elowav trumpets over the savanna.

By then five years had passed, and no word of Ragnir could be found; therefore Goraito took his knights onto a ship, and from Deulen sailed they to Maikhethlen, humid and covered in dense jungle, bordered at the north by the sky-scraping Dyuglebai range.

Onward the search continued, northeast to Mitho Gorikhwa, where the smallest clues were heard—great was Goraito's joy therein.

Now southward, down through Kebkhelin where the mountains belch forth flames, where the forests are only matched by those in Maikhethlen to the west.

Finally over the narrow neck of land the locals name So Vong, connecting Kebkhelin to Koraithlen in the south.

How long he searched, that Goraito Reu; how long his knights wearied of the quest; how angry was his heart at such a target, evading him at every turn; and so how great his joy when at last he found the man—the Baithas, Speaker, standing now before him, living in a Sun-baked village so far from all else, at the very end of the world.

As when the giant begwo bird finds a place to nest away from all predators, then lays her egg and leaves to find a meal, only to return to find a hive of ants have swarmed her chick, just so did Brenn Ragnir look upon the knights, concerned above all else for the safety of the Erkhesgur and the Kebkholenu.

Goraito Reu was first to speak, looking upon Brenn with relieved and tired eyes. "Gwennotir Ker, mine eyes behold a ghost," he said.

"No more Gwennotir, but Brenn," spoke the Baithas, hand resting on the sheath that hung at his side—though not touching the sword itself. "That name I left in Nugomor, along with my destiny."

At this the captain laughed and said, "Yet thou remainest a Baithas; thou canst not abandon that."

"I would if I were able." At this, Brenn looked upon the twelve Keulenu knights, none of whom he knew. "Tell me, Captain, how thou hast found me; I would like to know how my wish for peace and solitude failed."

"First offer me a drink," said Reu, "for we've seen no inn for three months and more, and all of us are weary and stiff from sleeping on hard ground and riding in the saddle."

"None asked you to come," said Brenn. "There is nothing I can offer thee; if ye thirst, return whence ye came. Keulen has water to spare."

But the captain did not move, only looking to Brenn's kinsfolk who stood alert with spears in hand, guarding the villagers who watched frightened from their huts.

Now these were the Erkhesgur—not all of them, for most had followed destinies in other parts of Edorath; but four remained, the closest friends

Brenn had: Thegikh and Perangorai, cousins born in Kebkhelin—mercenaries, they both were, until the day when they were caught and sold to slavers in Maikhethlen to mine for gold. Of all women on Earth, it is said that Thegikh was the fiercest; tall dark Tobëa, bulwark of the Erkhesgur, the man from Yenmiskelanë—that mythical land which our bards name Gelausi Khworeu; and there was Den, born in Skegyo and raised in Saulen; neither man nor woman—Den was more than mere flesh—and closer to Brenn than anyone else.

Brenn lay his hand upon the sheath of his sword, Pukhso, though he was careful not to touch the sword itself. "I would tell thee a short tale," said the Baithas to the captain, "for it seems that fate may yet be playing a part in thy coming; just yesterday I returned from fetching water, and there waiting for me on my doorstep were three children. Devils, these three children are, for they delight in tormenting me, and I have oft said to their parents, 'Keep your offspring away from me.' Yet there they stood, two boys and a girl hardly older than ten years.

"The girl held in her small hand a bird—just a chick, newly hatched and not yet feathered. It was dead. Aye, those little devils know just the thing to make Brenn Ragnir full of rage: slay an animal without cause. I hold the killing of an animal—lion, cow, or bird—in a lesser light than killing humans; for all humans are flaw, yet no animal is with sin. And yet these three gave me this bird, and I chased them from mine house.

"I did not bury the bird; why should I? Birds, like most animals, do not bury their dead, for they have no concept of an afterlife. Nature is a cycle, and all beasts understand the part they play after their breath stops and their heart ceases to beat. Therefore I placed the chick in a copse of brambles, so as to keep it from prying scavengers long enough for it to gain some well-deserved rest before entering that Cycle in which we all must one day join.

"Even before this, my mood was foul. I ate in silence and remembered when I was but a child, and I had discovered a dead bird near mine house. It must have fallen from its nest. I buried it, for I knew not then about animals' ideas of funeral rites. Kolewa helped me, yet he knew that such a deed was not needed, for he was thirteen years old and could by that time speak with birds. My older brother wept, and he sang; to him that bird had had a voice, a mind, relationships with other birds and beasts. I did not understand his thinking then, but I understand it now.

"The Sun then set, and I sat without mine house in the cooling night air, enjoying such solitude as I have been able to find in this land. But my peace was not for long, for three of my Erkhesgur came to me not long after dark. You see, my friends and I have played karkhro each week for these two years.

"'It is Nekhvodyeu,' I told them—for our games were on Therdyeu nights.

"'You have it wrong,' said Den, 'today is Therdyeu, and we've not seen our friend for ten days. Art thou not glad to see us?'

"Instead of wasting breath convincing them they were mistaken, I insisted that no matter which night today might be, my mind was ill and there was no place in my mood for games or friends tonight. Thegikh, ever fierce, did not feign disappointment. Tobëa, my stoic bulwark kinsman from Yenmiskelanë, made no move with body or expression. Yet Den, my closest friend, I saw was hurt; there was nothing to be done. I bade them all leave, and they, being good friends, granted me this wish. Before they turned to head back to this small village, Den said to me, 'Once thine heart was light, but these past years it's been as hard as steel; thou laughest or smilest not, nor enjoy thy time with friends. Would that I knew what happened to thee, my brother, my friend.'

"I had no answer, for I thought the statement strange. If anyone knew why my mood and heart were thus, it would be Den; they have been with me since the Taf-Waikht destroyed the gwerfegi on that fateful day five years ago, and they have stayed at my side through all manner of afflictions. But I said nothing, and Den went home with the others.

"Now I must confess, I lied to my friends; I knew very well which day it was." Here, Brenn turned to his four friends, guarding still against the knights with naught but spears. "For this I beg your pardon, though I regret not that I turned you away. The day before the Solstice is one I have ever spent alone; it is the anniversary of the day my life changed forever, damaged beyond repair. And what's more, as of last night it's been exactly ten years—ten years ago yesterday, my brother Kolewa returned to my mother and me as a corpse, and his Power passed to me, and my life has been little better than Hell since then. As I fell asleep, I wept—for myself and for my brother—and in my dreams Kolewa yet lived, and my own life was not a waking nightmare.

"So thou seest, Goraito Reu, it may be more than happenstance that led thee to this place on this specific day. Perhaps the Derevai have placed their wills in the destinies of us both. I ask thee yet again: What wouldst thou have of me? Why travel all this way?"—thus Ragnir; and Goraito answered quickly:

"Your king and liege hath sent me, bestowing this quest with urgent need; for he needs thee and thy Power in the war in Len Khalayu."

At this the Baithas felt his blood run cold, and his fingers played at Pukhso's scabbard. "What would the king of me, then?" he asked. "What must I do to rid myself of Easterlings? Knowest thou what I've done, how many miles I've walked, the friends I've lost, all to escape King Gwalo? What must I do to gain my peace?"

At this the captain said, "A donkey is born only to bear burdens; it has no say in its fate."

Then with a loud voice yelled Thegikh, "We will fight! Return whence thou camest, thou and thine horde of northern knights; Brenn will not bow to thy king's demands."

"The choice lies with Brenn," the captain said, "as to the outcome of this meeting. Brenn, I know thou hast wit inside that skill. We may settle this like savages, clashing one against the other like to bulls locked in combat. 'Tis true, we cannot kill thee—slaying a Baithas is the most heinous of crimes, when that Baithas has no heir—but how many of these Koraithlenu will be put to the sword before thou killest us all? How many unarmed natives dost thou suppose we knights can kill before thine Erkhesgur skewer us? We are on a mission of the king, Brenn Ragnir. If I do not return, if thou dost kill us to a man, more will come. This village is not safe so long as thou remainest."

"And what of my duty to the king?" Brenn asked. "How many Rilyun will die by mine own hand before Gwalo is satisfied? The last time I saw the king, he was but a prince, and Gwalo the Elder forced this very sword into mine hands and made me kill a man as his attendants watched. You remember, dost thou not? Perhaps not; after all, what's one ugly death among hundreds more? But I do not forget. I remember every life that ends by mine own will. By the eyes of Odol, I was just a child!"

"By my memory," said Reu, "thou wast fifteen winters old; hardly a child, I would say. And I remember well the day, for the pitiful stare in thine eyes has stayed with me longer than I'll admit. Has he told you of his blooding?" Here the captain turned to the Erkhesgur and the few Koraithlenu who tarried near.

"I have," said Brenn, answering for his friends. "And they know it's a tale I'd prefer to keep untold. I hated myself for what I did, and I hated the king all the more for the hate I held for myself. I have hated him my entire life, and his brat of a son as well. To tell the truth, I was happy when word came to me that the Elder died four years ago, but my joy was outweighed by the anger than came with the Younger inheriting the crown."

"A fine thing to consider," said Reu. "Now I await thy decision."

"Though thy words are close to sweet, the threats thou makest are bitter," said Brenn. "I would not have the Koraithlenu harmed, nor my friends who have no part in this dispute. Therefore to save them all, I give thee my decision: I will journey with thee to Jub Khewi, to that land of sand, rock, and heat—much alike to Koraithlen is Len Khalayu, though different in many ways—and there I'll treat with thy young king. Perhaps I can assist with whatsoever he needs from one such as me, and in return he may grant me the solitude and peace I've sought throughout my entire cursed life."

"A wise decision," the captain said. "We'll reach the Kala land by Spring."

"Give me but a moment to retrieve my things, then we'll be off," Brenn said, then returned to the path connecting village to his hut.

After Brenn ran the bulwark Tobëa and kind Den, who called after Brenn and bade him stop.

"My mind will not be changed," said Brenn. "This is the only way that ensures your safety, and the safety of the Koraithlenu."

"We do not wish to change thy mind," said Den, "for I deem thou hast chosen right; a difficult decision, though the right ones often are, and thou art brave for taking the right but difficult path. No, closest of friends, we come to tell thee this: Whithersoever fate takes thee over this wide earth, we will follow. We would not abandon thee to war and angry kings."

"I cannot ask you this," Brenn said, though a smile came to his lips. "This is my duty alone; neither Reu nor Gwalo hold concern for you—only me. It is into brutal war I go, perhaps to die."

"You do not ask, yet I affirm: we will accompany thee," said Den. "This will not be our first war, or hast thou forgotten? In Saulen we took part in heinous deeds commanded by our officers until we found the courage to escape that land. Then starving in Kebkhelin, we robbed a storehouse, which found us locked within a jail. Soon thereafter we came to Maikhethlen, cargo on a slave-ship, where we met our friends Perangorai, Thegikh, and Tobëa—and they themselves had seen their share before coming to that land to dig for gold beneath the whip. Then what—after we broke from bondage and took a ship, we made our way to Tobëa's home—the fabled Yenmiskelanë—in search of thine own father; there waiting for us was yet more war, which we foolishly took part in. Where would we be if not for war? None of us fear to see it again, if it be in support of our friend and leader and his courageous choice."

Stoic Tobëa grunted with a nod, which was enough to make Brenn grin; but still he said, "Ye know not what this war will bring, but I myself was there when it began, years ago before I met you all. I know the stakes, what we're likely to see, what might befall. A memory haunts me of an angry lordling who tricked me, lied, and used me to begin this fight. How many have died because of the war I helped to start?"

"Then let us finish it together," said Den. Laying a hand upon Brenn's shoulder, they added, "I'm with thee til the end."

Now let us follow Goraito's twelve, the Erkhesgur,

and Baithas Brenn: up the eastern coast of Koraithlen they rode, keeping in the shade of the Engwedigi Mountains. Then westward between the borders of Koraithlen's Nerro Desert and Nerlath to its north, where the Sun is cooler and many green trees do grow; to the narrow neck of land the locals name So Vong, connecting country to country, Koraithlen to Kebkhelin.

How to describe Kebkhelin, the country of islands and jungle? Green and mountainous, surrounded by oceans blue as the sky; the bays and jungles teem with life, filled with strange and myriad beasts that live in the trees and creep through the undergrowth. As fragile eggs sit in a nest between the branches of a tree and tremble in the wind, so do the Kebkholenyu villages sit nested in the mountains, shuddering in the constant storms that sweep the seas.

Up the western coast they rode, this band of knights and Erkhesgur, with the Magigekwa Mountains at their right, until after long weeks they came at last to Segai—capital city of Kebkhelin, trading port, and center of all activity. Here it was that Goraito hired a ship, a large vessel carrying goods from Gabmektu, Saulen, and Goreuhwo, bound for Maikhethlen and its neighbor Len Khalayu.

Now sailing with horses in stow, bunking with Kebkholenyu sailors, they traveled west across Maikhethlen Mor, making port in the state of Milridh.

"Too well we know this place," said Brenn to captain Reu; "for here it was we Erkhesgur were enslaved and forced to dig for gold. Here Den and I met our good friends, Thegikh, Perangorai, and Tobëa—and other Erkhesgur who've now gone their separate ways; they had been slaves here long before we two arrived."

"Yet here ye stand before me," said Goraito. "There's a story there, I sense."

"Aye," said Brenn, "though it's not a tale I'll tell, for it grieves me to recall the afflictions suffered there, the friends we made whose lives were lost in that rebellion I led, freeing more than two hundred slaves, putting our cruel masters to the spear. It's enough for thee to know that Milridh is the birthplace of the Erkhesgur, though we had not yet named ourselves thus."

"Wounds can run deep," Goraito said. "This I ken well, for I have many of my own—tales that I'll not tell another, lest those wounds reopen and bleed once more. I understand, Brenn Ragnir, and will not pry again."

The trading done, the ship departed from the port in cursed Milridh; then west again for many miles they sailed until their final stop in Ëogor. Here was the southernmost town of Len Khalayu; beyond it lay the desert spanning a distance few can fathom, that expanse they knew as Sakhdo Mor, the Sea of Sand. The captain and his knights, the Baithas, and his friends, unloaded their horses and mounted for the long and hot road before them. Directly north from Ëogor, they followed a narrow way that led through hills and rocks.

"I met a man from Ëogor," said Brenn for all who heard, "once, long ago, on my first visit to this land. I was alone and without water, shade, or food, with Aebakhmë's sakhnoë sailing toward Borheno-Gwega. He gave me water and safe passage to Jub Khewi, saving my life that day...and many others."

Riding beside Brenn, captain Reu then said, "You never spoke of your involvement with the lordling Aebakhmë. Is that a story thou wouldst care to share?"

"Nay," said Brenn. "Not when I may yet meet him near Borheno-Gwega."

At this Goraito laughed and said, "So thou hast not heard? The upstart lordling lost his head upon the field, many years ago, by our own Gwalo's royal sword."

"Truly?" Brenn asked. "I think it odd, where in mine heart there should be joy, an emptiness instead I find. What of Aebakhmë's army and ships?"

"To those who survived the battle, King Gwalo gave a choice," said Reu. "Return whence ye came, else suffer the same fate as your master. Many chose to die, though most departed this land. Wouldst thou share thy story now?"

"Not now," said Brenn. "Perhaps another day."

Not having gwarnyemith or kirvin, they instead tied bits of clothing about their heads to stave off the desert Sun. Another few day's ride through dry brown hills, then fifty miles south of Jub Khewi they turned northwest until at last they came to Borheno-Gwega.

A large oasis, it was—a cleft in the earth that stretched for miles like a canyon, filled with fresh water fed through the ground by some hidden spring. Yeshu trees grew thick and green around the lake, surrounded by steep cliffs. The Easterling camp sat on these cliffs, on the eastern side of the oasis, looking out over the lake while Jub Khewi looked upon the camp from the east.

The camp of Easterlings itself was more than camp; the Keulenu had occupied this land for the better part of a decade, and the tents gave way to huts of straw and mud (such was the style of the Badhyu who lived without the cities), and proper little roads now wound between the buildings so that neighborhoods and alleys were made. In the center of the camp sat the largest building: the house of the king himself, built in the style of the longhouses of Keulen, salvaged from the king's own ship in which he sailed down the Gwelulo to reach Len Khalayu; the hull now served as roof, its gunwales the walls.

More besides huts to live in lay scattered about the camp: a blacksmith, a hunter, a butcher, a tailor; there were booths owned by Badhyu who sold goods from Jub Khewi and the surrounding smaller towns. Several children ran and played, circling the newcomer's horses as they rode through the camp, laughing and shouting. A fair few of these children had features both Kalayu and Keuleno—brown skin, curly dark hair, blue eyes, or wide shoulders.

"I see the soldiers of Keulen have been busy," noted Brenn. "It takes much work and time to raise a family, does it not?"

Goraito laughed and said, "Hardly families, these—bastards of soldiers with too much time on their hands and Badhyu women with a dwindling supply of Rilyun men. We allow them to stay, for they know the land and the languages and they cause no trouble. There's ever work to be done and never enough hands to do it; the women want protection and the children want food."

"Hast thou any bastards of thine own?" asked the Baithas.

"I've been chasing thee eight years," said the captain with a frown. "Not much time to spread my seed. Still, eight years without a wife is enough to make any man take something on the side; but I'm not any man. Thou, yon boy!" Goraito pointed at a passing child, who paused in his game and looked up at the man on the horse. "I see an absence of soldiers, knights, and the king. Tell me, where is everyone?"

The boy did not speak, merely pointed eastward, and ran. Goraito and Brenn, Den, Tobëa, Thegikh, and Perangorai rode off in this direction, only halting when they reached the edge of the camp.

There stood dozens of people—Easterlings, all—in a circle around a clearing. Jub Khewi herself stood in the distance, silhouetted against the morning Sun. An army stood there on a rise of the earth, watching over the crowd and the clearing. Within the circle sat three Kalayu men facing north, armed and armored, praying as they knelt.

Dismounting their horses, Brenn and Goraito entered the crows. The captain said, "I see my old friend, Kregeth Gollapo! See him there, standing behind that armed knight."

Brenn saw the knight; he held a spear and small shield, and an ax hung from his belt. He wore no armor, and his hair was cropped short, though his beard was long and braided. Almost as tall as Brenn, the man stood, with lithe limbs and muscles like tree roots. His legs were apart as he readied to spring, not taking his eyes from the three Kalayu men.

Kregeth Gollapo was a man Brenn knew by a scar on his face: a horrid thing that began in his hair, then fell over his right eye and down his cheek, stopping beneath the jaw. Kregeth was the very same man who delivered that terrible news of Deugwer's disappearance to Brenn all those years ago. The captain saw Goraito approach, and a smile washed over this scarred face, and he embraced Goraito, and the two gripped arms.

"Goraito, my friend!" spoke the captain. "How long has it been? Too long, for I see thou hast grown thinner in the belly but thicker in beard. I was beginning to think the worst."

"I've lost count of the winters," said Reu. "Long have I been traveling, over all ends of Edorath, enduring freezing snow and blistering sands, searching for this one here." At this, he brought forth Brenn, and Kregeth took the Baithas by the arm.

"And who art thou?—though I have a guess," the captain said.

"Brenn Ragnir," said the Baithas, "though thou didst know me once as Gwennotir Ker."

Hearing this, the soldiers all around began to talk. The Baithas had returned! How long had he been missing? And why? All these and more the soldiers asked among themselves.

"By Odol's breath," Gollapo said. "Last time these old eyes saw thee, just a boy thou wast, no taller than a dog. Now before me stands a man, wide of shoulders and broad of chest! Brenn Ragnir it is—a fine name. I doubt that thou rememberest me."

"I remember," said Brenn, "though it's not a memory I hold in high regard—no offense to thee."

Kregeth slapped Brenn on the shoulder and said, "You've been gone a long while, Baithas! No doubt thou hast stories to tell; I cannot wait to hear them round the fire."

But here Goraito interrupted, asking his friend, "Kregeth, what's the game here? Wherefore the king stands at the ready inside a fighting ring? Is this a dauker?"

Now this was a surprise to Brenn; with another glance at the man who stood at the ready with his spear and ax, he recognized Gwalo the Younger.

Kregeth answered, "No dauker, this; every man and woman who claimed the title Easterling would fall upon a sword ere bowing to a Rilyun king. Nay, my friend, this is a simple duel. If Gwalo loses, we return to the snow-steppes of Keulen."

"Why would the king agree to that?" Goraito asked. "Go home? Forsake the fight?"

"Because this is the fourth Rilyun to challenge Gwalo," Captain Kregeth said, and at this many soldiers laughed. "You know as well as any the king's skill with a blade. We do not expect him to lose a duel until his hair turns white and his teeth fall out. Yea, there is wisdom in accepting these duels; our king slowly chips at the enemy's ranks, and they've too much pride to see it. Never long, these duels will last; blink and ye may miss it." Here, the captain pointed to the three Rilyun men praying.

"That's Commander Blod Abborader," said Kregeth, "the one who challenged Gwalo. His two lackeys, Captains Borndo Adlwidh and Rom Affelkhu. Look ye there, upon the hill." The captain waved toward the east, where Brenn and Reu looked, shielding the Sun from their eyes with their hands. An army of Kalayu soldiers stood atop the rise, near invisible in the shadow of the city. "Worry not about them," said Kregeth. "They come for every duel and only want assurance that we do not kill the other two—only the one."

Just then the three Kalayu men rose to their feet; their prayers were done. A cheer rose from the Easterlings who longed to see the fight begin. Beside Brenn, Thegikh spoke:

"What's happening, Brenn? I speak no Keuleno, nor Kalayo."

"That man's the king," Brenn said. "The same Gwalo the Younger who met my fists all those years ago. He's been challenged to a duel by that man, a Kalayo commander from Jub Khewi. If Gwalo falls to the Kalayo sword, the Easterlings will return to their homes. But fear not; this is the king's fourth duel, and his skills with spear and ax are the stuff of legend."

"Perhaps the duel will turn sour, and we'll join a fight against those on the hill."—this from Perangorai, itching to use his spear.

"Doubtful," said Brenn. "The king has not yet lost a duel, and none here would risk the lives of all at camp by killing the other two. Nay, my friend, we will not fight today."

"Thank the Six," muttered Den, who had not seen battle since Yenmiskelanë and had no desire for it again.

To the center of the clearing strode Gwalo and Abborader, each with steps of one confident in his success. Abborader wore better armor than the king: breastplate, greaves, bracers, and boots; in his right hand he carried a long curved klewaig, and in his left he bore a small round shield. King Gwalo wore naught but a shirt and short trousers.

Blod Abborader touched his thumbnail to his mouth and forehead, then said to all who could hear, "May God bless our duel, and I trust that the Easterling king shall honor his agreement when he falls."

Then Gwalo turned to his soldiers behind him, and with commanding voice he yelled, "As the four Derevai witness me, I will honor the pact made with Commander Abborader; if I am killed, all Easterlings will return to their homes in far-off Keulen. Art thou satisfied, Commander? Good; then let us begin."

The Kalayo man nodded, stepped back, held his klewaig aloft, and with a battle-cry he jumped toward the king.

Gwalo held his ground, his own shield raised at level to his eye, as Abborader brought down his klewaig from his right, using all his strength, and aimed at Gwalo's naked head. Gwalo shifted then his feet, lifted high his shield, and with a pivot to the left the klewaig glanced across the shield with a loud metallic ring.

The king then thrusted forth his spear, its aim precise and deadly, finding space between the rilyun's sword and shield. The spearhead found it; Blod felt the spearhead tearing through his breastplate, cutting him below the ribs.

Commander Blod cried out in pain and spun away, taking Gwalo's spear from the king's own hand. Blod pulled the spear from his shining armor—the tip was coated in blood. He dropped it in the sand as Gwalo took the ax from his belt. As a farmer long in years will grip a woodcutting ax and bring it down upon a log with all the strength and aim that uncounted swings have given, so too did Gwalo bring his ax down upon Abborader's helmet. A ring sounded forth, like the strike of a church bell, and the ax broke at the handle just below the blade. Gwalo cursed and tossed aside the useless weapon.

Now staggered Abborader, dazed by the mighty blow, and stumbled back. But Gwalo had no weapon; he used therefore his fist and punched Abborader in the mouth. The commander fell, his legs buckling beneath him, and he landed face-down in the dirt. But he was quick to recover, placing his arms beneath him to stand.

Some yards away lay Gwalo's spear, like a desert serpent waiting in the sand to strike. The king clutched at the commander's helmet, his fingers finding the space between it and the man's forehead and pulled the Kala through the clearing toward the bloody spear. But alas for King Gwalo!—for the helmet's strap did break within his grip, and with a muttered curse he cast the helm aside.

Forgetting now the spear, Gwalo drove a kick into Abborader's face. A heavy foot landed in the already bloodied mouth, breaking teeth; another kick broke the jaw; another broke the nose. Again and again the king stomped upon the man, until, panting, the king ceased, and Blod Abborader lay dead in a bloody pulp in the sand.

Then a cheer rose up from the Easterlings; all around, people chanted their mighty king's name and cursed the Rilyun commander and his army.

But Captains Adlwidh and Affelkhu looked on in abject horror. Affelkhu, the taller of the two, removed his helm and sank upon his knees in solemn prayer. Adlwidh glared at Gwalo with eyes that might set sand ablaze. On the rise to the east, the Rilyun army shouted.

"Thou man depraved!" spoke Adlwidh over cheers. "Thou hast no honor, no respect for thine enemy! What manner of king stands before me?"

Gwalo answered thus: "One who wins wars. If ye feel slighted, I offer you the same deal: fight me, and if ye claim victory, my army will depart this festering hellscape ye call a country."

Adlwidh spat on Gwalo's boot, and as the king looked down the entire crowd fell silent.

Then, Kregeth Gollapo, loyal but a fool, ran up to his king. He took a knife from his belt and into Borndo Adlwidh's neck he plunged the blade. The Kala captain fell, gurgling, and bled upon the ground beside his crushed commander.

Affelkhu stood and shouted, "The pact is broken!" then charged straightway at Kregeth with his klewaig outstretched. But the king intervened, parrying the blade with his spear, then brought it around to drive the point into the Rilyun man's throat above the breastplate. Rom Affelkhu puked dark blood, spraying the king, and collapsed and died beside the other two.

"That's done it!" cried Thegikh, choking up on

her spear's grip. "Although I have few Keuleno words, and fewer still of Kalayo, I know when I see it that a truce has been broken; the fight is on! How badly I have needed to scratch this itch."—then toward the Kala army she sprinted.

Brenn shouted after her, but Thegikh did not hear, and her cousin Perangorai laughed and gave chase after, his own spear in his hands. Brenn turned to his bulwark friend Tobëa and said to him, "Let them not be killed, my brother," and the man from Yenmiskelanë nodded and went after their fellow Erkhesgur.

Meanwhile the Easterling soldiers grew restless and confused, speaking among themselves as Gwalo shouted, "In the name of all thirteen Hells, what's happening? And whose soldiers are those running toward the enemy?"

Questions ran through the Keuleno army: Do we attack? Who is that running? Should we follow? They're advancing!

And advancing they were; whatever confusion had spread through the Easterlings had also spread through the Rilyun, and now a dozen broke off from the rest, sprinting toward the Keulenu to avenge their dead leaders. One by one at first, then a few at a time, and then all at once, the Easterlings drew their weapons and gripped their spears and hoisted their shields. As two waves at sea rise and fall toward each other, breaking and exploding as they meet in the middle, so too did the two armies race to the midpoint of the field between them and clash with one another.

"Idiots!" King Gwalo yelled. "Form a shield wall;

hold your positions!"—but it was too late, and his voice was drowned in the din of battle-cries and clashing metal and stampeding footsteps.

Brenn grabbed Den's shoulder, spinning his dear friend toward him, and spoke but one word only: "Run."

Tobëa led the Easterling charge, striding faster than any soldier from either army, scowling at the Rilyun before him as he all but flew up the hill with Perangorai and Thegikh at his heels. In his left hand was a small iron shield, and in his right was a long ash spear with a steel blade.

Within the Rilyun army, Kono Asskai stood on a large boulder with his tall shield. His fellow soldiers rushed onward below him. Kono spied the dark Tobëa and the growing distance between him and the pale Easterlings. Kono lifted his longbow, made from the horns of a wild goat, and nocked a long arrow. He sent a brief prayer to God that he would hit his mark, then drew back, pulling the bowstring to his chest so that the metal arrowhead touched the bow at his fingers. He released, the bow groaned, and the arrow soared.

The arrow drove against Tobëa's thick leather belt, ricocheting to his left after snapping in half. He paid it no mind, though he felt that the arrow had cut him below the navel.

Captain Ineikhë Kohol launched his long spear, and it struck through the helmet of Yewas Abel, tearing through the metal and into the bone, onward to the brain, and Yewas fell as the light left him—the first casualty of the day's battle.

Deuker Gudhoth watched Yewas die and ran after him to claim the abandoned klewaig, but Seroth Klisro, a friend of Yewas, saw Deuker pulling the sword from Yewas's dead hand. Deuker bent down and Seroth threw his spear. It landed in the small of Deuker's back, driving through until it emerged from his belly. Deuker fell over Yewas, and in just a few seconds more looting soldiers swarmed the two dead men.

Oënolai Akhes ran at Captain Kregeth Gollapo with his klewaig lifted above his head, but Kregeth gripped his own spear and thrusted it forward, hitting Oënolai in the right breast, and the point emerged beneath the shoulder. Oënolai dropped to the sand without a sound.

Eito Ammwinwo aimed his spear at Kregeth and threw, but the spear missed the Easterling captain, soaring over his shoulder, and pierced Gero Albo, a childhood friend of Goraito Reu. The spear struck Gero in the groin as he dragged a corpse to take its studded armor, and he fell on top of the body as his breath left him.

Captain Goraito Reu saw his friend fall and strode toward Eito, roaring in pained anger. When he came near, Goraito threw a spear at the Rilyun man. Baiso Abyewas tripped over a fallen helmet and stumbled into the spear's path. It sank into one temple and came out the other in a dusky pink spray.

Kelaino Affidisno picked up a stone the size of his head and hurled it at Greyo Reu, cousin of the captain. The rock struck Greyo's right shin, smashing bone and breaking tendon. He fell on his back and reached out to his cousin, but Goraito had turned away. Kelaino pinned Greyo down with a heavy foot and drove a spear through the Easterling's soft belly. Intestines popped, and Greyo saw darkness.

Maur Gwarndo ran toward Kelaino Affidisno as the Rilyun soldier bent to strip Greyo of his armor. Maur threw his spear, and it landed in Kelaino's chest. Kelaino cried out and pulled the spear from his ribs, and dark blood ran from the wound. Maur drove his sword through Kelaino's belly, and Kelaino grabbed Maur's arm as he fell to the ground. Maur fell with him, exhausted and wounded from fighting others. Kelaino died, and as his eyes looked at the harsh blue-white sky, Maur gasped and panted beside him.

Gworigaito Assogsetho ran at Perangorai, the swift killer from Kebkhelin. Gworigaito let fly his spear, but it fell short of Perangorai, landing in the sand in front of him. Perangorai picked up the spear and returned it to Gworigaito. It landed in the Kala's breastbone and knocked him backward like a kick from a mule.

Beside Gworigaito stood his brother Thedokha, who watched as Gworigaito fell on his back and belched up dark blood. Thedokha cried out for his brother. Perangorai saw him and sprinted to close the distance between them. Thedokha turned and ran through the lines toward Jub Khewi, leaving his brother's corpse behind.

Commander Shain Affag rode through the masses on his short-necked stallion, galloping toward King Gwalo. The king swung the butt of his spear and knocked Shain from the horse. The Rilyun commander landed on his belly, gasping for breath, and Gwalo shoved his spear between his shoulders. The spear broke through his breast, and the Kala drew his last gurgling breath as his blood pooled around him thick and warm.

Seryoth Ammikhlod watched Shain's horse run through the bloody battle without a rider, and he reached for the reins when it came near. As Seryoth placed a foot in the stirrup, trying to mount, Thegikh of Kebkhelin stabbed the man with a short sword that she had found in another man's belly. The sword ripped through Ammikhlod's shoulder, and the man dropped from the horse which swiftly trampled him.

Soldiers gathered to take Seryoth's armor and weapons, and Tobëa launched a spear through the back of Perlikhino Abbor. Perlikhino landed in a heap upon the dead Seryoth, and the scavenging soldiers took his belongings.

Theg Ellu drove his spear through Së Affag's buttock, pushing until the spear reached Së's bladder. Së screamed and fell as blood and urine and feces spilled out of him, draining his life away. For Së Affag, death came at a crawling pace.

Orr Denhwa threw his spear at Elëa Abbidayo. The spear landed in Elëa's neck just below the skull, continuing through the mouth, severing his spine and tongue. Elëa fell forward and bit the spearhead as he landed on his chin, shattering his teeth, but he had already died.

Orobola Erkho chased Esather Ammai across the battlefield as the Rilyun man cried for mercy. Orobola threw her spear but missed her mark, and the spear cut Esather's arm below the shoulder. Esather cried out and stumbled, and Orobola caught up to him, drew her sword, and hewed Esather's arm from his body. The limb fell to the ground. Esather puked, fell over on his side, and bled until he died.

Far-shooting Kono Asskai nocked an arrow and drew his goat-horn bow, aiming at his target Perangorai. He let loose the string, and the arrow flew. Perangorai grunted as the arrow caught his left shoulder, and he gritted his teeth as he pulled it out. Little blood flowed, and the former mercenary from Kebkhelin rolled his arm to ease the pain.

Perangorai fumed as he scanned the men slaughtering each other and yelled, "Who's the coward with the bow who won't come out and fight with honor?" but his Kebkholenu words fell on ignorant ears, and the clamor made it impossible to hear regardless.

Perangorai spotted Kono standing on a tall boulder with a shield in front of him. Kono nocked another arrow and loosed it into the battlefield. Perangorai roared and sprinted at the archer, and on the way he killed Eyo Addeudonu with a sword through the collarbone. He cut down Amgan Assogsetho and Mukh Abwi with his sword; two men on horseback—Igo Abboli and Perkho Abbeirtho—he knocked down with the spear in his left hand. Both men broke their necks when they fell, though Perkho did not die until ten other men smothered his paralyzed body as the battle continued. Perangorai continued toward Kono.

Captain Dunami Ammaëso stood at the bottom of Kono's boulder and shouted, "In the name of

God, shoot that man!"

Kono replied, "I already did, but he did not falter!"

"He bleeds like the rest of us," said Dunami, and Kono knew that God fought on their side.

But Perangorai did not fight on God's side, and as he reached throwing-distance to Kono, he hurled a spear at him. The spear hit Kono's shield, and the point came through the other side but did not touch him. Perangorai bent to pick up an abandoned spear, and Kono peeked over his shield.

"Thou didst miss, thou God-forsaken pagan!" shouted the archer, just before Perangorai's second spear caught him in the mouth. The spearhead broke Kono's teeth and severed his tongue and spurted from his neck. Blood sprayed and ran down Kono's neck and back and chin, and the archer toppled from his tall boulder and landed in a puff of sand and dust.

Dunami watched his best archer die, and looked back at Perangorai, who now sprinted at him with fury in his eyes and new weapons in his hands. Dunami dropped his own spear and ran toward Jub Khewi, away from the battle and his fallen comrades. Perangorai laughed in his belly as the Rilyun captain fled.

Dunami turned, saw that Perangorai no longer pursued him, and stopped running. He closed his eyes and whispered, "Forgive me, God, for being a coward."

Then, feeling courage rise within him, Dunami made for a thick group of fighting men. He picked up two bloody spears and threw them one after the other. They found their marks in the bellies of Thekkelo Ero and his brother Yodhedeu. Both fell and died together, just as they had been born together eighteen years earlier.

When the twins fell, Tobëa charged at Dunami to avenge them. Captain Ineikhë Kohol joined Tobëa at his side, and together the men pulled the brothers' bodies out of the fray. Dunami held his ground with klewaig extended. Other Rilyun soldiers stood at Dunami's side, giving him confidence.

Tobëa swung his sword at Baëlkho Abbango, cutting him through the collarbone. A horse and rider galloped by, and Ineikhë slashed out at Reudho Affyëa, slicing open his thigh. Reudho fell forward off his horse and died as the horse ran over him.

In the distance, off toward Jub Khewi to the east, a loud bellowing shout rushed over the battlefield, and all the soldiers, Easterlings and Kelai, looked up. There in the sky was the Prophet, the child of Khesi Addeu, Holder of the Power of Space, Mewas, wearing a black hood and robe. All fighting ceased as all eyes watched him fly overhead.

Perangorai watched the Prophet drift into the field like a storm-cloud and shivered. The hooded man hovered above the ground as a phantom, and around him rose a billow of sand that surrounded him like a shield, his robes flapping in the wind over his armor. Perangorai said aloud to himself, "That is not a man; that is a god."

The Prophet wielded no weapons but his Power. He reached a hand toward Mogwana Samdho and Sego Obë. The two Easterlings screamed together before sharp snaps burst from within them, and the two men fell limp in the dirt.

Kregeth Gollapo hurled a spear at the Prophet, but the Mewas diverted it with a twitch of his hand, and the spear instead found Khesi Ammeida, piercing him below the navel. Khesi died with a terrible cry.

Aumgan Assanami, the cousin of Ammeida, roared out and cast a spear at Kregeth after the Easterling ended the life of his kin. The captain dodged the missile, and the spear went through Thenglodo Sugor's neck. His elder sister, the shield-maiden Ikhter, threw her spear at Aumgan, piercing his thigh. Aumgan screamed in pain and limped away through the battle.

Goraito Reu saw his comrade Thenglodo fall by Aumgan's spear, and he roared in anger and sprinted after the limping man. With his sword in his right hand and a short broken spear in his left, he cut down Andhi Anneumi, Dyë Abbelo, Serothrë Adlwidheno, Methritho Asserothlug, Gwilo Assogsetho, Khes Adrilun, and Bil Abbubyui. Bodies lay in a trail behind Reu. Dark blood covered him from fingers to shoulders, painting his face and mixing with mud, his sweat drawing pink streaks down his arms and chest.

Seeing Goraito tear through his men, the Prophet flew toward the Easterling as only one who holds the Power of Space could. Aumgan Assanami, now crawling because of his wounded leg and loss of blood, saw him and called out, "My Prophet, save me! I don't want to die here!"

But the Prophet drifted past the man. Aumgan's Badhyo friend, Fano Bartheno, found Aumgan struggling and pulled him away from the battle beneath the shade of a boulder, beside the corpse of Kono Asskai. Fano squeezed Aumgan's bleeding thigh and looked into his friend's terrified eyes.

"Hold on," Fano said. "Don't close thine eyes, Aumgan, don't close thine eyes…"

But Aumgan closed his eyes, and he did not reopen them.

The Prophet selected a fallen klewaig, and the sword lifted into his right hand. With his left hand, he wielded his Power. In the wake of his slaughter fell Teudasseg Kegemsun, Pagpeder Senyudon, Kegem Norkerberg, Rudhro Redhedi, and Nido Perthu—all cut through with the Prophet's blade, or their bones broken with his thoughts.

Behind him, soldiers gathered like flies to the corpses to strip the dead Easterlings' armor and take their weapons. Seroth Abwiro speared Erugi Gavwero through the chest as the Easterling tried to pry away Nido's shield. Erugi fell dead on top of it, adding his own armor and sword to the pile.

Kregeth Gollapo launched a spear at Seroth Ammikhlod, striking him in the forehead straight through the skull, driving his brains out the other side.

Perangorai cut the legs of a horse as it ran by, and its rider Khes Addeg flew forward as the horse screamed and plummeted headfirst into the sand, and Perangorai gashed Khes's throat wide open. Blood flowed over Khes and his horse, and their blood mixed and pooled in the sand beneath them.

Tobëa punched Khwigro Adrilun in the mouth, breaking his front teeth, one of which Khwigro swallowed. Tobëa raised his sword to cut him down, but Khwigro fell to his knees and hugged Tobëa's legs, sobbing.

King Gwalo ran to Tobëa and said, "What art thou doing, thou skin-burnt savage? Kill him!"

But Tobëa had seen the pathetic light in Khwigro's eyes and could not bring himself to do it. With an enormous foot, he kicked the Rilyun man away, and Khwigro stumbled back. Gwalo cursed and plunged his sword into Khwigro's chest. The man gurgled as tears made trails down his dusty cheeks, blood bubbling from his mouth, and the king of Keulen pulled his sword free as Khwigro fell dead on his belly.

The Prophet drove his sword through the top of Thegmileth Aigwida's head, through his helmet, out through the bottom jaw.

Perangorai picked up a spear and hurled it at the Prophet, who hovered above the lesser folk. The spear missed, flying too low, and instead hit Sanami Angwai in the chest. Behind Perangorai, Sanami's half-brother Penno Affado cried out and ran at Perangorai. The Kebkholenu man swung his sword and cut Penno down the chest and belly. Penno fell to the ground several yards from his brother Sanami.

Now standing on the boulder that Kono Asskai had once taken as a vantage, Thegikh stood and aimed the dead Kala's bow at the Rilyun soldiers. With the experience of long years as a mercenary in her native Kebkhelin before she was arrested and sold into slavery to mine for gold in Maikhethlen, she nocked Kono's long arrows, drew the gut-string, and let them loose in swift blurs. Rilyun men fell all over the battlefield to her arrows. First fell Gwigo Abbruno, then Solkhwasi Akhisa and his son Paugo. Rilun Abbeferas, Elëa Affriyë, Odhyo Affedrë, and Pekuth Assereth fell dead with feathered shafts quivering in their necks, breasts, or eyes.

Thegikh spied the Prophet thirty yards away and aimed a deadly arrow at the Mewas. She loosed, and the arrow missed the Prophet, instead finding Asyu Angwilo, striking him in the chest. Asyu leaned over sideways and fell in a dead crash of armor.

Thegikh let fly another arrow at the Prophet, but the Mewas flicked a hand, and a head-sized stone lifted from the ground and flew at the archer. The rock struck Thegikh on her collar-bone, and she reeled back as burning pain spread through her arm and neck. Her hand and fingers went numb, the bow fell from her grip, and she toppled from the boulder.

Kregeth Gollapo saw the woman fall and ran to her. "Art thou dead?" he asked in broken Kebkholenu—for Kregeth was a learned man who spoke several languages.

"Not yet," Thegikh said through gritted teeth. She held her crippled arm against her chest. "Stop staring and get me out of here, thou bastard. I twisted my ankle."

Kregeth helped Thegikh to her feet, supporting her beneath her working arm. The two of them made their way through the battle until it was safe for Thegikh to limp back to the camp to find the medic, and Kregeth returned to the fray.

King Gwalo stabbed Yeyo Adredh between the eyes with a short broken spear, and Yeyo's brains splattered inside his helmet. Gwalo turned and killed

Magwod Ammwinoido, leaving the short spear in the man's chest, and cut down Eito Adrë with his sword. Gwalo killed Lwidheno Akhidho with a sword to the belly, then turned to Lwidheno's cousin, Trid Assantu, who fell to the ground and wept. The king kicked Trid with a booted foot, breaking the Kala's nose and teeth, then hacked away his arms and head and sent the limbless body rolling down a hill like a log.

Gwalo slaughtered the Rilyun, his eyes burning and his teeth white, his hands dripping with gore. Many turned and ran from him, but Gwalo chased them and roared like a mad wolf, with a spear in one hand and a sword in the other, until they had almost come within sight of Jub Khewi.

Seroth Abbam stopped running as the walls of the city appeared, and he turned to face the Easterling king. Gwalo hurled his spear at Seroth and missed. Seroth charged at the king and stabbed at him with his sword, cutting Gwalo just above the waist. Gwalo grabbed Seroth's hand and wrenched the sword free, then struck Seroth in the face with his forehead, breaking Seroth's nose and sending dark blood over the two of them. Gwalo took Seroth's sword and swung, making a deep red gash through the neck, the blade stopping at the spine. Seroth Abbam crumpled to the sand and bled. Gwalo sheathed his sword and took Seroth's klewaig.

When Seroth's younger brother Adlo beheld what the king had done, he rushed at Gwalo and cut him below the elbow. Gwalo shrieked with pain as his arm shuddered and bled, and he backed away from Adlo. The young man dragged his brother's corpse toward the city, but Gwalo picked up a spear with his left arm and threw it as straight as he could, though his left arm was less-practiced than his right. The spearhead grazed Adlo's neck, cutting the artery there, and blood poured freely from the wound. Adlo cried out and fell beside his brother, keeping one hand on his bleeding neck. Gwalo walked to the young man and thrusted his sword into his back, reuniting the brothers.

The king cradled his cut arm and flexed his fingers. He turned back to the thick of battle and walked around the field to avoid the soldiers on both sides.

The Prophet smiled beneath his hood as the king retreated, knowing that his injuries prevented him from fighting. He shouted over the battlefield with a booming voice, "Easterlings! Your king is abandoning the fight! Follow his example, and ye shall live to see another sunrise!"

With these words, the Rilyun found new courage and energy, and the Easterlings looked around to see their king making his way back to camp to tend to his useless arm.

From the center of battle, Reyo Deug lifted his sword and screamed at the Prophet, "Come down here, and I'll shove my blade so far up thine ass, thou'lt taste steel for days! Thou and thy god!"

The Prophet flew to Reyo in less time than it takes to draw breath, removing Reyo's head with a single movement of his sword. A dust storm rose around the Prophet in a surging ball, the wind and sand mixing in a blinding gale. The Prophet swung his sword and thrusted his spear, and a dozen more

Easterlings fell to his wrath.

Gerodol Erkhothlog, Segsaro Bakhmë, Enogwa Kro, Kerfoinë Iso, Poiro Allo, Ertho Nohyor...

Perangorai threw his spear at the Prophet, but once again the Mewas deflected it, and the spear killed Reseroth Abbameig, landing in his chest above the heart.

The sight of the spear that Perangorai meant for the prophet shocked Goraito Reu out of a lapse of hopelessness, and he joined the Kebkholenu man. Reu slashed Eith Akhala across the chest, and the man only grunted as he died. Perangorai killed Torek Abbartheno, and Reu killed Wenolai Akhedhro and Lwisna Affagir with two swings of his sword.

The Prophet roared at Perangorai and Reu and came down at them with his weapons raised high. Perangorai threw another spear, and this time the missile found its mark. The spear glanced off the Prophet's helm and spun away to land in the sand. The Prophet paused, hovering in the air. He felt his head, the tear in his hood. His hovering staggered, and he floated to the ground, shaking his pounding head.

Perangorai and Goraito ran at the Prophet, and many other Easterlings surrounded him. But the Rilyun stood between the invaders and their Prophet, holding spears and swords out to defend him.

Perangorai sprinted and jumped and kicked Kedhro Affoinas in midair, forcing him to stumble backward. Perangorai landed on Kedhro's chest and drove a sword into his soft throat. Several yards away, Sugor Aberëar pulled back his bowstring and shot an arrow. It landed in Perangorai's foot, and the Kebkholenu man screamed in anger and pain.

"Stop!" bellowed the Prophet.

Every man and woman—Rilyun and Easterling—paused. All were silent.

The Prophet rose into the air, his robes snapping in the breeze against his armor. "Enough for today," he said.

A high wind blew, and for a moment sand and dust filled the air like a scorching blizzard, and no soldier could see any other. When the wind let up and the sandy air cleared, the Prophet and his army were far away, headed back to Jub Khewi.

The Easterlings stood with their bloody swords and bloody spears in their bloody hands. Some panted, some cried, others puked, and a few allowed themselves finally to pass out and fall over. The flies and vultures had begun to stalk the place.

Now after the battle, the Easterlings who were neither dead nor injured joined in a feast with King Gwalo the Younger. They sang and toasted the memories of their dead brothers and sisters as they became drunk on mead and ate their fill of goat, which was plentiful in Len Khalayu.

Cuts had been sewn, bones set, and those healing from battle were now asleep with willow-bark tea in their bellies. The more grievously wounded lay in their beds with salves and ointments on their wounds, covered in bandages, smoking gannëa for the pain. A north wind blew the desert sands over the corpses on the battlefield, but still the flies and vultures and jackals found them.

The king himself sat at the table in his hall, and there he looked over the feasting soldiers who joined him. To his right sat Kregeth Gollapo, and to his left sat Goraito Reu. Beside those captains sat the many other leaders of Keulen, all from different regions of their country, who commanded sizable portions of the king's army.

As the night grew late, plates emptied and cups were drained and laughter rose high and loud. Some captains nodded slowly in their seats and drooled into their beards. Gwalo and Reu stood together, their cups spilling over, as they sang a song about dragons and women. Their voices rose louder until the tune was altogether lost. Then, when the song was finally finished, they drained their cups and laughed together.

The king steadied himself on Gwalo's shoulder and said, "By Odol's breath, I have missed thee, my friend; and thou hast missed much as well—so many battles, deeds worthy of song. But what of thy adventures? Pray, regale us with a tale or two!"

Goraito filled his cup—not with mead, but with the Badhyo drink ilo, which was clear and burned like fire in the throat. "Aye, my king," the captain said, "a story or more I could tell, but they'd pale beside those of Brenn. These past six months as I've ridden with him and the Erkhesgur from far-off Koraithlen, I've heard many of his exploits from his own mouth. I hope I've heard most of them, for if he has any more he'd be a proper hero in a bard's lay. Brenn, where art thou?"

"Here, Goraito," spoke the Baithas. He sat at the

far end of the table with Den and Tobëa. The three of them ate silently, sipping on mead, listening to the raucous singing. Perangorai and Thegikh now rested at the southernmost end of the camp, where Brenn and Den had made camp for the Erkhesgur; wounded and bandaged, the two Kebkholenyu now slept deep under the thick dreams of gannëa smoke.

Goraito spoke for all to hear: "Brenn Ragnir was in Goreuhwo the very day the Taf-Waikht destroyed the gwerfegi. Yea, he was there in the building itself. Now there is a tale, Brenn—tell it! Or tell of the war in Saulen, and what thou and Den did to that filth of a commander."

But Brenn said nothing and stared at his unfinished meal.

Then the king drained his cup and said, "Gwennotir Ker, it befits thy character to arrive after most of the work has been done."

The Baithas looked up and said with stern voice, "My name is Brenn."

"I saw thee not in the fray," said the king. "Delighted I am to see thee unharmed."

Brenn replied, "Tell me, King—why am I here? Why send Goraito and his knights to search the ends of the earth and bring me hither? What purpose might I serve thee, and thereafter be done with thy incessant stalking?"

At this the room fell silent, and the king glared at Brenn with cold eyes. "What manner of Easterling runs as thou didst? If thou wast not a Derotir, I'd swear thou wast bastard-born of a whore, and I'd never guess thou art the brother of Kolewa and the son of Deugwer—two of the most renowned men ever to have walked this earth. Were they here today, they would be ashamed of thee."

Color rose to Brenn's cheeks, and he said, "Were my father and brother here, the war might have ended years ago. What hast thou accomplished these past eight years?"

"Thou wilt speak not to me this way," the king barked. "I am thy king, and thou hast sworn fealty to me, though the memory may be lost on thee. Be not so quick to frame thy family in a light of innocence, Baithas. No man is without flaw, and thy father and brother did their share of frightful deeds while fighting the Mad Prophet, this I assure thee. Preach not to me of warcraft, Gwennotir; I've been at it since thou sucked thy mother's tit, rest her soul."

Brenn growled as a bear and said, "Thou dost dishonor to thyself by offending the Derevai as thou hast. They teach against needless violence, and all who kill for the sport of it they cast from the Shatter into the yawning void of the Nether."

"Quote not my own religion to me!" shouted Gwalo. "I will not hear it from a faithless whelp, from a man who stands as a god before his kinsman, letting them worship him without correction."

"I have never known any to see me in such a light," said Brenn. "And if I had, I would correct them. Being a Baithas is burden enough; to be a god would be a cruel fate worse even than death."

"And thou tellest tales of meeting a god that was not a Dorova." Gwalo the Younger paced around his table. "Sooth, thou art disloyal to the Keulenu and to the Derevai. Thou dost dishonor the Ker name, and thou nearest treason for speaking against me in front of my captains."

Here the king's eyes fell to the sword at Brenn's waist. At an impulse, Brenn's hand fell to the hilt. As lightning strikes a pond and the water is electrified, sending all life therein into a frenzy, so too did Brenn's sword vibrate with its Powers through his being, sending a low and sweet humming throughout the hall. As he held it, Brenn perceived the thoughts of each person in the room: Odol preserve...damn fool...he shouldn't fight...he's a traitor if he does it...dishonors his father...put it away, put it away...

Brenn released his grip from the sword, and the hall seemed to dim. The soldiers at the table stared at Brenn with awe, fear, and disgust.

"Worthless whelp," spoke the king. "I see now that mine hopes are unfounded; my aim was to bring thee hither and place behind us all enmity, that perhaps wisdom would find its way into thine heart, and thou wouldst use that sword for the good of Keulen. Alas!—where wisdom should sit, instead there is folly. Now I tell thee this as king of thine homeland, as thy liege and lord, as the one who commands the armies of the East: Give me the sword!"

Here King Gwalo drew his own blade, and all soldiers sitting near him straightway stood and fled the space. Now an empty room lay between Baithas and king, and Gwalo's sword trembled with a lust for blood as he pointed it at Brenn.

The Baithas felt a hand upon his leg—it was Den, begging with naught but a look in their eyes to cease this fight ere blood was spilled. Gently Brenn grasped his dear friend's hand and moved it aside, then stood and undid the clasp of his cloak, casting it over his broad shoulder and letting it fall to the floor. Long had he carried and worn that cloak: a gift from a sorcerer who saved Brenn's life after a bear drove him near to death in Saulen. Over land and seas, through war and slavery, Brenn had kept this cloak. Though now naked of it, still he stood before the king of Keulen as a bear on its hind legs.

"Before I draw forth Pukhso," said Brenn with a voice loud enough for all to hear, "I would speak of terms. Let this be a proper dauker; I desire no crown, nor title—only thy property. For I have discovered something thou keepest in thine hall which I greatly desire to possess. If I am slain, Pukhso shall pass to thy ownership, and none shall keep thee from taking it. But be warned! Such powers were not meant for the likes of us—mortal and fallible, we who are fragile of mind and flesh, with desires for vengeance and the will to dominate others. Use the sword to win thy war, then cast it aside and never use it again!"

"I'll use my sword how I see fit," said the king, "and I'll pay no mind to the worries of a lesser man; I am made of sterner stuff than thee. Now tell me—tell us all—what is it thou hast discovered in mine hall which thou desirest to keep for thine own?"

"Nay, I have no desire to keep it, but I would hold the right to do with it as I please—and I would release it."

At this the king's face grew pale, and he lowered his sword, though he kept his composure and showed not his concern; for he knew of what Brenn spoke.

"For nigh on fifteen years I have eluded you lot," said the Baithas to all who heard. "I am my father's second-born and was not prepared to take the mantle of Speaker; such was for my brother Kolewa. But he died, and the Power passed to me, and I have hated it ever since. Peace is all I want, and I have searched the ends of the earth for a land where Keulenu could not find me. I thought that I had found it in far-off Koraithlen, but Goraito Reu found me and brought me hither. I know that any deed short of my death would bring me no freedom from thy searching eyes and grasping arms, King Gwalo; therefore, I sought another way.

"While the Keulenu battle the Kelai today, I instead remained behind in safety. What leverage might I find, I wondered. Gwalo's hall was empty, for all soldiers were in the fray. There I searched, and I found no leverage; but I did find a grondeketh. A cursed man, more monster than human, locked in a cage meant as a rabbit hutch, a blanket draped over it, sitting in a corner by the wall. For what purpose thou hast kept him, I cannot begin to guess. But it is evil and wrong to keep such a being in a cage in which it can do little more than sit and crouch. Knowest thou what a grondeketh is, truly? Not mere children's tales; I have seen one in the flesh during my travels, and I tell thee this: he will bring nothing thou seekest."

"Thou knowest not what I seek," said the king. "What I keep in my private chambers are mine alone; what drove thee to search my things? This by itself is worthy of the ax. What wouldst thou do with the grondeketh? Release it? The monster would turn on thee and rake thy flesh from thy bones, then slaughter the entire camp. We are safe as long as it remains in the cage."

"Then why not kill it?" asked Brenn, and all eyes turned to the king to hear his response.

"A king need not explain himself," said Gwalo. "Now draw thy sword so that I may defeat thee in lawful dauker!"

"Make the oath first," said Brenn, "so that all may hear."

The king spat on the floor, then said, "If thou canst best the man most skilled with a blade in all of Keulen and Len Khalayu, then by law and divine right thou shalt inherit my things. And I hope they bring thee what thou seekest. As for thee: I'll not end thy life. I'll not commit the most heinous of sins by killing an heirless Derotir. But maimed thou shalt be; I will take thine hands and feet, yet alive thou shalt remain."

Then, for the first time since he had been in Yenmiskelanë when the Frog tribe were at his mercy, Brenn drew forth Pukhso from its scabbard. His own Power was then enhanced—he heard the horses without the hall, speaking to one another in hushed tones; but also, were the other three Powers brought to his spirit—Time, Space, and Thought. If he were to try, he knew very well that he could lift the roof from the king's hall and wind back the Sun in the sky, but he had no desire to do these things. The room cleared of people, tables and dogs, and the two enemies locked eyes.

"Thy grace may make the first move," said Brenn.

The king made an awful frown as one with rotten food on his tongue. "Think not that I fear thy magic blade, Gwennotir. I know how to kill; yea, I've been at it longer than thou hast."

But then the soft touch of a voice entered into Brenn's mind, not as sound but as rumbles of thought. A trick he saw before it happened: Gwalo reaching for the knife in his belt, hurling it across the hall to the Baithas. Brenn moved aside, the dagger flew by. Its aim was deadly, pointed at his heart, but Brenn moved just in time and the knife merely cut his shirt and shoulder. Blood seeped forth over his arm, staining the cloth and dripping on the ground. At this Brenn smiled; the king has cut him in the very place a certain bear had raked him to the bone so many years before in Saulen.

Now Brenn's turn, he closed the distance between himself and the king. Raising Pukhso, he sighed as the weight of the blade came down upon the Younger. But the king was quick, and more skill he had than luck; with his own sword he glanced Pukhso aside, and not a single cut had Brenn landed upon him. Gwalo lunged in reply, but Brenn parried. Again, Gwalo swung; again, Brenn blocked and moved aside.

An old tactic of his the king now used: with his bare fist he punched the Baithas in the face, knocking Brenn back with a daze and a sore jaw. Now Gwalo screamed, bringing down his sword over and over onto the poor Baithas. Like one crazed with rage the king went to his word, chopping as one with an ax into a fallen tree, his Keulen-forged steel against Brenn's otherworldly blade.

But then once more a soft voice came to the ear of Brenn's mind, and the Baithas learned a truth from the mind of the king himself: Gwalo was afraid. For a brief moment Brenn reconsidered this duel; why should he intend to kill a man filled with so much anger and fear? All those fallen by Brenn's hand in years gone by had meant to cause him and those he loved harm, and they had little good within them; certainly, they did not fear death as Gwalo did now. How long had the king feared the Nether? How long had a man's frame contained a boy's spirit? Brenn hesitated, and in that moment Gwalo punched him again.

Brenn stumbled, fell, knocking over a bench and twisting his ankle. Gwalo placed a booted foot upon Brenn's chest, pressing down with a force that spoke of the desire to see his foe suffer rather than see him give in so easily.

Then shouted a voice: "Stand up, Brenn!" Brenn saw from the side of his vision—it was Kregeth who spoke. Kregeth, the king's own right hand, the commander of the better part of Keulen's army, he who sat in confidence beside the king and shared his house in Nugomor—this man now cheered for Brenn to overthrow the king.

At Kregeth's voice, a wave of quickening shot through the hall, and several voices rose with the commander's. The Easterlings cheered for Brenn to stand, chanting his name—the one he had chosen, not the name he had left behind.

Then with a cry of his own, Brenn swung above his head shining Pukhso. A scream rang out, blood sprayed upon the floor, and Gwalo staggered back, cradling a bleeding hand. The first finger on his right hand was gone.

Brenn scrambled to his feet. Pukhso hummed and glowed with ethereality, giving him strength. The soldiers cheered as he stood, and Gwalo sneered like a wolf caught in a snare.

With all the speed of a man trained in combat since childhood, Gwalo crossed the space between himself and Den. Brenn saw it too late; he heard the king's thoughts not soon enough. Gwalo the Younger now stood behind Den, one hand gripping Den's arm behind their back, the other holding a sword to Den's throat. Den's eyes were wide with fear, though they dared make no sound.

"Yield!" shouted the king. A small cut appeared on Den's neck and blood trickled down over the blade as the king likewise bled upon the floor from his missing finger.

But did he yield, that fierce Brenn? As he saw his dearest friend within an inch of death, did he bend to the wrathful king's request? Nay—when had he ever given evil the satisfaction of having its way?

An anger of Brenn's own bubbled up within him; it came not from Pukhso, though the sword amplified his emotion. Brenn raised the sword, pointing it at the king, and fire erupted in his gaze. Yea, all who stood in that hall then felt electricity within their hair and upon their skin, such that happens when standing in an open field during a storm. The room crackled with astrality, and the king wavered in his decision to hold Brenn's closest friend as hostage.

Then, lo!—the Baithas Brenn Ragnir called down

lightning from the heavens, and the roof over the king's hall was straightway torn asunder as Odol's wrath shot through. It is said that for a moment Brenn's eyes turned white to match his hair, and in that time a bolt of lightning he directed through his sword, aiming it at Gwalo like an arrow from a bow. In an instant brighter than dawn's light on frozen snow, louder than a volcano bursting its top, the king lay dead and burned on the floor. Thus passed Gwalo the Younger, son of Gwalo the Elder, king of Keulen.

And it came to pass that Kregeth Gollapo knelt beside the dead Gwalo and took from around his charred neck the pendant of kingship, and Kregeth presented it to Brenn as he knelt, saying, "Hail, King Brenn! So shall the Baithais reign over Keulen as in times of old!"

Then the other Easterlings chanted together, "Hail, King Brenn! Hail, Baithas!"

But Brenn took the pendant and cast it upon the ground after he had sheathed Pukhso once more. He looked out to the hall and beheld the eyes upon him, and he spoke to them saying:

"Silence, all of you! Take this pendant of kingship from my sight; I have no need for it, nor any desire to wear it. Ye desire that I should rule over you?—then listen first to what I have to say. Ever have I wandered this Earth seeking to avoid all hints of fate. I became a Baithas and was not prepared nor willing, but this office was forced upon me because of the circumstance of my birth and the death of my brother.

"A soldier, the king wanted me to be, and so I

ran. But destiny placed me in the house of Aebakhmë, and he used me for his evil intent and started this very war in which ye fight. Again, I ran, but my countenance would not leave alone a mob in the streets of Jub Khewi beating to death a pregnant girl. I saved her, and together we fled the city; I left it to the throes of war—why should I not have? It was not my war, and still it is not!

"And then the Derevai placed in my path a helpless boy, strange and awkward, yet helpless; and so my friend and I adopted him and took him along on our travels. Yet another boy was found, this one fleeing from bondage in Saulen. For the first time, I used my Power to call upon a pack of wolves to chase away the boy's pursuers. And how was I rewarded?—with a mauling by a great bear in the woods. I was clawed and chewed within sight of death; yea, I may have died for a moment, for I thought I saw the Shatter, and a voice came to me saying, Thy task is not yet done upon this Earth. And I awoke; for a sorcerer had revived me and healed my wounds. This very cloak I wear was taken from the hide of that bear.

"Yet our second foundling boy was not safe, for his pursuers were none other than the Taf-Waikht, though I knew it not at the time. I took my found-family to Goreuhwo, hoping to evade the would-be captors. Then, alas!—that fateful event occurred, and we were caught amid the wreckage of that horrid attack. The boy, the first we'd found, his name was Laidho...he did not survive, and we buried him beneath an apple tree. But Gwidhotir, the other boy, was taken in the chaos by the Taf-Waikht, and I never saw him again. Little consolation I received knowing that I saved many people, carrying them from the fire and wreckage of the gwerfegi; I could not save my friends.

"Then came a summons from the chancellor himself—he wished to reward the man who saved so many lives during the Taf-Waikht's attack. Ai, but it was a trick; he discovered my identity and sought to use it as leverage against me. Fight for me in my conquest of Saulen, he told me, or I shall deliver thee unto Gwalo thy king. What choice did I have? I could not run, and so I went to war.

"I'll tell not of the horrors I witnessed there. Suffice it to say that my commander was a madman with a lust for blood and a disregard for human life. But there I met Den, my closest friend, and together we fled Saulen after I had taken our commander's head off with Pukhso. Together Den and I crossed the water into Kebkhelin, where we were starving. In a moment of weakness we stole some goods from a market and were arrested and thrown into jail.

"What happened then? The magistrate sold the two of us to a gold mine in Maikhethlen. Aye, we were enslaved, just as Gwidhotir had been. My count of days passed into months, every moment more miserable than the last. There we met many others who would later call themselves Erkhesgur. Together we overthrew our masters and put them to the spear, then took a ship and sailed across the Terunthleu to Yenmiskelanë. Tobëa is from that mythic land, and he had known my father there. Indeed, my father was in Yenmiskelanë; he had sailed across the Endless, the first to do so! Not dead was he, as ye all had assumed for those many years.

"We came to Yenmiskelanë, welcomed with open arms into Tobëa's childhood village. There we learned much: the truth of the ancestry of humankind, the origin of the Powers, and the fate of my father's crew. Their ship was damaged on the voyage from Edorath, and so they dwelt for a time with the Raven Clan while they made repairs. To some Easterlings were born children, half of each race. My father, too, begat a son, mothered by the Kleumas, the Listener herself. But a plague came upon the village, and many Easterlings perished. Those who yet lived took their new families onto the ship, now repaired, and sailed west toward Edorath. Tobëa was among them, scarcely more than a child. With them also were mine half-brother and his mother, who was called Sarkhangwena. But a storm came upon them, and the ship was destroyed. Many were drowned, and those who lived were separated and lost. Ye have heard where Tobëa's fate took him.

"But what of my father? I found his grave upon a mountain, and there I wept and cursed the Derevai that such should be his fate and mine, endlessly thrown into unwanted adventured. I slept beside his cairn that night, and again the Shatter came to me in a dream; for the night was cold and I was near death, and a person can behold the Shatter only when dead or close to it. In my dream a voice came to me, the same voice that came after the bear had torn me up. But now the voice spoke to me of other things, of destiny and fate, of cricket-song and the life of the world. I had a part to play yet, the voice said to me. I begged it to leave me alone to die; I wanted no more part in my own story. We must all be the main characters in our own tales, it said, no matter how strongly we wish to be left unwritten. I understood it not, but the voice left me, and I awoke with Den wrapped around me with a thick blanket, staving the cold from me, keeping me alive. Pukhso was changed after that night, having become the magic blade ye now see.

"Another clan came in the night, raiding the Ravens for Winter supplies. We must retaliate, I told the Ravens. This deed should not go unpunished! Yet they refused, for war is seen in a different light to those in Yenmiskelanë. If thou wilt kill a man, thou wilt take upon thyself the hunger and security of his family. But I did not listen; mine heart was angry at the fate of my father. We Erkhesgur attacked the Frog Clan, slaying all but a few of their brave men. Then their women and children and elderly came to the Ravens to beg for food and warmth, and the Ravens chased us back to our ship. Never return, they said to us. And if others from Edorath come, we will kill them as recompense for the blood ye have spilled here.

"Mine heart has pondered continually upon these things I have done and seen, and in living through mine horrors, mine heart cries out—O wretched life that is mine! Yea, I sorrow for each moment of every day because of mine afflictions. I am encompassed about by tales of adventure in which I want no part; and when I desire to live a life of solitude and peace, the universe laughs and mine heart groans. I am the subject of tales of such woe, for my life is not mine own to live. If I am your king, then here is my first and final decree: Give the crown to another! Leave the kingship to another more deserving and willing, and let me live in peace!"—thus Brenn to those who listened.

In silence the Easterlings considered his words, no more smiling and cheering his name. Then at last Kregeth raised his eyes to Brenn and said, "Tell us at least who should be our king, if not thou."

Then Brenn picked up the pendant he had thrown to the floor and threw it again—this time to the captain. Kregeth Gollapo caught it in his right hand and frowned.

"It would be a lie to claim I would not be willing," he said, "though it is something I have never desired for myself."

"That is why thou art my choice," said Brenn. "Now I will leave thee, King Kregeth, to thy business of war. By thy leave I will release the poor creature from its cage."

Kregeth nodded, and Brenn entered the king's bedchamber. There against the wall sat a cage cloaked in a blanket. Brenn threw it aside.

Now this is what this grondeketh looked like: it had the shape of a man, with skin pale and sickly, pulled tight over its long thin bones; a massive skull, pointed at the top; a mouth that stretched from ear to ear, drooling over dozens of long pointed teeth; fingernails long, dirty, yellow; enormous eyes, black, lidless, bulging from its face. It sat like an animal with hind legs bent beneath it, tapping with its claws on the floor.

Brenn made no startled move; he had seen a

grondeketh before, years ago in Maikhethlen just before he found poor Laidho. "I have not come to harm thee," he said. "I know thou wast once a man, and I would rest easier having released thee from this cage. I would ask thee to hurt none, but I know not whether thou understandest me."

But then the creature opened its wide maw, showing its rows of needle-teeth, and formed a single word close to human speech: "Brenn."

At this the Baithas frowned. "How knowest thou my name?" he asked, but the grondeketh made no reply other than speaking the name once more. "Could it be that I know thee, or that thou knowest me? Perhaps we met before fate took thee into this form?" Brenn sighed and said to himself, "Yet again I arrive at the threshold of a bard's tale, for here is the herald; and now I make my choice."

Then Brenn removed the latch from the cage and opened wide the door. Out leaped the grondeketh, and all people in the hall then gasped and moved aside. But the grondeketh made no move against them, but it turned to Brenn and said this time, "Come." And thus did Brenn make his decision, following the creature where it led.

The grondeketh bounded over the sands outside, running without hesitation or slowing as its feet and claws dug into the soft ground, but Brenn kept pace behind it. They came to the cliff-edge of Borheno Gwega; the canyon-valley spread out before them with its wide lake and small forest of leitho trees. But the grondeketh made no pause to admire the view, scurrying over the sheer edge.

Brenn looked down and saw the creature crawl

downward, using a narrow path set into the stone cliff. He followed as best he could, sliding on the loose rock and dirt. He came at last to an opening in the cliff wall behind a ledge that lay hidden by the cliffs above. The grondeketh waited there for him.

When Brenn had safely made his way to the ledge, the grondeketh rose upon its hind legs and placed a claw upon the wall, then ran the claw down the length of it. A series of clicks and whirs sounded from the rock within, and as the grondeketh's claw reached the floor a thud issued from behind the wall, and behold!—it opened inward, for it was not merely a wall, but a cunningly hidden doorway.

Now inside the cave Brenn looked around. A massive space it was, large enough that Brenn could see no end in the dark. But as the two entered, the cave sprang to life; lights of all colors and sizes flamed into being, illuminating the place—but they burned not with fire, and their light was steady and soft. Tables and boxes lay about the cave, stacked with tools and devices Brenn could not describe even to himself, though the boxes seemed to him more akin to paintings with moving images.

The grondeketh then jumped upon a table, knocking over objects that fell and broke on the floor, spilling liquids and powders; then the creature reached for a glass orb that hung on the wall in a sconce, containing a liquid the color of amber that swirled of its own accord. The grondeketh swatted, and the orb fell from the wall to the table below where its glass shattered and the liquid spilled out. Small grooves set in the table caught the liquid and led it into channels where it gathered at one of the table's corners and dripped through a small hole. The grondeketh jumped to the floor and opened its wide mouth to catch the liquid, which fell drop by drop until there was none remaining on the table or in the grooves. It swallowed, then was silent for a moment.

Then the grondeketh panted with harsh breaths like one sprinting, and its back and chest pumped as its heartbeat grew quicker. It lay on its side and clutched at its belly as it moaned with pain. Then the grondeketh's bones snapped and clicked, and the creature screamed. Its curved spine straightened, its long legs collapsed in on themselves and shortened until their proportions were not so grotesque. Its claws fell out and crumbled to the floor, and in their bloody places proper fingernails sprouted. Many sharp teeth fell out, and the ones that remained were small and ordinary. The eyes shrank, the black fading to grey, then to white, then blooming with blue irises and black pupils. The dark grey skin dried and split and sloughed away, revealing lighter and softer skin beneath. Brown hair sprouted from the scalp and grew down to the ears.

When the changing stopped and body pieces lay upon the floor among a pile of discarded skin, the grondeketh caught its breath and wiped its face with its hands; for it was not a monster, but an adult man. He dripped with sweat, and even in the warm cave room steam wafted from him. The man stood naked to his feet and coughed, pulled one last loose tooth from his mouth, and spat blood on the floor.

"Mother-trucker, dude," he said. "That hurt like a butt-cheek on a stick..."

With awe and confusion Brenn looked upon the man. Only moments ago he'd been a creature from a child's tale, yet now he walked upon two human legs to a bureau from which he took a set of clothes and dressed himself.

"Are you thirsty?" the man asked. "Can I get you something? Water? Coke? I think I need something stronger, myself." Beside the bureau stood a cupboard, and the man opened its doors to reveal bottles of a hundred kinds of beverage. He poured one clear liquid into two small glass cups, then handed one to Brenn. "Sorry, no ice. I assume the power went out sometime in the last two years. I should've hooked the fridge up to the emergency generator with the computers. Oh, well." He clinked his glass against Brenn's, said, "Prost," and drank it with one quick swallow; he grimaced, sighed, and poured another for himself.

Brenn sipped and felt his throat and chest burn—a strong liquor this was, akin to the Badhyo ilo. "Who art thou?" he asked at length.

The man frowned at Brenn and said, "You don't recognize me. I guess it has been a while. And I'll never look how I did then, even with my vaccine. Please sit, Brenn, you're giving me anxiety."

Brenn took a chair and sat across from the man.

"Maybe this will jog your memory. About two years ago, I think, in Saulen, you came down with a nasty case of got-mauled-by-a-bear. I saved your life."

At this Brenn's eyes went wide with recognition, and he cried out, "The sorcerer! Gaikhud is thy name, yes?"

The man shook his head. "That was the name I went by, but my real name is Adluo. How's that cloak I gave you? Still have it?"

"Indeed," said Brenn. "It remains above within the camp, for I removed it before slaying the Keuleno king."

Adluo laughed into his drink and said with a low voice, "I'll never get used to the way you all talk here." His teeth were white, his blue eyes bright. "How are your friends? The girl and the two boys who were with you. They aren't here, are they?"

Brenn frowned and said, "Laidho is dead, killed in the events at Goreuhwo when the Taf-Waikht destroyed the gwerfegi. Of Gwidhotir's fate, I know naught; he was taken by the Taf-Waikht on the very same day. Deubmeni...I hope she is safe. We parted ways after placing Laidho in the ground; I went to war in Saulen. She joined a caravan headed west, perhaps to return to Jub Khewi—though I doubt this was the case, for she was abused in that city and hated the time she spent there."

"I'm sorry, Brenn." Adluo shook his head. "It's been a crazy few years for all of us, huh? Ever since that day."

Brenn asked, "Wast thou there?"

Adluo nodded. "That was the day they took me."

"What happened?"

"Oh, you know..." Adluo refilled the two cups as he spoke. "The Taf-Waikht kidnapped me, put me in a crate, dragged me across Edorath, then locked me away for two years while some guy probed my mind for secret weapons-knowledge. And the more magic I was forced to use, the less human I became.

C'est la vie, ja?"

Brenn stood, putting his cup aside. "Who art thou, in truth?"

Adluo said, "There will be time for an exposition dump later, my old acquaintance. But right now I need your help." He motioned for Brenn to follow, and he led the Baithas through the cavernous room, past the strange devices which Brenn could not describe, even to his own thoughts. At the back wall they stopped; the largest of all the peculiar objects stood against the wall, reaching to the ceiling, silent as a bear in hibernation.

Adluo then went to a metal box that stood beside the great thing, moved a toggle, and lo! the room was filled with a soft white light; then more lights of all colors flickered on, spreading over the machine, outlining its shape in the dim cave. The central part glowed yellow—a giant Ring made of metal, large enough for the long-necked spotted deer of Deulen to walk through without ducking its high head.

"What manner of craft is this?" asked Brenn, looking upon the Ring in wonder.

Adluo here used a word that landed strangely in Brenn's ears, but he thought the Power within him gave the interpretation Entroër—that which allows passage between Earths. Confusion came upon Brenn's mind, for he understood not the meaning. "It's a doorway," Adluo said, seeing the bewildered light in Brenn's eyes.

"Whither does it lead?" Brenn asked.

"Anywhere," the sorcerer said. "I need your help, Brenn. I want to go home."

With a curt laugh, Brenn rubbed his face and

muttered, "I think I've gone quite mad, else thou thinkest me a fool, and this is some jest made on my account."

Adluo grabbed Brenn by the arms, forcing him to meet his gaze. "Listen to me, Brenn. I joke about a lot of things. It's part of my culture. I'm sarcastic more often than not, but not now. I'm more serious than I've ever been. You saw me change from that monster back into myself—do you need more convincing? What do you need me to tell you, or show you?"

"But why me?" asked Brenn. "Why needest thou mine help, and not that of another?"

"It's complicated."

Then Brenn pulled away from Adluo's grasp and walked around the room, inspecting the strange devices that blinked and whirred as he went by. "Tell me this: whither leads this Ring?"

Adluo sighed. "You wouldn't believe me if I told you. No? Are you sure you wanna know? Okay. I'm from a parallel universe. I came here by mistake, and this is going to get me back."

For a moment Brenn said nothing but looked upon Adluo with curiosity. "This intrigues me," he said; "not because I understand thee, but because I do not. Never have I heard this term before—parallel universe. Explain to me as thou wouldst a child, and then I will determine whether I might aid thee."

Then with one last exasperated groan, Adluo motioned for Brenn to sit and rest. "I'll give you a simple version, but I won't treat you like a child. I trust you to be smart enough to grasp what I'll say. Alright, here goes…"

Song of the Crickets

I took the name Gaikhud when I came here, when I found myself in the middle of a strange desert in a strange world. The machine that sent me here was gone, and I was stranded in what looked like a million miles of hot sand with no hope of rescue.

I guess you could say I come from Mithoër, though in my world it has a different name. I wasn't trying to go to Edorath. I didn't know that it existed, and I didn't care about finding out. The machine I built was for something else entirely. No matter how much I could attempt to explain what it was meant to do, you'd never understand, so I won't try. It's not your fault. This world is several hundred years behind my own world, maybe even a thousand or more, as far as technology goes. But that's beside the point.

Anyway, something out of my control went very wrong, and I found myself traveling between worlds for what could have been an eon or half a second. I appeared right here in this cave.

No matter how I think about it or try to apply reason to it, I can't figure out why I came to this spot. You'd think I would've stayed in Mithoër, where the machine was, where I was when it happened. But instead I ended up in Len Khalayu, of all places.

And there was Jub Khewi, not more than a couple miles away, filled with generous and caring people who found me a place to stay and helped me find employment cleaning dishes at a tea shop.

The language was the hardest part. Back home, I

can speak five languages, but I always used German to learn them. I had bilingual teachers and books to read. In Jub Khewi I was thrown into the deep end with no life jacket, and I had to learn Kalayo with absolutely no common ground with language. I learned like a child, slowly and painfully.

After a couple years, I was confident enough to apply for a teaching position at the university. That was also difficult. What could I teach these people that they would understand and not write off as black magic? At fourteen, I had already earned degrees in math and quantum engineering, then went on for a doctorate in theoretical physics, then hopped from university to university around the world earning degrees in ten other subjects (I love learning in the same way a junkie loves heroin), so I was definitely qualified to teach others—but I wasn't even sure the people here knew algebra, so I decided to teach that.

I chose the name Gaikhud Akheslen because I could claim to have come from the western end of Len Khalayu where the people are much lighter-skinned and more resemble Mithoëru. No one questioned my story of being abandoned by a caravan, but there were a few who held some kind of prejudice against me. I made an effort to demonstrate my adopted (but fake) Rilyun faith, and that ended the worries of most.

All the while, I was trying to find a way home. I had no idea how I had gotten here in the first place, though, so I redid all the schematics and calculations of my first machine, trying to find some flaw or an accidental breakthrough that I had created. It took years, but I did find it. The concept was simple, and I knew that with a little tweaking of the math, I could build a machine to send me back, on purpose this time. But I needed materials and tools that didn't exist anywhere in Edorath. How was I going to build my portal?

Of course, after living in Edorath for so long, I learned about the Holders. Four people per generation, each one born with one of four Powers: space, time, thought, and language. I didn't believe it at first, but then I learned that the prophet of the Rilyun religion lived in Jub Khewi, and he was the Space Holder, as were all his ancestors leading back to who knows when. I came to know of the other Holders as well, especially of your father, Deugwer Ker—the Wolf, they called him. And your older brother Kolewa the Fox. They're well-known in this part of the country, after wiping out Khesi Addeu's army.

We don't have anything like the Powers where I come from, or any other kind of magic. Not that I've ever seen, anyway. Discovering that magic was a possibility here in Edorath was an awesome moment, like a fish learning about birds. But I wasn't one of the Holders, and I never would be. Still, I knew there had to be an option.

I started in the library of Jub Khewi's university, searching through records of Holders throughout history. I read fairy tales and myths. I read the Kanakh-ri cover to cover a dozen times until I had whole sections of it memorized. I found nothing.

I traveled to Mithoër, seeking out every book or scroll or rune-carved rock I could find. I spoke to children for ghost stories, and old people for stories no one else remembered. My search took me to Dol-Nopthelen, Markhlen, Mitho Gorikhwa, and finally Saulen. That's where I figured it out.

Almost no one knows about the Una. They lived in Saulen before anyone else and left nothing behind except for a few strange things nobody would think to look for. It's no secret that Mitho Gorikhwa invaded Saulen a thousand years ago and wiped out all who were living there. Many of those people were descendants of the Una, and some had written down their oral histories. These records still exist in the lower levels of the Red Palace in Goreuhwo, and anyone can get in if their pockets are deep enough.

The records are sparse and often illegible, even when written in a still-living language. It's difficult to tell fact from fable, but I managed to stitch together what I thought made the most sense.

The Una spoke of nature spirits. They gave them names, talked to them like you would with friends, and treated them as equals. Sometimes a spirit would grant a favor to an Una, and these favors were usually spent on good crops or healthy livestock. There was really nothing special in those stories, but then it hit me.

Every single culture I had come across had stories like these. There was a time when people would converse with beings who were capable of the impossible. In Mithoër they're called mogans, in Dol-Nopthelen they're called yatten, and in Mitho Gorikhwa they're called shi-fai. This wasn't a coincidence.

I stayed in Saulen, building and fixing things for

people until I had saved enough money to travel back to Jub Khewi. Now that I knew what to look for, I found mountains of information at the university that no one else would have given a second glance.

On one moonless night, I hiked into the desert, drew some symbols in the sand, and spoke a few phrases in a long-dead language. I can't say for sure what happened, but a moment after my chant was complete, there was a crack in the air and the smell of burnt hair. Standing in front of me were a young boy and a young girl, both small and dark and older than mankind. I wasted no time in pulling out the special stone lock-box I had made. (Here it is. I made it into a necklace to keep it with me all the time.) After one more spell, the desert children were trapped, bound to me, and I controlled all powers that they possessed. (Don't look so appalled, Brenn. They aren't actually children, they're jinn. The same species that ancient peoples had lived alongside and would perform miracles of nature.)

Progress on my portal skyrocketed. I could conjure up the raw materials I needed, like metals and oil and things like that, and again use magic to refine them into plastics or alloys, and then shape them into the parts I needed. This cave filled quickly until it began to resemble my laboratory back in Austria.

I was enjoying myself far too much by the time I realized what was happening to me. It was slow, but definitely happening. Some of my teeth fell out and grew back longer and sharper. Same with my fingernails and toenails. Mine hair began to fall out like I was on chemo. My eyes grew bigger, my skin got leathery. I craved meat, and each meal was rawer than the last.

I took blood samples and studied myself. I sequenced my entire genome and took almost a year trying to pinpoint what was happening to me. Of course, you know now that it was the curse of the jinn. The more you use their magic, the less human you become, until you're only a monster with scrambled eggs for a brain.

I combined magic with chemistry and created a sort of antidote; though obviously, it would stop working after a while. It got to the point where I was drinking a liter of it every week, when before it was a sip every couple of weeks. I knew there was a considerable chance something could go wrong, and I might be forced to use magic for some reason away from my potion stash. I always made sure to keep a bottle with me, and I created the fail-safe you saw me use earlier.

It won't last forever. If anything, it's just a band-aid solution. I've noticed that I start to devolve, even if I go without using magic for long periods of time.

Anyway, where was I? Oh yeah, back here, working on my portal. I was here for several months before I decided that I needed a huge break. Mine hair was beginning to fall out again, and…well, I just needed to distance myself from my work for a while.

So, I went back to Saulen. I had a house there and friends. Only Belforeg knew about my…condition. I had to tell him. He's a doctor. I lived there for a while, working on random projects with materials I had created the last time I was there.

I built a steam-car for Belforeg as a thank-you for all he had done, and I made a few more things for a few friends, like a refrigerator for the inn, or a sewing machine for a nice woman who had mended a ripped shirt of mine for free.

I also made that stupid fire powder. It's called gunpowder in my world. Not a single moment goes by without me thinking of all those deaths I caused...

I needed money, and I thought the university in Goreuhwo would pay me for the formula. Why didn't I sell more sewing machines and refrigerators? I don't know. Maybe I wanted to be cooler than an appliance salesman. So, I became an arms-dealer instead? God...

In my world, fire powder was intended for fun purposes. Fireworks and sparklers. Maybe I thought there was a chance... I even included firework designs in my letters. I never wanted... (Sorry, I got some of this dust in my eyes...) It's like I tried to be Gandalf, but I ended up as Saruman...never mind, it's not important.

But the university never got my messages. The Taf-Waikht somehow intercepted them and wanted to meet me. I had no idea they had already made their own batch, and what they were planning on using it for... I swear it never occurred to me that something as horrible as that would happen.

They captured me, drugged me, put me in a crate, took me back to Len Khalayu. At first, they asked nicely for more weapon designs. When I wouldn't answer, they resorted to alternate methods. See these scars? Yeah, they used butter knives. And it's not just my arms. I'd show you the rest, but I'm really shy about that sort of thing, you know? Ha-ha. It's not funny.

They kept me chained up in some dark place for months. Then they brought in a specialist. You aren't going to believe this, Brenn, but it was the Mind Holder. He's in Jub Khewi! And they used him to get weapon information out of mine head. Luckily, they didn't understand any of it. And the things that were primitive enough for them to build, they already had. But there was no way they were going to build tanks or fighter-jets or AK-47s with their resources. So, they just kept me there, and that's about all I remember.

I devolved, even though I wasn't using magic. I could've used magic, but they didn't know that. This tattoo right here—pretty sweet, huh? Well, it's meant to connect me to my jinn-box no matter how far apart we are. I left them here in the cave when I went back to Saulen. Yeah, I used a little bit of magic in Saulen. You were there. (That was a joke, Brenn, you can laugh.) But the distance makes everything worse, so I made sure not to do it again.

I guess in hindsight, it might have been worth it to use a little bit to escape, but you know…whoops, I guess? I guess I wasn't exactly in the right mind to be thinking tactically.

Anyway, here I am. And here you are, as if everything happens for a reason, and life is a chess game being played by seventh-dimensional gods…

At the end of his tale, Adluo added, "They kept me in a little room. I think it was a closet or something, or maybe a room inside a closet. It had two doors—one that led into someone's house, I assume the Prophet's or the Listener's, and one that opened into a larger, darker room where they interrogated me. A few weeks ago, I experienced some especially bad pains in my joints. The grondeketh—I was becoming more it than me, you know? I was moaning and crying because it hurt me physically but also because I was lamenting the fact that soon I wouldn't be human anymore. Someone behind the door heard me and opened it, and I got out. Just ran out the door and hopped across rooftops until I escaped the city. Then I started running across the desert without a plan.

"That's when the Easterlings found and captured me. They didn't have any idea—still don't have any idea what I am. Hell, neither do I. In my world we have this philosophical thought experiment called the Ship of Theseus. The story goes, this guy Theseus and his crew were out on their adventures for so long that they ended up replacing every piece of their ship. So, is it the same ship? If all my cells are replaced one by one with grondeketh cells, am I still Adluo?"

To this Brenn could say nothing. He had listened to Adluo's tale with awe and wonder. The man standing before him seemed more alien than before, yet also more familiar. He now knew something about this man and therefore felt closer to him.

And Adluo said to him, "I really want to thank you, Brenn. For helping me with this, for listening to me talk. God, it's been forever since I've just had a normal conversation with someone. And I know you don't understand half the things I said, but you're smart and you'll catch on quickly. I like that about you. Stare into the void of ignorance and say, What lies within? That's what you do."

Many hours passed as the two men labored on the ring within the cave. And it came to pass that Adluo touched a toggle upon the table and behold! the ring shimmered to life with a hum like a swarm of honeybees. A veil of orange light shone from within, shimmering as water in a clear pond—yet within the veil, it swirled as if wind drove it about, and the color faded until shapes could be seen within.

Brenn saw what lay beyond. Great buildings they were, structures the likes of which Brenn had never seen. They touched the sky, filling the landscape from end to end. Flying things there were as well, like birds, yet not of flesh and blood—metal, they seemed, for the light of the Sun glinted from their giant wings. And on the ground between the buildings walked uncountable people, dressed strangely, yet their faces and forms were familiar.

The streets on which they walked were smooth and black, and upon them, the people also rode in wagons driven without ox or pony. No sound came through the ring, nor any smell, yet Brenn had seen enough to imagine the rest. His mind now felt stretched to the point of breaking.

"Now that," said Adluo, "is the capital city of my world's Gavwer. It's not where I want to go. I need to go home to Kersam. I'll have to change some settings. Brenn, come here so you know how this control panel works, just in case, okay?" Brenn looked away from the view through the ring with much hesitation. He went about learning from Adluo the ways of the toggles and slides and lights that controlled what was seen through the veil. "Theoretically," said Adluo, "this portal can take me anywhere, to any time, in any universe. But I've managed to narrow the scope down to my universe and my Earth. With the scale of the universe, landing in this city is next to perfectly accurate. If I ended up there, I could find my way home easily enough. I just need to make sure to end up in the right year. Again, with the entire timeline of the universe, ending up even a few hundred years before or after I want is pretty much exact, but I don't want to end up in King Arthur's court or the garden of the Eloi."

Then Adluo looked at Brenn as if for the first time, his eyes narrowing. "Oh man . . ."

"What's wrong?" asked Brenn.

"Your eyes are the exact color of Baja Blast, and I just realized how much I miss it."

Then came a voice from outside. Den spoke through the wall: "Open up, Brenn! Don't tell me that creature has eaten thee. I saw thee enter this wall—it's not a wall, but a hidden door. There's someone with me thou shalt be glad to see—an old friend thou shalt recognize."

Adluo waved a hand toward the door and said, "Eida, let them in."

The great door then opened, and in walked two people. Den stood with Erwo Abbidh; their faces amazed as they beheld the wonders of the cave. Then Erwo's eyes fell upon Brenn's, and he laughed.

"Odol's eyes," said Brenn. "Erwo, how farest thou?" He met Erwo halfway and they embraced.

"Last time I saw thee, we were in a Kebkholeno jail. Thou and thy two friends were released, and I never knew what became of you. As for Den and me, that magistrate sold us to a man in Milridh; there we were made to dig for gold as slaves until we rebelled and stole a ship. But that is a tale for later; what became of thee? And what of Rilun and Fehi? Did ye find the tomb of Pervikhseryedhi?"

Erwo answered not at first but looked Brenn over head to toe. "Thine hair's grown long and white," he said, "and thy beard as well. Do my eyes deceive, or hast thou grown taller?"

"Nay, not taller, though smaller around the waist, I deem. Did those Kebkholenu take you home? I thought for sure it was a ruse, and that they'd lead you into a trap and take your lives, collecting the bounty for rilŷn in Goreuhwo. I'm glad to see that's not the case."

At this Erwo laughed. "Indeed, they tried to kill us three days out, but we managed to escape through our wit. It helped that a great storm came through that night and destroyed all our tracks so that our would-be killers could not follow; the next day I met the mother of my child. There's a funny thing—when we met for that second time, all of us in that jail, thou and Den had just abandoned war in Saulen. There's a story as to why ye've found yourselves in another, eh?"

"Perhaps, though it must wait until later," said Brenn. "I've no time to tell any story; this machine thou seest must be completed."

Here, Den interrupted: "Is there water in this strange cave of wonders, or is there naught but metal and rock?"

Adluo, standing against a table with arms across his chest, nodded to a far wall. "There's a metal basin over there. Push the button and it spouts water."

Den went for the water as Erwo seemed to notice Adluo for the first time. "We've not met," he said. "My name is Erwo Abbidh."

Adluo made no move to grasp the hand that Erwo put forth. "We have, actually," he said. "You always wore a hood and mask when we spoke, but I haven't forgotten your voice."

Erwo's smile left him then as all recognition washed over him. "Gaikhud?"

"Not anymore. It's Adluo. My real name."

Erwo nodded and looked to the floor.

As the red autumn leaves of poplars will fall with the snow, leaving behind bare white trunks, so too the red blood in Erwo's face drained, leaving only the pale complexion of one who was sick. He lowered himself into a chair and dropped his face into his hands. He sobbed until his body shook.

"Ai, ai!" he wailed, "I am so sorry. Oh, Adluo, oh, God. I told myself that the ends would justify the means; it would not be the first time our God gave such a commandment. Sometimes evil can be used if the goal is a greater good. But the greater good never came. Long I wanted to glimpse any sign that my fell deeds might be worth their pain. I understood nothing, and I hated myself all the more for it. Who was I to question the will of God? If he commanded that I should keep a man in a cage and probe his mind, my faith needed to be unshakable to know the suffering I caused was for good reason. But there was no reason! Even the Listener could understand none of thy thoughts, thou who are from another Earth entirely, whose experiences and knowledge are alien to us all.

"Often, I wonder if the Dark One has not tricked us all. In Len Khalayu we have a saying: The Dark One will tell thee a thousand truths so that thou believest a single lie. Imagine, then, that the one lie he told was I am thy God. If God may use evil to accomplish a greater good, could the Dark One not also use good to accomplish a greater evil? Forgive me, Adluo; I did as my God commanded, and I realize now that fails as an excuse. The Kanakh-ri speaks of obedience, but what can one do when given a commandment one knows to be evil? What does one say when God permits one to sin for the greater good, but all consequences of such obedience are naught but death and war?

"I beg thee, Adluo: strike me, spit upon my face; do yet more than I did to thee. I deserve thy vengeance, and thou hast every right to seek my death. I know thou wilt not forgive me, but I shall wish for it every day until I die." Tears fell over his cheeks as water over a cliff.

Some moments passed as Adluo looked upon Erwo from his place at the table. Adluo saw a pathetic man, driven to vile deeds, too frightened of his god to refuse it. Adluo approached the weeping Erwo, then with swift movement drove a fist into the man's arm. Erwo flinched in pain and prepared for more, but none came.

"Help us with this thing," said Adluo to Erwo.

"With two Holders, we can finish it in no time. Anyone want Xanax? I sure could use some after that speech, hot damn."

Brenn looked at Erwo as the revelation came to his mind and lighted upon his face. "You," he said. "You are the Mewas? The son of Khesi Addeu?"

Erwo nodded, though he did not smile. "I have tried my best to abandon that name and legacy, though I cannot abandon the inheritance that is my Power."

Again, Brenn embraced Erwo and said, "I understand thee, brother. Let us finish this ring. Perhaps a better life awaits us elsewhere."

They worked for a time, and Den returned to the Easterling camp to be with their injured friends. As the day neared its close, Brenn said to Erwo, "I asked thee before, but thou didst not answer—didst thou find the tomb thou didst seek? I remember the first time we met in Beridh-Ostaith, ye three historians were on your way there. And thou didst mention thou hast a wife and child—who is she? Tell me."

Erwo smiled. "Perhaps I'll tell these two stories as one, for they flow together. But never have I told this tale in full, and it may be long."

"We have time while we work," said Brenn. "I am listening."

"Fine," said Adluo. "Just make sure you're actually working while you talk and listen, okay?"

Here Erwo began his tale, which has been hitherto told.

―――

Erwo's tale did reach sudden halt—for at the cave's great door there came a knock more frantic than before. Adluo swift the portal opened, and in ran good Den, with sweat upon their brow and breath labored.

"What's this?" asked Brenn. "Why lookest thou so distraught, so full of dark alarm?"

To which replied Den thus: "In brief I'll tell, for brief I must perforce be now—above, a battle rages 'twixt Keulenem and fierce rilŷn. But more, I bear a message for our friend Erwo—a woman to our camp did come ere battle was enjoined and bade me seek you out with utmost haste and urgency."

"A message? From whom?" Erwo inquired.

"Baiwieth is her name," said Den, "who speaks the tongue of Mitho Gorikhwa, Jongwo called, yet light of skin and raven-tressed, as folk of Sunless Dol-Nopthelen. From city walls to camp she ran, nigh spent of breath, and luck or fate did guide her steps to me, since I alone of Keuleno or Kalayo spoke. Of thee she asked, Erwo, husband dear to her beloved friend Pabelyo named."

"Aye, 'tis the same Baiwieth," Erwo confirmed, "who journeyed with us to Kollan ab-Kes, Pabi's most cherished friend, who by her side hath stood since that dread day in Goreuhwo when smoke of gwerfegi did Sun obscure. What word or tiding did she bid thee bear?"

Den then recounted all Baiwieth told: how Pabi, some weeks past, a noise did hear within her walls, and searching, chanced upon a hidden room, from which a creature leapt of fairy tale and myth, the grondeketh, invoked by mothers to affright their young. How Erwo, learning of this interloper, forth from his house did haste to track it down, while Pabi, all unwitting, refuge took with Fehi, her long-sundered brother dear. That night, as Pabi slept, to her appeared Tuláhujut in dream, dread angel winged and terrible, who bore a prophecy of unborn child, God's very Spirit cloaked in mortal flesh, to be as light unto the hearts of all the world's benighted host, and named Berem-Rë, Prince of Heaven and Earth.

When Pabi this strange vision did recount to holy men, the wadhestor Dannwi claimed the right to raise the child as foster-sire, since Erwo, steeped in learning secular, no fit custodian for the Godhead proved. Yet when fair Pabi to her house repaired to ponder this, a dreadful loss she found: the Pervikhseryedhi's pendant, hid within a secret hoard, was gone—purloined by none but Dannwi, who did boldly sport the potent charm in Pabi's very sight! Thus charged Baiwieth to seek out Erwo, warn him of the plot and peril dire afoot.

"Alas," sighed Erwo, "if 'tis true indeed that Dannwi now doth wear that baleful gem, then like a god he stands, with Power armed fourfold—and all who counter him shall fall. Would I had kept the trinket close! For though I ne'er would think to don it, knowing well the madness and the raging lust for might it breeds within the all too human breast, at least 'twould not in hands more ruthless lie."

Then Brenn in pensive silence sat, as one with heavy thoughts oppressed. At last, he spoke: "These tidings sore unsettle me, and like them not at all. This battle is not mine to wage—the Kalayu no wrong to me have done, save Aebakhmë, now cold in death. A friend I once did claim, fair Deubmeni, saved from the stoning in that far-off time, but she and I did part in Goreuhwo, and of her fate I've had no word since then. To earn my peace from Gwalo was my aim, yet he too lies in dust. Now I remain in this benighted land for one cause sole—to aid Adluo in his ring's fashioning, that I might escape with him to realms unknown, where Holders and their ilk no sway do hold…"

But Den broke in: "Think not of flight, my friend, when innocent lives hang in the balance! Your sword is wanted—take it now in hand and join the embattled Keulenem, who bleed and die upon the plain!"

To which replied Brenn thus: "An average hand am I with blade, and worse with spear. So, take this sword of mine, without its less than mighty wielder—give it to some arm more skilled, more seasoned far, like Kregeth or the bold Tobëa—they shall wring from it full value, where I could not."

"What, wilt thou then abandon this just cause?" cried Den, yet took the proffered sword, and held it close, still sheathed, lest inadvertent touch upon the grip should wake its fearsome Power. But Brenn, unmoved, rejoined: "It is not mine to quit, this battle—so begone, and bear the blade to worthier hands, that it may drink deep of its fill of foemen's vital blood!"

So, Den in wordless haste the sword bore forth, resolved to seek amid the struggling throng Kregeth or staunch Tobëa, and to them convey the weapon Brenn would not him wield. Yet on the battlefield's edge, Den paused, and scanned with anxious eye the heaving mass of warring forms—but though they strained to catch glimpse of Tobëa's towering frame, or hear Kregeth's stentorian rallying cry, the din and tumult of the fray defied their quest.

Then in Den's mind a sudden thought took shape, from which at first they recoiled, as one who fears to grasp a serpent bare—yet what recourse remained, save that which desperate need compelled? For far Tobëa fought, beyond the range of shout or wave to summon—so perforce must Den the fateful hilt of Pukhso clasp, and through the ranks of fierce rilŷn cleave bloody path unto that champion's side!

No sooner had that cursed hilt Den's palm caressed, than lightning through their veins did leap, and all their senses, mortal bounds overleaping, clarion woke—each sight and sound and smell, from feces-reek to clashing steel, now dim and muted fell, displaced by deep awareness of every soldier's sweat and laboring breath, the hot blood coursing, battle-fever high. With vision preternaturally keen Den marked each face of foe and friend alike, yea, even on the far-off city walls descried the dread and sorrow writ in lines of cheek and brow of helpless watchers old and young, who feared for kith and kin below.

The very tracks in sand, to Den's new sight laid bare, in winding rune and cipher told the tales of men who there did strive and fall, and who emerged triumphant from each bout. Then Den, the sheath discarding, Pukhso bared, its silver length in dawn's ambiguous light agleam, and thrumming in their grip as might some great cat purr, stretched languid in the sun. And as that blade from scabbard slid, so too did all of Den's old self, like husk, fall way—their mind a blank, save for the one drive sole to rend and cleave a crimson road ahead.

Thus transformed, as sinewy leopard swift and stallion-strong, did Den upon the foe descend—o'er heaps of slain they bounded light, the grin of battle-madness on their face, a rooster-tail of dust flung in their wake. And woe betide the first to bar their path—Ango Arrë, hapless wight, sword high in vain defiance raised, ere Pukhso lashed and sent his severed head in gory arc rolling amid the trampled dead...

And on Den plunged, unstayed by either fear or ruth, from stricken corpse a spear plucking to lance Esather's thigh from half a field away, and save Tobëa from the blade Esather thought to slip 'neath guard—a deed that gave the bulwark of the Erkhesgur pause, now spying Den as Pukhso's flashing edge swath bloody through the swarming ranks did mow.

"They have the sword," quoth he, at once relieved and rapt with wonder at their prowess fierce and fatal grace—then found within himself fresh heart to press the unrelenting fray. None could withstand the vengeance of that blade, or Den, become its living, raging sheath—ribs, throats, and skulls they pierced and clove and crushed, and men as wheat 'neath flailing sickle fell.

Their fellow Keulenem in awe descried this grim and glorious sight, and took from it both cheer and courage, laying to with might redoubled, that scant ground Den's charge had won they might preserve, and yield the foe no inch. But in that very hour, a cry rang out despairing—by the Prophet's hand lay Bortho lifeless, his neck in twain by force divine and hellish snapped—and Kalfro, brother true, upon that ruin flung himself, wild tears of rage and grief his stricken visage staining, there to expire, by Goraito's spear in the back thrust, atop his sibling's corpse.

Now Den, gore-spattered head to heel, surveyed the stricken field, deep-drawing labored breath—when sudden, words more foul than carrion upon their ear did fall, like sour milk curdling the throat: "It feels wonderful, does it not, all that Power in your veins thrilling like flame, like honey on the tongue?"

They whirled, and saw Dannwi Asakhdo, cloaked and hooded, his mismatched eyes aglow with avid malice through the mask's grim slit. "That sword—I would possess it," quoth the priest, one gloved hand stretching forth in dire command.

But Den, their fighting crouch assuming, cried: "Nay, villain—rather yield to me that charm thou hast purloined, Pervikhseryedhi's bane, and I perchance shall spare thy wretched life!"

A scornful laugh Dannwi for answer gave: "I see sweet reason finds in thee no home—so be it, then!" And with the merest flick of finger, Pukhso from Den's grasp did rend and to the Prophet's outstretched palm compel its haft, as lode to lodestone leaps—and Den, the blade's sustaining thrill of Power denied, gasping sank to their knees, all strength and sense drained sudden, til the world about them reeled in queasy flux, and battle-din overwhelmed their ringing ears—yet still some ember small of defiance inextinguishable burned in heart and mind, and gave them will to rise once more, fists clenched, though naked and disarmed.

"Stay down," Dannwi hissed, "I seek not thy doom, Ji-gua of Goreuhwo—live thou to see the Light prevail!"

But Den, swaying, stood fast, and spat the words, "Fuck you, false priest—come, slay me if thou wilt, yet know my spirit ne'er shall bend to thine!"

A fraught, tense beat—then agony exploded in Den's brave breast, as through it burst the point of a hurled spear, and down once more they crashed, the dry dust swallowing their broken form.

"Thanks for the sword," the Prophet mocked, and leapt with his new prize aloft, swift borne away on wings of stolen Power—while round Den's sight encroaching shadows crept, and mortal pain ebbed to a distant pang, a dying throb.

Yet in that extremity, one thought alone solace and succor to their mind did bring: "I really was brave, wasn't I? In the end…"

"It's finished," said Adluo. "The portal. It's done. It should work."

"Then let us bring it to life," said Brenn, "and together we shall leave this forsaken Earth in favor of thine own."

Adluo did not object, but he lifted a hand to bring pause to Brenn's offer. "Even with both you and Erwo," he said, "we'll need more power. Both of you are more than enough to keep it open but not to allow us to pass through. Pretty sure it would kill you if we tried now."

"Then I will go now to the surface," said Brenn. "Surely the battle is over; hours it's been since Den came to us for my sword, and I hear no din above. Be ready for me, for I will not be long."

"Shall I come as well?" asked Erwo, who himself was attached to the portal with strange ropes that glowed where his skin met them. They pulsed with his Power and fed the portal as an elowav drinks with its long snout.

"That's not a good idea," Adluo said. "I have the setting just about perfect. If you step away, I'll have to turn the whole thing off. And when we switch it back on it'll be difficult to calibrate again. Brenn won't be long, right?"

Brenn, with a nod, departed the cave then and climbed the narrow path unto the height of eastern cliff whereon the Easterling encampment lay. With a gasp he looked upon the scene of ruin—the camp nigh vanished whole, replaced by ash and dust in smoldering piles, the sky a cloudless grey, the air made thick with loss. Through camp debris he trudged, his boots acquiring sable soot with every step. His gaze strayed toward Jub Khewi and the field of battle and turned his stomach at the sight of innumerable corpses strewn about. Yet the fray had ceased, the living fled—but where?

Slow, careful steps brought him to the camp's north center nigh an immense crowd of Easterlings, who kept quiet vigil round the wounded and dying laid out on blankets as the healers worked. Brenn laid a hand on the shoulder of a man, who turned and looked on him with awe. "Where hast thou been?" he cried, "My young brother—alas, lies dead." Then to the throng: "The Baithas comes! Make way!"

A hundred heads then swiveled toward Brenn, all eyes transfixed, the crowd parting for him a path into their midst, where he advanced with steps of lead, foreboding in his heart some dreadful revelation. Tobëa, his back to Brenn, obscured his view. "My brother," Brenn addressed him, "Gladly I espy thee hale." He forced a smile, though it felt unfit. "But where is Den?" Tobëa turned his head, casting a despairing look, as a tear escaped down his cheek. He spoke no word but moved aside.

There lay the figure still and pale in death—'twas Den, their wounds washed clean, a sheet pulled up to chin, the blooming stain of blood in the shape of a sparrow's wing upon their breast. Straight locks of raven hue lay o'er their brow, eyes closed as one who merely sleeps, the slightest upward curl upon the still corners of their lips. Brenn knew not he knelt, but sudden found his knees in the dirt, his face drawn close to Den's. With a trembling hand he stroked beloved cheek and hair, and tried to speak, but his voice stuck fast like gravel in his throat, and Den's name formed on his lips, yet no sound came. Then Tobëa's steadying hand alighted upon his back. "The Prophet," he explained, "They fought…"

Brenn squeezed his eyes shut, pressing his brow to Den's, and wished for breath of life to stir against his cheek once more. But stillness reigned. He kissed the cooling skin, then gave way to grief, while Tobëa held him in a strong embrace, his mighty frame convulsing with sobs for love of friend and weight of tragic loss. The gathered host observed in reverence this pure display of manly tenderness, for even a heathen heart is moved by so deep a bond, though wretched be the severing.

When tears at last were spent, Brenn stood. "My sword, Den bore. Where lies it now?" "The Prophet seized it as his prize." Where Goraito Reu lay wounded then, the brave captain called: "Den's deed, most valiant I beheld! They gave us time, and so preserved my life." He held his blade high and bade the Baithas take it and avenge.

Then thronging voices rose as one, chanting Den's name in martial unison. Brenn accepted the sword from Reu, and vowed to all: "My friend, were it not for my own desire to shun the fight, might draw yet breath. This theme, perhaps, defined my life—that private ends permit such agonies. I rue it, friends—those led by me to doom and folly. No more! If final act is mine, I'll face our foe, reclaim my sword and talisman he stole."

"He'll slay thee—too much power he doth wield!" warned Tobëa, but Brenn replied: "Then I shall perish facing forward, not in flight." And thus, he strode forth alone, til voices faded, then sat on a stone, and from his boot pulled forth a long concealed, unopened note. "My dearest son," it earnestly began. "Know that I love thee..." Brenn read on and wept.

That's really all I wanted to say. I know not where thou art, but something within me knows thou yet livest and that thou are well. I miss thee, and I am sure thou missest me, but I'll not ask thee to come home. I envy thee, in a way. I envy thy courage. I find it difficult to fathom how someone could be so brave as to decide they need answers to questions so deep and burning that they would set out one day with naught but a rucksack. I'm so proud of thee.

Wind died a few months ago. He was old, and he went peacefully. I am sorry I can't pass on his last thoughts—if he wanted to say anything to thee before moving on to the Shatter. I am alone now. But don't worry about me. Thy father's and brother's bodies are not with me physically, but I feel their spirits here. I feel thine as well, sometimes, because I know thy thoughts are with thine home and family. Please do not think of me in any negative light; don't think that I assume thou didst leave because of something I did. Sometimes we just have to leave, and I understand that. Thou wast brave to leave, and if thou dost ever decide to do so thou wilt be brave to return.

I will wait for thee as long as I am able, but I will not expect thy return. Thou shalt come home in thine own time if thou comest at all. And if I am not there to greet thee, be sure that I will wait to welcome thee into the Shatter alongside thy brother and father, and of course Wind.

I love thee more than life.
—Miwë.

The letter done, Brenn felt his soul poured out, an emptied vessel, shattered, void of all emotion's hues. He wandered across the blasted plain, dragging the sword as a child drags a stick, and rambling to himself with addled tongue: "I see my father, mother, brother slain—my forebears lined in state behind. Their blood, their bones cry out to me from the earth. To them belongs this flesh. Their spirits summon me. Ye powers of the Shatter, take me hence!"

Then his dirge ceased, as a sudden shadow fell upon him, dwindling, til Dannwi stood before him. "Well met again, ere this world's end, O Baithas. Dost recall my visage now?" Brenn gave no word but stared as one struck dumb. The Prophet, tooth-bedecked and sword-begirt (its scabbard new, wrought with gems and silver), inquired: "This plundered sheath, doth it displease?"

To Brenn's unspoken thought—"My mind ye read?"—Dannwi nodded assent and spoke: "Thy brain an open book to me, and soon my Voice shall quell all foes. Swifter than planned, these Powers accrue—a sign of Heaven's favor clear." At this, Brenn gestured to the carrion-dotted waste. "Is this thy god?" The Prophet: "Yea, divine and manifold His forms—not least, the conquest of men's spirits in His name."

Brenn cried: "Then evil is thy lord—the one who grants no bread to starving child, who lights a rapist's eyes, makes women's wombs miscarry, and sends the just to early grave! If true He stands revealed, when I to Shatter pass, His pardon must He beg for deeds so foul!"

With head thrown back in mirth the fell priest shook, his brown beard and yellow teeth stretched in a rictus. "All things encompassed by the Godhead are! Both life and death, success and ruin stem from Him alone. To judge His ways by thy paltry conception is but vanity—His acts beholden to no human sense!"

The Prophet unclasped his robe and let it fall, baring a crossbow slung at one shoulder. Then he bared Pukhso too. Brenn drew a breath and exhaled deep—eyes shut, then snapped wide as he leapt forth! But ah, the Prophet stepped aside, and swung up his blade in counter. Steel sang on steel as Brenn did fend the blow, then whirling, chopped again—but Dannwi drew back laughing, arms outstretched. Now Brenn's dammed tears burst forth at last: "Thou whoreson damned!" he wailed. "My loved ones all—Laidho, Deubmeni true, Gwidhotir dear, and Den—thou hast destroyed! No more I have to cherish 'neath the sun!"

He aimed a head-cleaving slash, which Dannwi ducked. Then from the earth a spear up-leaped, as straight an arrow streaking for brave Brenn—whose blade did clip the haft in twain and send it askew. With a sneer, the evil priest flung his hands high, and desert grit arose in a blinding storm round the embattled pair. It stung Brenn's eyes, choked his nose and throat—he had no sight, as a voice sour as curdling milk assailed his soul:

"Imbued am I with godly puissance full! Thy misbegotten bones this waste shall strew, forgotten—stars I'll quench and Moon dethrone if He so bid! Avenger shall I prove and bane to all He deems unhallowed. Thou and thy fell creed to ash in this mine hand are doomed—my paean terrible shall blast this unclean earth and purge it by His will!"

A sudden snap of a bowstring—a searing pain in Brenn's unguarded shoulder! Swift the dust did settle, and the Prophet stood smiling, crossbow in hand still aimed. The shaft protruding from that soft juncture where the arm and breast conjoin, brave Brenn pried with numbing fingers, agony streaking through neck and torso. The sword fell clattering from his strengthless grip.

Yet in that dire extreme, stout-hearted Brenn thought on his Den—on that dear comrade's supreme and ultimate valor, their sacrifice... Could he, Den's sworn companion, do aught less? Nay, one sole path remained the Baithas now. The priest did abandon crossbow, and plucked Pukhso again from sheath, as Brenn, despite his skewered gut's white anguish, plunged forward headlong, desisting not til near his brow the Prophet's brushed. He sneered: "I fear I much overestimated thy poor threat." For lo! Pukhso had run Brenn through, back out to front!

Yet valiant Brenn, teeth gritted (cracking one), wrenched the arrow out from shoulder, and drove it through base Dannwi's neck, the gory point emerging far side! Dannwi gasped, at once unmanned by fear and shock, betrayal writ in bulging eyes as blood gushed down his beard. One hand clutched vainly at the shaft, one flew to tooth-bedecked throat as he slumped to earth, a plume of sand flung up to mark his fall.

In that instant, Brenn seized the necklace, snapped its cord, and beheld Dannwi prone until he too collapsed, a spreading scarlet pool beneath. Distant voices Brenn thought he heard but heeded not. A welcome darkness crept over his sense, as the lulling warmth of sand—not a hard bed, he mused, on which to die.

It chanced that Tobëa, with the Easterling host, did from the camp behold as Brenn engaged the Prophet fell in single combat dire. A cry of anguish tore from Tobëa's throat to see vile Pukhso pierce his comrade's flank, though Brenn in turn the wicked priest did slay ere both, it seemed, succumbed to mortal wounds.

As a fleet gazelle will quit her fawn a space to forage far afield, yet spying then some lion poised to strike, like lightning flies lest tender young to Death's embrace be borne—so Tobëa swift to fallen Brenn did run. Hot tears stung dark and anxious eyes to see his dearest friend in pool of mingling blood there sprawled. With gentle arms the mighty man did lift and cradle Brenn, and stroke pale locks.

"Ai, ai!" wailed stricken Tobëa. "Alas that I should watch thee perish, brother mine, when cruel fate this selfsame day took Den! Would Heaven grant that hale Thegikh stood nigh, Perangorai beside, on this cursed plain where lives unnumbered reap the thirsty spear! But distant lie they, mending grievous hurts, while Den... ah, Den is lost, their body cold, too far!" His brimming gaze to sky upturned. "O Brenn, if any puissance reside in god or Derevai, let them restore thy spirit to its mould, and us who keen!"

Then lo! the Baithas' azure eyes unclosed, and Brenn like diver from the deep did gasp. In ancient tongue of Yenmiskelanë cried Tobëa: *"Ihwuhkh kh'walhding yáhewtlhet!* Brought back upon the wings of the Raven! Dear one, speak—what vision unto thee in death was shown?"

Erect stood Brenn, by Tobëa's strength upheld, one hand pressed to his dripping wound. Quoth he: "A realm I trod, yet neither Form nor shade—some limbo at the fringe of substance, where much hidden truth to me lay bare. But hark! Aid me to gain the cliff, and I shall tell what may be told, for even as we speak, a child of destiny strains toward the light, whose advent shall transfigure all. But first—" He gestured, "Sword and amulet secure. Without them, vain our errand."

Tobëa the artifacts in haste retrieved, though doubt furrowed his brow. "The cliff? But Brenn, thy life hangs by a thread—that blade nigh cleft thee through! I marvel thou dost yet draw breath!"

His friend rejoined: "Breath shall not fail ere task be done. Come, I must lean upon thy steadying arm."

As one they limped across that corpse-strewn field 'twixt Easterling array and jeweled fane Jub Khewi, cynosure of Sakhdo Mor. Full many from the camp in wonder marked their passage, hailing maimed and ashen Brenn to learn what passed between him and the priest. Yet only "Time denies me leisure for the telling!" Brenn to each gave answer terse.

But to his sole companion he disclosed in transit of their trek: "Hear, Tobëa—that hour when vicious Dannwi 'neath my ribs cruel Pukhso thrust, ere I in turn a shaft through gullet drove to avenge the blow, both fell and I to death-like slumber plunged, yet 'twas not death in truth. My frame dissolved, I hung in orange void, burnt almond scent infused as vapor all about—yea, thou rememberest! In Yenmiskelanë that dreamlike fugue enfolded me, as Father's grave I found. And once before when bear-mauled flesh a leech in Saulen knit. Thrice now that voice hath cloven my bewildered mind.

"'Good morrow, Brenn!' it hailed. 'Dost thou recall our prior parley?' 'Aye,' thought I, 'Then am I sped in truth?' 'Not yet,' it answered. 'Let us speak as face to face.' The russet murk and spice-sharp bouquet dimmed, supplanted by a rush of hue and form, as scenery across a painted scroll unfurled, my leaf-like essence tossed and spun until a corporeal mantle re-assumed.

"In Albogorwë, in my childhood room I crouched, and by my knee lay open book—'The Windmill Man,' a ribbon 'twixt the leaves to mark my place. I scanned an inky plate which limned the Miller bargaining with Death for forfeit life of spouse. Pale lunar glow and lamplight warm the oaken chamber bathed. Heaped thick with furs the mattress, pillows plumped, cedar planks by rug concealed, the walls with woven fancies decked—a wolf, a bear, a tawny fox—my cabinet flung wide to show a lordling's rich habiliments.

"No higher than a weanling did mine head attain, as I to mirror drew. Bright gold, not blanched as now by care, my ringlets shone, for 'twas my natal day—around me strewn a wooden sword and shield, and battered tin as breastplate wrought and helm, in childish games of war. My chamber quitted, down the hall deserted, still as tomb, my small feet paced till round a bend a slice of light I spied beneath my parents' door. From lamplit room my father's voice in wistful canticle emerged, as sorathryu he plied:

Once when I was only a young child in Spring
I dreamed that I'd have somebody for me
And she would be beautiful, perfect, and lovely
And together we both would be happy

As I grew older and into my Summer
Mine heart grew a stranger and so did the child
I looked only for whose company's gift to me
Was priced high as only owls do fly

As company gave me, it took in the Autumn
And quickly I searched for the things I had lost
Winter I saw then was quickly approaching
I was not prepared for the storm that I saw

But Winter passed over like nothing but sunshine
For then when you touched me, I could not but smile
And for that I'm grateful, I'll always remember
The day that you turned me back into a child

Upon the covers sprawled my mother lay, dark tresses spilled like jet, transported smile suffusing her. But sudden at my back a hand descended, turned me round—'twas he, my brother! Scarce could callow eye discern Kolewa's face, near five and ten that night when I saw eight. His finger he did raise to shushing lips and led me thence away to mine own room once more. The latch secured, he did reprove: 'Thou knowest well 'tis banned to haunt our parents' threshold post-twilight.' Then wooden sword and targe I snatched, and hewed at phantoms, till my stance thou didst correct.

"'What ails thee, brother?' he at last inquired, as melancholy stole upon my mien. 'I miss thee sore,' I sighed, 'for times arise when I thy presence crave.' He shook his head: 'All things must end, or seemly or untoward; such truth should not bedew thy cheek.' I flared: ''Tis easy at remove to speak—thou art a god!' Kolewa then—or likeness mere of him—rejoined: 'No god am I, though thou mayst deem it so—as much I thee affirmed at our last congress.' Pensively I probed: 'Must I, then, perish now, to Shatter pass?' 'Thou shalt, when ordained term arrives—yet not by Dannwi's stroke this day. His coward thrust, by providence deflected, shunned thy vitals; no mortal craft such miracle requires.

"'Then wherefore hither summon me?' I pressed."—but Brenn here ceased. "What more to me was shown," quoth he, "I am constrained to not impart. The very stuff of god and man those themes encompassed—our twin natures, each one's cast and charge, and how those sunderings entwine. Erst unguessed springs of being to me lay bare; much, Tobëa, now to me is plain that ne'er compelled my mind to contemplate. But soft! yon cleft doth bid us enter in!"

On giddy ledge above the chasm's maw they paused, Tobëa's grip on Brenn still fast. "What, must we climb below?" the man exclaimed. "In thy drear state such hazard to attempt..."

"Nay," Brenn assured, "Mark there that wending track, narrow, yet sound—'twill guide us to the depths, and that hid portal we must straightway gain." With halting steps, each still the other's prop, the fissured stone they trod, till roof of vault lowered above them, swallowing the sun.

Brenn on the massive door a summons knocked. "Ho, Erwo, Adluo! The sword and charm I bear—make haste to grant us entry now!" Inward the valve swung wide on strident hinge, and Tobëa marveled to behold that trove of unknown mechanism—lights in blinding filaments that steady blazed, consoles of winking gem and mirrored pane where phantoms flitted in a dance obscure, and rife with strange puissance, the churning ring whose frenzied whorls a fearsome vigor voiced.

When maimed and ashen Brenn brave Adluo saw, "What in the hell happened?" he blurted, but the Baithas demurred: "That chronicle must bide its season. The sword, the amulet—place each upon thy rune-graven plinth, that eldritch bands of lambent force may plumb their mysteries, and that great vortex wake to life at last!"

So Adluo Pukhso and the necklace set where scintillating tendrils snaked and probed, sly secrets to unriddle. With a wail unearthly as the damned, the quaking ring blazed incandescent, lightnings green and red in spiral arms a-chasing, till a veil diaphanous as breath of dying man, yet luminous as nacreous inner vale of chambered nautilus, the hoop enclosed. A humming silence fell, anticipant...

Then Adluo touched a gleaming stud, and lo! within that lucent caul a world appeared in crystal clarity, as if through lens of flawless beryl! Miles on miles outspread a city vast—proud spires the welkin grazed, myriad souls in glittering rivulets flowed 'midst towers of glass and adamant that soared in weird asymmetries, and darkling chasms plunged 'twixt those monoliths to gnaw their roots. All scale and rule were shattered, as some haunt of titanic gods whose merest whim might rear a mountain range or rift the sphere!

To ravaged Brenn then Adluo spake: "We have really good doctors. You mentioned you wanted to come with me. Do you still want to? You need to get that wound looked at."

Into that veil the Baithas gazed and smiled. A universe undreamed there hung—no soul his name or visage marked as friend or foe, nor deed of his awaited, huge, or small. Safe anonymity those purlieus pledged, a second venture granted, in the hush and solace of a lifetime evening spent...

"Go thou before," said Brenn, "and find thy bliss. Some tie, perchance, yet binds me to this soil more prized than my sole weal. I stay behind." With grin of sympathy, and warrior's arm-clasp, the earthling bade him farewell. Lightly then upon the plinth he stepped, into the veil... And nevermore by Edorathian eyes was glimpsed, for good or ill.

A frozen beat the Baithas watched that slowly seething screen in silence. On the dais Erwo stood enmeshed in pulsing strands, his Power and those of sword and amulet combining might to feed the shimmering gate. His hand withdrew to loose that skein—extinguish screen and hoop and veil illusive.

Seeing time so short, in left fist Brenn the necklace seized, in right dire Pukhso's hilt. A flicker—then the veil wavered, as puissance fatal ebbed away. With roar of desperation, Brenn pronounced the forbidden, fell, unhuman name of

That which hath no form, nor face, nor voice, yet *IS*—the Lone God's true appellation, that no mind of mortal mould may harbor and stay whole.

What mangled, screeching din assailed their ears those witnesses could scarce encompass—yet one harsh and twisted sequence Brenn did force past bleeding lips: "*Gor'railyehotep!*"

The warmth of blood, the golden glow of life, seemed leeched from vault... Time crawled to gluey stop, and in the gravid murk a figure loomed—tall, anthropoid in outline, long of limb, yet blank of feature—no mouth, ear, or eye its awful visage bore. About the shape shimmered an aura crackling, fierce, so charged the very stone and metal of that crypt sang like glass harmonica, fine and shrill beyond the reach of human voice.

Each thread and fiber of the Baithas' mortal frame thrummed to that dismal keen. He knew full well what grim demise must claim all flesh that spake the secret name, or true face dared behold of any deathless Power, e'en Holders mighty. But he the path had chosen. Laughter bleak his throat escaped, as high he Pukhso heaved and through the apparition's sternum plunged.

A soul-pulverizing shriek of rage shattered the glassy air, the mountain's bones intimately convulsed, and heaven's vault threatened to rend and spill out flaming ruin. Brenn like a maddened bear his challenge hurled and, rallying a final lees of strength, thrust back that squalling godhead through the veil! Toward panel of controls he lunged, engaged a numbered key, a stubbornly hinged switch—and like a beaver's redoubt breached, the flood of Power his form abandoned, late sustained by Pukhso, all diverted to the ring for fleeting instants more! The gateway wailed, juddered as Brenn the calibrations changed—an eye-blink's space the veil near atomized, then settled placid as a winter tarn.

That beat for action seized the failing Baithas—necklace in hand, he hurled the ancient bane with fading breath into that turbid shimmer... Beyond the envelope it spun, was gone. Four thousand years and more that trinket cursed upon his native globe had spread its pall; now 'twould on other, unsuspecting sphere its malice wreak, for good or ill. Its fount expended, Brenn reeled back and senseless fell, the thwarted gate sputtering, dimming, doused to mundane vacancy of stone and shadow.

Erwo from plinth and cable-serpents tore, would fain have clasped his stricken friend—but found himself fast in Tobëa's staying hold. "Let him in quietude draw painful breath," the man implored. "Thou'lt mend apace, my Brenn, so let thy spirit rest!"

But Brenn demurred, swallowed the sanguine anguish blossoming from skewered gut to trembling fingertips. "That name by men forbid, by gods abjured, my reckless tongue hath spoken—mortal mind such burden was not meant to bear. Yet how could I abandon this harsh sphere that sired me, schooled me in gall of grief, in milk of love, absorbed my blood and tears, my kindred's dust? At brink of no return, some impulse cried 'Remain! Thy service here hath not quite lapsed, though solace for thyself be lost for aye. Those yet unborn thy deeds may profit still, though inward peace be e'er to thee denied!' What recourse then had I, save heed that call?"

Then Tobëa knelt, grasped Brenn's cold hand, the other laid on clammy brow, and said: "To thy well-earned repose now take thy leave—in Shatter, may thou lasting quiet find."

"My kindred throng to greet me," Brenn replied, as dimming eyes with unshed sorrow brimmed. He fixed his fading gaze on barren vault. "Father, Mother—there they patient wait! Kolewa, brother, how I've missed thy face! Even old Wind attends at Papa's feet. But soft—can I believe my swooning sight? 'Tis Den, dear heart! My fallen comrade true!" A beatific smile his lips overspread. "They bid me come—and now, methinks, I'm fit at last to join that blessed company."

With that, a sigh of deep content he breathed, let fall his lids and gently slipped away—and thus did Brenn Ragnir find his peace.

Coda

In Deulen's heat, where Mbeke's youth was spent, no snow had fallen, ice remained unknown. Yet now, in the Valk, a wondrous sight unfolded: the rain transformed to feathery white flakes, creating hills of strange and fluffy mounds. The child, amazed, beheld this novel world, her mind expanding with each passing mile.

"Close fast that window!" Mboka's voice rang out, as Mbeke, curious, sought to taste the snow. Reluctantly, she shut the wooden pane, though cold persisted, seeping through the gaps. Yet discomfort was far from Mbeke's thoughts, enthralled was she by landscapes passing by: sky-scraping peaks and valleys cloaked in white, while verdant trees defied the killing frost.

"How long, dear mother, til our journey's end?" the child inquired, her patience wearing thin. Four moons had waned since leaving home, yet still the road stretched on. "What manner of folk dwell in eastern climes?" she asked, her mind on strange new faces fixed.

"They're people, child, alike yet different too," came Mboka's cryptic answer, prompting more.

"In what way different?" Mbeke pressed to know, recalling how her mother hid their view when passing through the towns of foreign lands.

With sigh and hum, her mother pondered long, then spoke of Orominga tribes once seen: "Rememberest thou the folk of lighter hue, whose visage caused thee fright in younger days?" The child recalled, and deemed them sickly then, but Mboka swift corrected this false thought:

"Nay, child, not ill, but varied is folks' skin. The Oromingas, light compared to us, are but a shade 'twixt our own hue and those who dwell in lands where winter holds its sway."

Young Mbeke, puzzled, gazed upon her hands, imagining what shades might yet exist. "How light, dear mother? Tell me true," she begged.

"As white as snow?" her mother did suggest. The child's eyes widened, disbelief writ large. With gentle smile, rare on Mboka's face, she softened truth: "Not quite so pale, my love, but to thine eyes, accustomed to our shade, they may appear as light as driven snow. I tell thee this to quell thy future fears, for Easterlings will surely startle thee."

Thus ended talk, and silence reigned supreme, as carriage wheels bore on through frigid lands. Four months of travel neared its fated end, though Mbeke knew not journey's close drew nigh. Through Deulen, Len Khalayu, and lands beyond, they'd come at last to winter's icy realm.

As twilight neared, they came to Albogorwë's

gates, A city strange to Mbeke's wondering eyes. Unlike the simple huts of Deulen's lands, where animal hides draped over slender trunks, this eastern realm boasted stone and wooden towers, with multiple tiers reaching to the sky.

The streets, with rounded stones so slickly paved, bore witness to their carriage's approach. At last, the windows opened to the world, and Mbeke gazed in awe and nascent fear at people pale as milk, beyond her ken.

Through Albogorwë's heart they rolled, then to a wood of evergreens, and onward to the coast. The sea that greeted them was not the blue and friendly waves of Mbeke's childhood home, but grey and choppy, full of grim unrest.

Upon the shore, a multitude did wait, their numbers greater than her village whole. Great fires burned, and pavilions stood tall, while Mbeke searched the crowd for darker hues amid the sea of eggshell-tinted folk.

The carriage halted; Mboka donned her hat and tended to her daughter's appearance too.

"Mama," Mbeke whined, "I wish not to go forth."

But Mboka hushed her fears with stern rebuke: "These people mean no harm; be not afraid."

They stepped into the grey and wintry day, as servants followed, waiting their command. A man approached, in woolen suit attired, his beard close-trimmed, his eyes a warm brown hue. "Welcome, Tefwas Mboka," he did say, His Onobu tongue stumbling o'er the words.

But Mboka answered in his native speech,

surprising Kregeth with her mastery. No longer Tefwas, she corrected him, and introductions made, they spoke of rest and lodgings prepared in the nearby town.

Young Mbeke, shy before the stranger's gaze, sought refuge in her mother's flowing skirts. The king then led them to the stony beach, where waited those of import and renown.

A family stepped forth, their skin less pale, though still far lighter than the Deulenus' hue. Erwo Abbidh bowed, his wife beside, their children, Gwidhotir, tall, and Laidho, a babe, completed this more friendly-seeming group.

Of Holders past they spoke, of Space and Mind, and wondered when such gathering last occurred. "Ages have passed," said Erwo with a sigh, "and would that this were for a happier cause."

They spoke of one now gone, a friend to all, whose deeds had saved uncounted mortal lives. A Baithas he, who gave his life that others might endure.

Thus Mbeke stood upon that eastern shore, her world expanded, changed forevermore, as elders spoke of sacrifice and loss, and she beheld the vastness of the world.

Lo, as the Sun did touch the distant shore, and shadows stretched across the watery plain, stood Kregeth, king of Keulen, before the throng, between the crowd and pyre of solemn make.

"What words can honor Brenn Ragnir?" he cried, his voice resounding o'er the gathered host. "Say only this: a man he was, and valor he had; long may he find peace in the Shatter."

Then forward came the mourners, one by one, to lay upon the pyre their offerings: helms, shields, and swords of precious craft and make, surrounding him who lay in death's repose.

In finest raiment was the hero clad, a bearskin cloak draped o'er his noble form. His hands they crossed upon his lifeless breast, a sword replica of Pukhso (now lost amid the Nether's fell despair) lay clasped within his cold and stiffened grip.

Around him gathered friends and kinsmen true, the Easterlings forming the outer ring, while Erkhesgur pressed in close to mourn. Tobëa, Perangorai, Thegikh stood near, with Erwo, Pabelyo, Gwidhotir, and babe Laidho, all clustered 'round the pyre's somber height.

Upon a southern hill, a fire blazed, its smoke ascending to the darkening sky, as flames and weeping voices joined as one. Then Kregeth, with a knife of gleaming steel, did sever from the dead a lock of white, bestowing it on Erwo and Pabelyo, who shared the precious strands with Bear-folk three, the dearest comrades Brenn had known in life.

With torch in hand, the king approached the pyre, and set ablaze the wood with solemn touch. The fire leapt and roared, consuming all, as gathered guests bewailed their fallen friend.

Beside Pabelyo stood her sister-friend, fair Baiwieth, clad in wool of azure hue, her raven tresses bound in braided coil. Green eyes brimmed o'er with sorrow's bitter tears, as from her lips a mournful song arose, an ancient dirge in Dol-Nopthelen's tongue:

Song of the Crickets

What ails thee, friend? Thine hue is pale.
Great wounds, I ken, do weary thee;
thine helm is sliced, thy spear is snapped:
at an end is now thy life!

More tears never so well wept,
howled, or wailed, have been!
Nigh unto the bridge will I draw
and apply to thy withered arms
the balm of my words.

Where art thou? Knowest thou me? I knew thy name:
I saw thee in mine heart's bliss,
and tried thy powers of tongues.

Yet, when I heard thy kind voice
and saw thine eye shine
like stars in a clear sky,
then, the spark in mine heart ran low
but warmed my soul when beheld I thy face—
it hath kindled my life as heaven's touch.

Take me with thee, O man, my brother, O friend;
I'll stay the night and nigh thy pyre will be aflame,
and all thy songs I'll sing til morn,
when death doth take thee from my sight.

As smoke dispersed upon the salted air, the king, with reverent hands, did gather up the ashes of the fallen into an urn of silver hue, its surface gleaming bright. He led the solemn throng from coastal sands to Albogorwë's far side, where stood a house and by its flank, a modest hill arose.

There, on that verdant slope, more urns did rest, each marking heroes fallen in their time. One vessel bore a falcon's likeness, wings outstretched as if to soar beyond the veil. Here Segwi found her peace.

Beside this tribute, a bossed shield of copper-tinted steel displayed a fox's visage, bold and sly. 'Twas here that Kolewa, the Fox, in memory dwelt.

And further still, a simple sword stood proud, its blade supporting horned helm. In this spot, Deugwer the Wolf reposed, his spirit free to roam in wilder realms.

Then Kregeth, with a gesture grave and slow, bestowed the final urn to Erwo's care. With Pabelyo beside, they climbed the hill and placed the silver vessel near the Fox. Thus Brenn, the mighty Bear, joined his family.

From beneath her cloak, Pabelyo then revealed a smaller jar of clay, its seal intact. With gentle hands, she set it by the Bear, and there lay Den, the Lion, fierce and true.

Around this hallowed ground rode noble men, the scions of kings, princes, lords, and chiefs. Their lamentations rose on evening air, bewailing not just Brenn, but all who slept upon that hill, their deeds remembered still.

The eastern folk, with hearts weighed down by grief, bemoaned their Holder's fall—he who was friend to all who were willing, and of all the men on Earth one of the most generous and gracious, and to those who loved him most tender and humble.

Appendix A:

Keuleno calendar

The calendar used by the Keulenu at the time The Form and The Shatter takes place divides time into days, weeks, years, and eras. In place of months, days are counted in their respective seasons—for example, Brenn Ragnir's birth-date is 1 Summer 2E 4005, which corresponds roughly to June 21st 1987 CE (49 BA).

An estimation of the months are as follows:

1–93 Spring: March 20–June 21
1–95 Summer: June 22–September 24
1–90 Autumn: September 25–December 23
1–86 Winter: December 24–March 19
1–4 Dolseuk (Long-Summer): four days after Summer and before Autumn every sixteen years. In Keulen these days are reserved for festivals, as the number four is sacred to those who revere the dorovai. These days correct the calendar's lack of a leap-day.

The days of the week are:

Gwiodyeu (Life-day)
Tongdyeu (Thought-day)
Luwannyeu (Light-day)
Gwithodyeu (Mist-day)
Medwig (Midweek)
Nekhvodyeu (Cloud-day)
Therdyeu (Star-day)
Lwisnadyeu (Moon-Day)
Saweldyeu (Sun-Day)

Dolseuk days (named after the four dorovai):

Odoldhyeu
Naodyeu
Enodyeu
Parthudyeu

Each new season begins on a Gwiodyeu, no matter on which day the previous season ended.

Eras further divide the history of Edorath (as reckoned by Keulen), marking important historical events.

1E began when Panaikh Polekheft led his people to Keulen, settling near Nugomor. The dates are uncertain, as a land is not settled in a single day, but tradition holds that the day was 4 Winter 1E 4, being the fourth day of the fourth season in the fourth year of the era. The First Era lasted approximately from 4000 BCE to 2020 BCE (6036–4056 BA).

2E began when Kekhel, Baithas and ruler of the Keuleno people, married Brukh, a princess of the native Yaga nation. The Second Era lasted approximately from 2020 BCE to 2014 CE (4056–22 BA).

3E began when Brenn Ragnir, also known as Gwennotir Ker, ended the line of Holders after sacrificing himself to end the tyranny of the rilyun god. As he had no children and no extended family, the Power of Speech was lost and so the other three Powers were lost as well. The Third Era began in 2014 CE (22 BA).

Appendix B:

Glossary of Keuleno words appearing in this text

Aikhwë — lit. Ice-Waste; a massive glacier covering the northern part of Edorath

ayan (pl. eyain) — priest or shaman, usually associated with dorova-reverence

Baithas (pl. Baithais) — Speaker; Holder of the Power of Speech

begwo (pl. begwu) — emu or ostrich

dauker (pl. doëkir) — official duel, usually to win a contested rank or title

derotir (pl. deretir) — Holder; one who holds one of the four Powers

deukis (pl. deukis) — church or temple, usually associated with the rilyun faith

Dorova (pl. Derevai) — creator-being of the material

and spiritual worlds, humanity, and the four Powers

dorovayan (pl. dereveyain) — lit. dorova-priest; shaman of dorova-reverence

elowav (pl. elewaiv) — elephant

Erkhosgor (pl. Erkhesgur) — lit. Bear-person; one who took part in Brenn Ragnir's slave-rebellion in Milridh

gannëa — cannabis or marijuana

grondeketh (pl. grendekith) — monster appearing in many fables of Keulen and Dol-Nopthelen told as warning against the dangers of using magic

gwarnyemeth (pl. gwernyemith) — loose robe commonly worn in Len Khalayu

gwerfegi — large round building with an arena that once stood in Goreuhwo, able to host several thousand people

ilo — clear alcoholic drink made by the Badhë

karkhro — dice game played in Kebkholeni

Keugureg — Keuleno rendition of Adluo's country's name on Lighthouse Earth; keu (east) + gureg (realm; domain); Austria

kirven (pl. kirvin) — scarf or head-wrap commonly worn in Len Khalayu

Kleumas (pl. Kleumais) — Listener; Holder of the Power of Mind

klewaig (pl. klewaig) — curved sword commonly used in Len Khalayu

leitho (pl. leithu) — yucca or Joshua tree

Mewas (pl. Mewais) — Mover; Holder of the Power of Space
Miwë (pl. miwes) — diminutive of mikhter "mother"; mama; mommy

sakhnau (pl. sakhnoë) — lit. sand-ship; mode of transport used in Len Khalayu and Deulen resembling a sailed ship with skiffs or wheels that moved upon sand

sorathryu (pl. serethrŷ) — instrument played by cranking a wheel against strings, akin to a hurdy-gurdy

Taf-Waikht — lit. First-Tribe; group of rilyunë zealots prone to terrorism and violence in the name of their religion

Tefwas (pl. Tefwais) — Efter; Holder of the Power of Time

wadhestor (pl. wedhestur) — preacher, priest, or pastor of the rilyun faith

Emmett Burgess is a student of history, linguistics, geology, and literature. He spends his time writing, reading, studying dead languages, and sharing a quantum-entangled id with two other beings. He lives in Illinois with his spouse and daughter, ca. 12 BA.

Emerson Grey was born and raised in Jemston, New Amrika. He attended the University of Jemston where he studied literature, history, and linguistics, earning advanced degrees in Ancient Terran History and Culture. He is now a tenured professor of Terran Literature at the University of Jemston, as well as a senior member of the Windmill Writing Fraternity. He lives in a small cottage on the Robert Grey Memorial Estate with his wife Matilda, ca. 9340 AA.

John Talbot saw a cool rock once.

You can connect with me on
Instagram @**authoremmettburgess**
Facebook @**emmettburgessauthor**
TikTok @**authoremmettburgess**
and at **www.windmill.ink**

Reviews are always appreciated.

Thanks to Andy for putting up with my shit, even when I can't.

Thanks to Lilith for giving me a reason to get out of bed every day.

Thanks to Holly for loving what I write, even if I don't.

Thanks to Ellie for being a supportive friend.

Thanks to Mom for always being the first to read.

Thanks to Dad for keeping me grounded in reality.

Thanks to Andrew Wilmot for being a great editor.

Thanks to Julia for being an invaluable beta reader.

—Emmett

Printed in the USA
CPSIA information can be obtained
at www.ICGtesting.com
LVHW031459081124
796065LV00012B/856